THE MASADA PLAN

THE MASADA PLAN

a novel by

LEONARD HARRIS

Crown Publishers, Inc. | New York

Printed in the United States of America

Published simultaneously in Canada by General Publishing Company Limited

Library of Congress Cataloging in Publication Data

Harris, Leonard, 1929-
    The Masada plan.

    I. Title.
PZ4.H31392Mas [PS3558.A6467] 813'.5'4 76-22557
ISBN 0-517-52799-5

Dedication

for Sally and Dave

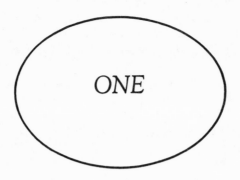

ONE

Eight stories below, the traffic moving up Madison Avenue and along Sixty-fourth Street intruded softly and intermittently, a faraway horn or a racing motor pushing its way through the low hum of the air conditioner and the subdued sounds of a Schubert string quartet over the FM radio. A patchwork bedspread, cool summer cotton, green and white, was pulled back from the iron-and-brass double bed. On the white sheet lay a man and a woman, both naked.

A black enamel-and-chrome digital clock on the bedside table read 1:30; ninety minutes into July 12, 1979. Outside, the night was warm and sticky, but the room had an airy look; three walls and the ceiling white, the fourth wall papered in a pink-and-white pattern, a white shag rug on the floor, pinks, whites, and more than any other color, greens, dominating the room.

Photographs were everywhere, hanging on the walls, standing on the bureau, the desk, and assorted tables. In size and framing they were an amiable chaos, but three faces reappeared regularly. In one large portrait standing in a filigreed silver frame on the dressing table, all three were seen: a blonde girl of about ten, a brown-haired boy slightly younger, an ash-blonde woman in her mid-thirties. The resemblance and the attitudes in the photo said they were mother and children. The youngsters both had blue eyes, the woman's were grayish green. Three individual sets of photos of the children could be seen; they suggested the boy was an extrovert, smiling brightly from frames of chrome and brushed aluminum; the girl seemed reserved. On a small antique table standing near a green-and-white zebra-striped love seat was a portrait of the children when they were younger. They wore matching outfits, the boy in Black Watch shorts, the girl in Black Watch jumper, both in white shirts with Peter Pan collars. Clearly they were the children of the woman in the pictures; the absence of a father was equally clear.

1

In more businesslike frames, most of them clear Lucite, could be seen pictures of the woman with other adults, most of them eminently recognizable. On her desk she stood facing Henry Kissinger, she looking grave, he jolly. Next to that she posed between President and Mrs. Ford, all of them facing the camera. In other photos she stood or sat with senators, diplomats, best-selling authors.

The face in the pictures belonged to the woman stretched out on the bed. Except for the bands of white skin where a bikini would be worn, her long body was moderately tanned. She took care not to expose it to too much sun because she knew, at thirty-six, overtanned skin began to look like creased leather. The body was remarkable; it and her face had always been eye-catching and both had grown more attractive as she moved elegantly into her thirties.

She had always ridiculed the possibility that, physically, anyone could improve with age. She'd answer such assertions with "What you mean is I'm not falling apart as fast as most of the others." No one would mistake her for twenty-five, but certainly she was in better shape than many twenty-five-year-olds. A half-hour swim each day and regular calisthenics kept her waist lean, her abdomen flat, and her long legs slim and hard.

The man on the bed appeared in only one photo, which stood on her bedside table in a horizontal wooden frame painted in glossy green enamel. The two of them were seen in three-quarter profile, she grinning at him, he smiling but unsure whether to look at her or the camera. Obviously he was not the father of the children, but his presence in only one photo undervalued his presence in the room. He was there often, on the bed often, although seldom ensconced in it, for the demands on both their lives usually kept him from spending the night with her.

This evening's lovemaking would soon be over, he would be leaving; that prospect was in both their minds as he reached an arm across and put his hand on the small of her back. His arm was wiry and strong, as was his entire body. His shoulders, thighs, and calves were as thin as hers; he was a mere three inches taller and perhaps twenty pounds heavier. Where the sun had not reached, he was darker than she; elsewhere she was darker, although with tinges of gold to her color that he did not have.

His hair was brown and curly, gone to gray at the sides, with gray beginning to spatter the brown everywhere. His eyes were a cool blue, and they looked at her the way a lover's sometimes do, asking gently: Shall we? Leisure together was not one of their luxuries, and at first the need for hurrying had caused tension and anxiety. After a while, they realized they'd have to learn to accept the hurriedness, the sudden departures, the last-minute cancellations—on both their parts. "Just until we can spend our nights together," he had said confidently. Privately, he was not so sure, and she even less.

This warm summer's night she answered the Shall we? in his eyes by kissing his mouth and running her left hand down his side and along the buttock and thigh. With the hand on her waist, he pulled her toward him, and as their bodies touched all along their lengths, she could feel he was indeed ready to make love again. And she knew she was.

She rolled her body onto his, pushing him onto his back, she on top of him, both their bodies still stretched at full length, legs together, parallel. Then she opened her legs and sat up. Easily she slid him into her.

This had become their favorite position. He found the weight of her body on his hips and abdomen exciting, she found the freedom to move herself freely on his penis an aphrodisiac. Some of the time she sat up, others she leaned over him, her breasts near his face, her nipples within reach of his lips.

Her orgasm came before his, deep and delicious, and she wallowed in it, her words, "Oh darling, darling, darling," more exultant gasps than articulated syllables. Then she took painstaking, enthusiastic delight in bringing him to orgasm. I'm a craftsman, she said to herself, no, an artist, and she felt wet and warm and almost drunk as she worked on him, watching him climb higher and higher and higher, until, with his eyes closed, his face in a smile, almost a grimace, of ecstasy, he took the sighing, groaning breaths that came with his climax.

Lazily, she fell on top of him without letting him slip out of her, and their bodies again parallel and pressed full length, they kissed. For a long time they lay still, both stretching their time, trying to make it leisurely and luxurious. At last he rolled her off him, intending to get up, but as she rolled she held onto him and they lay side by side for another fifteen or twenty minutes before, finally, they released each other.

He rose, the hair on his chest damp with his sweat and hers. Drowsily, indolently, she pulled the top sheet over her, admiring him as she did. "Anyone ever tell you you've got a hell of a body—for a man your age?"

He sucked in his belly and slapped it hard. "I've got to watch this," he answered, giving a second slap to make sure she knew what he meant.

"Oh cut it out," she said. "You're beautiful, and you just want to hear me say it."

"What's wrong with that?" he replied, then leaned over and kissed her and turned and headed for the bathroom. Inside, he showered, wrapped a large, striped towel around himself, and walked out. He could see she was headed for sleep.

"It's the old story," he said as he dressed. "The woman just rolls over and goes to sleep, and the man heads out for the long cold trip home."

That woke her. "Is it that way at all your stops, eh?" she asked. "A quick fuck and out into the cold?"

He shook his head. "This is the only stop I've made in, how long has it been, almost two years?" It had turned serious and he wanted to move it away. "Quick fuck. Slow fuck. But always out for the long cold trip home. Poor wandering Jew. The poor male."

"Not if he marries the fuckee," she answered, sitting up. "Not even if he's in residence. Anyway, eight blocks on an eighty-degree July night is not exactly long and cold. And besides, who told you to leave?"

He touched the small box hooked to his belt, then picked up the jacket of his gray summer-weight suit and held it by the hook at the collar. "There's no damn reason for me not to stay, it's just that things are so touchy, I want to get back; I'm a little nervous when I'm not on the premises."

"It's as bad as if you had a wife waiting up for you," she told him.

"Worse," he answered and walked over and kissed her.

She kissed him back. "Talk to me tomorrow, will you?"

"Of course," he said. "Good night. It was lovely."

"I hate to have you leave," she said, lying down and curling her legs up into a fetal position, but continuing to look at him.

"And I hate to leave," he answered. "Well, that may change soon," he added, looking at her hard.

She just stared at him without answering. How many times had she heard that? And she knew he meant it, and maybe it would happen, but offhand she just couldn't see how . . . or when.

Finally she said, "Yes, talk to you tomorrow," and she threw a kiss at him.

Slowly, reluctantly, he turned and headed out of the bedroom, along the green-carpeted hall to the foyer, then through the front door. He rang for the elevator. Waiting, he slipped his jacket on and buttoned one button of it. The white-gloved operator slid open the heavy door. The details of the turn-of-the-century building, inside and out, were ornate and heavy, and prospective apartment buyers were told proudly it had been built by Stanford White. It hadn't; rather it was one of the many buildings in New York that made invalid claims to being his, and when a newspaper article a few years earlier identified it as one of the fakes, there were long faces on the elevator and in the halls for days afterward.

She had moved in shortly after that article; nonetheless the agent who showed her around told her the Stanford White story. She hadn't been able to resist saying "You're close, but you haven't got it quite

4

right. Actually this building was designed by Evelyn Nesbit."

The agent didn't get it, but apparently remembered the name Evelyn Nesbit and repeated it to the building's board of directors, because a couple of the stuffier directors, she found out later, had wanted to deny her application to buy an apartment.

The elevator door slid open, and he walked out of it and onto the street, smiling. He had heard the Stanford White story two years ago, in response to his remark about the pretentious grandness of the building. It was the first time they had walked into it together, and since then, as he approached, or left, he often thought of the story and smiled at it.

Then he looked at his watch, and the smile faded. It was 2:20, and he hoped nobody was looking for him. Heading west toward Madison Avenue, he decided to walk. Although it was hot and sticky, a slight breeze had come up, and he felt the desire, the need to stretch his legs. He had skipped his two-mile jog in the park that morning; too much work had piled up. Whenever he couldn't run, he felt restless. So he decided to walk, although he had made all sorts of promises he would not go out on the street alone, especially not late at night.

Oh, hell, he said to himself, who's going to bother me tonight? It would raise too much of a sweat. Even the walk was making him perspire; he loosened his tie, and unbuttoned his jacket.

He reached Madison Avenue and headed uptown along the east side. As he walked, the traffic, also going uptown, passed him in waves—small ones, for at 2:20 a.m. on a summer's night, traffic was light along Madison Avenue. Controlling the frequency of the waves was the pattern of the traffic lights, which sent the bunched cars by him at intervals of about ninety seconds. Since the traffic was coming from behind the walker, he heard each wave before he saw it. And then his internal alarm system, which had been fine-tuned by years of use, rang faintly. This time one car was not moving with a wave; its sound told him it was just behind him, moving at a speed suitable for window-shopping, restaurant-hunting, or address-finding. But where he was now walking, the shops were closed and mostly dark, and there were no restaurants or residential entrances. Why the slow car? Something asked the question, but faintly.

Then the car slowed to a standstill. He heard a car door open and slam shut. The alarm sounded a bit louder. Again, he heard the car, this time gaining on him. As he started to look to his left, his search was simplified, the car was moving slightly ahead of him. It was a black, four-door Mercedes. In it were a driver and a man sitting next to him. The passenger was looking at him, but turned away quickly when he stared back. The volume on his alarm was turned up.

The Mercedes pulled twenty yards ahead of him, until it was halfway between Sixty-seventh and Sixty-eighth streets. As it stopped, the right front door opened and the passenger got out, slamming the door after him. The man was short, dark, slender, wearing a gray raincoat, even though the night was far too warm for one. Both his hands were in his pockets. North of him, up Madison Avenue, not another pedestrian could be seen. Raincoat headed for a shop window and pretended to be looking in.

Ridiculous, the walker thought. By now the alarm was shrieking. He whirled around and looked behind. Ten yards back was the first man who'd gotten out of the car. He was as swarthy as Raincoat, no taller, but much heavier and stronger looking. Passenger Two had a hand in his jacket pocket. To his left, the Mercedes matched the walker's speed, and, as it did, effectively closed off each space between the parked cars as he reached it.

Well, they did this neatly, he said to himself. Men in front and back of me, probably with pistols; closed stores to my right, their car to my left. They probably would rather not shoot, he thought, but they might before they let me get away. His heart was thumping. They had him.

Hell, I've got to give it a try, he thought. He suddenly broke into a run, not toward either man, not to look for an open door in the building fronts, but straight at the Mercedes gliding along next to him. For a moment the men in front and back of him were startled; he had moved in the one direction they hadn't anticipated. Then both moved toward the street, expecting he would try to slide through the narrow space between the side of the Mercedes and the parked cars to its right, to go around the front or the back of their car. Again he surprised them, for without slowing down, he leaped for the roof of the Mercedes, and using his hands and arms as if the car were an oversized vaulting horse in a gymnasium, he propelled himself onto its roof and half slid, half vaulted onto Madison Avenue.

He landed on his feet, stumbled for an instant, and sprinted into the middle of the avenue, crossing it and slanting north, moving in the one direction that would place his pursuers behind him. That direction was west, onto Sixty-eighth Street, toward Fifth Avenue and Central Park.

The three pursuers broke out of their startled inertia and went after him. Raincoat started running. The stocky man jumped into the car, and the driver headed for Sixty-eighth Street.

But the quarry had two bits of luck. First, his attackers were momentarily slowed by a wave of traffic going up the avenue, and he added a few yards to his lead. Second, Sixty-eighth Street was an eastbound street, and the Mercedes turned onto it going west, so it would take only one eastbound auto to block the Mercedes. And that one car came along. A cab, having dropped a late fare in the middle of the block, was riding east when the driver saw the Mercedes accelerating toward him. "Jesus Christ," the cabbie shouted out loud, although there was no one to hear him. He stamped on the brake pedal and pushed the heel of his hand onto the horn, hard. The two cars stopped less than five feet from each other. The cabbie stuck his head out the window ready to argue, but, to his astonishment, his prospective opponents abandoned the Mercedes and raced toward Fifth Avenue.

By this time, the man they were after was near Fifth Avenue, his heart pounding madly. Uncontrollably, he thought. Why is it, he asked himself, I can run so hard exercising and not have all this trouble breathing?

He heard a shot fired behind him. That's why, he answered. He was half frightened, half detached, waiting for the sound of the next one, zigzagging, hoping for traffic to slow down his closest pursuer. A few cars came down Fifth; he weaved among them, making a tougher target.

He heard another shot, felt nothing. And now he was at the low stone wall bounding Central Park. He vaulted it, as he had the car, only more easily; the wall was less than four feet high, but the drop was farther than he had estimated and he half landed heavily in some bushes; a branch caught on his right pants leg, tearing it, then slipping inside scraping the outside of his calf. He fell, got up, stumbled. He couldn't see very well. There were few lights here, but he wasn't complaining. It meant they couldn't see either. Where were they? Probably along Fifth Avenue, trying to guess where he'd come out of the park.

In the dark he staggered forward, headed uptown because that was the way home. His breath was ragged, his heart thumping, his footing unsure. His scraped leg hurt. All this goddamned jogging, he thought, why am I so short of breath? He knew why: fear. Nearby he saw the path, paved and lighted. He had run along it many times; it was a lot better than stumbling through this underbrush. He also knew it could be seen clearly from Fifth Avenue, which would make him an easy target.

And they would shoot; that he knew, too.

Plowing along, tripping, moving as quickly as he could, he figured he was stupid to keep going in the most predictable direction, toward home. But he couldn't think of a sensible alternative and the adrenalin moved him forward. Keep out of the light, he told himself. Don't leave the park at Seventy-second Street, that's where they'll be waiting for you. Keep going north, he thought. Then get out of the park and double back.

Now he was near Seventy-second, and he moved deeper into the park. There's light here, move fast, he told himself. He jumped over a bench, was on the Seventy-second Street park road, ran across it. Think invisible, he told himself. But there was lots of light. He was exhausted. And I've only run a little more than a quarter of a mile. I don't think I can outrace them again.

Then for the first time, he asked himself: Why are they after me? Why now? Has something just happened? Something in the last few hours, something I don't know about? Hell, it's not over, he warned himself, no postmortems yet. Make sure to get the hell away, then look for the reasons. Then as a kind of cryptic answer, his beeper sounded. Quickly, without slowing, he fumbled to turn it off. Someone wants me. Why? To warn me? Well that was one worry he'd have to postpone. Don't worry, he thought. I'm coming. As fast as I can.

On and over another bench and he was on park grass and dirt again. Downhill he loped, parallel to a paved pedestrian walk. He might just be out of it, he thought. Give it another block or two and then over the wall, back out to Fifth Avenue, and home. And find out why. And no more solitary walks late at night. He slowed a bit, breathed easier, suddenly aware he was drenched with his own sweat, his shirt sticking to him, wetness dripping down his face, his hands clammy and—amazingly—cold in this summer heat. The downhill helped him relax; he felt better. He felt safe. He was going to make it.

Then from the rear, the car was upon him so suddenly, he had no chance to evade it. It appeared all at once to him as a pair of blinding headlights, high beams flicked up, flooding the park around him, burning through the back of his head. It had come down the pedestrian path; the scuffling of his own feet, the roaring of his own breathing had kept him from hearing it.

He froze, unable to run, knowing he was caught, unsure whether to raise his hands. The car door opened and closed. A figure came around to the front and into the glare of the headlights.

A New York City police sergeant stood in front of him, the nameplate under his badge said Guardino. Sgt. Guardino, tall and bulky, looked at him angrily. "You know you're not supposed to be in this park in the middle of the night? Who are you and what are you doing here?"

He smiled at the sergeant, wanting to say, I'm damned glad to see you. Instead he replied, "My name is Dov Shalzar. I am the Israeli Ambassador to the United Nations, and three hoods have just tried to mug me. Would you drive me back to my embassy, please?"

"Could you describe them?" Guardino asked.

"Not a chance," the ambassador replied. "Didn't see them well enough."

That was not quite true. He had seen them well enough to know one thing for sure, but he saw no point in telling the sergeant.

Shalzar was certain his three attackers were Arabs.

8

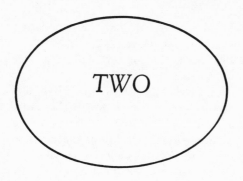

TWO

On the Sinai Desert in the early morning of July 12, 1979, an Israeli patrol made its way across the soft, trackless sand. Moving in single file, a jeep, followed by an armored half-track, then two more jeeps emerged on the horizon and then disappeared as they mounted the crests of the dunes and descended into the troughs. The night on the northern Sinai was clear and, for summer, surprisingly cool.

In the lead jeep, the lieutenant in command of the patrol looked at his watch; it was ten minutes past three. Since it would take forty-five minutes to return to their camp, he'd have to order the patrol to start back in five minutes if they were to be off duty at four, as scheduled.

The lieutenant was jumpy; he had heard the Egyptians were bringing up tanks to the Suez Canal, even into the limited force zone, which violated the October 1975 agreement, and that the ambassador had protested in the UN. A lot of good that will do us, he thought. Besides, he had just heard those things. All he was told officially was to be specially alert. But then they always told him that.

The wind was rising, whipping up the sand. The jeeps, among the last things Israel had received from the United States before it began its Middle East arms embargo nearly two years ago, were not built for luxury riding, and the lieutenant would be relieved when he could climb out and stretch, and then lie down on his bunk. Being young, he was not comforted by the Israeli folk wisdom that Arabs did not like to fight at night. He would feel easier back at camp, easier still when his tour was over and he was far from this vulnerable forward position.

Again the lieutenant looked at his watch. Time to turn. As he was about to reach for the mike on the two-way radio, a voice sounded over it.

"Lieutenant, this is Levi." Levi was in the jeep behind the half-track, which held an infrared detector designed to pick up moving objects in the dark, such as planes and tanks. Levi sounded excited.

"Lieutenant, I'm getting six or seven blips on my screen, coming from the west and moving very fast."

They were fast indeed, eight Russian MIGs, flown by Egyptian pilots, headed for the same camp to which the patrol was returning.

The lieutenant would radio back to the camp; first, however, he would tell his patrol to prepare to fire at the approaching planes. He got to do neither, for the planes had spotted him, and all eight fired off heat-sensitive surface-to-ground missiles, received from China only three months before.

They blew the patrol to pieces. It was a clear case of overkill; for the missiles were designed to destroy tanks. But then it was small loss to the Egyptians; they had missiles to spare.

Nor did the lieutenant's failure to phone his command with news of the attack constitute a loss to the Israelis, for by this time they already knew that the Arabs, in devastating force, were attacking Israel along its entire land border.

The Old Man's hair was standing wildly on end as he walked into the cabinet room; on top, the few remaining hairs were in a snowy chaos; along the sides, the curls looked as if electric charges were running through them. The five men sitting around the teak conference table were startled. Tempestuous though he could be, the Prime Minister was famous for his composure in a crisis. Now he did not look composed, decidedly not.

In varying degrees these five members of what the press called the kitchen cabinet knew that the fighting, which had begun five hours ago, at a few minutes after three in the morning with massive Arab attacks, was going badly. But all were surprised by the Old Man's disarray and by the grimness of his face. The lines between his nose and down-turned mouth were as deep as troughs, the brow was glowering, the body in its wrinkled white shirt and tan pants was a mixture of rigidity and fatigue.

Even the Defense Minister and the Chief of Staff were upset by the Old Man's appearance and they, of course, had been following the war since its first minutes. What they, and the three others, knew was that the Prime Minister's mission throughout the night had been to prevail upon the United States to intercede, with troops, or diplomatic pressure, or, as in '73, with an airlift of supplies. And everything about him said it hadn't worked. And as soon as he got to the head of the table, he said it for himself.

"Good morning, gentlemen," he began, the growl in his voice accentuated by his tiredness. "It's bad. No, not bad, critical. I don't see how it could be worse."

None of them expected a miracle, but there had been some hope for American support in extremis, even though the alienation of the two countries in the past years was known to every schoolchild. No one said a word, although none of the five was known for shyness. On the Prime Minister's left sat the Foreign Minister, the urbane, eloquent Itzhak Weismann, to millions all over the world, the voice of Israel. Next to him, the Defense Minister, Shmuel Arit, a former Chief of Staff of the Israel Defense Forces and, like Weismann, a member of the Prime Minister's Labor party. Beyond him, the current Chief of Staff, General David Benot. On the other side of the table, to the PM's right, sat the two representatives of the left and right fringes of the coalition, Labor Minister Lev Shapira, a dove and a radical, and Finance Minister Uri Gonen, of the right-wing, hawkish Likud group. Of the six men in the room, only Weismann had no combat experience.

Looking at the five, the Old Man knew they were reading his own despair, and unwillingly—foolishly, he said to himself—he tried to temper it by running his hand through his hair to make it, and therefore the whole situation, seem a little calmer. Then he went on.

"First to bring you up to date on the fighting. On the Lebanese front we're up against regular army units as well as the PLO; in Syria, Iraqi units are already up there with the Syrians, and more are pouring in. We have identified Libyan planes flying with the Egyptians, and Saudi troops with the Jordanians and Syrians."

He lowered his head to look at some papers on the desk in front of him. "Let's see. We've slowed the Jordanians down on the West Bank, but not much, and we're paying for it. We may have to move the government to Tel Aviv, but let's not take that up now."

"Our boys are doing splendidly, it's a wonder they're doing as well as they are, but the fact is, the missiles are doing incredible damage to our tanks and planes. I have to tell you, we're lucky if the kill ratio is one-to-one."

To the five listening, the one-to-one may have been the most devastating information of all. They knew that the Arabs now had a four- or five-to-one advantage in tanks and planes; they remembered the glories of '67 and even '73, when kill ratios of ten- and twenty-to-one were not unusual; on the contrary, were expected.

Now they were lucky if it was one-to-one! That summed up what had happened in the six years since the Yom Kippur War: the loss of their special relationship with the United States, the hostility of the African-Asian bloc, their growing isolation and friendlessness throughout the world, their financial and military weakness—the entire concept of a Middle East balance of power slipping away on skids greased by Arab oil. Their arms superiority of the early and mid '70s had dwindled and then been reversed, as the United States moved from friendship to so-called even-handedness, to an arms embargo on the Mideast. With Soviet help the Egyptians and Syrians had set up missile screens denser than the ones protecting Moscow, in short, the densest in the world. In late '75 as part of the accord, they had returned the Abu Rudeis oil fields to Egypt, which meant the loss of 55 percent of their supply. The difference was to have come from Iran, backed up by American guarantees. But the Iranians had staggered Israel just a year ago by signing a pact with its Arab neighbors to embargo oil to Israel, and the United States, under pressure at home, had jumped through the loopholes in its "guarantee." And then there was the effectiveness of the Arab boycott on suppliers to Israel, and the cutoff on credit as the Arabs had begun throwing around their petro-dollars.

But what had been worse than all the rest was the return in the late '70s of the Arabs' "drive-them-into-the-sea" rhetoric. To see even moderates in Egypt, Jordan, and Lebanon, encouraged by UN anti-Zionism, join in the cries of "wipe out the Zionists," was most hateful of all. The tension at the table spoke for all Israelis; the country was like a clenched fist, and, perversely, it seemed to delight in shaking that fist at the Arabs and the world.

Isolated, poor, weakened, friendless, surrounded, Israel braced its back to the wall. Somehow no one considered surrender. Throw everything at them, was the spirit of the nation. Fight to the end.

The men at the conference table were part of this spirit, yet facing the end, as they now seemed to be, even they, leaders and generals, were appalled.

Then the Chief of Staff, General Benot, took over, pouring on the details. "The Egyptians must have every helicopter the Soviets made in the last four years, and a few American ones, too. In three spots in the Sinai they landed commandos behind us with wire-guided missiles; it was either pull back or lose a brigade in each place.

"Over the Golan Heights it is nearly impossible to get a plane through, which means we can't touch the replacements they're bringing in. We've got no depth along the West Bank. We need reserves, we need equipment, we need ammunition, we need fuel." Benot went on as if reading a laundry list.

But the Labor Minister, Shapira, his chin on his hand, had already stopped listening. He knew where this was headed and he didn't like it. Nor did he know how to stop it. He'd just wait, he decided, to see what he could do.

The Prime Minister put a question to his Chief of Staff. "What will it take to stop them?" From the way he watched the others, rather than Benot, as the general answered, it was clear his mind was on rhetoric, not information.

"Three months of resupplying, two years to build up our own armaments production; right now we're practically hand-tooling tanks and planes." The general's eyes stayed on the Old Man. The PM did not look back; his eyes swept the table as Benot spoke.

"But we don't have two years," added Benot. "We don't have three months."

The Old Man's eyes never left the others as he asked, "How long?"

"One week. Maybe less."

The Prime Minister had made his point and he sat back in his chair, as if for the moment the question period were over. One week. Of the four listeners, Arit, the Defense Minister, was not surprised. The other three were shocked, and Lev Shapira, the Labor Minister, grew hostile.

"You're trying to stampede us down this road," he said. "For God's sake let's not be in too much of a hurry; it only goes one way, we can't come back. Let's talk to Washington again. Let's think some more."

The Prime Minister began his answer in anger, his piercing brown eyes glaring from under the bushy eyebrows, but that quickly turned to weariness as he spoke. "What do you think I've been doing the past four hours, fixing my hair?" He ran a hand over his disordered mane.

"Washington will not supply us with military aid. Washington *will* go to the Security Council and urge an immediate cease-fire. Since the UN has been dying to drink our blood, we don't have much hope there. But even if by some miracle we got the votes, the Arabs could stall for a few days, and by then, the way we're using ammunition, we'll have a unilateral cease-fire.

"From the Russians we can expect nothing, except broad smiles at the way their weapons are testing out. The British are mealymouthed, as usual; the French and the Germans are sympathetic, mildly; not that those three matter.

"To me it looks like everybody's going to watch, and maybe deplore, while the brave little Israelis get wiped out."

He reached a lumpy, thick-fingered hand to the heavy oval table and picked up a gold medal encased in Lucite. It had been struck to commemorate a great battle fought in Israel 1,900 years earlier. On one side, in Hebrew and English, was a line from an Israeli poem: "Masada shall not fall again."

Because the paperweight was always on the table, no one in the room had to be shown what was on the medal. Everyone knew. The Old Man just turned it over in his hand, then let it drop with a thud.

"Masada is about to fall." His eyes were on the medal.

It was a fine dramatic moment, meant to stir the blood. For the Labor Minister it didn't work. "Look," Shapira said, being as commonplace and reasonable as he could be, trying to show he hadn't been swept away. "Stop trying to make out anyone who's against you is in *favor* of Masada falling. Look, we all know what you're working around to, so come and say it straight out."

Shapira believed in facing things squarely, and he had the face and the physique for it: square jaw, shoulders, hands. He was a radical socialist, an idealist, and, as far as it was possible to be one in Israel, a pacifist. He was a Sabra, and a labor leader, and at thirty-eight, young enough to be the Prime Minister's son. According to the Old Man, who had arrived in Palestine during the Second Aliyah and had worked on the roads as a laborer for the first four months, Lev didn't appreciate the struggle to establish the state.

The Old Man valued Lev, though, because he needed his radical support, because he wanted to know what young people were thinking and because he knew Lev was not a yes-man. And despite their frequent arguments, which the PM usually won with his heavy Eastern European irony, he liked Lev.

One would never know it now though, as the Prime Minister, one finger aimed at Lev's nose, responded, "You look! I'm not working around to anything. I'm trying to come up with some ideas to get us out of this. What can you contribute?" His look was accusatorial; clearly he didn't expect anything.

Shapira was never cowed by his venerable adversary. He pointed back with a gesture that faintly mimicked the Old Man's. "If we had been willing to debate the PLO, instead of being stupid; if we had given back the Sinai and the West Bank, and some of the Golan Heights, we'd be in a different position now."

Half shouting, the Finance Minister, Uri Gonen, interrupted. "Yes, different! Instead of fighting in the Sinai we'd be fighting in the Negev; instead of on the West Bank, we'd be fighting in Jerusalem. We'd be two or three days away from the end, instead of five, or, if you can imagine such luxury, seven!"

Shapira swiveled his chair to the right to face Gonen. "And do you know what you're suggesting?"

Then the Old Man took control back, slapping his hand on the table, hard. "All right," he said, addressing Shapira as if the Finance Minister hadn't even spoken. "You're so anxious to talk about it, let's talk about it. It's a plan. Desperate, yes. A last resort, yes. To be used only in extremis, yes. All right, you show me we're not desperate, not in extremis, not ready for the last resort. You tell me, what's the next-to-last resort? Tell me!"

This last resort, this desperate scheme that came to be known as the Masada Plan had been formulated five years earlier, just after

14

the Yom Kippur War had given the Israelis a new sense of mortality. Six persons, two politicians, two scientists, two generals, had sat down in secret at the Weizmann Institute to work out a Doomsday device. Nowhere was it recorded who they were: that was agreed on in advance, although their identities were the subject of much high-level gossip. People who knew seemed to agree the two scientists were the youngest of the six, and that one of the two was a nuclear physicist and the other, a woman, an engineer.

At first the six had laughed when one asked the other, "Who's going to be Dr. Strangelove?"

Then, when the plan was suggested, reportedly by the young physicist, there was little doubt he deserved the title.

The plan was so daring, so deadly and yet so simple, at first the other five laughed at it; they could not believe it did not have a flaw in it. And they began to pick it apart. Or try to, at any rate. In short, their debate took the form all the subsequent debates were to take in the tight little command circle, whenever the plan was discussed: initial ridicule; apparent flaws that turned out not to be flaws; final, reluctant agreement that the plan was as threatening a Doomsday device as Israel, given its limited power, could hope to come up with.

At the start the plan would have been voted down, five to one, the objections ranging from the technological to the moral. The former, the young nuclear physicist disposed of first, showing that the plan's biggest apparent flaw, its delivery system, was actually its strength, because it was within Israel's capability, and its effectiveness could be assured in advance.

The catastrophic effects of the plan he demonstrated, using a map. And soon the logistical and technological objections were all answered. That left the moral, which were not completely and finally answered then—or since.

The young nuclear physicist found himself being assaulted by the other five, with ethical objections he felt it was not his function to refute. He did say a couple of things, though, which turned out to be persuasive. One was that a Doomsday device was a last resort, designed to be so frightening and awesome it would dissuade others from provoking it, and as such it was designed to violate all the rules of chivalry.

And second, their committee had been charged by the government with the task of finding a feasible plan. "We," he told the other five, "are not the nation's High Court of Ethics. For us to judge the plan's morality would be to usurp the government's function. Our job is to come up with a plan that works. I think we have done that. What to do with it is the government's decision."

Eventually, the Committee of Six voted unanimously to "pass the plan along," the use of the word "endorse" having been voted down.

15

And each of them, even the nuclear physicist, voted yes with the mental reservation that the plan would never be used, and therefore the entire project was an academic exercise.

But on the morning of July 12, 1979, in the cabinet room in Jerusalem, the exercise was no longer academic.

The Labor Minister leaned forward pugnaciously. "Why are you in such a hurry? We were hurt badly by their opening offensive in '73, and we bounced back and won. How are you so sure, only six hours after an attack begins, we won't do it again?"

For the first time, the Defense Minister spoke. Shmuel Arit was a fighting hero, a famous general, one of the few who had come out of the '73 war with good grades. The '73 war, in fact, had made him Chief of Staff, and later Defense Minister.

"First, all the indicators are different: the strength analyses, the weapons matchups, the intelligence reports, the kill ratios. Second, in '73 we started with a partial mobilization; this time it's total and not helping. Third, even with the Arab weaknesses in '73, we might not have won without the American airlift. This time the Arab weaknesses are gone, and so is the airlift. Fourth, we're missing the clout to get it stopped through diplomatic channels. Is that enough?" Arit said it clinically, his beefy, muscular face impassive, as if to show there were no emotional investment, just a marshaling of facts.

Then the Prime Minister took over again, apparently summoning help against Shapira, but secretly hoping for more opposition, so he could be sure every view, every supposition, was exposed to the most demanding attack before it was accepted. "So what are our options?" he asked.

When Gonen, the hawk, jumped in, though, it was to attack Shapira, not the plan. "I'll tell you one option," he shouted, his jowly face quivering with righteousness and excitement. "There's always a long swim in the Mediterranean—for the lucky ones. My pacifist friend," and here he took a quick, annoyed look toward Shapira, "doesn't seem to believe the Arabs when they say they're going to destroy the state of Israel and drive its people into the sea. As I recall, a lot of people didn't believe Hitler. They read *Mein Kampf* and said he didn't really *mean* all those nasty things about the Jews; they said power would make him more responsible.

"Well, I believe the Arabs. I believe that when they can, they'll do what they've promised. And right now they can." The Finance Minister stopped talking, but his face went on quivering for a moment or two.

Then, for the first time, the lean, elegant Foreign Minister, Weismann, spoke, using privately the same florid eloquence he was known for at the UN and at fund-raising dinners the world over.

"I should be in total agreement with the Labor Minister's position,

16

could he show me a solitary acceptable alternative to the plan. My God, the mere thought of it is an abomination. Are there alternatives? I could formulate three worth discussing. First, we could defeat the enemy in the field. I accept the expert military determination that we cannot. Given half a chance, God knows, we could, but we haven't been given even that." Praising the armed forces was, for Weismann, a ritual; among the leaders, he alone had never been in combat, and was defensive about it.

"Second, we could secure an immediate cease-fire vote in the Security Council. Immediate. And have the Arabs respect it. I am leaving soon for New York to try to achieve that, but I hardly need say we don't have the votes. And even if we did, the Soviets have a veto. And even if they didn't use it, the enemy could simply ignore the vote, as they have ignored others. Or they could signal compliance and then stall until we were supine.

"You'll recall how in '73 we managed to delay while we encircled the Egyptian Third Corps, even under heavy pressure from the United States. For the Arabs today, there is no such pressure. And the stakes are far higher, not a mere army corps, an entire nation.

"Clearly, the only way to secure a cease-fire would be for the US and the USSR to threaten the use of force. Equally clearly, neither is sufficiently concerned to do that. From the Soviets of course we expect nothing. Which leaves the United States, and I hardly need recount for you how their concern faded in the face of petrol and petrodollars.

"Were these two powers to *be* sufficiently concerned, of course . . ." The Foreign Minister let his voice trail away. He had come close to speaking of the plan itself, which, with the Prime Minister sitting there, would have been presumptuous, and Weismann was never presumptuous. With a glance toward the Old Man to make sure his deference had been noticed, he went on.

"The third alternative would be to, in effect, throw ourselves on the tender mercies of our Arab neighbors. Eight, perhaps five years ago, I might—I say *might*—have preferred that to the plan. Today, and here the Finance Minister's analogy to *Mein Kampf* is well taken, I should not trust this nation to the mercy of Arab armies, much less to that of the PLO. Our neighbors have been trumpeting their intentions; why shall we not take them at their word? Where are the responsible voices in the Arab world of 1979? And in the rest of the world, from whom can we expect help as abject captives, if we cannot get it as an independent nation?"

About to sum up, Weismann looked around at the others. His ability to compose an extemporaneous speech was formidable and he always liked to be sure others appreciated it, no matter how grave the subject.

"No," he concluded, "I should not want the fate of three million

Israelis to ride on such speculation. I should not want such a decision on my head!"

Whatever his egotism, the Foreign Minister was an extraordinary speaker, clear headed, vivid, and graceful. For a moment no one spoke. Then the Labor Minister responded.

"No, you would not want that on your head. But the plan. *That* you would want on your head."

To himself, the Prime Minister congratulated Shapira for keeping up the fight. Privately, he shared most of the Labor Minister's questions, and moreover resented Weismann's glibness and delicate sycophancy. Most of all, he felt this was too serious a decision to be railroaded through. Aloud, he attacked Shapira.

"Let's think for a moment about whose head the plan is really on. Ours? Or the Arabs', who are not looking for accommodation and peace but fire and destruction. Ours? Or the Americans', who caved in when the Arabs grabbed them where it hurts, Wall Street and Detroit. Ours? Or the Common Market's, which dropped us to please their oil suppliers. Ours? Or the Africans' and Asians', who deserted us for economics and pretended it was principle."

The Old Man looked at Shapira, as if to say: Your turn.

And the Labor Minister took his turn.

"I know, I know, it's all the world's fault. But we're the ones who are talking about using the plan, not the world. We're the ones playing with dynamite, only worse."

The Prime Minister waded back in, caught in the argument and trotting out his famous irony. "I'm glad that our Labor Minister is reminding us of the dangers of the plan. Because otherwise none of us would have thought of them. We always looked on it as a magic wand we could wave to get us out of trouble.

"You mean it's risky, Lev? You mean we're taking a chance? You mean there's actually some danger? Why didn't we think of that?"

The Old Man looked around the table. His face was red and his wiry white hair seemed even more electric. He thought Lev had made some strong points, and now he was trying to provoke more debate and defend his own position, and most of all, counterattack.

"So now the answer is obvious! We don't use the plan. It's settled." He paused. The others all looked shocked, which was what he wanted. Then he went on.

"But first answer me one question. What do we do instead?"

Despite the PM's wishes and efforts, it had become a tennis match, he against Shapira, with the other four swiveling their heads from player to player.

The Labor Minister said simply, "Does the end justify the means?" He knew that the Old Man, as a youthful democratic socialist, had loved to ask the same question.

The Prime Minister whacked the ball back. "Ah ha, Lev! Answering a question with a question! You sound like an old Eastern European Jew!"

The Russian-born PM knew that kind of remark infuriated the younger Sabra, who had a certain contempt for the "Jewishness" of the Diaspora. He kept right on speaking, not giving Shapira a chance to answer.

"Well, first," he said, "I'll answer your question. Then I'll tell you why you couldn't answer mine.

"The answer to your question is, no, the end doesn't necessarily justify the means. Sometimes it may, sometimes it may not. However, this particular end, preventing the annihilation of the state of Israel, does justify these particular means, a warning to a complacent world."

Shapira wanted to jump in; the Old Man was too fast.

"Now let me tell you why you couldn't answer my question. Because you could not bring yourself to utter the only alternative to the plan, which is to let Israel die. You won't say it. You'll keep your sanctity right to the end. And why will you stay the Jewish saint, and refuse to make the decision? Because you know that *we* will make the decision for you, and leave you untainted. I just wonder what you would do if *you* had a majority, and your view were about to prevail."

If the Prime Minister had begun this exhortation to keep the discussion alive, he was ending it with the intent to win over Shapira.

"Don't worry though, you won't prevail. We'll do what we have to. Not because we are less high minded than you are, or more ruthless. Or because we don't see the dilemma. It's because someone has to—what's that expression that always makes my mouth dry up?" He looked around impatiently, and with a touch of amusement.

"Oh yes," he answered himself, "bite the bullet. And *we'll* do it to spare *you* the taste of powder."

Then he sat back momentarily, but only to take a deep breath before firing off one more round. "I wonder what you would have done at Masada, Lev? How would you have voted?"

With this kind of salvo, the Prime Minister had leveled many opponents, in elections, meetings, debates, in the Knesset. But this opponent remained standing.

"A *warning* to a complacent world," answered the Labor Minister, nodding his head and smiling faintly. "What a nice way to put it! And suppose the *warning* doesn't work and we have to go beyond warning?"

"We'll worry about it then," the Old Man replied. "We'll have another meeting. The alternative you seem to leave open, jumping into the Mediterranean, will still be available to us later."

Lev Shapira could see he had no allies at the table. His only hope

had been Weismann, but the Foreign Minister had made his one eloquent statement of conscience and then said no more. And even if he
got the Foreign Minister, a third vote would be needed just for a
deadlock. He had no hope; nonetheless he tried once more.

"And do you want us to be remembered for all time by that *warning?*" he asked. Shapira looked at Weismann as he said it, but the
Foreign Minister looked only at the Prime Minister. And it was the
latter who replied.

"And do *you* want us to be remembered for all time with memorial
candles and prayers for the dead? Or do you consider this just a tem-
porary defeat? And do you hope that maybe in another 1,800 years
there'll be another Jewish state? That's how long it took this time.
And that's how many? Sixty generations? Is that the legacy you want
for your children?"

Up to then the Labor Minister had kept his powerful, stubby hands
on the table, using them to gesticulate as he spoke. Now he dropped
them into his lap, a signal of defeat. He didn't want to stop, but he
didn't have the support. He was one against five.

The Old Man saw the signal and, oddly, was disappointed. He
waited, to give Shapira a last chance, but the hands remained in
the lap; he was mute. Again, the PM waited, and then said, almost
expectantly, "Does anyone have any other reservations, or comments?"

Silence around the table. Everyone looked around at everyone else.
Except for Shapira, who stared straight ahead.

"Then," said the Old Man quietly, "I'll add one more thing. We're
taking on a tremendous responsibility. We'll have to answer for it—
to the Knesset, to the people. To ourselves. And for us old-fashioned
ones, to God. I wish none of us had it; I wish we could have a referen-
dum, I wish there were a better answer. But the lack of an alternative,
unless you count extinction as an alternative, in a way makes it easier.
So, it comes to this: Someone has to do it, and I'm willing to take it
on my head. Are you willing?" No one answered.

The Old Man stopped and looked around. "If there are no further
comments, we'll vote." He waited. Silence. "Remember," he said, "any
way you vote, you are making a decision. You can't avoid it."

The hush in the room was awesome. Nobody moved. Then, as if
cued by the Prime Minister, from the street the low rumble of moving
tanks could be heard. He let the moment stretch. Then looked at each
face around the table; from his left, Weismann, Arit, Benot, Gonen,
and, last, Shapira.

"All those in favor of the plan," he said softly, "raise your hands."

Without hesitation up went the hands of Arit, Benot, and Gonen.
Weismann, giving himself another moment of conscience, paused
briefly before raising his hand. Only then did the Old Man put his
hand up.

Five hands. Five faces looked at the sixth.

"So," said the PM, "*We* have made a decision." He accented the word "we" and looked at the Labor Minister as he said it.

Shapira understood. He put his hands over his face as if to rub the anguish from it, and then slowly shook his head from side to side.

"I know what you would like," he said, his voice suddenly turned hoarse. "Unanimity. Solidarity. I cannot give it to you. I cannot bring myself to vote for this plan. I ask myself, am I another Pilate, washing my hands of responsibility? I have no sure answer. I wish I did. I only know I cannot say yes to this plan. I'm sorry."

And then, in a touch of melodrama that was totally out of character, the earnest Labor Minister himself spoke the question. "All those opposed to the Masada Plan?"

And head down, eyes closed, he raised his hand.

To everyone's surprise, the Old Man leaned forward, reached his right hand to Shapira's thick shoulder and gave it a squeeze.

Then, turning brisk, he went on.

"The question is how to put the plan into effect. As you may know, we have worked out a scenario. I'll outline it for your comments."

From his portfolio the Old Man took out a set of papers stapled together. He glanced at the top sheet briefly, then the second and third, and spoke again.

"Delivery will be on three levels. The first will be official, presented to the UN, the US, and the USSR. It will ask an immediate cease-fire. It will say we are victims of aggression, that the Arab invasion affects the peace of the world, and could trigger a nuclear world war."

Wetting a gnarled finger on his tongue, the Prime Minister turned a page, looked again, and continued.

"The second level will be unofficial, and authoritative, and will get closer to the real nature of the threat." He no longer used the word "warning"; now it was "threat" and the others noticed it.

"We will say that we have nuclear weapons and that when a nation's life is at stake, it reserves the right to use *any* weapons in *any* way it sees fit, with *no* limitations on its response."

The PM looked up to see if there were any comments. None. Again he turned the page, looked at it briefly, and spoke.

"On the third level, the threat will be conveyed precisely and specifically, but irregularly, which is to say in such a way that it does not appear to be coming from our mouths. To be specific, we'll have it leaked, only there'll be no question of its authenticity."

Then he spoke a gentle aside, directed at Shapira.

"You see, Lev, we too wish we didn't have to do this. We don't want it inscribed in history, not unless the record of the world's broken pledges, the shabby expediency, the desertion of our friends, the Arabs' attempt at a final solution are all inscribed with it. But you know and I know they won't be. So by leaking it, we keep it unofficial; we can always deny it for the record."

The Old Man was defensive about this tactic. Although his explanation of it seemed to be meant for Shapira, he was really defending it to himself.

"Pragmatic?" he asked, and then answered, "Yes. Immoral? No. And who makes this judgment? We at this table, we who are in charge, responsible. We do not shrink from it. We do it when it must be done. Now! We cannot wait for an ultimate verdict, chiseled in stone, handed down from Mount Sinai.

"Now is when it must be done. Let it be on our heads. Let the country's young writers and philosophers vilify us for it later. I just hope they're around to do it, and there's a country around for them to do it in. I'll take my chances. I'll be satisfied."

The vote was past; this was not campaigning, this was from the heart of an old man who had built a nation from nothing and now at the end of his life again saw the specter of nothingness.

"But I've said enough." The Prime Minister snapped himself back to the business before them. "Now give me your reactions to the three-level delivery of the plan. Any comments, objections, changes?"

He put down the document, sat back and waited. He wanted it absolutely clear he was not rushing this.

Silence.

Again the Old Man spoke. "All that remains, then—and I say this as if it were a mere detail, which I assure you it isn't—is how to carry out the second and third levels. To whom. By whom. Again, we have worked out a scenario, which I offer for your reactions.

"We are expecting, hoping, the primary response to the Masada Plan will come from the United States. The first level of the plan will be delivered officially to the UN by Itzhak, to the USSR through the Swiss and to the US by our ambassador in Washington. Therefore, he should not handle the unofficial second and third levels. They should go through Dov in New York."

Sitting at the table, papers in hand, the Prime Minister was prepared for some argument on this. But the substantive discussion of the plan itself and the tensions of the situation had drained all six of them. No one was prepared to debate tactics.

"Any thoughts on this?" he asked wearily. Pause.

Arit, the Defense Minister, spoke. "This third level, this leak, why only in New York? Why not Moscow, too?"

For an instant the Old Man's eyes flicked toward Weismann, who looked back and quickly glanced away. Then the PM replied, "Because we can't work it with the Russians, we don't have the right kind of contact. I wish we did. Anything else?"

Silence.

The six men around the table looked at each other. They knew that in the next day the Masada Plan would decide the life or death of their country. And more. Much more.

"So then it's settled," said the Old Man, suddenly as brisk as if they had just agreed on the main speaker at their annual banquet.

"We'll let Dov do it."

Again, silence.

The Prime Minister shrugged and got up, indicating the meeting was over. The others stood, too.

"For now, there's nothing more to say. As soon as there is, we'll talk." The others started to leave, and the Old Man spoke loudly, so all could hear him.

"Itzhak, you stay behind for a few minutes so we can call Dov." He said nothing more until the four were out of the room. Then he looked at Weismann.

"And the Russians?"

"Hours ago, as you instructed," Weismann answered. "You were quite sure of yourself, weren't you?"

"Sure I was sure." The Prime Minister shrugged and looked at the places where the other four had been sitting. "What other way could they go?"

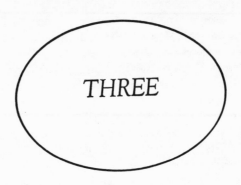

THREE

Dov Shalzar slammed down the library phone as if it had suddenly become too hot to hold. He had never liked the damned curlicued thing anyway; brass and mother-of-pearl, it looked as though it belonged in a call girl's bathroom. Years ago it had been ordered by a precious New York interior decorator because one of Dov's predecessors thought it would give the place the chic needed to impress wealthy friends of Israel.

He loathed it and kept meaning to have it changed to phone company standard, the latest of these intentions having come last year when the UN mission and the ambassador's residence had been combined in a town house on East Seventy-second Street. Once again he had let it slip, perhaps because he realized the phone had its uses. It had become the messenger he could blame for the bad news. When he heard something he didn't like, he could vent his anger at the phone, slam it down, blame its tidings on its ornate, pretentious ugliness.

This time he found it grotesque indeed. Shalzar slumped low in his wing chair, sliding his slim legs out in front of him, his hand rubbing his forehead. Well, at least now the ambush on Madison Avenue made sense; it had been a microcosm of a larger attack by Arabs on Israelis. Only he had escaped with his life. His country might not be so lucky.

When he got back to the embassy, with the help of the two policemen from the Central Park precinct, he found out his beeper had been signaling a call from the Prime Minister. He picked up the phone and got the Old Man. First he apologized for his unavailability, and described the attack on him. Then he heard of the Arab invasion. Then he was given the most repugnant task of his life.

He had to put the Masada Plan into effect.

A delivery scenario had come along with the birth of the plan. The

UN ambassador was the prime operative and he was brought home and briefed. Two years later, when Shalzar assumed the post, he, too, was instructed carefully in the plan, and part of his briefing was the oral shorthand by which he'd be ordered to carry it out.

The ambassador first had to be sure he could recognize two voices on the other end of the line. So after the Old Man spoke briefly, the Foreign Minister got on. Weismann had said only, "Your old friend wants to tell you about the dinner invitations. We agree he's doing the right thing."

Then the Prime Minister had come back on the line to give him the orders.

"We have decided," he said, using the preset language, "to invite those people to dinner. As planned. You send out the invitations."

The UN ambassador felt an iciness, a contraction in his chest and stomach at hearing the orders. It hit him first when Weismann got on the line, and it grew with the Old Man's words. Shalzar could barely breathe, and he had to concentrate on inhaling so he could answer.

"Don't you think we should put the dinner off a couple of days?"

"No," the faint voice came back at him. "Send the invitations right away."

Shalzar concentrated on regularizing his breathing for a moment. Deep breaths, in, out, in, out. "Supposing they won't come?" he asked.

"That's up to them. You just send out those invitations. You tell them we've got to hear from them by 9 a.m. tomorrow, or we'll assume they're not interested; 9 a.m. July 13, your time. Thirty hours from now. Understand?"

Oh yes, he understood. There was an icy hand in his chest cavity, squeezing. He understood.

When Shalzar was briefed on the plan, in the summer of '77, he had found its enormity and deadliness stupefying, but like most of the tiny number of Israeli diplomats and officials who knew of it, he was not disposed to argue because he couldn't imagine it would ever be used. It was a Doomsday device, nothing more, and like people all over the world, even those who knew of the brinksmanship of power politics and the destructiveness of modern weaponry, he had never believed Doomsday would come. And now, even though he knew of the fighting and heard the orders, he refused to concede Doomsday was here.

"If we invite them this way, they may think us rude," he said, desperate to break out of the jargon and scream his protest. "They may never talk to us again, or invite us anywhere. Do you want that?"

He wished he had the Old Man there, growl and all, so he could stand nose-to-nose with him and fight, but all he had was the small, faraway voice that clearly was not disposed to argue.

"Listen to me, Dov, this is not a matter for debate. Either we invite them at once or we may never be in a position to ask them again. In which case it won't make any difference whether they ever talk to us, or invite us back. I hope that's clear." The Prime Minister did not pause to give him a chance to reply.

"Send out the invitations exactly as we discussed earlier."

By this time, Dov Shalzar was standing at the phone, grinding his feet into the thick tan carpeting like an athlete about to start a race. "Please think about it, old friend," was all he could manage. "Please think."

This time the Old Man's voice had a touch of melancholy. "We have thought, and we have decided. How soon will you be sending them out? Give me a definite time."

Shalzar looked at his watch. "It's 3 a.m. here; I'll start first thing in the morning."

"And how many will you send?" asked the PM.

"Well, I assume the first is being taken care of, so I'll be responsible for the second and third. Is that correct?"

"Yes, that is correct. Good. Any more questions?"

Yes, Shalzar wanted to say. Do you know what you're doing? All he said was, "No, sir," to make it sound like a soldier obeying orders.

"Good, then that's all for now. Please tell us the moment you have a response, or anything else happens."

"Yes, sir."

"Dov, we're counting on you."

"Yes. Goodbye, sir."

"Goodbye. God bless you." The Old Man was an atheist who never let a tight moment go by without invoking the Lord's blessings at least once.

The ornate receiver banged into its cradle. Shalzar rubbed the bony fingers of his right hand over his temples, then his eyes. The plan came with the job. He had always known that; he had just never believed it would ever leap from those papers in his safe and become real.

Sitting in the quiet of the embassy library, with its subdued tans, browns, and golds, its walls of books, all of which he had chosen, and its telephone, which he had *not* chosen, he thought back to another room, in Jerusalem, where he was briefed two years ago. On hearing the plan, he'd said, "If we get to the point where we have to use it, we can't win anyway."

And the Prime Minister had answered, "We know all that. We hope never to have to use it, but if it comes to it, we'll have to know how, and there'll be no time to learn. So get it all down in your mind, now, and make sure it stays there, letter perfect."

And Shalzar knew it, every last detail. And wished he had never heard of it.

He slumped back onto the velvet of the wing chair, and for a moment sat there, staring straight ahead. Suddenly he was aware that his shirt was still sopping wet from the run along Sixty-eighth and through the park. The Arabs hadn't wasted any time in carrying their war to Madison Avenue, he thought. He jumped to his feet, walked quickly out of the library into the hall, and bounded up two flights of blue-carpeted stairs.

In his third-floor bedroom he showered quickly, daubed some merthiolate on his scraped calf, put on a solid gray suit and a fresh blue, short-sleeved shirt, and striped tie.

He sat on his bed, picked up the phone and dialed the number of the apartment on Sixty-fourth Street he had just left.

It was 3:30 when her phone rang. Kate Colby knew that because even before she answered it she looked at the illuminated face of her digital clock, so she could decide how annoyed to be. Then she reached out and drew the receiver to her ear.

"Hello, it's three-thirty in the morning," she began, trying to fend off the strands of blonde hair that kept getting between the phone and her mouth.

"Ah, but it's nine-thirty in Israel," replied Shalzar.

Her voice was still groggy, but she was coming around fast. "I'm not in Israel. *You're* not in Israel." She hesitated, then perhaps because she hadn't come around enough, went ahead and said it. "Only your wife is in Israel. But who's complaining?" At once she wished she hadn't. As it turned out, it didn't matter, because he ignored it, which is how she knew something serious was afoot.

"Kate," he began, and she heard the urgency, "I want you to stop the tape and not start it again until I tell you. That may be a long time, and it may hurt. But I need your assurance, right now. Please!"

"Oh boy," she said, the cobwebs gone and a mock brightness taking over. "This has got to be important. A divorce." She paused for effect. "No, not *that* important. Maybe just a war in the Middle East."

"Yes." And then he paused. "And that's only part of it. Now Kate, for God's sake, stop being so clever. Stop it."

It was hard for Kate Colby to stop her quick cleverness, even when she wanted to, but then it was hard for her to complain about it, for it had helped her in her climb up the greased pole of TV journalism. And at the moment she had gotten as high as any woman ever had. Once she had been called "a witty Walters" and she had answered, "There already is a witty Walters, and her name is Barbara. Could I be a caustic Colby?" She feigned annoyance at the comparison; secretly she was pleased.

Kate was a UBC correspondent who anchored specials, covered major international stories, and had her own syndicated talk show, "Today's Woman." Aside from Barbara Walters, she was the only woman in television news with the clout, on the air or in executive offices, of those alpha magnitude stars, the anchor men.

And she had done it all in seven years. At twenty-nine, freshly separated from Ed Colby, with two small kids, no occupation and almost no money, she had walked in off the street to the offices of a New York radio station and said to the news director, "I want to be a reporter." After chatting with her for twenty minutes about broadcast experience and her lack of it, he said, "Honey, I've got a desk and a tape recorder. What I don't have is money. If you want a chance to cover stories just for the experience, you've got it."

She jumped at the desk, the tape recorder, and the chance.

Two months later, when she got an interview with a reclusive corporate president nobody else in New York had been able to come near, the news director found a salary for her. Three months after that, she was working for a small, independent TV station; another year later she was hired by a network station, which started her on news and soon gave her a talk show. Then the network stole her from its own flagship station and assigned her to network news. By the time she had been in broadcast journalism four years, her popularity was second only to the veteran who anchored the UBC evening news.

Kate Colby was clever; she was also intelligent, well informed, hardworking, and thoroughly prepared. She could match wits with anyone. And she could be tough.

And without question, her looks hadn't hurt. She was nearly five-foot-nine, slim, with long, elegant legs. "I just hope you're a leg man, as opposed to a you-know-what man," she had said to the ambassador soon after they met. At thirty-six she had the kind of aquiline features that would improve with age, skin stretched over bone with no padding in between: a nose that was a plastic surgeon's dream; strong chin—perhaps too jutting when she got angry. Her eyes were a pale gray green, her hair dirty blonde with gray in it, but touched up to an ash blonde. All of it looked terrific on TV.

She sounded good, too, a Southern girl with just enough of Georgia left in her speech to give it a softness that made the wit sharper by contrast.

By now she had been divorced for six years, and lived with her two children in a roomy cooperative apartment on Sixty-fourth Street between Madison and Park avenues. Joanna was ten and Charlie nine and they went to private schools. Each day Kate set aside time to spend with them, reading, playing games, or just lying on her big bed, the three of them, talking. Because of her live-in house-keeper, she was free to race off on short notice to cover big stories wherever they happened.

She had worked hard to get away from "women's stories" and gradually she strengthened her credentials in politics and international news. Soon she was getting invitations to the UN cocktail party circuit and it was at an Israeli reception she had met Dov Shalzar, two years earlier.

"I'm sorry," she told him over the phone, the sleepiness and the cleverness gone from her voice. "The tape is off."

She had hit upon the phrase as shorthand for saying she was tuning out as a journalist. At first he had used the term "off the record"; they had both laughed at that, he because it sounded stuffy, she because it reminded her of reporters in 1930s movies, with press cards in turned-up hatbrims.

"When you videotape something," she had told him, "stop the tape means they're not recording. It's better than off the record. *Anything* is better than off the record."

Kate Colby and Dov Shalzar had been lovers for nearly two years, almost from the time he had arrived in New York to take up his post. The reception at which they met was held to introduce him to the press and the UN community, or such of it as was still going to Israeli parties. Glass of white wine in hand, she had been talking to the lean, handsome man with the New York accent for twenty minutes before she realized he was the guest of honor.

What fooled her, she had confessed to him, was the accent. "I come by it honestly," he had assured her. "Oh, I believe you," she shot back. "Who would bother to come by that accent *dis*honestly?" She smiled as she said it, to soften the sting, and, she admitted to herself at once, to do more—to see if she could get a response from this attractive man, who looked as if he could be the ambassador from any one of a number of European countries: France, Italy, Belgium, England, as well as from Israel.

Also, she was happy to see he was two or three inches taller than she, and slim and athletic looking. Happy because two situations she tried to avoid were walking hand in hand with a short man and sleeping with a fat one. The walking part was damned silly, she thought, but she had spent the last three years of her married life sleeping with an increasingly paunchy Ed Colby, and it hadn't helped a marriage that was already shaky for a dozen other reasons.

Her mind ran through all this like a computer, until she had to tell herself: my God, slow down, walking around at this reception is probably a dark-eyed beauty named Mrs. Shalzar, and a covey of stalwart young Sabras.

Shalzar had grinned back after her quip about the accent, which pleased her. The man doesn't look like a stuffed shirt, she thought, so I shouldn't be surprised, but after all, ambassadors do tend to be overstuffed with dignity. And she had lost her appetite for stuffed dignity.

For his part, the ambassador hadn't missed the resonance of her smile, and his in return had been part of a cautious response. Another part had been to prolong the conversation by asking, "Shall I explain the accent?"

And he did explain, starting then, and continuing at the many meetings to follow.

David Seltzer came by his accent in Manhattan, on West End Avenue, where he was born, and where he lived for the first seventeen years of his life. He was raised on Zionism without realizing he was paying much attention to it—until the Israeli war for independence in 1948. Then, already a freshman at Harvard, he took the train home, packed his knapsack, and told his startled parents, "I am going to fight for Israel." Neither Bernard nor Ida Seltzer was prepared to see their Zionism carried that far, but Dave was not to be stopped.

When the war was won, Dave Seltzer decided to stay in Israel, and like many of the new Israelis, Hebraicized his name. As Dov Shalzar, he finished college there, joined the diplomatic service and rose quickly, an advance that was not hurt by illustrious combat service in three more wars, '56, '67, and '73.

Shalzar was a perfect choice for the New York post; not only did he speak the language of the natives, he had the medals and the glamour the job needed and the eloquence and sex appeal to woo Hadassah ladies and other friends of Israel at lunches, dinners, receptions, or wherever funds had to be raised and Israeli positions explained.

About a Mrs. Shalzar and children, Kate was right—yet not right. Twenty-five years earlier, Dov had married a fierce Sabra, and had regretted it almost at once. No red-necked country boy could spit out the words "New York Jew" with the venom Ruth could. She and the three children managed never to be with him at his embassy posts. The children he missed, but felt a strong relief at being far from the teeth-grinding tension of life with her.

For the conduct of his private life, this left three options. The first was divorce, which for years he had dismissed as potentially harmful to his career, and because of Ruth's combativeness, potentially bloody. The second was abstinence, which his morality told him was unnecessary and his body told him was unthinkable. The third, which was the option he chose, was what he delicately characterized in his mind as "relationships."

Shalzar was neither a flirt nor a womanizer. Wherever he was posted, however, he managed to set up liaisons, some lasting the duration of his assignment, but none longer, which combined sex with esteem, compatibility, and an understanding of the limits of the affair. None was, for him anyway, "serious," until he met Kate Colby, and even then, for a year, he permitted himself no thought of divorce. Only when she broke off with him for a while did he allow himself the thought, hopefully, apprehensively.

Kate, of course, had thought about it, too, as they began talking of it, even joking—at any rate *she* joked. He took the first step, a separation, but never seemed to go on to the next. Sometimes she wondered whether he wanted to.

"I'll be right over." Dov's voice on the phone, she now realized for the first time, was as tense as she had ever heard it.

Reflexively, she started to be funny. The line started out as, "You men never get enough." But she swallowed it, and instead said, "You come ahead, if it's that important."

"It is," he said. "I'll be there in ten minutes, maybe less."

He was there in eight. They walked him into the living room, wondering what she'd hear, and just how bad it was, he looking pale and tough and a little haunted, wondering how much to say and how to say it. Often she had conjured up pictures of what this gentle, civilized man could have looked like in combat, a machine gun in his hands, killing people. Now she thought she knew.

Kate sat on the end of the sofa, her bare, tanned legs curled up under her. Dov leaned over and kissed her on the top of the head, with unexpected softness, as if he were saying this was the last touch of intimacy he could offer for a while.

Then he sat in the easy chair that had become his favorite; it was set at a right angle to the sofa so they could look at each other. He began speaking.

"We have been invaded. By the entire Arab world—Egyptians, Syrians, Jordanians, Lebanese, Iraqis, PLO, Saudis, even a few token Libyans. Not to mention regiments of oil money and the best Soviet and Chinese equipment money can buy. And, oh yes, American equipment, too; that's an irony, and one we could do without. Our planes and tanks are under the heaviest missile fire in the history of warfare. Arab aircraft have hit Tel Aviv, Haifa, and a lot of other places, including Jerusalem. We've never seen anything like it. The jihad is on."

His narrative had flowed like a stream, and when, finally, she had a chance to say something, all she could utter was "My God, not again!"

He managed half a grin and repeated her words, "not again." Then shook his head. "No, not *again*."

" 'Again' would be bad enough. Right now, though, I'd settle for it, because in spite of the losses, that would mean, eventually, a happy ending, a successful ending. No, not 'again.' "

He hesitated, ran a hand across his chin, seeming suddenly to question whether to go on. Then he did.

"The difference is, this time we shall lose."

He stared at her and very carefully began explaining, knowing he had to divulge important material, yet afraid to say too much. Down on the street a police siren sounded; he heard it as a warning. Be careful. He waited for it to fade, giving himself a moment longer to get set.

"What sounds like the dismal ending to this story may really be just the beginning—maybe no less dismal, but the beginning. We have a plan.

"Its justification rests on four assumptions. The first is that it's to be used only in the face of the imminent annihilation of the state of Israel. *Only* then. Think for a moment, Kate. Suppose the United States were about to be wiped off the face of the earth. What would you, as a nation, do to stop it? Or to put it a better way, what wouldn't you do?

"Israel is looking Doomsday in the face. If you can't understand that, you can't understand any of the rest." The ambassador paused, his eyes warning her: Get ready. He waited for a response. Kate got the warning, and wondered what the details of the horror were, and how she was involved. All she did was nod. He went on.

"You know what a Doomsday device is, don't you? Dr. Strangelove told the world about it. It says: If you destroy us, you will trigger a response that will, in turn, destroy you. By making the price of a first strike exorbitant—so high no one will want to pay it—the device keeps the peace. At least that's the theory."

Shalzar stood, stretched, walked a few steps toward the window, then back, trying to loosen up. She watched him; he was not having an easy time, nor was he a man given to confiding.

"May I put some music on?" he asked, and barely waiting for her yes, walked to the record player, fished a couple of discs out of an album of Beethoven piano sonatas, and without looking to see which they were, put them on the changer and started it. Before continuing he waited for the first quiet sounds of the piano.

She listened. A late sonata, one she could never remember the number of. She was more interested in him; he seemed as taut as she had ever seen him; she thought if she had touched him she'd feel only rigid muscle. He waited for a few bars, then perched on the arm of the easy chair, and spoke.

"The second assumption is the memory of the holocaust, a memory that is, for us, like an indigestible meal, long since swallowed, but tasted over and over at the smallest upset. In spite of all you Americans have heard, or read, about concentration camps and gas chambers and ovens, you have been spared the actual taste of annihilation. Your response to it is genuine, but abstract. Think of the difference between my discussing the pain of childbirth and your discussing it. I can sympathize. You've felt it.

"The Jews have felt it. I don't want to be another Jew who keeps throwing up that awful number, but six million of us were murdered. That's twice as many Jews as there are in the entire state of Israel.

"This brings us to the third assumption, which we have reached only after disbelief and then agony. We are alone—just as in the 1940s. No one is going to help us, which means, of course, the United States. What special despair that gives me, because I'm still so much an American, I can't tell you. The fact is, though, this country has cut us loose for convenience. For the convenience of its bankers and automobile manufacturers and commuters and Sunday drivers. Not out of fear, mind you, because America is strong enough to stand up, and to do more, to pressure a solution in the Middle East. But that would hurt its oil supply and its dollar. You'd have to make some adjustments, and that would be inconvenient. No, not fear. Convenience."

The closest Kate Colby and Dov Shalzar ever got to genuine battling came when they argued over the Middle East. She had to be careful, she knew, for Dov, in most things a moderate man, was intransigent on his nation's position, and this was not the time for a debate. But she couldn't keep still.

"Don't you think Israel should have been more willing to compromise rather than sitting there with chunks of occupied territory? The Arabs have rights in the Middle East too, Dov."

Never would he let that pass, and she knew it. She was surprised at the mildness of his sardonic answer. "We have given up the passes and the oil fields as a compromise. You see what good it did us. *We* are not the ones, after all, who have threatened to wipe out the *Arab* nations. Yes, the Arabs have rights, but they do not extend to the right to murder us."

He stood and smiled, a grim, bitter smile. "Arab rights is one hell of a rationalization for what you are doing—throwing us to the wolves and sitting back while they tear us apart."

Kate couldn't quite understand his response. She had expected more anger. As he went on, though, she began to understand.

Shalzar was quiet and didactic when he spoke again.

"If we can expect nothing from you in this crisis, it follows that we owe you nothing. We have no obligations to you or anyone else." He stopped himself. He did not want to go any further at the moment.

Something in him wanted to stop being so guarded, to open up and tell her everything he knew about the plan and his role in it. But he couldn't, not if the plan were to have a chance. Later he could tell her more, he'd *have* to tell her more.

He went on to the fourth assumption. "Finally, there is our awareness of our own power. We're just a tiny country, but never before in history has a midget had the destructive power he can have now. To say it's like a flyweight having the punch to knock out the heavyweight champion approaches the comparison without really coming close.

"So if you take the imminent annihilation, the memory of the holocaust, the total friendlessness and you add the lethal punch, you get a little guy who is dangerous. Very, *very* dangerous."

Shalzar looked at her, waiting for a reaction.

"If you're trying to frighten me, Dov," she said at last, "you're doing a hell of a job."

He walked to the sofa and sat next to her, reaching out to take her hand. "It would take a fool not to be, Kate. This is scary stuff."

Then she added something that made him fear he had said too much. "Whom else are you trying to frighten? And with what?"

If Kate was scared, she was also exhilarated, sure she was hearing something monumental, trying to find out more by emphasizing the fright, which wasn't hard, and playing down the curiosity, which was.

But he sensed the probing in her voice and face and knew he had to be careful. "So far you're the only one I've told."

"I'm not sure I want that honor," she replied.

The ambassador smiled at her. "It's too late now, and besides you won't have the honor for long. We're going to frighten a lot of people." He hesitated. "In a way, everybody. In another way, as few as possible, but the 'right' people. Even 'righter' than a network correspondent."

His smile became a grin; yet as he continued, she got the clear impression he was on tiptoes.

"So the 'who' is ambiguous and the 'what' even vaguer than that." He took her hand and squeezed it. "And if I knew, I wouldn't . . . I couldn't . . . tell you."

"Well thank you, Dov," she replied. "Thank you very much. You feed me enough to scare the hell out of me, without letting me know just what it is I should be scared of. And you half admit you're hiding the gory details, or would if you had to, which is the same thing. And of course I can't use a word of it to win an Emmy. How did I get so lucky?"

To disguise her groping, Kate had turned light and ironical. To disguise his concealment, Dov took on the same tone.

34

"I guess you know the right people," he answered. "Anyway, you've already won an Emmy."

"Two," she answered with a smile. "But that's beside the point. The point is that I, the reigning Queen of Flippancy, suddenly am not going to let you get away with being flip. Why did you tell me all this?"

She was pressing; he was standing firm. "Because I don't have a wife to tell. That is, I have a wife, but not to tell." He paused, and then said something she was to remember long afterward. "Because it's important that you know."

Her inevitable question was, Why? But before she could ask it, he went on.

"Look, an hour ago I got a phone call from Jerusalem that made me think the world was coming to an end, a call that told me a war only six hours old was going against us so badly it was no longer a question of *if,* only *when,* a call that told me a plan—one I've fought against since it was created—was going to be used.

"I don't want to sound melodramatic, but there's nothing in this for you, Kate. I'll just ask a lot and drain a lot and give nothing back. I'm drawing on my credit all the way, with no promises to repay. How much do I have?"

Kate lifted his tense hand to her face and kissed it on the knuckles, very softly, barely touching it to her lips.

"Unlimited. What can I do?"

"For now," he answered, "just listen, hold on tight, don't make me feel too guilty about the things I can't tell you."

The ambassador leaned over and kissed her lips. "When I can, I'll tell you; when the time comes, I'll use you." He hesitated, and decided against saying more. Not at the moment, anyway. She saw it. Why is he waiting? she asked herself. Shall I ask? No, she decided, if he wants to wait, I'll wait.

Then, to change the subject, he said, "It is called the Masada Plan, in Hebrew, *metz-ah-DAH.* Does the name mean anything to you?"

She shook her head.

"Masada was, and is, a fort, and historically and symbolically one of the most important places in Israel," he began.

"You know the tank units are particular heroes in Israel. When you read about the Six-Day War in '67, you read about tank battles, in which we destroyed the Arabs. The Yom Kippur War, in '73, had what was probably the biggest tank battle in history, bigger than El Alamein. Even on the Golan Heights, tanks were the key.

"Now on the other hand, when we fought for independence in '48, we didn't have many tanks." He laughed and shook his head.

"No, not many. To put it mildly. But as soon as a tank corps was formed, I made sure—being very pushy—to get armored service, and in the '56 war I was a tank captain. By the end of the '67 war I was a general, and in '73 I commanded three brigades.

"In Israel you can be a general and a civilian, too, and military distinction can mean a lot to your career. In fact, if Golda Meir had been a general, they'd probably have made her queen. Being a general certainly helped me. To some extent I'm ambassador to the UN because I'm a general and I'm a general because I'm in the armored force." Shalzar did not use the past tense here, and Kate noticed it.

"What I'm saying is," he went on, "the tankers are an elite. They ride, they don't walk—except at one place, where they do walk, and which they always remember. And which, in case you are lost in my elliptical yarn spinning, ties in with Masada.

"After you've taken your tank training, you go through a swearing-in ceremony, and to do that you go for a walk, uphill, and the walk is steep and rocky and takes nearly two hours. The place is Masada, and part of the oath the recruits take there is a line from a poem: 'Masada shall not fall again.'

"Masada is a rock plateau, it's a fortress, it's the scene of a famous battle, one of the last great Israeli battles for nearly 1,900 years. And it's a symbol that has indescribable emotional impact in Israel, for two reasons. First, it represents a defeat, which is why the line 'Masada shall not fall again' is part of the oath. But much, much more important is the victory it represents."

By this time the two Beethoven sonatas had finished playing, so Shalzar stood, walked over and flipped the records. And he lowered the volume, so that when the next sonata came on it was barely audible.

"It's easy for you to believe Jews can be fighters. Ever since you were a child there's been a state of Israel, and it's been pugnacious. But for centuries before that, many people had questioned the bravery of Jews—including a lot of Jews. Maybe that's the reason, as much as any other, some of us went off to Israel to fight: to find out how tough we were. As men. As Jews. You see, in New York, the Jewish boys of my generation were supposed to be good students, and play a musical instrument, and become doctors and lawyers. Being physical, being tough—that was left to Irish, and Italians, and Polish, and blacks.

"The stereotype of the wily Jew, who could avoid military service, or at least stay away from combat, had permeated the thinking of many Jews as well as Gentiles. When Moshe Dayan was training the Israeli Defense Forces, soldiers were drilled to attack, attack, attack, even to the point of recklessness, because he wanted to obliterate from the military all traces of 'Jewish cleverness.'

"In all this, that rock in the Judaean desert called Masada plays a big part. It's why we chose the name the Masada Plan.

"Let me tell you about Masada," Shalzar said. "It's important that you know, so you'll understand better what we're doing." And he stretched his legs out in front of him, and put his head back on the sofa.

Kate uncurled her legs, patted her robe in place, and turned to half face him. She was curious to hear what he'd say about Masada, but even more curious about what he'd ask afterward.

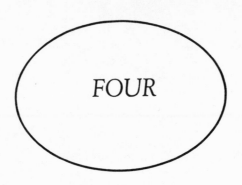

FOUR

Masada is a boat-shaped plateau in the eastern Judaean desert, about thirty-five miles southwest of Jerusalem, on the shore of the Dead Sea. It is a little more than a third of a mile long and about an eighth of a mile wide. Its steep cliffs and rocky terrain give it an austere beauty, and, more important historically, make it a superb natural fortress, difficult to approach, even more difficult to climb.

There is archaeological evidence that Masada was inhabited 6,000 years ago, and first fortified a century before the birth of Christ. The fortification we see the remains of today was built by the Roman puppet King Herod, who feared that the Jews would depose him, or that Cleopatra would march from Egypt and seize the kingdom of Judaea.

Around the rim of the plateau Herod built a double wall; on its northern end, a luxurious three-level palace-villa, on the west a large administrative palace. Elsewhere within the walls he built three smaller palaces, a large bathhouse, apartments, storerooms, and cisterns to catch rainwater, even a vegetable garden. In short, he designed the fortress for comfort and to withstand a lengthy siege, and with the help of the natural forces which had roughhewn the topography, Herod did his job well, as the Romans were to find out a century later.

From the time of Herod, Masada was manned continuously by Roman soldiers, until the eventful year A.D. 66, when one of the periodic Jewish uprisings against the Romans erupted into a war of revolution.

One of the first strongholds the Jewish revolutionaries attacked was Masada. A group of Zealots under Menahem took the fort and wiped out the Roman garrison. Throughout Israel, the Jews fought bitterly. At first they were successful; then the Romans, pouring legion after legion into the battle, dragged them down. Finally, in A.D. 70, the Roman general Titus retook Jerusalem, tore it apart, destroyed the Temple which was the heart of the nation, and drove most of the Jewish survivors out of the country.

By A.D. 70, the revolt was crushed all over Israel, and the Romans were back in control—except for Masada, where the Zealots holding the rock fortress had been joined by Jewish insurgents who had managed to get out of fallen Jerusalem and make their way across the Judaean desert. The fort became a base for raids into the surrounding countryside and so harassed the Romans that the Roman governor, Flavius Silva, decided in A.D. 72 to take Masada.

Silva set out with his Tenth Roman Legion plus auxiliaries and thousands of Jewish captive slaves carrying food, water, supplies, and timber. Counting those slaves, who were vital for construction work as well as transport, the Roman force amounted to about 15,000 men.

Defending Masada against them were 960 men, women, and children.

Although he had overwhelming numbers, Silva knew the Jews were tough and desperate, and well supplied with food and water. So with characteristic thoroughness, the Romans prepared for a siege.

First Silva built eight camps around Masada for his men, then a siege wall encircling the plateau, so no one could escape. The wall was an engineering marvel, six feet thick, its eastern section studded with 12 towers built at intervals of 80 to 100 yards, its total length more than two miles, even covering slopes so steep that in any event no one could have used them for escape.

With the camps and the wall completed, Silva took on the problem of attacking the fortress. He found one point at which he could construct the ramp needed to move the troops and siege equipment up Masada. It was on the northwest face of the plateau, an outcropping called the White Promontory because of the color of the rock. With the promontory as a starting point, the Romans filled in earth and huge stones, in some places using scaffolding, until they had a ramp that was about 215 yards long and at its broadest part the same distance wide. At the top of the ramp they constructed a high siege tower, and a battering ram with a catapult.

Presumably the Zealots tried to stop the construction, but because it offered such a narrow front for attack, they couldn't bring much force to bear on it. Presumably, they tried to crush the Romans by rolling stones down the ramp, and the Romans responded with fusillades of arrows. In the end, the Zealots were unable to halt the building of the ramp and the siege tower.

Despite the resistance of the Zealots, the Romans, their catapults hurling darts and stones to pin down the defenders, brought up their battering ram, which after some difficulty breached a section of the casemate wall.

To the surprise of the Romans, the Zealots quickly repaired the breach, using lumber and earth, so that the wall was less rigid, more yielding and therefore less susceptible to the effects of the battering ram. But since it was made of wood, it was vulnerable to fire, and Flavius Silva ordered his soldiers to throw torches on it. Soon the repaired section of the wall was ablaze.

Then a strange thing happened, but one that modern visitors to Masada, who know its tricky weather conditions, can verify. When the fire at the wall started, the wind was blowing it toward the Romans, driving them back, threatening to engulf their siege machines, and causing them to despair of success. But suddenly, as if by the hand of God, the wind changed 180 degrees, pushing the flames back against the wall, causing its entire thickness to catch fire, and driving the defenders back.

The Romans were now joyful; they took the shifting wind as an augury of divine assistance. And they marched happily back to their camp. They set a heavy guard that night, to keep the Zealots from escaping, and they went to sleep knowing that the next morning they would attack.

On Masada that evening in the spring of the year 73, the Jews, like the Romans, felt the hand of God, but, unlike the Romans, they were not elated. They thought that somehow they had failed Him, that He had caused the wind to turn on them.

The leader of the Zealots, Eleazar ben Ya'ir, never for a moment considered fleeing. When he saw the repaired section of the wall aflame, he knew their situation was hopeless, and so he called the most courageous of his men together. He told them there was no way out, that they were certain to be taken, that God had proved to them their hopes were vain by turning the wind against them. He called it God's anger for their many sins.

Eleazar reminded them what the Romans would do to them and their wives and children, should they capture them. "Since it was God's will," he said, "let us not allow the Romans to execute God's punishment. Let us do that ourselves.

"Let our wives die before they are abused," he said, "and our children before they have tasted of slavery; and after we have slain them, let us bestow that glorious benefit upon one another mutually, and preserve ourselves in freedom, as an excellent funeral monument for us."

Some of the men at the meeting that night on Masada agreed with their leader wholeheartedly, others wept at the prospect of killing their wives and children. Eleazar flailed at those who showed weak-

40

ness. In a long exhortation he questioned their manliness and courage, detailing the cruelties the Romans had inflicted on the Jews, reminding them it was God's will, and that the Romans were hoping to take them alive to inflict torture and misery upon them. According to the Jewish historian Josephus, Eleazar said, "Let us make haste, and instead of affording them so much pleasure, as they hope for in getting us under their power, let us leave them an example which shall at once cause their astonishment at our death and their admiration of our hardiness therein."

Not only did Eleazar's oratory prevail, it was so convincing, Josephus writes, his hearers would not even let him finish before proceeding with "demoniacal fury" to the grim and pathetic task.

"Nor indeed, when they came to the work itself, did their courage fail them as one might imagine it would have done; but they then held fast the same resolution, without wavering, which they had upon the hearing of Eleazar's speech, while yet everyone of them still retained the natural passion of love to themselves and their families, because the reasoning they went upon, appeared to them to be very just, even with regard to those that were dearest to them; for the husbands tenderly embraced their wives and took their children into their arms, and gave the longest parting kisses to them, with tears in their eyes. Yet at the same time did they complete what they had resolved on, as if they had been executed by the hands of strangers, and they had nothing else for their comfort but the necessity they were in of doing this execution, to avoid that prospect they had of the miseries they were to suffer from their enemies. Nor was there at length any one of these men found that scrupled to act their part in this terrible execution, but every one of them despatched his dearest relations. Miserable men indeed were they! whose distress forced them to slay their own wives and children with their own hands, as the lightest of these evils that were before them. So they not being able to bear the grief they were under for what they had done, any longer, and esteeming it an injury to those they had slain, to live even the shortest space of time after them—they presently laid all they had in a heap and set fire to it. They then chose ten men by lot out of them, to slay all the rest; every one of whom laid himself down by his wife and children on the ground, and threw his arms about them, and they offered their necks to the stroke of those who by lot executed that melancholy office; and when these ten had, without fear, slain them all, they made the same rule for casting lots for themselves, that he whose lot it was should first kill the other nine, and after all should kill himself. Accordingly, all those had courage sufficient to be no way behind one another, in doing or suffering; so, for a conclusion, the nine offered their necks to the executioner, and he who was the last of all, took a view of all the other bodies, lest

41

perchance some or other among so many that were slain should want his assistance to be quite despatched; and when he perceived that they were all slain, he set fire to the palace, and with the great force of his hand ran his sword entirely through himself, and fell down dead near to his own relations."

When the sun rose over Masada the following day, the Romans put on their armor, climbed the ramp, laid bridges of planks on their ladders and readied their machines for the assault, anticipating fierce resistance. But they met none. They saw no enemy. They heard no sound. They encountered only silence and blazing fires within the fortress.

The legionaries entered through the break in the wall, and met two women and five children; when the suicide had been agreed on, the women had taken the children and hid in a cave on the side of Masada. The women told the Romans what had happened that night, and it is their account which became the basis of Josephus' writing.

At first the soldiers did not believe the women; they forced their way through the fires and found the bodies, but, according to Josephus, "could take no pleasure in the fact, though it were done to their enemies. Nor could they do other than wonder at the courage of their resolution, and the immovable contempt of death which so great a number of them had shown."

There was no jubilation among the legionaries; nor was there a celebration back in Rome. In fact, no mention was made of the fall of Masada, for in the Roman records, Judaea had already fallen, three years earlier, in 70. The triumphal arches had already been built, the commemorative coins already minted and circulating. The words on those coins were Judaea Capta.

Dave Seltzer had changed his name to Dov Shalzar, fought two wars, and attained a colonelcy when in 1965 he first visited the fortress. In seventeen years as an Israeli and a warrior, he had cried only once, and that once was on Masada.

In '65 Dov prevailed upon an archaeologist who had served in the army with him and was one of the leaders of the Masada excavation to let him tour the plateau, which was closed to outsiders while the digging was going on. With his friend guiding him, Dov examined the ramp, the walls, the ritual baths, the living quarters, all with a growing lump in his throat, until they reached Herod's luxurious, triple-tiered palace on the northern end of the rock.

The archaeologist stopped and spoke to Dov almost reverentially. "Here," he said, "we found some things I want to show you. They made us feel we were suddenly there, at the final hours of that night in the year 73.

"First these." And the man picked up a wooden case, laid it on the ground, and carefully opened it. There, in individual pockets, were eleven small pottery shards. He picked one up, delicately, and held it so Dov could see it. "These are called ostraca, they have lettering on them, and we found hundreds of them. But these eleven were found together at a central location; each seems to have been inscribed by the same hand, and each is a man's single name, or nickname—which means they were notable enough to have been identifiable by that single name.

"The one I am holding says on it ben Ya'ir. Do you know who he was?"

"Of course," answered Dov, his voice thick. "He was the leader of the Zealots." Then suddenly, as the archaeologist was about to explain, Dov realized what the eleven ostraca could mean. And his friend saw it.

"Yes," said the friend, "we think the same thing. These could be the lots of the ten warriors chosen to kill the others. That could have been their last meeting with their leader, ben Ya'ir. Can we ever know for sure? No. But these *could* be." Then he silently returned the bits of pottery to the case and closed it.

I mustn't, Dov kept telling himself, trying to bring his emotions under control. I've seen men, my friends, die next to me, and I haven't cried. I mustn't.

Then, gently, the archaeologist resumed. "There is one other place I want to show you." And with that he patted the attaché case he had been carrying during the tour. Together they walked to Herod's cold-water pool.

"Here," said Dov's friend, "we found the remains of three skeletons. One was that of a man of twenty; near him were armor scales, arrows, bits of a prayer shawl, and a shard with Hebrew lettering on it. The second skeleton was that of a small child."

The friend knelt and put the attaché case on the ground. "The third was that of a young woman," and he snapped the case open. "Because of the dryness, her scalp and her hair were preserved intact." Dov stared down at the case. There was the scalp. There were the rich, beautiful black braids of hair. There, from nearly 1,900 years ago. There.

"A warrior, his wife and his child. Near him, armor bits and iron arrows. On the plaster near where her remains were found, stains that seem to have been blood. I have seen and spoken of all this a number of times," said the archaeologist. "It still gets to me.

"We have no doubt that this was one of the last defenders of Masada. What I have lain awake nights thinking about is: Could this have been the last man, that warrior who killed the other nine, set the fires, went back to his own loved ones, ran himself through and then fell next to them? Again, we'll never know. Again, it *could* be."

Now Dov could not trust himself to speak. He knelt next to the case and very gently touched two fingers of his right hand to the braided hair of that woman who had died here because a band of Jews in 73 refused to be slaves. Dov's touch was so light he could barely feel the texture; he feared the hair would crumble if he pressed it. And yet, and yet, through his fingers he could feel a current flowing, as if a circuit had been completed, a circuit linking him over the miles and the centuries with this woman at Masada, and his Zionist parents and seventeen-year-old Dave Seltzer, who had gone off to fight for Israel.

Quickly, Dov got up and turned his back to the archaeologist to hide his face. He walked off to the west and stood watching the sun beginning to set behind the Judaean hills, tears rolling down his cheeks.

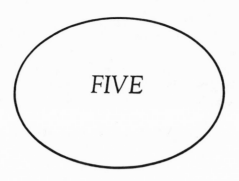

FIVE

Telling the Masada story softened and saddened Shalzar's face. For a while the jaw muscles stopped clenching and unclenching, the tight creases around the eyes melted, the tense downturn of the mouth eased.

Kate's reaction began in wonder and anguish. Could she ever yield meekly to the knife, or worse still, stand by while her children were killed? While Joanna and Charlie had their throats cut? While their blood ran down their soft necks? Was there any cause more precious than life? She couldn't share the Zealots' fanaticism. One thing she was sure of—Dov was zealous enough to choose death. His face had taken on a kind of exaltation just from telling the story.

"They're a lot braver than I am," she said, "or more committed, or something. I guess I can't think of *any* reason, any cause, I'd let my kids be killed for. Can you, Dov?"

"Every child in Israel is facing that right now, Kate." He was calm as he said it, and she realized she was sitting next to, staring at, a zealot. And then the rest of her reaction to the story welled up in her. Why were they calling it the Masada Plan? And what part would he ask her to play?

"So at Masada, they committed suicide," she began. "What does that say about your plan?"

The ambassador had an arm up on the back of the sofa; the leg nearest her was bent and on the cushion between them, but the relaxed pose belied the stoniness which had returned to his face. "If you mean, are we sharpening our knives, the answer is no, we're too advanced a civilization for such primitive methods. If you mean, are we making dangerous, desperate decisions, involving life and death, we are."

He smiled, a pale, gentle smile, and for a moment he was again her love, nothing else. "If you're asking just what the Masada Plan is, I can only say again, as I will each time you ask, there's no more I can tell. But I don't mind your asking. I know you didn't get to be a UBC star on looks."

Shalzar leaned to her, reached over and tousled her hair, pushing a strand of it over onto her eyes, where, fine and silky, it stayed until she sent it back with a toss of her head and a pat of her hand. Then Kate reached to him with the same kind of gesture, bouncing a hand off his curly, wiry hair, which not only failed to slip over his eye, but barely moved. She kidded him about that hair.

"Mine blows in the wind," she'd said on one of those rare days when they had the chance to walk together in Central Park. "Yours just stands there and fights back."

Gently, she grabbed a handful of hair and used it to tug him toward her on the sofa. She leaned in and kissed him on the lips, her mouth soft, almost open, a reminder that only a few hours ago he had been there to make love, not talk about Armageddon.

"Wouldn't it be boring," she suggested, half teasing, "if the only reason you came over here was to get into bed and make love and spend the night? Wouldn't that be dull?"

"Stifling," he replied, with a mischievous grin. "Almost as bad as if I were all those other dull things, a WASP millionaire investment banker, with a Park Avenue triplex, a Southampton beach house, a private jet, a schooner that sleeps eight, and a frameable divorce so I can publicly parade you to 21 and Palm Beach and Cap Ferrat. All those things you detest."

There he goes again, she thought. Back to Bill Brewster, even now, for the hundredth time, worrying it like a cat tossing a mouse, never finishing it off, never giving it up. Would he ever stop?

For the moment he did, quickly. In his eyes she saw a transition. He said nothing, but she knew what was happening. He was preparing to answer the question she had never spoken after his telling of the Masada story: What does he want of me? And she knew, too, he was having trouble beginning.

Shalzar looked down at his watch, and unthinkingly she echoed his movement, glancing down at hers. The delicate hands of the jeweled Tiffany watch on her wrist showed her it was 5:15 in the morning, and reminded her of Bill, for it was a birthday gift from him. A yacht, and a summer house, and Palm Beach, and 21—how boring do I find all that? she asked herself.

Still, Shalzar hadn't spoken. His eyes had followed hers. He knew the watch, too. She waited for him to ask. He remained silent. Finally, he said, "Odd you should do that just now."

"Do what?" she asked.

"Look at that watch."

"Whose watch should I look at?"

46

"Oh, don't be funny," he said. "You know what I mean."

"No, for God's sake, I don't!"

"You will in a moment. I have something to ask you. Are you ready?"

"Yes," she half shouted. "Ready, ready, ready! Go on!"

"I want an introduction. Strictly business and very important. And I want a Triple-A rating." Shalzar paused.

Furious with impatience, Kate said, "Do you want me to write one out and leave the addressee blank? Or are you going to tell me who?"

He smiled. "I almost feel I should extract an OK in advance, before I say."

"My God," she said, "you're doing more tiptoeing around this than you did about the invasion of Israel. How important can it be? Tear open the envelope, please!"

"I want you to introduce me to Bill Brewster."

Kate stared at him.

"I should have gotten the okay in advance!" he said.

Finally she managed to say only: "Bill Brewster?"

"Yes," he replied. "You remember. William Schuyler Brewster, you used to . . ."

"Shut up," she said.

William Schuyler Brewster was all those dull things Shalzar had just spoken of: a WASP investment banker, president of a huge financial house, owner of the yacht, the jet, beach houses in Southampton and Palm Beach. He had been Kate's lover, briefly, before she met the ambassador, and then again, briefly, a year ago, when she had broken off with Shalzar because she grew tired of sneaking out back doors.

Her disenchantment with the furtiveness of their romance budded during their first year together, and it blossomed one week in the spring of last year, when Dov broke four straight dinner dates. She had had enough, and Bill was available, tall and aristocratic and handsome and divorced and one of the catches of the year. A WASP, too; his hair fluttered in the wind, like hers. In the past nine months, since she and Shalzar had come back together, Brewster existed for Dov as a bugaboo, a hobgoblin, a straw man, a personification of entrenched privilege and capitalistic evil—anything Shalzar needed him for, which most often turned out to be windmill to Shalzar's Don Quixote. Yet the two men had never met.

"Dov, are you sure you're not crazy?"

"Listen, Kate." He leaned forward, launched himself to his feet, and walked across the room and back, in a semicircle around the glass coffee table in front of the sofa. Returned, he stood over her, picking nervously at the candle standing atop a tall, carved wooden candlestick on the table. "I'm not crazy and I'm not fooling around. I want to meet him . . . no, I've *got* to meet him. And as soon as the hour is decent. Maybe sooner."

"You're going to have to give me a little more than this, Dov. I mean, I assume it has something to do with Israel, and Masada, and frightening people and the end of the world, but all it reminds me of is the endless talk about Bill Brewster we've been through, and the thousand times I heard 'What happened?' and 'How could you?' and all the other picking at scabs that still makes me bleed."

The adrenalin was surging, and though Kate knew it had to be more than the scratchy old jealousy record being played again, she was beginning to think she heard that familiar tune. "And stop picking at the goddamned candle!" she shouted.

He stopped. And stretched the hand out to grab hers.

"Listen to me," he began, swinging around the table and sitting next to her again, without letting go of her hand. "Why do you think I told you to get ready, and went through all the preliminaries? I knew this would happen, and I can't say I blame you. Look, this is Israel I'm talking about. And Masada. All of it. It's also, if you have a sense of humor, one of those damned amusing coincidences that pop up when you intrude into the haut monde." His left index finger pointed at her as he said it, while his right hand continued to grip hers. "As I sometimes do.

"Let me tell you the requirements of the man I've got to meet. Then you tell me the name of the man.

"I need someone who is very close to the Secretary of State, yet does not work with him. Who is thoroughly familiar with government, yet not in it. Who is considered by the Secretary to be politically 'sound' and knowledgeable, yet not a political animal with a big R or D branded on his hide. Most of all, I need someone the Secretary can thoroughly, unequivocally, absolutely trust. Now, make up a list. Go ahead. How many names are on it?"

Kate looked down for a moment. "Just one." Then she looked up, her face set in the "You're-right-but-I'm-still-not-going-to-do-it" look that meant she was digging her heels in like a southern mule.

"Look," he said, reaching across her, grabbing her hand so that he was now gripping both of hers in both of his, "you're embarrassed. One minute you're overwhelmed by the global impact of the Mideast war, the next you're flustered because it is possible two men are going to meet, each knowing the other has made love to you. That's why, don't say it isn't."

She was looking across at him, still rebellious, he could see, but slightly chastened, and softening. He pressed ahead.

"Kate, I hate to say this, but aren't you playing right into the hands of the men who think women aren't ready for self-government?"

48

She flinched, hardened for a moment, and tried to pull her hands away. Dov got angry, let go of her in disgust.

"Suppose we set up a cloture rule. We'll promise to spend no more than five minutes talking about what you're like in bed . . . you goddamned egomaniac!"

"Who's an egomaniac?" she shouted, then paused. "Five minutes? Would that be for each of you, or both?"

The tension was broken, the hostility put aside. They looked at each other and laughed.

"Supposing I had said no?" she asked.

"Then I would have had only two choices."

"What were they?"

"The first thing I could have done was to keep you captive in the embassy and throw my Aunt Sophie's gefilte fish at you until you changed your mind."

"Would that have been so bad?"

"Bad? You never ate my Aunt Sophie's gefilte fish, I can tell that. They're like rocks. I can now reveal to you a secret for the first time. During the Yom Kippur War, when our tanks ran out of ammo, we fired Sophie's gefilte fish at the Egyptians for three days. It was the turning point of the war."

"And what was the other choice?"

The ambassador shrugged. "Why I'd have to locate some other beautiful woman he's slept with and dazzle *her* until she was ready to give me anything I wanted."

A dangerous thing to say, but he had always been a verbal brinkman, confident, even arrogant about his talent for taking risks and escaping. Instantaneously, he regretted it, though. Then said to himself: It's just as well. It will occur to her sooner or later; let it occur sooner.

The possibility that she was being used did not occur to Kate just then (because for one thing, she knew nothing of the delivery scenario for the Masada Plan), but later she would often think back to his words. He, not sure how she was reacting to his risky remark, stepped back from it, just to be safe.

"Kate, to be honest I hadn't thought of an alternative. I don't know what I would have done. I was counting on you to say yes."

She was about to reply, yes, count on me, always, when something he said choked off her answer and chilled her, a chill starting in her throat and descending to her chest, her stomach, her gut.

Shalzar said, "And I have something I want to give you in return."

My God, she thought, a quid pro quo, a tit for tat! This man I love wants to make sure I get fair measure, as if he were a tradesman and I a customer! All she said was, "And what is that?"

He heard it, and squeezed her hand. "Look, this has nothing to do with anything about us. You understand. There's a way I can help you, just as you can help me. And I want to do it. Understand?"

"Yes, Dov. Understand." Her caution and hostility remained, but he had no time to deal with them. He had to go on, but he was not sure how.

Kate made it easier. She squeezed back with her hand. "Look, I *do* understand." This time it was a lot warmer. "And I do appreciate it. Now, go ahead."

He nodded. "Okay, start the tape rolling."

"You're not joking are you, Dov?" The chill of her first response to his offer of a return favor was now replaced by the tingling nerve endings of a reporter.

"I guess I don't blame you for asking, but I really haven't time to joke. Ready?"

"No," she shouted, jumping to her feet. "I need a pen and paper. Give me fifteen seconds." And she raced out of the living room, down the hall, to the desk in her bedroom, where she snatched a pad and ballpoint pen, and dashed back to the sofa. Fifteen seconds was all it took.

She sat, composed herself as if she had never left, made an exaggerated motion of setting her pen at the paper, and said, "Ready."

"We haven't released this to the wire services yet—or to anybody. We won't until after the fact. But here it is. At 7 a.m., New York time, the government of Israel will hand notes to the US, the Security Council, and, through the good offices of the Swiss ambassador in Moscow, to the Soviet government, urging them to act immediately to stop the Arab invasion of Israel, on the ground that it constitutes a grave threat to world peace.

"The note warns that the repercussions could extend beyond the Middle East, and raise the chance of nuclear war."

Scrambling to write as fast as she could, Kate muttered "Hold it! hold it!" a few times as she wrote. Then, when she was finished, "Am I allowed to ask any questions?"

"No."

"Am I allowed to interpret that statement in the light of information I already have?"

"Is that a question?"

"Yes."

"That's what I thought. I said you weren't allowed any questions."

"For God's sake, Dov!"

"What?"

"Say something!"

"All right. Stop the tape. Now, what is it, dear?"

"Is that fair?"

50

"No. It is strictly discriminatory. In favor of UBC. The ones who should be complaining are the other networks, the wires and the *New York Times* and the Washington *Post*. Now, it's nearly six, which gives you better than an hour's head start on your competition. So go ahead, use it wisely. And don't ask any questions. And the tape *is* stopped."

"Dov, thank you. I guess I'm greedy."

"That's all right. It's how you won all those Emmys."

"Just two."

"What will you do now?"

"Phone this in, for a bulletin. If you're sure no one else will get it, till after seven, we can use it to lead the morning news."

"Then will you phone Brewster? We don't want to wake him too early, but we simply can't wait."

"Yes, Dov. Of course." But Kate was already distracted, scribbling a couple of sentences she could dictate over the phone. Then, for an instant, she stopped and looked up. "Thanks, Dov. Really. Thanks."

Without waiting for an answer, she looked down at her notes again, finished writing and then stood up. "I've got to phone this in, which should take three minutes if Hannon is in passable shape and an hour if he's hung over. I'll use the phone in my room. Want to come in with me and listen—look Ma, no secrets—or sit out here?"

To show he was no less open than she, Dov answered, "Thanks, I'll wait out here—and think of what to say to Bill Brewster when I meet him."

"That's what I was afraid of," she said, with a smile to show she didn't really mean it. "Be right back." And then she disappeared down the hall.

In her room Kate sat in the Victorian wicker chair she kept at her desk. Cradling the phone between her jaw and left shoulder, she used her right hand to dial the private home number of Richard Hannon, president of UBC News. With her left she held the pad up, so she could reexamine her copy.

After four rings, the phone was picked up, and the thick, groggy voice of Dick Hannon said something close to "hello."

"Dick, nudge your wife, will you, and ask her if she found the pantyhose I left in your bed the other night?"

By now coarse banter was a tradition between them. It had begun with Hannon's trying to shock her when she was new at the network; it continued when she showed she could give as good as she got, maybe better. Even this time, at six in the morning, with this kind of news, it was automatic.

"Who the hell . . . Kate, is that you? What the hell time is it? What's happening?"

"Are you awake, Dick? Are you sober? I've got something important." She told him what she'd learned. His reaction startled her.

"So what?" he began, amid heavy throat clearing. "What do you expect Israel to say? That it's only a little teapot war and the rest of the world should ignore it? They'll probably come back and whup the Arabs again anyway in a week or so."

Immersed in the situation as she was, Kate was amazed at how little he understood the Middle East power balance. She also knew that to brief him properly on its dangers might involve moving into the stop-tape areas where Dov had spent so much time. But when would she be crossing the line? Certainly she had known, even before the early hours of this morning, that the Israelis couldn't "whup" the Arabs in a week or so this time. Beyond that, though, what was safe and what wasn't?

She was in a bind, and Dov had put her there; he had co-opted her. By letting her into the inner circle, he had prevented her from sending any messages without his approval, so, as a journalist, she was in a worse position inside than she would have been outside.

All this whirled around in her mind as she groped for a way to convince Hannon UBC should run a bulletin he rated as "so what?"

Finally, she fell back on clout, which had worked before.

"Dick, take my word. It's not pro forma. There's a kind of threat in this, I smell it. I don't know exactly what kind, but let's read a bulletin with just a whiff of that to it. I'll stand behind it, Dick. It could be something like," and she read from her pad, " 'Israel, which has had a nuclear arsenal for at least four years now . . .' "

"Hold it! Stop right there!" Hannon interrupted, shouting. "With that opening phrase, don't bother to go on to the second. Not unless you've got some mighty convincing documents."

"But Dick!"

"Forget it!"

"You haven't even heard the whole . . ."

"I said, forget it."

She let out a snort of derision. "OK, then this. It won't be much more than what's on the AP and UPI wires, and damned soon, ahead of us, if we don't get cracking. Listen: Israel will warn the US, the Soviet Union, and the Security Council this morning of the danger of a nuclear world war if fighting in the Middle East is not stopped at once. The warning will come in separate letters delivered at 7 a.m., New York time, in Washington, Moscow, and New York, and it falls short of the direct threat many observers felt the beleaguered Jewish state would make."

"The first sentence is fine, Kate. Forget the second. Unless you know something you're not telling me. Do you?"

"I know that I've won a lot of goddam awards for this news organization, and never got you in trouble once. Isn't my word worth anything around here any more?"

"A lot, beautiful, a lot." He knew she hated that, and he was trying to get her off the track onto a male-chauvinist-pig chase. When she wouldn't go for it, he continued. "But this is a nuclear threat. And this is Israel. And we don't mess with them."

"I see. You *would* take my word, then, if I got an exclusive on next week's school lunch menus in Levittown? Could we mess with *them?*"

"Listen, you're the one who wants to get this on ahead of AP and UPI. Do you want to lose that while we filibuster over a nuance in a twenty-second bulletin most of our sleepy viewers will miss anyway? I'm willing to go on; I've got three hours sleep under my belt."

"Oh shit . . . if I may be unladylike. I'm tired of arguing. Do it any way you want, Fearless Fos-Dick."

"One of these days I'm going to get pissed off at that kind of stuff from all you heroic frontline correspondents who think I'm sitting in the rear echelon. One of these days I'm gonna drag you into a meeting with the corporate types and show you where the front lines really are." Hannon's Irish temper had broken through, but he stepped on it. "But it won't happen now, or to Kate Colby because she's just too goddamned important to this organization. Nice going, Kate."

"Yeah, thanks and goodbye." Kate slammed down the phone. She stood, catching a quick look at herself in her dressing table mirror; for an instant she paused and put a hand to her hair, stared at it again in the mirror and examined briefly the tired face beneath. She made a pass at her hair, knowing it wouldn't do much good. Then she shook her head and smiled. Surely, she thought, I'm not worried about Dov seeing me this way. It's Bill; the prospect of talking to him—even on the telephone—makes me want to spruce up. That's one of the things I like—about Dov.

Kate headed out of the room and down the long hall toward the living room, where she found the ambassador sitting on the edge of the sofa, watching her, waiting for the next step. "OK," she said. "Now it's your turn. And this is one call I insist you hear, so come on back to the bedroom with me." She strode toward him as she said it, and reached her hand out.

Shalzar shook his head. "Don't you think it better that I let you handle this one by yourself?"

"Most certainly, definitely, and unequivocally not." Kate's lips tightened as she said it, but she tried not to let the tension go too far. "You know how prone I am to work up an assignation every time I talk with Bill Brewster. I need you listening to keep me moral. Come on."

Again, she extended her hand. Shalzar took it, but would not let himself be lifted from the sofa. "I trust you."

"Don't do me no favors. Listen, I've got you this time. You want one of my invaluable contacts, you do it my way. Now come on."

Reluctantly, he let himself be lifted. Kate kissed him on the cheek as he got up, to keep things affectionate, to show it was not a mere battle of wills. As they walked back to the bedroom, she asked, "What makes you think he's in town?" In fact, she had not spoken to him in months and was, in her way, as apprehensive as Shalzar about speaking to him, perhaps more. Perhaps Brewster was in Southampton. Perhaps Maine, perhaps Europe. And she'd be off the hook. Damned selfish of me, she thought.

Shalzar got rid of the conjecture. "He is in town. Do you want his private number?"

The question was as much a test as an offer of information. And she was not going to fake her answer—well, maybe she would, slightly. She started to reply, I know it, which she did. Instead she shifted ground slightly, and said, "I have it." And when they reached the bedroom, she reached into a desk drawer for her personal phone book and made a show of looking it up.

Shalzar sat on the edge of her bed while she sat at her desk; out of habit she played with a loose end of the wicker caning as she tucked the phone between jaw and shoulder and began dialing.

"Where do you want to meet him and when?" she asked Shalzar as she dialed.

He looked at his watch, 6:18. "Let's make it seven-thirty if that's all right with him. And, let's see, it shouldn't be here, or at his apartment, it'd be safer at some third place." He hesitated. She stopped dialing after five digits and waited. An ironic smile came over his face.

"The Unity Club," he said, almost triumphantly.

"What?" She slammed down the receiver.

"Well," he replied, shrugging. *"I'm* not known for spending time there. And William Schuyler Brewster sure as hell isn't."

She sat, staring at him. So I was worried about my egotistical reaction to their meeting, she thought. So I was worried about being too feminine, worried about betraying the incapacity of women to do objective, hardheaded things. Hell, he's worse than I am, and he's a man, an ambassador.

The Unity was the leading Jewish club in the city, organized just before the Civil War by the German Jewish "crowd" in response to the anti-Semitic policies of the older WASP clubs. The Unity had come to be known not only for the prodigious wealth of its membership but also for its anti-Gentile policy. In the last few decades, several of the newer members had put up WASP friends, most from their own Wall Street houses, for membership in the Unity, and they'd been thunderstruck to have them turned down. Somehow they had thought the admissions committee would be flattered to embrace the very group whose snobbery had caused the formation of the Unity a century earlier. They were wrong, and even more wrong, it turned out, to have brought the issue before the club's board of directors, where they were roundly beaten. Several of the new people had resigned; one had gotten a WASP friend to bring a suit before the state's Human Rights Commission. Since the Unity was a private club, he had no case, but the directors, extremely sensitive to charges that they, as Jews, were no better than anti-Semites, issued a declaration of nondiscrimination on ethnic grounds and invited the WASP plaintiff to join, an invitation that was refused.

Well, hell, she wasn't going to argue; if Dov wanted to ask to meet at the Unity, she'd ask on his behalf. If Bill wanted to refuse, she'd refuse on *his* behalf.

All she said to Shalzar was "I didn't know you were a member."

"I'm not, but I've been offered the use of its facilities any time I need them by the one and only Maxwell Seligsohn, media giant, friend of Israel, and Unity Club grandee. I wouldn't join an organization that was discriminatory, you know that."

Kate looked to see if he was serious. He smiled back at her, but added, "I mean that! I wouldn't."

She responded to the smile. "It's not only anti-Gentile, Dov. It's anti-women, too. And here I am female and Gentile, and I don't think it's funny."

Now he was impatient. "I don't either, and I'm against clubs entirely, but this one is quiet and nearby and relatively safe."

"This is the second time you've brought up safety in the past three minutes. Why?"

Shalzar spent only an instant deciding not to tell her about the attack on Madison Avenue a few hours before. "Just because we've got to be careful, that's all. Now, please phone him, Kate."

She nodded and shrugged and dialed the number. This was the line he'd answer personally. In the middle of the third ring, it was picked up.

"Hello." No throat-clearing for Bill Brewster. At 6:25 in the morning the voice was already as lucid, cool, and controlled as if he were addressing a business meeting. And the rampant Ivy League intonation of that one word triggered a flood of memories in her. Of those elegant, quietly luxurious moments with Bill and his friends, the powerhouses. How heady their company had made her. How easy she felt with them; how well, she knew, she handled herself, how proud Bill was of her. Memories, too, of private aridities, the stone walls of conservatism, the condescension toward women, the soft-spoken snobbery—all of it expressed in the cocksure tones of the East Coast Establishment.

"Bill, it's Kate."

"Why, hello. My goodness. Have I overslept? Or are you up early? Well, never mind, it's always good to hear from you." There was real delight in his voice, the accent didn't conceal that, and she was happy to hear it.

"I'm up early Bill; it's not quite six-thirty. And it is awfully rude of me to be waking you. But I have a very special request that is really terribly, terribly important." Kate heard herself turning on the southern lady voice she often used with Bill and others she considered aristocrats. Shalzar, sitting there, heard it, too. She hated herself for it, but she was not about to abandon it now.

"I must introduce you to somebody, and almost at once."

"Almost at once?"

"Yes, Bill, within the hour, if you possibly can. Actually, let me say it more urgently. I'm asking you more intensely than I've ever asked before."

"More intensely than ever? Ah, well." If Bill had a way of being stuffy when others were light, he could be unexpectedly arch when others were serious. "And does that intensity preclude any advance disclosure of the person to whom I'm to be introduced? Or shall I venture a guess?"

"Well, Bill, since you're going to meet him in an hour, I hope, there's no point in keeping it a secret. Would you like to guess?"

"Why yes, why don't I? Could it by chance be His Excellency the Jewish ambassador?"

Bill had a way of pronouncing the word "Jew" or "Jewish" with something close to a built-in sneer, she thought. He put extra "e"s in it to stretch out the vowel sound, which was the way many Southerners said the word. Early in her New York life, Kate had heard it in her speech and forced herself to change it. Bill Brewster, though, was not a Southerner. He was born in Connecticut and had gone to Groton, Princeton, and the Harvard Business School.

"If you mean the Israeli ambassador, you are exactly right."

He pretended the exchange hadn't occurred. "And where shall we meet in one hour's time? Shall I go to the embassy or would the ambassador care to come here?"

"Neither." She hesitated. Could she really bring herself to say it? She had to. "Would you be horrified if I were to say the Unity Club?"

There was a moment of silence and then a chuckle at the other end of the phone. "Horrified? No, but my sense of fair play would be offended, and I'd not feel comfortable in an establishment where so many of my fellowmen were excluded merely on . . ."

"Yes, Bill, all right, Bill, but another time please!" Brewster had been mimicking one of her liberal manifestos. "Please do this because I'm asking it of you. Which by the way is not easy for me to do."

"I shall meet your request, as always, Kate. Which by the way is *quite* easy for me to do."

"And as always I am grateful to you, Bill." The conversation would have been tough enough for her at the best of times. Now, with Shalzar sitting and watching, hearing at least half of it, perhaps more, it was all the tougher, and she wanted it done with.

"Do you know where the Unity Club is, Bill?"

"Why, Kate, what a strange question! Would it surprise you to learn that I have had lunch there on several occasions? With no hard feelings? You see, I respect the right of people to associate privately as they see fit." Bill was enjoying this. "I don't know if you realize that two directors of our corporation are of the—let's see, now, is it Israeli?—persuasion."

"No, it's Jewish . . ." She realized, an instant too late, he had been teasing her.

"Yes, Kate. It is truly amazing how the humorists in our midst fail to recognize wit from any source other than themselves; and liberals, particularly, cannot imagine it coming from a conservative."

Yes, she could be as rigid as any right-winger, and she knew it, but again, this was not the time. "Guilty, Bill. And glad you can meet with the ambassador. I can't tell you how grateful we . . . I . . . am. He, too, of course." She didn't want to make them sound like a team, she knew how that hurt Bill. But she already had. Again, no time to worry now.

"Then we'll make it seven-thirty?"

"Yes," he answered. "Seven-thirty. If the Unity is ready for me, I am ready for it."

"Fine, see you there, Bill. And thanks. Really. Thanks."

"I'll look forward to meeting the ambassador. Goodbye."

"Goodbye."

Kate hung up the phone and looked over at Shalzar. He was relieved and happy to have the meeting set. He was also curious; the conversation with Brewster had not been neutral; it had been charged—a negative charge, probably—but he knew that was more threatening than nothing at all. And there was something in Shalzar that kept asking: Why should she prefer me to this man? Not that he denigrated his own appeal, but Brewster seemed so much the perfect match for her. In the nine months since he and Kate had resumed their relationship, Shalzar had raised the question often, and each time he did, Kate took it as a denigration of her value system, not his assets. And each time she did, a conversation that began as an easy exchange of compliments became tense and defensive. Even then, Kate could see the ashes of the tension smoldering. A tiny breeze and there would be a flame. She wouldn't let it happen.

"As you heard, it's all set. On your . . ." It had started to come out as, "On your turf." But she thought, No, no. And switched in mid-word, adroitly, she thought, to: "On your terms."

Shalzar stood, and took her hand. His face suddenly opened up, relaxed, smiled, and he bent over and kissed her hand, then her mouth. I love this man, she said to herself. I do.

"Good," he said. "Thank you. I can't tell you how important this is." His face got serious. "Will you come too, please? I'd like a third person there."

Kate realized then she hadn't given an instant's thought to whether she'd be asked or not; also she realized she wanted to go—desperately. For a journalist the opportunity was precious, even if she couldn't immediately report what she learned.

"Yes, of course. But I've got an eleven o'clock taping, so I've got to be at the studio by nine. I don't know how long I can stay."

"Stay as long as you can," he said, squeezing her hand. "And my car will drive you to the studio," and he smiled, just a bit tightly, "unless you get a better offer from Wall Street. But at any rate," and he started out, not letting go of her hand, so that she had to stand and walk with him, "I get to drive you over there. First, though, I'm going back to the embassy, to talk to Jerusalem, and to shave, so the Unity Club won't be embarrassed for me. Why don't I pick you up at seven-twenty? That's," and he looked at his watch, "forty-five minutes from now. All right?"

By then they were at the front door. "Seven-twenty downstairs, okay." And she leaned forward and kissed him. Then she stood smiling as he pressed the button and waited for the elevator. It came, the big door slid open, he stepped in, and it closed behind him.

Kate watched it and then closed her apartment door.

What fun this is going to be, she said to herself as she stood looking around her foyer, not quite sure what to do next. Part of the world going down the drain, maybe more to follow, and of all the men meeting to try to jam in the stopper, it had to be these two. And she'd be there to see it, to see the tension, the springs wound tighter because of their relationship to her.

Or was she just flattering herself? Would they forget her in manly pursuit of more important issues?

My God, she said to herself, they *are* more important. Much more than my goddamned romances. Why call that "*manly*"? What does that leave for feminine?

She had to shower, dress, get ready. She wanted to turn on the morning news, to check on the bulletin she had phoned in. But there, a step away from the door, she was frozen, her body unmoving, her mind racing, revving up, wheels spinning.

Maybe she should feel triumph at the meeting of those two, one her lover, an ambassador, the other, her former lover, president of an

58

investment house, former Cabinet member, confidant of the Secretary of State. And *she* had decided which would be the lover and which the former lover. No sense of triumph came. Instead there was anxiety, a responsibility to see that they got along, that none of the combativeness broke through, especially not from Dov, to derail their meeting.

In her flimsy silk summer bedjacket, tanned legs showing from mid-thigh down, she stood in the foyer and stared around her. Her eyes picked out a small, gleaming stainless steel sculpture by Ernest Trova. Bill Brewster had given her that last year, for her thirty-fifth birthday; it was the fulfillment of a promise made to her a year earlier.

They had seen the sculpture in a gallery window while out walking on one of their first dates. She thought it beautiful, brilliant without being slick, and she said so. "When's your birthday?" he had asked with a grin. "You just missed it, by a couple of weeks," she answered. "Too bad for me. I do love it."

"All right," he replied. "Next birthday." And next birthday the Trova was delivered to her, even though she and Bill were not seeing each other. Dov had come along.

That first stroll past the gallery window had come more than two years ago. Bill's marriage was breaking apart; he had moved out of his Park Avenue co-op and taken a suite at the Waldorf Towers. He was very vulnerable, yet painfully reticent about discussing himself.

They went to dinner often, to the theatre occasionally, to concerts rarely. Once they even tried dancing at Le Club, but that hadn't worked too well; he was a graceful dancer, but self-conscious and conservative, and obviously he didn't approve of the kind of people in the discothèque.

And they had made love. Bill Brewster made love the way he danced. He was elegant but inhibited, never abandoned. Even when he was letting go, she had thought, he couldn't let go.

Behind that stuffed shirt, she kept telling herself, a warm, spontaneous man was trying to bust out. Bill never could quite make it, though, which stunted their relationship. So did the frequency of his business trips, which took him away from New York as many as three weeks out of the month.

He had just gone away for two weeks on business when she met Dov at the embassy cocktail party. By the time Bill returned she and Dov were lovers, and she told Bill so at a mournful dinner, in the course of which he came close to exploding, without ever quite making it.

Not that it would have done any good then, for Dov had arrived with the brilliance of a meteor. The newness, the excitement, the humor, the splendid lovemaking, the power of adventure, of the exotic, overwhelmed everything . . . for a while. For a while she hadn't minded the furtiveness, not being able to take him to dinner parties, or to be taken by him. Not being able to walk into public places together. On those rare occasions when they were out in public, both of them half hiding to keep from being recognized, so that no one spotted the TV celebrity out with the glamorous ambassador —who had a wife and three kids back in Tel Aviv.

For a while it hadn't mattered. For a year. Then the sneaking around began to add up, and the nights she spent sitting home while he was out at places suitable only for a man and his wife. Not that she wanted to go, not at all. She knew most of those dinners and parties and they were dreadful; what she wanted was to be *able* to go.

And no divorce or separation from his wife seemed possible, at least he never sounded as if it did.

Then Bill became president of his banking house and the traveling stopped. He was now divorced, and, according to *Women's Wear Daily,* one of the five most eligible men in America. He began calling her again. At first she said no; then she had dinner with him, and again and again. It was so relaxed; she could walk into Sardi's with him after the theatre without worrying about who might see them. She could walk everywhere with this tall handsome man, sit with him, hold hands with him when she wanted to, easily.

This release of tension, almost explosive in force, began translating itself into affection for Bill. Love? She didn't know, but she was more than willing to give it a try. A part of her whispered: Wouldn't it be nice if it were love? Wouldn't it be splendid? Wouldn't it be comfortable? Wouldn't it be convenient?

Bill asked her to Haiti for a long weekend, to the super-rich new resort, Habitation LeClerc, in which his firm had invested; she started to say yes. Instead she said, "Let's go to Oloffson's." Oloffson's was the rococo, almost seedy hotel in Port-au-Prince favored by the literati, and the setting for Graham Greene's novel *The Comedians.*

To her surprise, he said yes, enthusiastically, and contented himself with one long lunch at Habitation LeClerc.

They made love, for the first time since they had started seeing each other again. She had decided she couldn't go without that; the alternative was not to go at all. But she found herself looking forward to it. And it was better than she had remembered it.

Was it love? She needed full time to find out. So she made up her mind to break away from Dov, a course she had been toying with for several months, as the frustration mounted. Just as she knew she wouldn't go to Haiti with Bill without sleeping with him, she knew that once she did she could no longer sleep with Dov. She told Dov she was going to Haiti, without telling him with whom, and that she'd call him as soon as she returned. She tried to inject, into her voice and words, clues to a new remoteness.

That Sunday-night ride home from Kennedy airport was a nightmare; she was petrified at the prospect of phoning him. She got home and walked in, looked at the phone in her bedroom, realized she was exhausted and pulled back the covers and went to sleep. The next day she was very busy, and could not seem to find the time to call. Finally, Monday evening, five minutes before he had to walk onto the dais at a UJA dinner, he called her.

"Hello there, welcome back. You did say you were going to call me, didn't you?"

"Dov, I've honestly been so busy, I haven't had a minute to breathe."

Dov had been trying to convince himself he was imagining her recent aloofness; this time he heard it immediately and unmistakably.

"Did you have a good weekend?"

"Yes. Lovely." Then she was tongue-tied.

"Well, what else do you have to say for yourself?" With moments to go before he had to make a speech, with a sinking feeling spreading in his stomach, he tried jocularity.

"I've been doing a lot of thinking over the weekend, Dov."

He sensed what was coming and was trying to delay it. "Showing off, eh?"

All she said was "Dov."

So he went on, "Did any of the thinking involve me?"

"Yes," she said grimly.

"Well," he said, trying to sound bright as his despair deepened, "tell me about it."

"Oh, I'd rather do it at lunch tomorrow."

"Am I going to like it?"

"No."

"You're going to break off with me?"

"Yes."

She had to laugh to herself at the teen-age expression he'd used, "break off." Yet it was exactly what she would have said. She supposed people stopped inventing romantic dialogue after they left their teens and had to make do with leftover terminology.

The next day, at a maudlin lunch at the Russian Tea Room, irrigated by a torrent of tears and wine—tears for her, wine for him—she told him why, leaving Bill Brewster out of it for the moment. He accepted sadly, gracefully. They agreed they'd have lunch once in a while.

Dov confessed, as he made feeble passes at a plate of cold borscht, that he'd been expecting it, but that its actual coming felt like—the closest he could come to describing it was a punch in the belly.

Oddly enough, as soon as she managed to do what she had so feared, to tell Dov, the promise of her romance with Bill started to wane. Part of the reason, she thought later, was that Dov filled more of her heart and mind than she had realized, and without his taking up huge chunks of both, Bill just seemed to rattle around, unable to fill the spaces she had cleared for him.

And then there was Bill himself. Etched into his fine, analytical mind was a profound pattern of conservative attitudes, especially toward women. More and more she could see herself being displayed as a trophy, the latest and most impressive acquired by a man who had three residences, a fifty-five-foot schooner, and the presidency of one of the most important Wall Street houses.

Clearly, Bill wanted to marry again, and she was willing to play with the idea whenever he broached it in his cautious, elliptical way. When he started putting forward his reasons for wanting to remarry, though, she found it tough to believe she was listening to a 1978 New Yorker. What *he* wanted, always what *he* wanted. A hostess, a housekeeper, someone he could be proud of, someone to stand in front of his fireplaces, in New York, Southampton, and Palm Beach. A trophy. And what a special trophy, she would think as she listened to him, if he could get Kate Colby to quit television to marry him.

And oh yes, he would want her to quit. That became clear one evening when they met for dinner. She arrived at the restaurant ahead of him and was sitting admiring the snowy white tablecloth, when he walked up to her, shaking his head. Carter Lipscomb, one of his bright young analysts, was quitting to go to San Francisco. And why? Because his wife, who was an architect, had been offered a good job there. Can you imagine? he said. Giving up a splendid future at Patton and Company, probably a partnership in ten years, to follow your wife to a new job!

"And suppose," she'd asked, "you'd wanted *him* to move to, let's say, London, for your firm. Would you expect her to give up her job to go with him?"

"Of course, but that's a thoroughly different situation."

"Why?"

"Because, obviously, Lipscomb is going to be the breadwinner in that family, and a formidable one, I should add, and Betsy is going to have two or three children before too long, and put away her architectural career."

"And that," she'd said with a smile, "is woman's fate."

"I shouldn't put it that way," was his answer.

"And suppose," she'd continued relentlessly, knowing she was upsetting him and their relationship, "you were to answer the call from GM or Ford or Chrysler to become chairman. Would you expect your wife to go with you to the wilds of Michigan?"

"Why of course I would!" He'd looked at her as if she were mad.

"I didn't know that Bill Brewster, who's pushing fifty, well forty-seven, anyway, was planning to grab off a childbearer in her twenties and start a new family!"

"Well, that's ridiculous; I'm not."

"So a woman's career is not the point, and childbearing is not the point. I suppose the point is that old 'quo vadis', 'whither he goeth she should goeth, too.' "

"Yes, I guess that's what I believe." He'd said it sadly; he'd been led into a cul-de-sac, had seen it and been unable to, or hadn't wanted to, back out. They never really came close to the possibility of marriage after that.

There were times, though, when she'd think, what the hell, he wasn't a bad trophy either, one of the five best in the country, WWD said so. Then she'd say, if I ever marry at all, it won't be so the man and I can display each other like trophies.

The parting of Kate and Bill was a time of great sadness for her parents, down in Atlanta, who had been rooting for Brewster decorously, but with a fervor that approached pompon waving and backflips. But her direction was inevitable, and as soon as Bill realized exactly what she wanted, so was his. Once having decided, she wasn't willing to ride along too far with him, because at no point, not even the best, did their relationship have the intensity of the one with Dov. The end of the road came sooner, though, because of something Dov did.

Two weeks without her and the richness, the joy of his life in New York faded. He dragged through his daily routine, brooding when he should have been concentrating on the tightrope he was walking on behalf of his nation. Suddenly he understood he had been enduring his barren, fractured marriage because his contentment came from Kate. Without her he had no further interest in the status quo. In the next of his biweekly transatlantic phone calls to his wife, he refused to back away from a fight, as he had always backed away before.

Suddenly, the personal tightrope he'd been walking no longer frightened him. Let him fall off. Hell, he'd *jump* off.

For two weeks he pondered that, finding himself walking the streets of the East Side alone at night, to the despair of his security man, replaying scenes with Kate. He spent other lonely hours considering the options, what they'd mean to him personally and professionally. Then one night, when he'd made up his mind, he sat down at his desk and wrote two long letters, which he sent in the next diplomatic pouch. The first was to his wife, saying that after fifteen years of de facto separation, he wanted to make it official. He explained his reasons fully, although she knew them all. He sent a copy of that letter to his lawyer in Tel Aviv.

The second letter was to the Foreign Minister in Jerusalem. It declared he was separating from his wife, with the intention of getting a divorce, for reasons of long standing personal incompatibility; that he understood it could be embarrassing to the government, especially with the orthodox groups in Israel, and that he was, therefore, offering to resign.

Both answers surprised him. The Foreign Minister said he saw no reason for a resignation, that he was essential in his post and that the government expected it could handle whatever protest was forthcoming, which, he anticipated, would be minimal. In a separate personal note, the Foreign Minister expressed surprise the separation hadn't occurred years before. His wife's answer was even more surprising, because it came, not from her, but from her lawyer, setting forth a list of demands.

Then he waited until he and Kate had one of their infrequent lunches. When he ordered a martini, she knew something was going to happen, but Dov passed the time as casually as he could until they were almost finished, and then trying to be offhand, told her about the letters. By this time, Dov had learned about her and Brewster; in fact, for anyone who read newspapers, it was hard *not* to know—Suzy, Eugenia Sheppard, the "Eye" column in *Women's Wear,* all mentioned the pairing of these two beautiful people—and he was ready for her to say, in a tactful way, it's too late.

Even when the affair with Bill was at its height she had fantasized about Dov's becoming available to her, but only to try to lay the possibility to rest. She'd thought she was succeeding, but that day at lunch her reaction was so strong it left her no doubt where her real emotions were invested. The pangs she felt, the elation! She said nothing. Then, all she could manage was "It's a serious move, Dov." She desperately wanted him to exculpate her.

He understood, and did. "Kate, I hope you realize that this move was a long time in coming, and it was something I had to do—having nothing to do with my feelings for you." And then, taking another sip of his second martini—an indulgence for him—he went on. "My feelings for you are still there, though. I'm afraid to ask you about yours, but if my new situation is still pertinent, perhaps we could spend some time together."

Two nights later they were in bed. That was nine months ago.

As the past year unrolled in her mind, Kate wandered aimlessly through her apartment, plumping sofa cushions, performing minute adjustments on picture frames, moving plants and vases a millimeter to the left or right, looking into the empty rooms of Joanna and Charlie, both of whom were away at summer camp, and finally ending in her bedroom.

Somehow her bedside clock intruded into the reverie. One minute before seven. The morning news was about to go on, with *her* bulletin.

Kate raced across the shag rug to the portable TV set on her boudoir table; she snapped it on; it was already set on her channel. The closing credits of the early morning educational hour were just fading to black, and a commercial came on the screen. She had at least a minute.

She sprinted down the hall to the front door, which she opened, made a grab for the copy of the *New York Times* on the floor, slammed the door, and ran back to her room. Another commercial was on the tube, so she glanced at the front page, and saw a four-column, three-line headline: ARAB NATIONS ATTACK ISRAEL; ADVANCE ALONG ALL BORDERS; JERUSALEM, TEL AVIV BOMBED.

She started reading the story, then heard the voice of the UBC anchorman. "Good morning. It's July 12 and here is the news. UBC News has just learned, exclusively, that at this moment, 7 a.m., Israel is delivering notes to the United States, the Soviet Union, and the UN Security Council warning of the possibility of widespread nuclear war if Middle East fighting is not stopped immediately."

Then came two sentences of background, and the entire bulletin was repeated.

Of course, she said to herself, some son of a bitch in the newsroom has got to change a few of my words to show he's earning his paycheck. They'd rewrite the Gettysburg Address if I phoned it in.

Still, it was on, and first. Kate walked over to the set and switched the dial to NBC; she wanted to see how soon they'd get it on. She had to smile at the thought of what was going on in the other newsrooms: Wondering where UBC had got the story. Wondering if it was accurate. Frantic calls to Washington, to Moscow, to UN correspondents, to the wires, to check it. Probably they'd still be puzzling over it when the wire services sent the story out, which would be in a few minutes. They can't get it on before a quarter after, she thought, pleased with herself.

Then: My God, it's nearly five after now, I'd better get moving. Quickly Kate moved down the hall. She headed for the kitchen, threw some coffee into her little coffeemaker, poured water in, and pushed its plug into the socket. Just as quickly she headed back, jumped into the shower, then dressed, in a tan linen skirt and white blouse, and worked on her hair.

I can't give this too much time, she thought, but I've got to look presentable. I haven't seen Bill in months. Oh cut it out, she said to herself, almost aloud. She slipped into a pair of sandals, no stockings in the summer heat, grabbed for her purse and the *Times* and went back into the kitchen, where the coffee was ready.

She poured herself a cup, added milk, no sugar, and sat on a high stool, reading the *Times*'s coverage of the fighting. From the Arab joint command, reports that would be taken by the public as extravagant claims, but which she knew from Dov were not far off. From Israel, inconclusive reports, heavy fighting, losses on both sides, bombing. She knew both sides were censoring, carefully, but even so she could see the difference. The Arab tone was exultant, the Israelis' sober.

Immersed in the paper, she sat in the kitchen until the doorman rang her from downstairs, telling her someone was waiting. Then she stood up, clutched at her purse, and left the apartment.

The ambassador's car was double-parked in front of her building, Shalzar in back, one security man at the wheel, a second standing alongside the right rear door. For reasons of security and modesty, Shalzar had a medium-size, two-year-old black Buick; no Cadillac, Continental, or Mercedes.

The bodyguard opened the door for her, shut it behind her and got in the right front seat. Kate had never seen him before, but she did recognize the stocky, thick-necked driver, Yehuda, an ex-tank sergeant who went with Shalzar wherever he was assigned.

As the car moved forward, Kate turned to Shalzar. "What news?"

Before responding, he said, "Tape is still off." And she said, just a touch annoyed, "Of course."

Spotting that, but ignoring it, Shalzar said, "Same. Bad. Worse." Then he added, "By the way, I heard your bulletin. Very proper. Well within bounds."

Kate smiled. "Well, my fearless leader, dickless Dick Hannon, has to share the credit for that. I would have been a little less proper and pushed the boundaries a little more. But I'm glad you liked it. And I'm glad you let me use it."

"NBC didn't have it on till about twelve minutes later."

Then Kate remembered, she had forgotten to look for that. In fact, she had forgotten to turn off the set! What a thing to think of, she said to herself. Hell, the housekeeper will turn it off.

To Dov she said, "And thanks for letting me come along to the Unity to listen."

"There are only two conditions," he said, smiling. "You've got to look like a Jewish man."

"Listen," Kate answered, "if you're going to try to pass Bill Brewster through those portals as a Jew, I'll make it. Anyone would make it. Bill is someone than whom nobody looks more goyish. But as for the man, there we have a problem. At least, I *hope* we do."

"You couldn't fool me for a moment," said Shalzar, squeezing her hand. And for a second or two they just stared at each other.

"It really means a hell of a lot to me, Dov, to be there," she told him.

"If you're important enough to arrange the meeting, Ms. Colby, you're important enough to sit in. Besides, I told you I wanted a third person there." Again, he managed a smile. "Three sets of memoirs will come out of this meeting, and I want yours to confirm the accuracy of mine—about how, if things work out, Dov Shalzar averted a world crisis—and if they don't work out, how Shalzar's brilliant efforts were botched up by an intransigent banker."

He repeated, "If they don't work out." And he stopped smiling.

The car was pulling up to the entrance of the Unity. She was going into a confrontation only a half-dozen people in the world knew about, and which any journalist in the world would sacrifice his mother to be at. Why had she said "his," she wondered.

She was lucky, she thought. Going into the Unity, for this. But she could just as well be going into Clarke's, or the Stage, or "21," or the Irish bar where the news cameramen hung out. She felt at home with journalists, diplomats, bankers, and show-biz types. Eclectic. And exciting. Even the meeting of these two men, the Israeli soldier-diplomat and the WASP moneyman, was her doing.

Shalzar snapped her out of her daydream. "I'm surprised you haven't asked for a preview. It's not like you."

Yehuda, the driver, opened the left passenger door, and Shalzar started out, as she thought of an answer. The truth was, and she was embarrassed to say it, she had been lost in her egocentric reverie. As she got out, helped by his outstretched hand, she said, "I thought that since I'd be at the main event, I didn't need the preliminary, but just so my press card isn't revoked, tell me what you hope to get while you're defiling the hallowed halls of the Unity."

They started across the sidewalk, under the blue canopy with its intertwined white letters, UC.

"I hope I'll have the ear of the man the Secretary of State trusts and listens to above all others. Into that ear I'll pour a message of the extremity of Israel's situation, the desperation of its mood, and the determination of our nation to do anything it can to save itself from annihilation. I will definitely use the expression 'stop at nothing.'"

"And what do you expect to happen then?"

"I should hope Brewster will take what I say seriously enough to convey the gravity of it to the Secretary, who will then ask of Israel, 'What can be done?' We shall then make some suggestions on what can be done, and hope and expect the United States will use its influence, its muscle, to carry out our suggestions. If not . . ." He shrugged and kept staring at her, his mouth open as if there were an ending, but he couldn't bring himself to speak it.

Kate supplied the ending. "If not, you put the Masada Plan into effect."

"Not quite," responded Dov, this time looking straight ahead, his face as taut as it had been hours before in her apartment. "The Masada Plan already is in effect. Now our problem . . . America's problem . . . the world's problem . . . is to turn it off. Before it's too late."

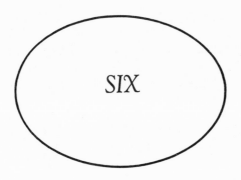

SIX

Three stories high, its white marble grayed by time and New York air, the Unity Club stood as a celebration of its membership's wealth and taste. Unlike Kate Colby's apartment house, it was genuine Stanford White. When, in 1890, its original home, a brownstone, was outgrown, the Unity commissioned White to build it a new midtown home. The building was completed in 1893, a date memorialized in Roman numerals on its second-story entablature.

Inside and out, the Unity had the grandeur, the luxury, the ornamentation of a Veronese palazzo of the early Italian Renaissance; in fact, White used just such a palace as his inspiration. Architecture students visited the edifice often, because some of its characteristics recapitulated those of White's extinct masterpiece, the first Madison Square Garden. The students especially admired the arched loggia on the second story, which, fortunately for them, could be seen from the outside, for the Unity's functionaries did not take warmly to droppers-in. Even a new member could feel chilled by his reception until his face came to be known.

As she and the ambassador walked through the entrance foyer, headed for the majestic wooden staircase which led to the second floor, Kate gawked at the lofty coffered ceiling, and was startled by a "May I help you?" from the clerk, whose frigid tone indicated help was the last thing he had in mind.

He thawed and turned deferential at the ambassador's "We are guests of Mr. Seligsohn." They were expected, it turned out, were led to the huge second-floor library and shown to one of the alcoves formed by the library's series of vaults. No one else was in the room, and to Kate the awesome space more resembled a cathedral nave than a library, a funny feeling to get in a Jewish club, she thought.

"A waiter will be up to see if there's anything you'd like," said the clerk after they had seated themselves in two oversized leather arm-chairs.

"Thank you," replied Shalzar. "We're expecting a Mr. Brewster to join us."

"Very good, sir, I'll look for him," said the clerk, and walked out.

Kate looked at Shalzar, waiting for him to speak.

"Do you think Brewster will object to your being here while he and I talk?' the ambassador asked briskly.

"I wouldn't be surprised," she answered. "He has strong ideas about a woman's place, and one of the places he thinks it *isn't* is where men are discussing international politics. On the other hand, he knows I brought you together and he knows my feelings about a woman's place . . . so it'll be interesting."

"And Kate, what should I know about him so that I can best deal with him? You can skip the romantic secrets."

"I was planning to." Her answer was patient, but not amused. She went on. "First of all, try to forget he's a Gentile."

"And what's that supposed to mean?"

"He'll be here any minute. Do you want to hear it quickly and bluntly?"

Shalzar expelled air through his mouth sharply in what was a cross between a sigh and a snort. He was impatient and prepared to fight. "Yes."

"OK. In the two years I've known you the only serious misjudg-ments I've seen you make have come when your Jewish chauvinism acts up to the point where someone's intelligence is underestimated merely because he's a goy."

Shalzar's face got combative.

"Want to debate it or hear about Bill? Either one is OK."

"Go on," he told her.

"Bill tends to be . . . dignified . . . slightly courtly and stiff—deliberately, proudly. But elegant. And there's a quick, flexible, imaginative mind working behind that stiffness, using it as a screen. Don't think you have to explain too much. Don't think he isn't anticipating, working out the next two or three steps, perhaps even before you announce them."

"You make it all so simple. I'll just sit back and let him tell me what it is I want. No point in trying to keep up with him; I've just been living this . . . myth of Jewish intellectuality."

"You want to debate, don't you?"

"No, sorry, go on. Tell me more."

"Stately, maybe even pompous. Conservative, chauvinistic, smart, quick—for a Gentile. Not much on wisecracks. The rest you're now in a position to find out for yourself." Kate was looking toward the doorway as she finished, and his eyes followed hers. With the black waiter, who was nodding in their direction, stood the tall lean figure of Bill Brewster. Quickly he scanned the room and took in the chunky security man, Yehuda, sitting near the door. Then he started toward them, a reserved smile on his face.

Kate had always chided him about that smile, symptomatic of the way he held a part of him back when he met people, particularly women.

"What are you afraid of?" she'd asked the first time she saw it.

"Sometimes I wonder," he'd replied, "do I know that person, or, more often, does he or she remember me, because to be immodest about it, I have an extraordinary memory for names and faces, and I generally assume that others, not being equally favored, will not remember me merely because I remember them."

"And suppose they didn't remember; what would happen then, do you suppose?"

Bill had chuckled and said, "Why then they'd probably respond with the kind of halfhearted half smile, which is aloof and repugnant —the kind I usually give people. And I, of course, would dislike it."

One of the world's more self-aware stuffed shirts, she'd thought. To him she'd said, "Bill, you're crazy. You are handsome, charming, sexy, bright, rich, eligible. One of America's dream men. You could walk into a room full of women you'd never met, smile, start talking and, nine times out of ten, walk out with anyone you damn well chose. But it would have to be a smile that said 'I'm delighted to see you,' not one of those half-assed attempts that say 'I'm not sure you know me, and until I find out, I'm not risking anything.' "

And he *could* walk out with anyone he chose, he's an attractive devil, Kate thought as he came near. Six three, with broad shoulders and slim waist accentuated by the cut of the gray pin-striped suit, he looked like the tennis player he was in college. Responding to style, but not precipitately, he had let his hair grow long enough to touch his collar; the blondness had faded with age and turned to gray at the sides. But it didn't hurt, not at all, she said to herself. As always, he was tanned; tennis, skiing, and sailing took care of that the year round. His eyes were a startlingly light blue. Although he was not a matinee idol like John Lindsay, he was often called "a Lindsay type." There was a resemblance. Moreover, the two men shared a look of patrician disdain both could have done without.

Now he stood over their low table. Shalzar got up; Bill Brewster reacted almost as if Kate had rehearsed him. First he leaned toward her, bending over, arms out, smile welcoming. He kissed her warmly on the cheek. "Kate, my dear, how good it is to see you! You look marvelous, especially for this businesslike hour of the morning."

"Bill, I'm delighted to see you; it's so good of you to come. I'd like you to meet Ambassador Shalzar. Mr. Ambassador, this is William Brewster."

Again, as if trying to show her, Bill jumped in first. His hand was out; again, he smiled warmly. "How do you do, Mr. Ambassador. I'm pleased to meet you. I've heard so much about you."

"And I am pleased to meet you, Mr. Brewster, and happy you are able to be here, particularly at this time of day, and on such short notice. I'm grateful to you, and to Kate, whose powers of persuasion have once again proved redoubtable."

Watching them, she thought, by God, it's Dov who's a bit tense, the ambassador, the general, the after-dinner speaker, who's a touch unsure of himself, pushing a touch hard to impress the competition. And how funny, she thought, that each of them, trying so hard to skirt their obvious link—her—should each brush it lightly in his first few words, Brewster with "I've heard so much about you" and Shalzar with "powers of persuasion" and "redoubtable."

And then Bill just stood in place and she didn't understand why. "Kate," he said, "thank you for getting us together. It's a meeting I've long wished for, and I hope, especially at this difficult moment, that some good may come of it."

Still he stood there, towering over Dov, who remained standing too, apparently confused as to why Brewster was not sitting. Then at once Shalzar and the woman understood. Brewster was waiting for her to leave! The ambassador responded.

"I've asked Kate to stay, Mr. Brewster. She realizes everything said here will be . . . off the record. I'd like her to be present if that is acceptable to you."

It wasn't acceptable; she admitted that to herself with a pang. He didn't know quite how to express his reluctance; nor could he hide it.

Gingerly, tiptoeing through every word, Brewster began. "I hardly need say there's no third person I'd sooner have here than Kate, but my experience has been that the presence of any third person places a burden on the two who are talking, as well as on that person . . . and therefore gets . . ."

He seemed not to know how to continue, so Kate broke in.

"It's up to you two." And she rose, because it had all seemed so awkward, both men standing, she sitting and staring up, waiting to be disposed of. "If you want me to go, I'll go willingly, with not a word to the Human Rights Commission or NOW. If you want me to stay, I'll stay. I'd hate to be the cause of any friction between you." She realized, and almost smiled as she did, that she, too, couldn't stay away from the romantic triangle, despite her determination; it was like the way you always stubbed the sore toe you were trying hardest to protect.

Then Shalzar spoke decisively. "Mr. Brewster, while it is desirable to me that Kate be here, you have been kind enough to come at my request, as a favor to me. If you are determined that she not be here, I'll yield to your wish."

Score one for Dov, Kate thought. By offering it as a matter of personal privilege, Shalzar had put Brewster on the spot. He could accept it on that basis and seem high-handed, argue it on the merits or yield gracefully.

Gracefully, he yielded. "Since personally I'm delighted to have Kate stay, and since my tactical objections are not shared by you two, who are clearly far more expert in this sort of thing than I, and since the Unity Club doesn't seem to object . . ." He said the last with a wry smile.

"Listen, fella," she interrupted, "if they don't object to *you* . . ." She smiled, too, and didn't finish. And he concluded, "I defer to your judgment, happily."

Brewster took the third of the four leather armchairs around the coffee table, which left the ambassador in the middle of the group, Kate on his left and Bill Brewster on his right.

"Mr. Brewster," Shalzar began, when he saw the gray jacketed waiter approaching them. He paused.

"Can I get you folks something?"

Shalzar, impatient but now in the position of host, looked at the other two. Neither said anything, so the ambassador said, "I'll have some coffee; what would you like?" He looked first at Kate, then at Brewster. Kate answered, "I'd love some." Bill said, "Fine."

"Coffee, please," said Shalzar. The waiter walked away and he went on.

"Mr. Brewster, as you may know, a half hour ago, our ambassador in Washington delivered to your Secretary of State an urgent note from our government. It said the fighting going on in the Middle East—in my country—is extremely dangerous, not only to the participants, but to all the world; it could result in a nuclear world war." Between each of those last three words he paused, his bright blue eyes staring into Brewster's as if trying to burn each word onto the banker's optic nerve.

"What my country wishes to do, at once—and let me impress upon you the urgency, and the lateness of the hour—is to amplify that note in an informal way so that your Secretary may understand more fully what we mean and what we do not mean, and how critical we consider the situation in the Middle East to be at this moment.

"In order that the Secretary might be told, free from the delays, the formalities, and the posturings of an official communication, my government has asked me to do it, rather than our ambassador in Washington. And it has asked me to function through an intermediary contact, one whom the Secretary and I both trust unreservedly.

"By now, I hardly need say I hope you will be that intermediary. If I'm wrong about your capacity or willingness to help, please tell me so." The ambassador hesitated, shrugged, and smiled disarmingly. "Another thing I hardly need say is that I hope I'm not wrong."

Bill Brewster looked first at Kate Colby and then, longer and harder, at the ambassador, his face registering two feelings: First, what have I gotten into? Second, I'm pleased to be asked and to have the capacity to deliver. Seeing Brewster's hesitancy, and guessing at a conflict behind it, Shalzar tried to get him to commit himself. "If you agree to listen to and transmit this amplification, there is of course *no* implication that you endorse it, or are not free to comment on it, to me or to the Secretary. Nor is there any implication that you are compromising your own freedom—in any way but one."

Bill was looking more and more interested; he loved clauses and complications. "And what is the one restriction?"

The parquet mahogany floor of the club's old second story creaked and the three of them looked up, startled. The waiter had arrived with the coffee. He in turn was startled by the way they had all jumped when he walked up, and he said, "Excuse me, folks!"

Trying not to show his impatience, Bill looked to the Israeli. He wanted to tell the waiter, put the stuff down and leave, but his sense of propriety told him that was Shalzar's function. Shalzar did it for him.

"Just put the tray on the table; we'll handle it. Thanks."

"Would you like me to pour, sir?"

"No, thank you." Unlike Bill, the ambassador let his impatience show. The waiter turned and walked away. Dov looked at Kate, and asked, rather imperiously, she thought, "Would you pour us all some coffee?" Without waiting for a response, he turned back to Bill, and grinned.

"Now that we've disposed of *that* important issue . . ." Bill grinned back.

Kate, leaning over the low table to pour, saw the exchange of smiles, the first real personal contact between the two men, and she felt a touch of jealousy; relegated to the coffee detail while the men warmed up to business. She put a cup in front of Bill, another before Dov and took a third for herself. "Black the way you like it, and milk, no sugar for you," she said to the two in turn. She thought, oh my God, I shouldn't have done that, remind each I know how the other likes his morning coffee. Then, to herself, Oh, screw, it'll remind them I'm here and I do other things besides serving coffee.

But neither man had any inkling of her reaction, and she didn't do anything to let them know about it.

"The one restriction," Bill reminded the Israeli.

"It is the same one I have placed on Kate, that you respect the confidentiality of everything said, no matter if you agree or disagree, no matter what the outcome."

Brewster nodded his head and then sipped at his coffee; idly, belatedly, he looked toward Kate for a moment and said, "Yes, this coffee is fine, thank you."

Shalzar echoed him with "Yes, thank you."

Then Bill went ahead. "I understand, indeed I should expect, both the freedom and the restriction."

Dov took a sip of his coffee, and nodded. Did the American's answer imply an acceptance of his mission? Dov decided to go ahead on the assumption that it did.

"I don't know if you're aware of the nature of the fighting in Israel at this moment, Mr. Brewster, very few people are. The war—the invasion—is only six hours old and its pattern is already decisive and irreversible: Arab advance and advance and advance. In case you didn't know it, although I'm sure you do, Israeli military superiority has been a myth for nearly two years and a joke for one."

He paused to see what effect that news had on Brewster; Bill did not seem surprised. Dov picked up his coffee cup, went through the motions of sipping at it, and then continued.

"As you may gather, some of this I have already discussed with Kate, but some of what I am about to say not even she knows; some I heard in a telephone conversation with Israel minutes before I got in the car to come over here." This Dov said looking at Kate, a warning he was going to spring something on her.

"The desperation of the military situation is such that the government is contemplating its removal from Jerusalem to Tel Aviv, and I don't think I have to tell you how extreme a situation it would take to cause that. We've been thinning out our forces in the central sector to defend against the Egyptians in the south; the Jordanians surprised us by the total commitment of their opening attack. Now we fear Jerusalem may be taken soon, or bypassed and cut off. Things are not better in the Sinai or the north; our planes and tanks have been hit with unimaginably heavy missile fire. I could go on giving you all sorts of unpleasant facts, but the Arab advantage is so compelling, we envision defeat within the week. Within the week."

Shalzar repeated these last words because he saw the impact they had on Brewster. The tall banker's face seemed to pale beneath his tan. This, clearly, he had not known.

The Israeli paused, and then continued. "Now, you must believe these words are not being said for effect; that is precisely why we are doing this so informally, so that you may be assured by the context, as well as by my statements, that nothing I say is exaggerated or even shaded for dramatic or diplomatic reasons. When I say within a week, I don't mean a month; I don't even mean *in* a week. I mean *less* than a week. When I say we're considering the removal from Jerusalem, I don't mean in a week, I mean in the next forty-eight hours."

Shalzar was leaning forward, eyes blazing, but speaking softly and deliberately. Kate was shocked by the vividness of the way he was describing it, even though she had heard some of it before. Brewster looked concerned; he was careful not to show anything more.

"As sure as we are of our military situation, we're even surer of Arab intentions. They mean to annihilate the state of Israel; their words proclaim it, our intelligence confirms it. They have the intention; they have the capability."

Brewster saw it coming; he grew more guarded. Shalzar grew more tense. Then there was a break. The waiter was back.

"Mr. Salazarro, sir?"

"That's close," the ambassador answered, annoyed yet amused at the approximation of his name. "Yes?" He noticed as he said it, the waiter was carrying a small silver tray with an envelope on it.

"A message for you, sir."

Quickly, the ambassador reached into his pocket, fished out a dollar, threw it on the tray, and picked up the envelope. Too big a tip, he thought, but he didn't have any change with him, and he wanted to end the transaction.

The waiter said, "Thank you, sir. I have been told to wait for a reply."

A message at eight in the morning? Here? With a reply demanded? The questions began to be answered when he turned the envelope over. It was cream colored, blue bordered, expensive vellum, with the address 815 Fifth Avenue, and in bold blue, Seligsohn.

To every Israeli fund raiser, Maxwell Seligsohn was known as Big Mac because he had probably done more for Israel over thirty years than any other private individual in the world. He was also a member of the Unity Club and a power there, as he was at any institution on which he chose to spend time and effort. One hour earlier Shalzar had called him to arrange for that morning's meeting.

Shalzar tore open the envelope, murmuring an "excuse me" to the others as he did so. He pulled out a note card. It read, "How soon can we meet regarding American response, governmental and private, to the invasion?"

To himself, Dov said, Goddammit, that's one of the last things I've got the time for today. To the waiter, after a moment's hesitation, he said, "Get me an envelope, please."

"I have one right here, sir, and some paper." The waiter reached into his pocket and pulled out a few of each. Dov took only an envelope, and then on one of his own cards he wrote, "Eleven, at the embassy." He thought for a moment and added, "If that's all right." One never said no to Mac Seligsohn, and one didn't even say yes too imperiously.

As the answer was being carried away—to Seligsohn's waiting limousine, Dov was sure—he turned back to Bill Brewster. If Bill and Kate expected him to explain the note, they were disappointed.

"But desperate though our situation is, we too have certain intentions and capabilities." The ambassador picked up where he had left off, as if the message had never arrived.

This was the real beginning. He spoke slowly and paused, because he was on a tightrope, and because he wanted them, Bill especially, to start listening hard. Bill knew, and was ready. So was Kate.

"Our bedrock intention is that the state of Israel shall not perish. For that we shall stop at nothing. Nothing." Dov tried a smile, which came out more a grimace. "I warned Kate I would use that expression. There it is." He looked at her, bleakly.

"Now, as to capabilities. As you may know, we have had nuclear weapons for some years now, so when I say we'll stop at nothing, you must take into account *all* our capabilities."

Well, it didn't take him long to get to that, thought Brewster. OK, but their official statement strongly suggested nuclear weapons, so he didn't set up this private warning just to repeat *that*. Besides, it was no secret the Arabs had a small nuclear stockpile and the tininess of Israel made it peculiarly vulnerable to retaliation. So Shalzar was saying something other than: We'll hit the Arabs with nuclear weapons. But what? the American asked himself. Well, that's the point of this meeting. He'd wait and hear.

"If this sounds fierce, warlike, even ruthless," Shalzar continued, "please remember the world first deprived us of much of what we need to defend ourselves—money, arms, oil. Then it reneged on promises, indeed guarantees, spoken and implied, legal and moral, assuring Israel of its right to exist. Now it is standing by, doing nothing to stop this . . . holocaust. And so we are left to ourselves.

"Can you reasonably expect us to accept any limitation on our freedom of action in order to please other nations? Can you?" He stared at Brewster.

"I'm listening, Mr. Ambassador, and I respect the extreme gravity of the situation. Beyond that, I know you are not expecting any answer, any statement of personal agreement or disagreement from me."

Shalzar's answering look agreed.

"Mr. Brewster, I've stressed this with Kate and now I want to do the same with you. Israel faces the certainty of defeat and, therefore, the certainty of destruction. Perhaps I should spell that out. I mean the end of the Jewish state. I mean the total subjugation of the people of Israel. I mean the loss of hundreds of thousands of Jewish lives. I mean the forced emigration of hundreds of thousands of others—to where, God only knows. Tell me, Mr. Brewster, after the American reaction to taking in Vietnamese, how many hundred thousand Israelis would the United States be willing to take in?"

He barely paused for breath before resuming, quickly. "Nor am I expecting an answer to that."

But Bill Brewster would not let the ambassador's assumption go unchallenged. "Since it is really not material to the point we're considering, I don't feel I'd be moving out of my neutral position by answering. And I want to. It is my feeling this country would offer to take in large numbers of Israelis, should the unthinkable eventuality occur. Perhaps all of them. I don't see why you presume an antagonism that doesn't exist."

Dov Shalzar's eyes widened. "Doesn't exist, Mr. Brewster? Doesn't exist? Obviously we see the thing from different sides. Don't forget I know America—as a Jew. I know the antagonism toward Jews. And I assure you your government's position vis-à-vis Israel in the past few years has fortified that antagonism."

They were off on a tangent. And into a personal argument that was worse than immaterial; it was poisoning the atmosphere. Both knew it, yet for the moment neither could pull back. Kate spotted it, too, and decided to help.

"Can the coffee girl say a word?" she asked. "Well, I think you're both right. Dov, you're right in your implication that Bill is numb to latent anti-Semitism in America. It's a pain that has never pained him. Bill, you're right in thinking Dov tends to see an SS man hiding inside every Gentile.

"To reconcile your two rectitudes would take a learned panel of six a month in Aspen. Why don't you drop it for now? And while you're at it, why don't you drop the Misters? You'll save a lot of syllables, and save yourselves the trouble of calling me Ms. Colby, which I'm going to insist on if you maintain the formality with each other."

Both men seized on the names as a way out of the earlier question. "Fine," said the ambassador. "Call me Dov, Bill. Dov as in peace." "Dov it is," answered Brewster. "And peace sounds lovely to me."

"More coffee anyone?" asked Kate. And the two men answered, almost together, "No thanks, Ms. Colby." The three of them smiled. Then Dov resumed, and there was no more smiling.

"And for those not dead, and who would not or could not flee the destroyed nation, I am talking about lives of poverty and abject serfdom. So I suggest to you that unless you are talking about the death of every last man, woman, and child, the fate I have outlined meets the definition of the destruction of Israel.

"Again, no answer required." But Dov paused and waited for Bill Brewster to volunteer one. Bill knew no further tangents were needed, so he remained silent. He just shook his head and smiled slightly. Dov smiled back, and then an odd thing happened. Both turned to Kate with self-satisfied looks that said, unmistakably, Aren't you proud of the way we're getting on?

Yes, she was. Proud of each, and his closeness to her. Proud she had been able to bring them together. In a way, each one "belongs" to me, she thought, then chastised herself for the rampant egocentricity which intruded, however briefly, on the gravity of the meeting.

Dov went back to work. "Bill, I can't divulge to you the exact nature of our nuclear arsenal—anyway, with your intelligence-gathering apparatus, the Secretary may know more about it than I do. What he may not know, although it shouldn't surprise him, is that we shall *not* go to our deaths leaving our nuclear arsenal untouched. Any more than the Soviet Union would, or the United States would. Would you? And *that* does not call for an answer, Bill.

"Now, we don't *want* to use nuclear weapons, and their use would be particularly tragic if some step might have been taken to avoid it. We are much more interested in using nuclear force by *not* using it, if you understand what I mean."

For the first time since Dov had begun his narrative, Bill volunteered a substantive response. "I think I do. You want to use it as you are at this moment, as a threat to us that if we do not intercede you will blow up a few bombs."

Dov smiled. "This is why I am so glad our talk is private and informal. Otherwise, I'd immediately object to the word 'threat.' But you're right; it is a threat. Please remember, though, we're doing it only to keep the noose from tightening around our necks; we're not doing it to help us tighten the noose around anyone else's, as the Arabs have done with their oil threats. Nor are we threatening on a them-or-us basis. If we are successful in saving Israel by this means, it will not have been on the basis of destroying any Arab state; the possibility is really too ludicrous to mention; nonetheless, I'm raising it to underline what the quid pro quo is *not*. The Arab states will merely be deprived of the emotional and symbolic satisfaction of wiping the state of Israel off the face of the earth. They will lose nothing strategically or economically.

"So, yes, it is a threat. One that, if it works, essentially harms no one. But now I've gotten off the track and I want to get back on it.

"What heightens the chance of a misstep and tragedy is the shortage of time. We can't wait too long for you or anyone else in the world to intercede—and here we're really talking about only one other possibility, the Soviet Union. And this is in no way a threat to use them against you—we assume anything you decide to do you'll do in consultation with the Soviets.

"Naturally," here Dov smiled as if to say something lighter was coming up, "since we have been called a client state of yours it's only fitting that we come to you first.

"That will take time, and time is critical. When I say we can withstand the Arab attacks for as much as a week, that could as easily be four or five days as six or seven. However, we can't wait even that long, because at that point our country would be in ruins, cities destroyed, thousands upon thousands dead, industrial capacity shattered, armed forces nonexistent. We must set a deadline, which, should it be met, would leave us with a substantial part of our nation intact. And I assure you, as we sit here, the destruction goes on.

"So we have set a deadline of twenty-four hours from 9 a.m., New York time, which is," Dov looked at his wristwatch, and, as if compelled, the other two looked at theirs, "less than twenty-five hours from right now. If we have a negative response, or no response by then, we'll consider that all our options are open and that we have complete freedom of action."

Gone now were the playfulness and the personal closeness of the past half hour. Bill's face was set, carefully noncommittal, the negotiator who was not allowing himself the luxury of showing any emotion, lest it get in the way of his efficacy. All that showed was the habitual clenching and unclenching of his clearly defined jaw muscles.

Kate was wide-eyed, trying not to show it, failing. Looking from one man to the other, awed by the immensity of the threat without actually knowing its size, a network of antennae trying to absorb all the words, faces, feelings, meanings of the moments, wishing she could be taking notes, knowing she couldn't.

Dov's attitude was the strangest. The serenity was back, the exaltation that had taken over when he was telling the story of Masada. He now no longer had the agony of considering alternatives. His face was almost beatific as he looked straight at Bill, waiting for the question he knew would come next.

It came. "I understand everything you've said up to now, Dov. What you have not yet explained is what you want, what Israel envisions as the kind of response that would satisfy it."

He looked at Brewster, their eyes met, and for the first time that morning in that hushed sitting room overlooking Fifth Avenue they saw each other as adversaries.

"Would you expect us to stop the Arab attack?"

"Yes, of course. That and more. We would expect it to be noticeable within one hour after acceptance; we would expect all Arab firing to cease within six hours, although we would understand and make allowance for the unruliness of guerrillas; after all, they have not stopped for thirty years.

"Will this be difficult? No question. Not beyond the capabilities of the US and the Soviet Union, though. How will you do it? We leave that to you. We could suggest steps, but that would be presumptuous of us."

Brewster nodded his head slowly. "I see. You would expect that. As for the 'and more' . . ."

Dov smiled faintly and said, "I thought you'd never ask. We have given it a bit of thought. It just happens we have made up a list. Here is the 'and more.'

"We want a rollback of Arab forces to the borders as they were before last night's attack.

"We want a multinational patrol force to begin landing within twenty-four hours of the cease-fire, and within one week to be large enough to cover every inch of border Israel shares with Arab nations, which means all of Israel's land borders. They will patrol a DMZ made up of equal five-mile strips on each side of the borders I've just mentioned, and they will not be removed without the agreement of both sides.

"We want guarantees of investment capital to, among other things, build up the Israeli armaments industry. We want similar guarantees of raw materials and heavy machinery.

"We want guarantees of arms from the US which will maintain us at parity with the Arabs.

"We want guarantees of oil and other energy sources to be specified until we are sure our own sources are ample."

Dov had gone smoothly over the words "other energy sources," but Bill had not missed the phrase. "May I interject a question here?" he interrupted.

Dov smiled. "I'll just answer it to save time. We'll not ask you for weapons-grade fissionable material. We don't need to."

Bill touched the fingertips of his right hand to his forehead in a mimed salute of congratulations to Dov. Dov nodded back and went on.

"Finally, if you've been getting bored with the routine nature of these . . . requests . . . here's something new. We want the creation of an international hostage community on Israeli soil. In it will live leading citizens of many other nations; in it will be held precious art objects and artifacts from all over the world, the Declaration of Independence, for example, the Magna Carta, the Mona Lisa, the Pietà, any of several paintings from the Hermitage. Both the people and the objects may rotate on a sensible basis.

"Those in the hostage village will be able to pursue the same productive, creative lives they had been leading, perhaps even richer lives; in fact this may turn out to be a kind of MacDowell colony or Aspen, with people fighting to get in." Dov couldn't resist the tangential bit of fun. But not for long.

"By locating this village centrally, let's say just outside of Jerusalem or Tel Aviv, we shall do the best we can to make retaliatory attack— you see, we realize that after what we are doing, Israel may not win the world's Congeniality Award—a matter of concern to all the world, in a way that it is apparently not at present."

Brewster was moderately startled, although he was doing a fair job of not showing it. "Yes, that is a new one. I must admit I've never thought of it." He shook his head ruefully. "It certainly means to me that you expect there'll be some who'll want to retaliate, which in turn means your threat, which you are clearly not specifying, is more threatening to non-Arabs than I at first took it to be."

Dov replied: "The use of hostages is, of course, old stuff. We watched sundry Palestinian terrorists, and at Entebbe Airport we showed the world how they could be stopped. Then we decided there was a way the concept could be used less viciously, more creatively, a way that would make nations and peoples realize their mutuality of interest rather than their antagonism. We think we've found it.

"As for the specifics of the threat, I can do no more than repeat 'freedom of action,' which means the decision to use any capability in any way we see fit, without restriction, to save our nation from annihilation."

For more than half an hour, Brewster had done little more than sip coffee and listen. Occasionally he had spoken, usually to question or clarify a point. But mostly he had listened, impressed by the deadliness of what Shalzar was saying and by the adroit, thorough, committed way he was saying it. Now for the first time he prepared to respond. He ran a large, powerful hand through his hair, looked at Shalzar, seemed to set himself, and began: "Dov, I could characterize your nation's course of action. It might satisfy my ego, but it would be pointless, indeed harmful; I could not affect it. If I were supportive, that might give you an optimism which I assure you would be unfounded; if I were critical, that might create an antagonism, which is the last thing in the world we need now. I hope someday we may have the leisure and the goodwill to thrash out the issues and the morality thoroughly . . . the three of us." And he looked to Kate to show he remembered her presence and her role.

Then he looked back at Shalzar. "Right now I'll confine myself to the function for which you've asked me here, and which I've agreed to fulfill.

"First of all, do you realize how little time you are giving us? I must present your . . . information . . . to the Secretary. He must then consult with the President, who must then authorize him to contact the Soviet Union. There will be furious meetings in Moscow, I promise you, and then assuming an affirmative result occurs, indeed I'm assuming affirmative results all along the line—we must then approach the Arab joint command, which if it agrees—I should say can *be pressured* to agree—must turn off the spigot in a matter of hours. As you know, that takes time, and even after it's off there are drips."

Brewster shook his head from side to side. "I don't see how . . ."

Shalzar's answer came without hesitation. "That's all the time there is. I shouldn't say this, but because we're being so private, Bill, even the time we have represents a triumph for the doves, with a small 'd.' There were others who wanted less. If this turns out to be not enough, we fail—all of us, we fail. There is no more time.

"What I am assuming is that you are listening to me; the Secretary will listen to you; the President to the Secretary—he usually does—the Soviets to the US and the Arabs to both. And that you will all listen to reason.

"For your information, the Secretary is on his way to New York, to go to the UN about the Middle East; in fact, he may already have landed. The UN will do no good, of course; but that he's here for it is lucky, because you must really talk with him face-to-face, within a very few hours.

"And Bill, I'll be available every minute of the next twenty-four hours." He reached into his breast pocket for a pen, fished for another calling card and wrote a number on it. "Here is my direct line. Call me at any time, for reaction, clarification, any reason at all."

Then he glanced at his watch. "Kate, you should have left fifteen minutes ago. You'll be late for your taping. It's five after nine."

She looked at both men and rose. "I'm going to call the office and tell them I'll be late and they should book extra studio time. There are things, not too many, mind you, but there are, more important than the 'Today's Woman' show. And this is one of them. I'll be right back. Sorry, Bill." She looked over at him and grinned. "And for heaven's sake, don't say anything important."

Dov looked up with a mischievous smile. "The next five minutes will probably be crucial to your memoirs."

Feigning worry, Kate started back to sit down, then grinned, and kept on going.

Bill spoke first. "I resolved that the first words I said would *not* be 'that's quite a girl,' but they keep popping out anyway."

"You'll get no argument from me on that," Dov answered. "But I would put it 'quite a woman,' especially if she were in a position to overhear."

Bill looked concerned. "You see, Dov, I never could, I never shall understand that. Insofar as it has any connotation at all to me, 'girl' in this instance signifies how young and beautiful Kate looks for a . . . person . . . of thirty-six . . . or have I given something away?" Bill seemed genuinely worried.

Dov chuckled and said, "No, I am acquainted with the grisly number."

"But mostly," Bill went on, "my feeling is that it is so trivial, why bother?"

"Trivial? Maybe," Dov replied, "but your problem, Bill, is that you're just not in a position to know. As a Jew, I have some frame of reference in which to understand how some can resent, and strongly, 'trivial' remarks that do not seem offensive to others. Call a black 'boy,' and though it may seem harmless to others, it infuriates him because it bespeaks slavery and menial work. Call a Jew 'clever' or 'a shrewd businessman,' and it reminds him of 'moneylender.' Call Kate a 'girl' and it hurts like hell because it reminds her of the days she and other grown women were sent out of the room after dinner to discuss babies and diapers while the men began the 'heavy' talk. Kate is not a trivial person, Bill, but she is as sore as a boil about 'trivial' references that put down women.

"Your problem, Bill, is that there is no trivial reference that can put you down, because you're not a member of any disadvantaged group. So 'boy' or 'shrewd businessman' you would honestly take as a compliment and 'girl' you'd honestly offer as one."

"Now wait a minute, Dov." Bill pretended indignation. "Haven't you ever heard the old saying 'New York is built by the Italians, run by the Irish, and owned by the Jews.' Of course it's no longer true, if it ever was, but the point is, we WASPs don't even, as they say at the racetrack, get a call in that group. Haven't you heard, *we* are the minority in New York."

"Yes, I've heard the old saying; you forget I'm a native New Yorker. I was roaming the streets, East Side, West Side, while you were safe within the cloistered confines of . . . where is it? . . . Darien?"

"Westport."

"Westport. And you see, Bill, even the old saying uses three stereotypes, the Italian as laborer, the Irishman as Tammany hack, and the Jew as moneylender. As for the WASP, minority, yes; disadvantaged, no. A minority like the British planter on Jamaica, like the plantation owner in the Mississippi Delta. A member of a small, privileged club, with lots of people waiting in line to get in."

Bill looked at Dov. "How can I cry ouch if I don't feel the pain?"

"You can't," Dov answered. "It would be phony. All you can do is learn where it hurts others. And don't poke them there."

"Well put. I'll try to make use of it."

Dov looked frankly and openly at Bill and replied, "Don't use it *too* well."

Bill was about to say, "I don't think it would help," when Kate came back. He was relieved; he knew he would have regretted saying it.

"Well," she announced, "*they* don't seem to think anything is more important than 'Today's Woman,' especially since I couldn't tell them what it was. "So I said"—she started to add "screw them," when she remembered she didn't say things like that in front of Bill, so she quickly edited that and it came out instead, "to hell with them. ABC has been trying to hire me for two years now.

"OK," she added as she sat down and leaned forward as if she had just caught two boys with their hands in the cookie jar. "What were you talking about? Anything important?"

"Just you," Dov answered, with a wink at Bill.

"Just *boy* talk," Bill chipped in, and then grinned at Dov, pleased at his own wit, thinking, not bad for a WASP.

It was now 9:10 and Dov said, "I think we should get out of here. There's just not enough time and there's no more to say at the moment; and we don't want to get Kate into any more trouble. Unless there's something else you want to ask, Bill."

"My final request for the moment would be to learn a bit more about what your 'freedom of action' envisages, Dov. I know the Secretary will ask. What shall I tell him?"

"Tell him," Dov answered carefully, "that if I circumscribe it by specifying in advance, it either stops being freedom of action or it becomes misleading, and I don't want either to happen."

"In other words," Bill summed up, "tell him there's nothing more you'll tell him."

"You could put it that way," Dov said pleasantly, as he started to rise, Bill rising with him. Dov reached out a hand to the taller man. "I can't tell you how much it means to us that you are making yourself available. And I don't have to tell you how important this matter is, and how essential speed is."

"I'll do what I can," said Bill, careful to make no commitment. "And get in touch with you as soon as I can."

As the three left the library and started toward the broad staircase, Dov saw the waiter standing off in a corner. "Is there anything you'd like me to sign?" he asked.

"No, sir."

"Thank you," the ambassador said.

As they started down the stairs, Dov said to himself, Seligsohn doesn't miss a thing. And at eleven on the busiest day of my life he succeeds in getting me to see him.

On the sidewalk, Dov turned to Bill and asked, "Can I give you a lift?"

"No, thank you," Brewster replied. "I've got a car." A few feet behind the ambassador's modest Buick stood a huge Rolls, with uniformed driver at the wheel, but Brewster carefully avoided pointing it out, as if that would amount to a "that's *my* car" gesture. He did add, "In fact, if it will save you time, I'll be delighted to drop Kate."

For an instant, Shalzar felt competitive. Then he merely answered, "No, thanks, that's quite all right."

"Of course." Brewster said it gracefully. He leaned to Kate, put his hands delicately on her shoulders and kissed her cheek, while she performed a mirror image of his actions.

"Good to see you. Hope to see you again soon," he said.

"We really must," she responded. Then Bill turned to Dov and stuck out his hand. "I'll be talking with you very soon."

The ambassador reached out and squeezed Brewster's hand, giving extra pressure to make up for their disparity in size. Without letting go, he said, "I hope so. I pray we'll be talking soon, and fruitfully. Because if we don't . . ."

Dov let his speech remain unfinished. He squeezed Bill's hand even harder, then turned, took Kate's arm and guided her toward the Buick. For a second or two, Brewster watched them go. Then he strode toward the Rolls. Both car doors closed, both cars moved slowly off.

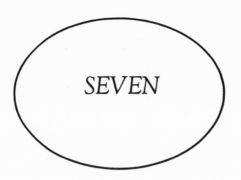

SEVEN

As soon as they settled onto the Buick's vinyl upholstery, the ambassador turned to Kate and asked, "Do you mind if the car drops me first and then takes you on to the studio?"

She answered, "Of course not; I delayed the taping so I'm all right on time now."

Then she waited. She sat looking straight ahead, at the thick neck of the security man in the passenger seat, expecting Shalzar to say something, to offer an opinion on the way the talk had gone, to make a pronouncement on Brewster—he was not hesitant about forming and proclaiming first impressions—or to ask for her opinions.

When he stayed silent, she turned and looked at him, as if to milk an answer from him by her expectancy. Still he didn't speak, nor did he look at her. Finally, knowing the ride from the club at Sixty-second and Fifth to the embassy on East Seventy-second Street would take only a few minutes, she couldn't wait any longer.

"All right. I heard the whole thing. Some I didn't understand; some I didn't believe."

She stared at him, still waiting. Dov looked remarkably fresh, she thought, for someone who'd been up all night; his thin face was taut, but the eyes were clear.

She continued to stare at him; he continued not to return her look. Nor did he speak. So she tried again.

"Since you're not going to ask me just what it is I don't understand and what I don't believe, I'm going to tell you anyway."

He seemed to tear himself away, coming back from wherever he had been. He smiled faintly, turned to her and said, "Why don't you tell me?"

She grinned. "If you insist.

"Well, the part I don't believe is how you can possibly expect to get all you've asked for. Do you? And why didn't Bill ask which were negotiable and which weren't? Shall I stop there while you explain fully and patiently, or go on to the part I didn't understand?"

His reaction began in annoyance, but as he listened he realized she was once again being useful as a straw man—person?—sounding board, against which he could bounce his ideas and then reformulate them as they came back at him.

"Since you've stopped," he said, "why don't I explain, partially and impatiently, OK?"

"I'll take what I can get."

"The answer is, none is negotiable." Shalzar seemed guarded, almost crafty, as he responded. "The terms are a package and Bill knew it. Of course the time may come when he'll ask me to take the package apart, but we'll be talking often, I suspect, and there's no point in his raising the possibility until he talks to the Secretary of State, who, for all Bill knows, may give him a quick yes or no to the entire package. In other words, he knows there's no reason to cross that bridge till he comes to it."

He relaxed. "You see, Bill's a better negotiator than you are. And almost as good looking."

Then his guard went up again. "You want to know if I expect to get everything I asked. If I knew, I'd be feeling a lot more euphoric than I do now. I'd be sitting back contemplating the happy ending. The answer is, I don't know. But I will within twenty-four hours. Does that take care of the first part?"

Kate felt the eggshells under her feet, and kept walking. "Dov, wouldn't you do better to say you'll take something less than the whole package? Wouldn't that improve the chances of an agreement?"

He gripped her upper arm, firmly, without hurting her, and leaned toward her as if to reveal a confidence. Then he changed his mind. A wild and, he had to admit, totally baseless suspicion ran through his mind. How much of this will get back to Brewster? Had he asked her to pump the Israelis? Had she agreed? Ridiculous, he thought, but he underlined his answer anyway. "This is a package and it is not negotiable. Now let's go to the part you didn't understand."

Kate saw and heard the change; her first question was being dismissed. Why? She didn't know. She went ahead.

" 'Freedom of action.' "

"Why," he said, "that means just what it says. We reserve the right to do anything we see fit to save ourselves from the extinction we believe is less than a week away."

By now the Buick had turned up Park Avenue, on its way to Seventy-second Street.

"How in the world can you expect anyone to meet your demands when he, or she, doesn't know what he or she is being threatened with? Couldn't you at least give an example? I mean, if you tell the world that, let's say, you're going to blow up all the bagel bakeries, at least we know what we're in for and whether we want to react or not."

Her example gave Dov, who was tense and edgy, the chance to blow up at something peripheral. He spoke with a cold anger.

"You know, Kate, bagels are not a Jewish universal, not at all. You'd be amazed at how many Israelis have never even heard of them, let alone eaten them. People who judge Israel according to the customs of New York Jews are in for big surprises."

Her eyes widened at his anger. "That was only a joke, for heaven's sake!"

He didn't want to give any ground. "Yes and no," he replied. "For your joke you were groping for an image that was prototypically Jewish and you came up with the bagel. That's the kind of premise that leads to faulty and dangerous conclusions, even as part of a joke."

"Okay, okay," she answered, getting a bit warm herself. "To hell with bagels, I retract the image. Please get back to 'freedom of action.'"

"As I told Bill, the minute we give an example, we begin limiting our freedom. Suppose, to pick a nonbagel example, we say we're going to kidnap Robert Redford. Either it could mean we're going to do something *like* that, thus limiting us and tipping our hand, or it could mean we have no intention of doing anything of the sort, in which case we are misrepresenting. Either way we're in a bind."

"But Dov, you did make a point of stressing your nuclear arsenal."

"Now wait a minute, wait!" He did not want her to pursue that tack. "The reason for mentioning nuclear weapons is merely to remind everyone of the full range of our capabilities, not to give an *example*. We use it to *broaden* the possibilities of our response, not to narrow them.

"Besides, the phrase 'freedom of action' was presented to me by my government. I can't go beyond it. Not a word. Remember, Kate, what I said in your apartment about not knowing, and even if I knew, not being able to tell you?"

"You mean your version of the Fifth Amendment?"

Dov Shalzar looked out the car window; they were at Seventy-second Street and Park Avenue. "Fifth Amendment? I don't care for the comparison, but you can say that if you want to." Then he turned to her. "Sure it's all right for me to get out first?"

She nodded and smiled. "Sure. Is that called changing the subject?"

"No," he answered, smiling back. "That's called ending the subject." He glanced at his wristwatch. "Just as well, I'm almost there. Our foreign minister is en route; he should be at the embassy in about an hour. I can use the time to lay in a fresh supply of bagels."

"I'm sorry about that, really."

He laughed. "Weismann, it just so happens, really *does* like bagels."

89

"I'd love to break bagels with him some time."

Dov looked at her searchingly for an instant, then said, "Actually, I can't make any culinary promises, but since we're going to be spending a good part of the next twenty-four hours waiting, why don't you come for an informal dinner tonight? Just you and I and Weismann. About seven. All right? Needless to say, the tape remains stopped."

"Supper with the Golden Throat, the Voice of Israel? You bet it's all right!"

Yehuda turned the Buick into Seventy-second Street. Ahead of them, groups of people clustered around the embassy; above the knots, several TV newsmen's film cameras could be seen. There was no movement. They were waiting; so was the New York City cop on duty. The ambassador could more easily have gone in the building's rear entrance on Seventy-third Street, but perhaps a few hortatory words for TV wouldn't hurt, he thought. He began preparing something in his mind, when he noticed the car was moving slowly.

They were approaching a double-parked car, which they'd have to move around. Yehuda looked to his left; just to the rear, a gray Audi moved slowly with them. The Israeli driver-bodyguard became impatient. Why didn't the damned car either go ahead of them, or stay back to let them move around the double-parked car?

The trunk of the parked car stood open, and two men appeared to be looking in it. A hell of a place to make repairs, Yehuda thought. Again he looked to his left; the Audi had not changed position.

Something was wrong.

The bodyguard smelled it. A veteran of four wars and innumerable ambushes, he did not need a second sniff. Savagely, he stepped on the gas, cutting his wheel to the left as he did, and shooting through the fast-closing space between the parked car ahead of him and the Audi to his left. Simultaneously, he shouted, "Get down!"

Frozen by surprise and fright, Kate felt herself grabbed by the ambassador and shoved to the floor of the car; then his body sprawled over hers.

As the Israelis' Buick shot by the double-parked car, the two men at its trunk straightened up. One was holding a stubby submachine gun, the other a pistol; the first lifted his weapon and fired four shots. But the speed of Yehuda's reaction threw him off. One round went through the right side passenger window, the second through the rear window and out the left side. The third and fourth flew across Seventy-second Street, hitting no one but sending a doorman diving into his front entrance.

The second gunman, blocked at first by his partner, never did get into position to fire, for Yehuda's move quickly turned their angle of fire from bad to impossible, as the Audi, now racing to catch the Buick it had failed to block off, got between the street gunmen and the target.

On the sidewalk, the policeman, hearing the shots, started to push his way through the dozens of news men and women, who moved toward the shots themselves, cameramen lumbering forward with their bulky shoulder braces, shouting "Watch it!" and "Get out of my shot!"

By the time the cop could get to the curb, the two gunmen had jumped into their car and started off. He pulled his revolver, but would not fire on busy Seventy-second Street. Hurriedly, he pulled the two-way radio from its case on his hip and called the Nineteenth Precinct.

In the Israeli car, Yehuda muttered "slobs," in anger and in professional contempt for the botched job. Then, "Everybody OK?"

From the floor of the back seat the ambassador answered "all right" and Kate managed a muffled "yeah!" The security man next to Yehuda was silent, so he said, "Avram?" Still no answer. He looked glancingly to his right and saw why.

Avram was slumping forward. The first shot had hit him in the side of the neck and been deflected upward into his skull. He was unconscious and in a few seconds would be dead.

"Avram is hit!" shouted Yehuda, but could do no more about it than that, for in his rear-view mirror he could see the Audi, with three men in it, close behind them. Ahead of them, waiting for the Madison Avenue light to change, stood two taxis, blocking their way. Cutting his wheel sharply to the left, Yehuda drove onto the wrong side of the street and around the cabs. He shot through the red light into the middle of the intersection.

One bus coming up Madison, Yehuda thought, and we've had it. But there was no bus. Three of them, traveling in their customary caravan, had gone by an instant before. The Audi was there, though, and still close; it had followed their maneuver, and they had not gained any ground.

The bodyguard wrenched the wheel to the right, heading the car up Madison Avenue, simultaneously shouting to Shalzar, "Stay down, for God's sake!"

He knew he mustn't give their pursuers a straightaway on which to fire at them. These Arabs—Yehuda called them that without knowing who they were—wouldn't hesitate to fire amid cars and people; they had just demonstrated that.

Fleetingly, the Israeli considered attempting a right turn onto Seventy-third Street to get to the embassy's back entrance. At once he rejected it. The one-way traffic went the other way, and chances were he'd run head on into another car. But even if the Israeli car made it, Kate and the two men would be an easy target as they tried to clamber out, unlock the rear door, and get inside.

Instead, Yehuda went the other way, sharply turning left into Seventy-third Street, wheels screeching, frightening a day-camp counselor and a covey of six-year-olds headed for Central Park.

Shalzar rose and pulled the slumped Avram back against the seat; his hand felt the stickiness of blood on the security man's neck and shoulder. Shalzar slid the hand up, feeling for a pulse in the neck. Nothing. The ambassador was used to battlefield casualties; he was almost sure Avram was beyond help. He reached his bloody right hand into the man's jacket, found the shoulder holster and removed the automatic pistol. Then Shalzar turned, staying low, asking, "Are you all right, Kate?"

Scared, cramped, and humbled on the floor, Kate didn't honestly know the answer. "I guess so," she replied. The ambassador wasn't really listening; he was peering through the rear window at the pursuing car.

As they turned, Yehuda knew that if Seventy-third Street were blocked by traffic they'd be in trouble. And it was. A garbage truck was stationary while the maw in its rear was being fed. Behind it, a panel truck and a cab honked their horns redundantly.

So far his movement and his turns had prevented the pursuers from getting a clear shot. In a moment the Buick would be stopped with the gray Audi right behind them. Yehuda had to get around the tie-up ahead of him.

All that remained to him was the sidewalk, and he went for it. He hit the brake and, using a garage driveway, sent the car charging along the sidewalk, which on this hot summer morning was almost free of pedestrians. Horn sounding, the Buick raced forward, sideswiping a delivery cart, just missing a lounging doorman, heading right for a delivery boy on a bike, who saw them and threw himself onto a parked car as they went by, then turned to yell "crazy mother!" Even as he did, the Audi went by, a man with a submachine gun leaning out of the left passenger window. The delivery boy rolled off the parked car into the street.

On the floor of the Buick, unable to see where they were going, why they were turning and jolting, Kate was terrified, the more so when she got a glimpse of Dov's right hand. In it was the automatic pistol from the dead bodyguard's holster; all over it was blood from the man's mortal neck wound.

"Dov, let me up. I can't take this down here!"

The ambassador had one knee on the back seat as he peered through the rear window; the other knee was on her rib cage, holding her down.

"You'll have to. There's going to be more shooting."

So far not a single shot had come from the Audi; there had been no chance, and Yehuda had to keep it that way. As the bodyguard reached the corner, he hit his horn, again ran through a red light, and bounced the car off the sidewalk onto Fifth Avenue, almost hitting a cab. The hackie honked back angrily, only to have his rage diverted from the Buick by the Audi careening off the sidewalk right behind it.

On Fifth Avenue, headed south, Yehuda moved the Buick right into Central Park. At that point he stopped improvising and began following a preset escape plan, one of several prepared by Israeli security men to cover many eventualities. This one made use of the winding Central Park roadway to provide them with opportunities to escape or, if it was possible, to turn and ambush their pursuers. No one knew if the plan would work; no one had ever used it before.

As Yehuda drove into the park, approaching the first of several curves, he could hear the oscillating wail of sirens as police cars rushed to the Israeli embassy a block and a half away. That's too far away to help us, he thought. And it will take too long for them to pick up our trail. We can't count on them; those guys behind us will shoot as soon as they can.

Tires squealing, the Buick rounded the first turn on the Seventy-second Street park road, shooting by the spot Dov had crossed in his escape earlier in the morning. I'm getting allergic to this place, he thought, watching the Audi behind them.

Then Yehuda chose the left fork, which headed west. In about forty yards, he remembered, they'd have to make a sharp left onto a kind of service road. He got ready. It was close. It was there.

"Hold on!" he yelled. He hit the brake, turned his wheel hard to the left, and half skidded onto the service road, which was one of two parallel lanes used by pedestrians, bicyclists, and park vehicles. Between the two lanes ran two stone walls, about ten yards apart. Where the lanes and the walls ended, the Central Park Mall began.

Slowing as little as possible, Yehuda drove about thirty yards, to the end of the stone wall, and made a right turn. He stopped the Buick; now it could not be seen from the road.

For a moment, the pursuers in the Audi had lost sight of the ambassador's car on the tight curve and, approaching the spot where the service lane began, would have to make a quick decision to turn left, or else go shooting by. Seeing the road ahead of them empty, they braked frantically, and managed to get onto the service lane. Still, they could not see their quarry, for the Israelis had turned around the wall and were out of sight.

As soon as the Buick turned, Shalzar leaped out and, pistol in hand, ran to the stone wall and peered around it. When he saw the Audi turn, too, he waved to Yehuda, who then drove the Buick to the second wall and turned behind it. The Israelis were now facing back toward the main road, the pursuers' car headed away from it, and two walls separated them. Shalzar, as soon as he waved to his car, sprinted the ten yards to the second wall, and he, too, got behind it.

Yehuda drove his car about twenty yards along the second wall, stopped, leaped out, grabbed his own pistol from its holster, and joined the ambassador, who was at the second wall now, waiting for the Audi to appear.

If their pursuers appeared beyond the first wall and kept going away from the main road, the Israelis would merely return to their car, head back for the main road and out of the park. If the Audi followed their path, making the two tight right turns that would get it where the Buick was, behind the second wall, it would have to slow down drastically. And waiting for it would be two combat veterans, with automatic pistols.

The Audi made the turns, slowing down to less than ten miles an hour to do so. As it went into the second turn, Yehuda and the ambassador each steadied his weapon in both hands. Yehuda, on the right, went for the driver; through the window he could see his dark, bony face, eyes hidden behind a pair of green sunglasses. The security man's first shot crashed through the windshield and hit the driver in the lower neck, just above the left collarbone. His hand dropped off the wheel. The second shot shattered the right lens of his glasses and went through the eye socket into the brain. His head, which had started to slump forward with the first shot, was kicked back with the second. Then Yehuda swung toward the man in the right rear seat.

Simultaneously, Shalzar had gone for the man next to the driver. He, like the passenger in the rear, carried a submachine gun. Dov saw the man's flattened muscular face, noticed he needed a shave. He saw the searching look turn to surprise at the sight of the two armed men, saw him begin to raise his weapon to fire. By then it was too late, for Dov had gotten off two shots. The first grazed the gunman's neck, wounding him superficially; the second hit him in the middle of the forehead. Then Dov too went for the man in the rear, who by then had his weapon up for firing. But he never got to fire. Possibly, Yehuda thought later, the dope had forgotten to release the safety. Maybe he was just slow; actually it had taken almost no time for both Israelis to fire, and he had not expected to confront weapons; his quarry was supposed to be fleeing.

In any event, each man hit him once, one bullet striking his left cheek, the other his chin; Shalzar fired a second shot, which missed, shattering the rear window; it was not needed.

No longer having a hand on its steering wheel or a foot on its accelerator, the Audi rolled gently ahead until it nudged up against a huge oak, where it stalled.

The ambassador looked around. On the far end of the mall, two boys on racing bikes had turned and were pedaling away furiously. In the direction of Fifth Avenue they could hear police sirens.

"We'd better get out of here," he told Yehuda. "I don't have any time to spend at a police station."

"First I want to see who those guys are," the bodyguard answered. "See if they're dead. I want to make sure they are. For Avram. It'll only take a minute."

"No, dammit!" Dov shouted back. "We don't have a minute. And they won't have any identification. Let the cops do that for us. We've got to get out." He had Yehuda by the arm and was pulling him toward their car.

It was an odd sight, the two men with pistols, arguing, and Kate, trembling, pale with fright, wondered if she understood any of what happened. She had sat up when the car stopped, saw Avram slumped over, with his bloody wound, saw the two men racing to the end of the wall, saw the other car come around, saw the shooting.

Her eyes flashed horror at Dov as he climbed into the back seat with her and Yehuda took the wheel; they moved from his face to the gun in his right hand. Watching her, he shifted the weapon to his left and then slipped it into his jacket pocket.

The Buick moved forward to the main road, deliberately but quickly, made a left and then headed west, out of the park.

"My God," was all she could manage. "My God."

"It's OK," he answered, and then repeated that in the same cadence she had used. "It's OK." What was OK he couldn't have said.

"Is he dead?" She nodded toward the slumped form of Avram.

"Yes."

"And those other men. Are they? Who were they? What happened? Where are you going? Shouldn't you wait for the police?" She was wringing her hands in anguish. When Dov reached out to hold one of them she pulled it back. He looked down; he had reached out with his right, which was covered with dried blood.

"They look like Arabs, but it doesn't matter. And I don't know if they're dead, although I'd say they are. They're men who tried to kill us and in one case succeeded." He held out his hand. "This is Avram's blood."

He put the hand down. "And we're getting out of here, back to the embassy, because I can't spend time talking to police now—we'll explain that later—and because their friends might try again. We're at war."

The ambassador looked down at his bloody hand. "Avram would

have laughed if I told him he'd get it on East Seventy-second Street in Manhattan." Then he shrugged and put the hand and the thought away.

By then they had reached Central Park West and he turned to Kate. "Chances are the police are looking for this car. I'm going to put you in a cab to your studio and take another cab back to the embassy. I just cannot be stopped now. I'll let Yehuda take his chances on getting the car back." Shalzar turned toward the front seat. "You hear, Yehuda?" Then as an afterthought: "The car—and Avram."

The driver nodded, then turned the car onto Central Park West and brought it to a stop, to let the two of them out. Shalzar waved at a cab. When it pulled to a stop, he opened the door for her. "This has been an experience for you; I know it. Right now, we can't stop to talk it over."

Kate was shivering as if it were January. With one hand she clutched the cab door; her knees were so weak she was afraid she'd fall down. "I feel like I've been on a battlefield."

"You have," he replied. "For a few minutes. Just think of the thousands of Israeli women and children whose country is a battlefield and who can't get in a cab and leave."

"Am I leaving the battlefield now?"

"I hope so. I can't guarantee it. You want tranquillity—find yourself a beachcomber." Then he softened. "It'll be all right. I don't think they're after you. Call me when you're finished taping."

"You expect me to tape now?" she asked, astonished.

"Of course. The show must go on."

"Speaking of tape," she said. "I assume I can start it again to the extent of reporting this shootout."

"Uh uh. You assume wrong. I said I didn't think they were after you, but your 'scoop' this morning, combined with the certainty they know about 'us,' could make them suspect you're involved. Another scoop, about the shooting, might tell them for sure. It's not worth the risk."

"Suppose it is to me?" she asked.

"I'm the roller of the tape and I say it's not worth it." He leaned forward to kiss her; all he got was her icy cheek. Then she stepped into the cab, he closed the door, and she was off.

He stopped another cab and climbed in, wondering how long it would be before they were after her.

As her cab headed south toward her studio on Fifty-sixth Street, she thought of his words: "You want tranquillity—find yourself a beachcomber." Strangely enough, she thought she had found a kind of tranquillity when she met Dov. Sure, she knew he had been a soldier, but such a gentle man! Dov. How often she had said to him his name ought to have an "e" at the end of it.

And ten minutes ago, in Central Park, with a dead man in his own car, he and Yehuda had shot three men. And he hadn't even wanted to find out if they were dead!

Well, she thought, at least the last fifteen minutes have answered a question. Kate had become a network correspondent too late to cover Vietnam and the Yom Kippur War, but she had clamored to cover the civil war in Lebanon. She had wanted it as an assertion of her feminism and as a test of her stomach. Could she function in danger, amid the blood of battle?

Today she had come up with a tentative answer, and she didn't like it, for the answer seemed to be, not too well.

When the Buick had come to a stop on the Central Park Mall, she had disobeyed orders and sat up; she had looked through the rear window and seen Dov and Yehuda firing. Seven shots they had fired, and had killed three men. But the one shot she would never forget was Dov's second, which had hit the gunman in the front passenger seat square in the forehead.

She had seen the man's face, already surprised, frightened, and in pain from the first shot that had grazed his neck, suddenly contort as if trying to squeeze itself into a smaller space. It reminded her of Oswald's face, tightening, grimacing, as Ruby's shot hit him. She wondered if all men who were shot looked like that. And women.

Then the blood from the forehead, spurting like a fountain. This isn't real, she had thought; it's a parlor trick. Blood doesn't shoot out of you that way. Then, mercifully, the moving Audi had taken the sight away from her eyes.

And Dov had walked back to the car as if he had just stepped on an ant. Three ants. At least Yehuda had paid the men the attention of wanting to identify them. Dov hadn't even cared that much, hadn't even been curious to see if they were dead. And the civilized thought that the three might have been helped by medical treatment—might have been worthy of the consideration given to prisoners of war—that had apparently never even occurred to Dov. No instant of remorse, no hesitation, no shakiness, no shadow of regret, no recognition that these were humans he had shot.

Hell, he hadn't even given a second look at his own man, shot in the front seat of his car, whose blood was barely dried on his hand. It was all business.

Four men killed, one, maybe two, by him, and all he had said was, "We'd better get out of here."

Why am I surprised? she asked herself, sitting in the cab, still shivering, although the day, nearing 10 a.m., was getting fiercely hot and muggy. It wasn't that he hadn't warned her, early on. Four wars, he had said on their second meeting, had turned many Israelis into cold-blooded warriors.

"I like to think," he had told her, "that we care for the Arabs as fellow human beings when we're not at war. And I know that whenever Jews and Arabs have been allowed to live side by side, without ideological propaganda, we have coexisted splendidly. The Jews have given jobs to the Arabs, and education and medical care.

"I also know that when we are fighting, we are obsessed by the statistic that it is three million Jews against fifty million Arabs; we are obsessed with the knowledge that if one Arab soldier can cancel out one Israeli soldier, we are done for. We train ourselves to think in kill ratios—of planes, tanks . . . and men. One of ours to five of theirs, ten of theirs, twenty of theirs. One Israeli fighter cannot spend too much time on one Arab fighter. If they can match us one to one we cannot win."

Yes, she had been warned, but seeing it was something else. She looked down at her hands, and held the right one out, palm down, fingers apart, to see if it were any steadier. Her fingers vibrated. With her left hand she seized the fingers of her right and squeezed. How was she going to get through that damned taping?

The taxi stopped short for a red light on Central Park West and she burst out with "For Chrissake, watch it!"

"Sorry Miss Colby," said the taxi driver, a chubby red-haired man named Phil Goldfarb. "We can't let anything happen to a TV star."

"That's all right," she said.

She'd have to pull herself together. She had just seen for herself the things Dov had been warning her about. She could remember well the first time he had warned her, because it had also been the first time they'd made love.

It had been a summer's day, like this one, hot, sunny, sticky, lethargic, almost slow motion, but unlike this one, bathed in a romantic haze. The streets of the East Side were almost empty and the people in them were operating at half speed; the city all seemed to be beginning or ending vacations. It had been a summer's day when one is especially susceptible to romance.

On that day, two years ago, Kate had known Dov less than a week, and had been with him twice. The first occasion was the embassy party when they met. The second was two days later. She had walked into her office and found among her messages a call from the Israeli ambassador to the United Nations, asking her to call the embassy.

Her heart was thudding as she picked up the phone and dialed the number; when she said: "Kate Colby of UBC," she was immediately shunted to the press office. Well, she said to herself while waiting for the press officer to pick up the phone, so much for your expectations, old girl. But the PR man knew nothing about the call and switched her to the ambassador's secretary, and in an instant she was talking to Dov himself.

Again, her heart beat faster and she feigned a seriousness, trying to assume this was business unless he let on it wasn't.

He had let on right away. "Can you have dinner with me tonight?"

She had gone, eagerly, and had found, on that first evening, many of the elements that were to enthrall and irritate her throughout their relationship.

They had met in a little-known but first-rate Italian restaurant in the West Thirties, small, dark, simple, expensive. First he apologized for the anonymity of it. He said, frankly, he had to be careful about being seen in public, especially with someone as well known as she, and he explained his marital situation, the de facto separation from his wife, the strict sense of propriety he felt in his post, particularly because of its importance to American and New York Jewry.

Sitting there, drinking Valpolicella, eating pasta, she found in him a devastating mixture of reserve and sensuality. And the wit, which, coming from an ambassador, surprised her, she confessed.

"Listen," he had answered, putting on the touch of Jewish inflection he often used to punctuate humor, "if a shiksa can be funny, anyone can. Even an ambassador."

This had led to a discussion of Jewish and Gentile humor, and to Dov's talking about army humor. She had asked him at that first dinner about his army experiences and he had replied, "There were many and they don't really belong in a humor conversation."

He called the next night and said, "About those army stories, could we combine them with dinner in what should be a fascinating evening? I hope."

"You hope what?" she answered snappily. 'That I'll go or that it'll be fascinating?"

"Both. How's that for greediness?"

"When? How's that for aloofness?"

"Tomorrow evening. How's that for eagerness?"

"Great. And do you suppose these verbal pyrotechnics will end?"

"Let's hope not," he replied, chuckling.

There was one other thing he wanted to say. "I think we might make love tomorrow night."

But he didn't. Maybe I misunderstand the vibrations, he thought. If I'm right, we'll make love, whether I say it or not. If I'm wrong it would be embarrassing.

As it turned out, they did make love.

Dov picked her up at the studio; it was seven o'clock, a half-speed summer evening, and they walked across Fifty-seventh Street. His delight at being with her was heart-stopping. She felt as fluttery as a teen-ager, and as innocently happy. Both sensed they had made a quantum leap in intimacy during the two days they had been apart.

Kate was not surprised when, after walking hand in hand with her for half a block, he put an arm around her shoulders and squeezed her gently toward him. Then he leaned and kissed her softly on the mouth. The enthusiasm of her response surprised him.

Kate was slim, but tall and strong; when she kissed back and, for emphasis, put her hand behind his neck to draw him close, she startled him with her strength. Then they walked on, his right arm around her shoulders, her left around his waist, neither looking at the other, neither saying anything, both breathless with the closeness and the newness of it.

When she turned to him to speak, there was—he would never forget it—a florist's shop behind her head. Flowers by Richards. "Look, let me make you an offer. Instead of a restaurant, why don't we go to my apartment. First, I'll cook dinner, then you tell army jokes."

They walked five more strides before he answered. He turned—this time there was a liquor store, Buy-Rite, behind her. "Instead of a restaurant, why don't we go to your apartment? First you cook dinner. Then I'll tell army jokes. Then we'll make love. How's that for a counteroffer?"

In spite of herself she blushed, and started walking again. Her eyes were downcast like a maiden's when she answered, "I accept."

His impulse was to want to kiss her again. No, he thought, I can't do that, it's too much like sealing a bargain. Instead, he tightened the pressure of his arm around her shoulders. That way, they walked to the corner, both pretending they didn't have a new purpose, both knowing they did.

He signaled to a cab; she remembered it was a big one, a Checker.

"Sixty-fourth and Madison," Dov said to the driver, and then slid across the seat to kiss her. The taxi started forward with a lunge and their heads snapped backward without their eyes losing contact. It was almost choreographed; they grinned at each other, both breathing deeply, anticipating.

Then they kissed. How prim of me, she thought, as at first she wouldn't open her mouth. Here I am going to take off all my clothes with him, to get into bed with him, to take him inside me, and I won't open my mouth. She did. The warm, wet taste of his mouth and tongue was delicious. This kissing, she had always thought, with tongues, with the in and out, was just like the sex act, except that the woman could do the in-and-outs, too.

Their bodies tilted as the cab turned off Fifty-seventh Street, north on Madison Avenue. Suddenly she was frightened that when they stopped kissing she wouldn't know what to say. He solved that by speaking first.

"If I may quote an aggressive remark made by Ms. Colby yesterday, I can hardly wait." Gently, he stroked her face with the fingertips of his right hand, caressing her forehead, eyes, nose, then around her mouth, out to her left ear, down her jawline. The touches made her shiver.

When they reached the corner of Sixty-fourth Street, paid the cabby, and stepped onto the street to walk the few yards to her house, she was sure the entire world knew what they were on their way to do, together and for the first time. She was sure she could see it in the cabby's eyes, as he gave Dov his change.

An old man and woman on Sixty-fourth Street leered at them. Their look said: We know where you're going! Tom, her doorman, was trying to look detached and clinical, but Kate knew *he* knew.

"Where are your kids?" Dov's question startled her.

She tried to make the answer nonchalant, so he didn't get the idea she had invited him to an empty house for reasons of seduction. "Oh, away at camp." She was sure the nonchalance hadn't worked, that he was leering, too, that he thought she had set this up.

And dammit, he's right, she said to herself. The admission made her smile, and she turned it on him. He grinned back; she got on the elevator sure that Louie, the elevator man, had spotted their purpose, too, but not caring.

On the way up he edged closer to her, reached down and grabbed her hand. It was going to be okay, she knew it. At her floor, the majestic door slid open with the solid sounds of heavy metal, let them out, and then closed again.

Of course her keys would not be reachable, she knew that. Down into her oversized bag she dug, nervously wading through the comb, change purse, compact, checkbook, wallet, Kleenex, pens, pencils, steno pad, hairbrush. They weren't there—and the children were away and the housekeeper was off. She knew it!

And then there they were; she sent a nail file clattering to the floor getting the keys out, and after he picked it up, she felt the keys vibrating in her shaky grasp as she tried to find the right one for the right lock and then insert it. Sensing a mini-crisis, Dov turned to her and gave her a warm, brisk kiss that said, OK, get down to business now and open that door.

With that she managed the locks, first the upper, then the lower. They stepped into the foyer and she switched on the light, accompanying it by the obligatory "Oh I hope the place isn't too much of a mess." She was embarrassed at the compulsiveness of the remark. Besides, all was orderly. Admit it, she said to herself, you fixed everying up this morning, just in case.

He looked around, at the portrait of her kids, the tile floor, the small bookcase. He said: "Hmmmm," in a tone that meant: I like it. At least she hoped it meant that. The two of them stood still and she thought, anxiously, neither of us knows quite what to do next. A TV star and an ambassador, and neither of us quite knows.

She was, after all, the hostess. "Would you like a drink, or shall we . . ." She didn't know how to finish that and she knew what it sounded like. She had led herself into a trap, and as she groped for a way out, her skin grew redder and redder beneath the tan, although the pause, the groping, and the blushing all took a mere instant, before she finished her sentence: "go on a tour of the manse first?"

Dov had heard the pause and spotted the redness, and mocked them ever so gently. "Why don't we get some wine and carry it with us while we . . . go on a tour of the manse."

Maybe the mocking hadn't been so gentle, he thought, and to cover his embarrassment, he leaned forward to kiss her—just as she, to cover hers, took a vigorous step around him to get the wine. He had been standing behind her and to her right, and her vigorous step brought the side of her head into vigorous contact with his nose.

"Oh, I'm sorry, did it hurt?"

"No, no, it's all right," he responded, putting a hand to his nose. Two fingers came away bloody. Dov looked at them and then at her, and smiled. "You Americans have some strange sexual customs. Does it get better after this?"

Recovering her wits, and her wit, and thankful for the chance to break away from the awkwardness, she asked, "You mean there's more?" Then she noticed the blood still flowing and she got worried. "Come, you'd better lie down." She took him by the hand, led him through the foyer, down the long hall and into her bedroom. She walked him to her bed and gently shoved him onto it, not stopping to pull off the patchwork spread. "You know you didn't have to pull this kind of thing; I was going to let you come in here anyway."

"Funny," he answered, holding his nose. "I thought you were the one who was pulling something."

"Stay there; I'll get you a washcloth."

She was back in a moment. The washcloth was green, of course. Kate folded it and leaned forward to put it on his nose. Dov knew the bleeding had already stopped, but he let her care for him, and as she did, he put his hands on her ribs and drew her down to him.

With her face close to his, and her eyes looking straight into his, he said, "Do me a favor and go easy on the nose. You started one side bleeding, but I'm going to follow a Christian precept and turn

102

the other nostril. I know you don't want to add red to your bedspread." Dov kissed her on the lips; this time both their mouths were open.

Bending over was awkward for her, and without taking her mouth away, she swiveled her lower body so she was sitting on the edge of the bed. Dov, without taking his mouth from hers, slid his body toward the center of the bed to make room for hers, and gently, persuasively, his hands at her waist half turned and half pulled her onto the bed so that she was lying on her right side, her body stretched out at full length and parallel to his.

Slowly, Dov kissed her eyes, slowly moved down along her nose, to her left ear, the lobe, down her neck along the jawline to her chin, then her mouth again. He ran his hand down from her waist along her hip and then back up, pressing to get their bodies closer.

Dov still had his jacket on, and she could feel the bulk of something in his breast pocket—wallet, glasses, she couldn't tell—pressing her breast. She felt the pressure of his ribs on hers. No sign of a belly, she thought, with pleasure. Not a trace. How delightful.

Below, she could feel the hardness of his thighs. And another hardness . . .

Still pressed up against her, Dov curled his right arm in and slid his hand into the scoop neck of her jersey blouse, into the flimsiness of her bra. Just for an instant a remembered tension ran through her, a conditioned defensiveness about the size of her breasts —"small but perfect" is the way she jokingly referred to them. Small they were, no doubt about that. Then the tension was replaced by shivers of delight as his hand delicately played with her breast, pressing, rubbing, his fingers on her nipple.

Oh God, he knows how to do that. Oh God.

She kissed him harder, then drew her face back. "I've got to leave you for a couple of minutes. I'll be right back."

"Should I stick around?" He feigned surprise as he said it, and then opened up into a grin.

Standing above him, she shrugged and threw back a deadpan reply. "If you want to. If not . . ." She shrugged again. He sat up quickly, grabbed her hand and kissed her fingertips.

"I might stay. I might even change into something more comfortable."

Kate looked down at him tenderly. With her free hand she grabbed a handful of his curly hair, the first of many times she was to do that.

"While I'm gone, why don't you make yourself useful by pulling back the bedspread and getting into bed . . . if you decide to stay."

Then quickly, as she was turning away, she blew him a kiss, and added, "Don't you dare go 'way!"

Pretty flip, she thought as she walked into her bathroom and closed the door. So why are my hands shaking? And why, Goddammit, am I off the pill?

She undressed quickly, and turning, spotted herself in the full-length mirror. Will he like that body? she asked herself. Then answered. Why not? It's not at all bad—for a woman of thirty-four. She was not displeased. Long shapely legs, strong thighs, well shaped and not at all flabby. Flat stomach, well, fairly flat; good wide hips, slim waist, cute breasts, she said, maybe not big, maybe not perfect, but cute.

She opened her medicine cabinet and reached with unsteady hands for the round case holding her diaphragm, playing a tattoo with it on the aspirin bottle to the right and the bottle of nail-polish remover to the left.

Never, she muttered, never will I get this thing fixed right. It's been too long, I've forgotten and he'll be wondering where the hell I am. She fumbled at the case to get the disk out. Pull yourself together, old girl.

Kate had been off the pill for several months because her doctor suggested it and, simply, because there had been no steady man in her life recently. She had long ago found that casual affairs were not for her. Sometimes, in her more rebellious moments, she wished they were, but her one try at disconnected sex—when she was newly separated, lonely, and depressed—convinced her it wouldn't work. There was, of course, Bill Brewster. What was he? Casual? No. Steady? Definitely not.

Finally she had the disk in her left hand, and with her right she reached up and took the tube of cream. Then she stood for a couple of seconds, stupefied, before she realized she couldn't open the tube with one hand. So she put the diaphragm down on its case on the edge of the shelf above the sink—and knocked them both to the floor.

She looked at her face in the mirror over the sink. Pull yourself together, old girl.

She bent over, picked up the diaphragm and its plastic case, put the case securely on the shelf, washed and dried the diaphragm, and once again placed it on the case. Then she opened the tube.

Steady now, she said, almost aloud. She picked up the diaphragm in her right hand, and with the tube in her left squeezed cream on the rubber circle. Now put down the tube, she ordered herself. Now spread the cream. Now pinch the diaphragm, carefully.

Not carefully enough. The disk squirted out of her hand and landed in the tub.

All right, she said, you can cry, you're entitled to. Or you can go out and say, Would you mind coming back in a couple of weeks so I can get back on the pill again? That's provided he's still out there, and not asleep. How to kill a romance, she said. Or put it to sleep, anyway.

Well, start over. Pick up the diaphragm. Wash it. Dry it. Spread cream. Insert. Carefully. There. Done. She couldn't believe it. She put on a short green dressing robe and walked back out.

Dov was lying under the sheet, his thin, muscular arms folded under his head. He turned and smiled at her. "What's your hurry?" Then he stretched out his arms for her and pulled back the sheet from half the bed.

Kate started to climb in.

"Hey, take that off. Please!"

Just for an instant, she hesitated. Then she slipped out of the robe quickly and slid under the sheet.

For twenty seconds which seemed like long minutes, they lay there, barely touching, staring into each other's eyes. Then he put a hand on the small of her back and pressed her to him. They kissed, and she could feel the length of their naked bodies close, the hairiness of his chest, the flesh of his stomach, flat and hard, the muscular thighs —and, yes, the hot hardness of his penis against her pubic bone and the insides of her thighs.

His hand moved to her breast, cupping it, fondling the nipple. The shivers came back; she sucked at his mouth, fiercer, wetter.

After a while he pulled his mouth away, kissing her face, her ear, her neck, as he had before. Oh, this was going to be all right, she knew it. Better than all right. She breathed deeper as his mouth moved down to her collarbone, kissing along it from side to side, as if to trace it. His hand moved from her breast to her buttock, caressing it, then cradling the seam between it and her upper thigh.

And his mouth was on her breast, kissing, licking, sucking at the nipple.

Oh, her nerve endings cried out. Oh, the blood surged through her. Her hands went to his head, rubbing the sides of it, stroking his hair, sliding down the sides of his face to stroke his shoulders. His hand on her buttock slid up to her hip, pivoted her off her side and onto her back. Then it was stroking her abdomen. Oh, the chills! And it moved down between her thighs, stroking, feeling, probing, so delicately, the lips of her vagina, her thighs opening to make room for his fingers.

Oh Oh! Her right hand reached for his penis, so hot, so hard. Carefully, she said. It's dry. And so hot. So hot. Twenty degrees hotter than the rest of his body. She rubbed it, gently. She stroked the under side of the head, gently, gently.

And his fingers were sliding into her. Oh! And she was wet. Oh! Sopping. And his fingers were slipping up over her clitoris and around it . . . and Oh, God, how good. Good. Oh God. God plus O equals good, she thought; what a thing to think, she thought, at a time like this.

She wet her fingers in her mouth and put her hand back to his penis, rubbing harder now that she had wet it. Oh but it felt so good, long and hard. And hot. Then it slipped from her hand, because his body was sliding down in the bed, his mouth was on her belly, and then he was kissing her abdomen, her pubic hair, the line where her thighs met her abdomen. And then his tongue touched her clitoris, oh! and then her lips, and into her vagina and then back to her clitoris, oh! rolling around on it Oh! Oh! OH!

It was too good, too juicy, too fast, she was coming along too, too soon.

Kate grabbed the sides of Dov's head between her two hands and got it away from her. "Come up here, Dov, dearest, I want you in me."

His muscled arms braced on the bed; her hands slid down, from the head to the shoulders, to the tensed triceps in the arms as he hauled himself up so that he was on top of her and face to face and kissing so that she could taste her own juices in his mouth. Salty, good, yes, good.

And then he was in her. Neither of them had to guide it. She was so wet, he just slid in. He was in her, moving gently in and out. She had dropped back from the brink of orgasm when she took his head away, but now she was coming up there again. Coming, up there.

He was sliding in and out, and she slipped down so that he would rub her the right way. Rub me the right way, she thought, that's funny . . . it was better than funny . . . better, better, better . . . it was all boiling up up up, oh yes, yes . . . and then an explosion. A flood . . . yes . . . yes . . . yes yes yes, his mouth on hers, her arms tight around his sweating back, his penis in her . . . and all of it coming together . . . NOW! NOW! DOV! DOV! DOV!

And then to stay up there, that exquisite plateau, high and warm and wet . . . and heaven! Up there! Up there! In there!

She opened her eyes.

Dov's face, strong, red, happy, smiling down. His sweat on her chest. Or was it hers? His sinewy body on top of hers. He still in her.

"Oh Dov, I can't tell you. Dov, it was . . ." What could she call it? "Dov, I never thought it would be this good, not the first time. I was ready to throw this one away. But Dov, oh Dov!"

He shook his head no. "I knew it would. From the first time I touched your hand. From the moment I put my hand on you . . . there . . ." And he did it again, and they were on their way up again, so they stopped talking.

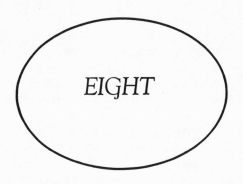

EIGHT

Bill Brewster's drive downtown from the Unity Club lacked the gunplay of Dov's chase through the park and the sexual reverie of Kate's cab ride to her studio. It was calm, ordered, and efficacious, the way almost everything was for Bill. When he'd read Portnoy's complaint about being caught in the middle of a Jewish joke and not finding it funny, Bill had reflected that *he* was caught in the middle of a WASP straight line, and he didn't find *that* funny.

Looking around at the carefully understated gray luxury of his Rolls-Royce, having just left the woman he loved, and lost—melodramatic but true, he said to himself—he wondered if inside the stuffed shirt of the investment banker, there was a swinger fighting to get out. No, he thought, crossing one shiny black Oxford over the other and stretching his long legs in front of him. No, inside the stuffy shell there's the real Bill Brewster fighting to get out, or at least partway out.

He didn't deny his desire for order, for efficacy. Precision turned him on; he had a kind of passion for dispassion. No, he didn't believe chaos was the only road to adventure; his problem, he had come to realize, was that he couldn't find *any* road to it. Occasionally he'd say to himself, to hell with the excitement, someone's got to run the machinery. Bill did, and well, and was proud of it. And had come to want more.

The meeting with Kate and Dov set several notes reverberating in his mind. First there was the shock, the hurt, of seeing her, and with the man she apparently preferred to him. Then came the instant realization that here was a chance to *accomplish* something and perhaps get a whiff of adventure, too. Bill was pleased and invigorated, especially because this was the kind of job he could do better than anyone else. And that he could be seen doing it by Kate. Was he being a boyish showoff in thinking that? Sure. What the hell. Bill was, of course, ignorant of the qualifications Dov had listed for the man who would contact the Secretary of State; had he known them, he would have agreed with each, and then added, with no immodesty, that he was the only man who met every requirement.

Bill and Secretary of State Peter Maloney had first met at the Harvard Business School and to the surprise of almost everyone who knew them, became roommates and remained close friends in the nearly twenty-five years since. An odd couple, the patrician from Groton and Princeton and the tough half-Irish, half-Italian kid from the parochial schools of Brooklyn and New York University. Each looked to the other for something; each offered something; each envied the other certain attributes and was gratified to be accepted by the other.

Paradoxically, it was the stocky, swarthy Pete—he got the olive skin from his mother's side and the snubby features from his father's —who gave the tall WASP lessons in how to charm Ivy League women. At the first graduate mixer the two attended, Pete looked around at the ethereal blonde beauties from Radcliffe and Wellesley and almost licking his chops said to Bill, "We're going to go through them like a knife through warm butter."

And Pete did, while Bill watched with awe. The sheltered 1950s maidens of the Seven Sisters colleges had never encountered Pete's combination of brains, ingenuity, irreverence, and New York chutzpah. And Bill, along for the ride, did just fine with those young women whom Pete found too tame, or who found Pete too exotic, or who were drawn in by Pete's radiating energy waves, but when they got close, preferred Bill's more conventional assets.

Pete provided the daring, the imagination, the touch of vulgarity —chutzpah was the word they both learned to use for it—and Bill the easy social grace that Pete called "class" and Bill described modestly as "merely fitting in." Each valued the other's contribution and was flattered that the other would want to borrow his qualities. If Bill came to rely on Pete for introductions to the most attractive women, Pete depended on his "classy" friend for guidance on their care and feeding: the kind of dress they favored, the cuisine, the music, the sports—and how to "fit in" at the country club when such pilgrimages could not be avoided.

Though both learned, and profited, neither was ever able to—or wished to—take on all the characteristics of the other, which was the cement that held them together. Had Bill fully assumed the brashness of a street kid from Brooklyn, Pete would have lost interest. Had Pete been able to "pass" completely at the yacht club, he would have become common currency to Bill. So, neither transformation occurred totally, although Pete, as he did in all their exchanges and unspoken rivalries, got a bit the better of it.

Bill Brewster never came close to Pete's level of chutzpah. Pete, on the other hand, learned to "fit in" so deftly he was soon acceptable at all but the most carefully protected of the *derrière garde* strongholds.

After graduation, to the cement of their differentness was added a new bonding material, rivalry. For two years Pete stayed in Boston to work on a doctorate in economics at MIT, while Bill returned to New York as a junior banking executive. Ironically, those two years, the subtle competition absent, were the coolest of their friendship. When Pete came back to New York and, with his PhD, found a job a millimeter more prestigious than Bill's, the rivalry assumed the pattern it was to follow thereafter. It was always unspoken, and always marked by each man's affection and generous acclaim for the other, and by the slight but noticeable lead Pete seemed to maintain.

Pete was the one who jumped ahead, and Bill the one who caught up. Maloney was a vice president at twenty-nine, Brewster at thirty-two; Maloney a senior vice president at thirty-three, Brewster at thirty-five. For two years they were neck and neck—although neither would have been indelicate enough to describe it that way—until, at thirty-seven, Pete became executive vice president of Union Consolidated, the corporation he had been instrumental in building into a multinational.

Bill didn't achieve that title at his banking house, Patton and Co., until he was forty—Pete casually pointing out that Wall Street firms were much more conservative about advancing young men. But Bill had no sooner caught up than Pete, in that same year both men reached forty, jumped two steps.

Because of his brilliance in moving Union Consolidated into international markets—his coup in securing a trade agreement with the Soviet Union got him on the cover of *Time* magazine—Pete was made president of the firm. He had been in that job only three months when a power struggle among the directors put the two sides in a position of seeking a compromise choice as chairman, and Pete Maloney, just turned forty, became president and chairman of the board of the twenty-third largest corporation in America.

It was only last year, when Bill was forty-five, that he became president of Patton and Co., and with a sixty-year-old member of the Patton family in the chairman's post and younger Pattons on the way up, Bill couldn't expect to catch Pete if he stayed at Patton.

In this gentlemen's duel, only once had Bill Brewster gained a step on his friend. Five years ago the President had asked Bill to serve in the Cabinet, and he took a leave from Patton to become Secretary of Commerce. And he noticed, or thought he noticed, a tiny rent in the magnanimity Pete had always shown as a front runner. Pete had given a lavish dinner party for Bill in his Park Avenue penthouse and despite Pete's toasts and congratulations, Bill noticed his joviality was a trifle forced; he overemphasized by a hair the headaches of government service, he spent a touch too much time on the overtures made to *him* by the Administration. These were merely nuances, though, in a pattern of Pete's customary generosity and support, and Bill told himself he could well have imagined them.

Before long Pete had regained the step and gone back into the lead. Bill served at the Commerce Department for eighteen months before the bureaucratic and political infighting got to him. "It's not a banker the job needs," he had told Maloney two months before resigning, "it's a street fighter."

Less than six months after Bill quit, Pete accepted the President's invitation to become Secretary of the Treasury. Unlike his friend, Pete thrived on the infighting, and was so successful at it, and so imaginative in his ideas on the use of trade and credit as foreign policy instruments, that when the new administration took office in 1977, Pete was offered and accepted the post of Secretary of State. If there was some question about Treasury's being higher than Commerce, there was no question that State was. Pete Maloney had finished first again.

Throughout all this, their friendship not only survived, it grew stronger. Whenever Bill was in Washington or Pete in New York, they dined together; they spoke on the phone at least once a week. When Pete was interviewed for his second *Time* cover, he said to the reporter, "There are three people who can get me any time, anywhere, for any reason: the President, Bill Brewster, and my wife. In that order." When his wife Muffie held up the magazine, pointed to the quote and said, "What's this?" he laughed and answered, "All right, all right, next interview I'll move you up into a tie with Bill."

In fact, though, there was a whole range of discourse for which Bill was far closer to him than was his wife. On such subjects as corporate affairs, governmental maneuvering, economics, money, people in Wall Street and Washington, the two men spoke a kind of shorthand, skipping many preliminary steps. Were either to try to talk to his wife on the same subjects, laying the groundwork alone would be exhausting. Nor was this merely business talk; to these two, both of them ambitious and successful, the world of business affairs was highly personal, indeed intimate.

So it followed naturally that each man became as well the other's confidant in all personal matters. As close as Bill had ever come to revealing himself to anyone, he came with Pete. When Bill's marriage began breaking apart, it was the Secretary of State, burdened by crises of détente, arms limitation, oil embargoes, Middle East conflagration, and brushfire wars, who from all parts of the world at odd times of day and night, was calling two apartments less than a mile apart on the East Side of Manhattan, trying to get Bill and Penny Brewster to work things out. And when that failed, it was Pete who held Bill's hand, sometimes long-distance, through the separation and divorce.

And it was Pete who knew more about Bill's feelings for Kate than anyone did; in a way, more than she did, for Bill had never felt free enough to uncork his real emotions and set them flowing in her presence. Pete was the one to whom Bill reticently unburdened his desolation when he and Kate parted, although this time Pete made no attempt to intercede, for he barely knew her.

So it was a simple thing for Bill to pick up the phone in the car, and while driving slowly down Park Avenue, to reach Pete through the White House switchboard, which was proud of being able to contact any member of the administration anywhere in the world within four minutes. This time it took only ninety seconds, and had Bill been at home, he could have traveled the distance between the two men in that time, for at the moment home to both men was the Waldorf Towers. Both had left their Park Avenue apartments, which had been a block apart, Bill when he was divorced, Pete when he moved his family to Washington. Now the suite kept by the State Department for the Secretary was three floors above the one Bill used as his impermanent, uncomfortable home.

"Well, hello!" Pete's voice had a three-octave range of mood, and now it was at its gentlest.

"Pete, sorry to bother you, know how busy you are."

"Never that busy, old boy, how are you?"

Pete first took on the "old boy" habit at the Harvard "B" School, when it had seemed to him an elegant alternative to the déclassé salutations the guys had used on the streets of Bay Ridge. He kept it because it covered one of the few weak spots in his armor, an inability to come up with first names quickly. As protection he called every male "old boy," even young boys and old men, even his closest friends, even Bill Brewster. When a nervous subordinate would ask Bill, "When do I graduate from 'old boy' to a first name?" Bill could reply, truthfully, "I've known him for over twenty years, and I haven't fully graduated yet."

The phone held in his right hand, Bill leaned to the car window to see where they were—Park and Fifty-third, the Racquet and Tennis Club, of which he happened to be a member, to his right. "Pull over right here, will you please, John?" he said to the driver. There was no point in getting too far downtown until he worked out an appointment with Pete; the Waldorf was only a few blocks away.

"I'm fine, Pete, but I have a problem that's extremely serious and of major concern to you. I need some time with you."

The Secretary looked at the schedule book on his desk, then at his watch: 9:20. His eyes went back to the book; he flipped the page, looked again.

"I'm going to be here three days, old boy, and today and tomorrow are really tight. How about—" he paused, turned another page—"how about lunch on Saturday before I go back?"

Standing at the entrance, his administrative assistant, Steve Phelps, shook his head in a frantic no and gave him a thumbs-down signal, which the Secretary answered with a slashing motion across his throat, meaning the scheduled lunch could be cancelled.

"No good, Pete. This is of *major* concern to you. To all of us, and we must talk about it within the next couple of hours."

"Wow. You're not kidding, are you?"

"No. I'm not."

Pete flipped back to the schedule for Thursday, July 12. "The next couple of hours? Boy, oh boy." Phelps was mouthing the word "No!" vehemently and repeatedly. "I don't see how . . ."

"Pete, you have to." In the car, Bill Brewster had gone into body English. His legs were no longer stretched in front of him; he was upright in the seat, body leaning forward as if straining across a conference table to win a point.

"All right, hold on, old boy."

He took the phone away from his face and turned to his aide. "Steve, something's got to go. Before lunch."

Phelps's eyes widened. "Mr. Secretary, you're crazy! You can't!"

"Yeah, I am crazy. Getting crazier every day. But I've got to. Which one? Who's the lunch with?"

"The two oil company people."

"With the Middle East fighting, it's better if we give that one a couple of days. Move them to Saturday."

"You have a lunch Saturday."

"I'll have two lunches Saturday. And move today's nine-thirty and the ten into the lunch opening. Play with it, you know."

Phelps shook his head. The Secretary said: "Do it." That was that. Then he lifted the phone. "How soon can you get here, Pete?"

"Five minutes."

"Where are you, for Christ's sake, downstairs?"

"No, but close."

"All right, so you'll be here by nine-thirty. That'll give us an hour. Fifty minutes for you. Ten for me. Okay?"

"Fine, Pete. I'm on my way. Thanks." Bill hung up the phone and leaned toward the driver. "We're going to the Towers entrance, John."

The big gray car started forward, sliding to its left as it went so the driver could make the left turn onto Fiftieth Street. Within two minutes they were in the driveway of the Waldorf Towers. Bill was out of the car before his driver could open the door. "Wait for me, John." He pushed through the revolving door and stepped into a waiting elevator. Felipe, the operator, expecting to take him up to 15, was surprised when Brewster said brusquely, "Eighteen, please." He was moving as soon as the elevator door slid open and pushed the buzzer of Pete's suite even before he had come to a stop in front of it.

Phelps answered the buzz with a rueful look that said Why did you have to do this to us? Bill pretended not to notice.

"I'm Bill Brewster and I have an appointment with the Secretary."

"Yes, I know, Mr. Brewster. How do you do? Come in, please. I am Steve Phelps, the Secretary's administrative assistant." Phelps smiled. "You're two minutes early. Please have a seat and let me tell him you're here."

Bill walked to the French provincial sofa and sat on one end of it. It was just like the one in his suite and he detested it. But he didn't have long to contemplate it. Within a minute, Pete Maloney appeared from the hall, covering the ground between them with his choppy, energetic stride and reaching out a broad, stubby-fingered hand to shake his. The Secretary threw an expectant smile at him. "Well, old boy, I guess you've got something on your mind."

"To put it mildly." Bill smiled back at him. "Where can we talk?"

"Confidential?"

"Totally."

"Worried about being bugged?"

Bill was surprised at the question. "This is your turf, Pete. Are you worried?"

Pete laughed. "What I meant was, is the subject matter worth listening to?"

Bill just nodded his head, slowly and decisively, three times. He was startled; the possibility of being bugged had not occurred to him.

"Actually," Pete answered, "this place is pretty secure; it's just been checked out. I guess what I really want is an excuse to get out of here. I need to take a walk; I need ten minutes of deep breathing and un-important talk before I go back to taking on the world—or else I'm gonna start taking on the world with my fists." And he balled both hands into fists. Bill saw his old friend was haggard and as tight as a drum.

"Of course, whatever you'd like, and take your ten minutes."

"I'll be right back," answered the Secretary, and he launched his stocky frame back toward the bedroom, reemerging in thirty seconds with his seersucker jacket on, holding a wide-brimmed Panama hat. Behind him came a broad-shouldered man, almost as tall as Bill, with a neat, styleless brown suit, dark glasses, and an unfashion-ably short haircut. A Secret Service man.

"Hope you don't mind if a friend comes along."

"Of course not." Bill nodded to the agent, who nodded back pleasantly. No introductions asked or given.

In the elevator, Pete put on a pair of sunglasses and the hat.

"So you won't be recognized?" Bill asked.

"To keep the sun away," the Secretary replied. "I could walk up to most people on the street and tell them my name, and they wouldn't know who I was. Kissinger was really the only visible Secretary of State I can remember. I'm one of the others. Do you suppose John Foster Dulles or Dean Acheson or Dean Rusk had to fight off autograph hounds?"

He looked at Bill and for a moment his face relaxed. "None of us patricians ever attracts a following."

As they walked out on Fiftieth Street, the agent dropped a couple of paces behind them. Pete, who was only five-foot-eight, and had put on extra weight in the last few years, set a strenuous pace, as if trying to outdo his taller friend at walking as well as everything else. He turned north on Park Avenue and for a block said nothing. Bill waited. Impatient though he was to begin, he realized Pete had made a point, twice, of telling him he needed a breather, and Bill could do nothing but await his cue. And Pete was not yet ready to give it.

"You know," the Secretary said after a few minutes. "It's nuts, but I love Park Avenue. They could fill it with glass towers from top to bottom, I'd still love it. I walk along it whenever I can; been doing it ever since I was a freshman at NYU. Did I ever tell you that?"

Bill shook his head no. Pete was determined to talk about himself.

"I don't know what the hell got me interested in business administration—an eighteen-year-old, lower class kid from Brooklyn, the son of a longshoreman, but when I started learning about money and business, I wanted to see firsthand what life was like for those 'entrepreneurs' I was reading about. I asked myself where I should go to have a look. Pretty much the only places in Manhattan I knew were Times Square, Madison Square Garden, and NYU. But of course I had heard of Park Avenue. So one afternoon, I took the Lexington Avenue subway up from Astor Place and, not being sure where to start, got off at Fifty-first Street. Of course, I should have gone a couple of stops more, but I didn't know. I walked over to Park, and headed north, just the way we're doing now. What an eye-opener it was! Women having limo doors opened by chauffeurs in uniform and building doors opened by doormen in uniform. Kids in school uniforms, walking dogs. Men with tans and pinstripe suits that fit perfectly. And sleek hair. You know, they *walked* differently from the way we did in Bay Ridge. Their faces were composed. So self-assured, even the schoolkids. They seemed to own the world."

Bill could see his friend loosening up as he spoke. Suddenly Pete turned to him and laughed aloud.

"What I didn't know then, but learned before too long, was that they didn't just *seem* to own the world. They *did* own it.

"Then came the biggest revelation of all. The kid who wanted it, suddenly, unexpectedly, got a look in. A second-story window was open; I guess they were fixing the air-conditioner or something. This was back in the fifties, maybe they didn't have an air-conditioner yet. I wish I could show you the apartment house but I think it was torn down; it was in the low sixties, big, gray stone, huge windows. This one was wide open, and through it I saw what looked like the biggest room I had ever seen outside a museum, and on the walls were paintings, just like in a museum. Landscapes, I think they were, kind of dark."

Without slowing down, Pete again turned to Bill, looking up at the taller man. "Now this may amuse you, old boy, but until then I had never seen a painting hanging in anyone's home. Certainly no one I knew had one of *any* kind, let alone the kind in that apartment. I was ignorant as hell about paintings then—still am—but I've always had a feeling for what's expensive. I could sort of sense it, I don't know, maybe *smell* it. Anyway, I knew those were worth a lot.

"I was just standing there, looking in, when someone came to the window and my eyes left the paintings and met his eyes. He was about my age, but what a difference! He had on a double-breasted blue blazer, and a checked shirt, and a maroon knit tie. He was looking down at me, in more ways than one. At me, a kid in a sweatshirt with the letters NYU on it, and a pair of chinos. Already he had begun to take on the insolence that was in those older faces I had seen getting out of and into the limos.

"He knew I was goggle-eyed, and I knew he knew; our faces were giving us away. I was embarrassed; I felt like an intruder. It was a classical confrontation of the ins and the outs, and I suppose right then is when some kids become socialists or communists . . ."

Pete smiled to himself. "Not me. I wanted *in*. Probably that's why I was majoring in business, not political science.

"I turned and walked on, but the apartment had been a revelation, I couldn't get it out of my mind. I kept thinking, My father is a longshoreman and does all right; what can *his* father do to be able to afford that?

"Soon I was staring at everyone I saw going into or coming out of those apartment buildings, asking myself, What does *he* do to be able to live here? What does *he* do; what does *he* do?

"Every few weeks after that, I'd take the subway up from NYU and make that same walk, never feeling I belonged, but using it to psych myself, setting a goal: to be able to walk along Park Avenue as someone who *did* belong. And now that I do, I still get a kick out of the walk, and out of belonging.

"And when I got my penthouse apartment, with the paintings, you know the one thing I missed, Bill?"

Brewster had begun to think Pete Maloney had forgotten he was there and why they were walking.

Pete looked at him, almost colliding head on with a chubby woman in a print dress as he did. "Instead of being thirty stories up, with a view of the East River, I wished I had an apartment on the second floor, so I could leave the window open and walk out on the street and look up into the big living room with all the paintings and be able to say, They're *mine*.

"And you know, Bill, when I leave Washington—and the way things are going now, it'd better be damn soon if I want to walk away instead of being carried—when I leave, I'm going to buy another apartment right here on Park. I don't care if I find one on Fifth with twice the space at half the price. Park means I belong."

He looked at Bill as if amused at himself. "OK. I don't know where all that came from, but as the commercial used to say, 'Thanks, I needed that.' Now let's get down to business." The Secretary's mind had a way of zippering and unzippering compartments, abruptly and definitively. "I took fifteen minutes; you've got forty-five."

"Pete," Bill began, "what's the outlook in the Arab-Israeli fighting right now?"

Suddenly, the Secretary looked wary. Arguments between the two men about the Middle East had brought them close to hostility. Pete did not share the Administration's lack of sympathy for Israel, which the President called "evenhandedness." He had protested privately but strongly when the United States declared an arms embargo nearly two years ago because he felt it was one-sided rather than evenhanded, since the Arabs continued to depend chiefly on Soviet arms rather than American. But he had not resigned, as Bill had urged him to do, first because he felt it would do no good, second because he was simply not as pro-Israel as Bill was. He blamed what he called Israeli intransigence and bludgeoning of the United States for their perilous position of the late '70s.

Once or twice he had come dangerously close to calling Bill an unpaid lobbyist for Israel and Bill had come equally close to calling him an anti-Semite. "I'm the best goddamned friend the Israelis have in this administration; if I leave they'll have nobody," Pete had shouted at a stormy dinner a year ago. "With friends like you . . . you know how that ends," Bill had answered, almost shouting in return.

So walking along, by this time at Sixty-third Street and Park Avenue, Pete's answer was cautious. "It's very early to say, but Israel doesn't seem in too good shape." He knew how weak Israel was and had been for the past year; he was somewhat regretful to think he had played any part in it. But he didn't know how much Bill knew, and was waiting to see.

He didn't have to wait long. "Two hours ago," said Bill, "just a few blocks away from here, I met with the Israeli ambassador to the UN, Shalzar. He told me the Arab invasion is so compelling and so successful, the advances so deep along the borders, the effectiveness of Arab air and missile attacks so devastating, that Israel doesn't believe it can last more than a week."

He watched for Pete's reaction. None. The Secretary seemed not one whit surprised. And Bill knew that had Pete questioned the description, he would have spoken up strongly. So he took the silence as an affirmation and went on.

"The ambassador believes no intervention is forthcoming from the United States or the Soviet Union, or indeed from anywhere in the world—certainly not from the United Nations." Again Bill paused to wait for some disputation. When none came, he went ahead.

"He says that Israel will stop at nothing to save itself from extinction. It considers it has total freedom of action—'freedom of action' are his exact words—to prevent the annihilation he is certain awaits Israel at the hands of the Arabs. And he reminds us—this is the heart of it, I think—of Israel's nuclear arsenal. What exact use would be made of it, if any, Shalzar would not say, although I pressed him on it."

Again, he waited for a reaction. This time Pete nodded, nothing else. Bill continued.

"However, Israel will not take action, whatever it may be, before 9 a.m. tomorrow, New York time. At that time, it will do whatever it sees fit to save itself, *unless* we give it the following assurances." And here Bill recited the demands Shalzar had made, the rollback of troops, multinational peacekeeping force, guarantees of finances, arms, and energy—and the international hostage community.

As he did, Maloney walked more and more slowly until, at Seventy-fourth and Park, he stopped.

"That's quite a list, Bill. Shalzar must have something really nasty in mind. What's your impression of the threat, old boy? Is it nuclear, or just bluster? Does it go beyond the Middle East?" As he asked, he took Bill's arm and steered him across Park Avenue so they could reverse their direction and head south toward the Waldorf, only this time on the west side of the avenue.

"I can't answer," Bill said, "without your first answering several questions of mine. First, we can accept the proposition that Israel has a nuclear arsenal—but how big is it? Second, is the Israeli situation as precarious as they say it is? Third, do the Arabs have nuclear capability, and if so could an initial Israeli strike nullify it?"

"The right questions, you quiet son of a bitch, every one of them.

And so lost in admiration am I for your perceptions, I might even answer them. We estimate their nuclear arsenal as being between a dozen and two dozen weapons. Second, they *are* in as bad shape as they claim to be. And third, we believe the Soviets have given the Arabs nuclear warheads, to be used defensively, and the Israelis could not nullify them with a first strike. The Israeli weapons, as far as we know, are primitive by our standards, but their big problem is delivery. Their rocketry is not developed enough to be counted on, certainly not in the face of the radar-missile screens the Soviets have helped the Egyptians and Syrians set up. And of course the Israeli air force, as much of it as is left at this point, is even more vulnerable than their missiles.

"So by asking those questions, Billy boy, you answer the question: Are they threatening to attack the Arabs with nuclear weapons? If the Arabs can retaliate, which they can, and if because of the relative landmasses and population concentrations of the two sides, one nuclear weapon hitting Israel will do as much damage as, let's say, ten hitting Arab countries—which it will—then the Israelis are not threatening merely the Arabs. They've only got one strike, and a limited one, and they've got to make it count."

Digging into the problem, the Secretary seemed almost exultant with the challenge. "The question is, what will they do to make it count? And why should the United States be worried enough to exert the tremendous pressure it will take—if it's indeed possible at all— on the Soviet Union and the Arab countries to meet the Israeli demands?

"In short, what I'm asking, Bill, is are they actually threatening to hit us?"

"How could they be?" Again Brewster answered by asking. "How can a country with a couple of dozen dinky bombs and a delivery system of questionable efficacy against countries on its borders, threaten us? They're desperate, Pete, don't discount that for a moment. But they're not stupid."

At Sixty-sixth Street, Pete almost stepped into a stream of traffic; Bill had to grab him under the left arm and yank him back onto the sidewalk. The Secretary barely noticed.

"Well then," he asked, addressing the question to himself as much as to Bill, "who the hell are they threatening? Albania? Angola? Outer Mongolia? Lower Slobbovia? If they're not worried about the whole world's feelings, or, to be gross about it, the world's retaliation, why are they talking about an international hostage community? But they don't have the delivery systems, so how are they going to get the bombs wherever they're going? In a suitcase with 'Fragile' painted on it? By parcel post, with a Do Not Open Till Armageddon sticker?

"And how do I go to the President, much less to the Soviet premier, with a vague threat of who knows what harm, to who knows who—a threat passed along by a friend who heard it from the Israeli ambassador to the UN over coffee? How, Bill?"

Again, the Secretary stopped and turned to face Brewster. "We need more, old boy. I don't for a moment question the seriousness of it. I don't question the Israelis' desperation. What I do question is my ability, anybody's ability—not to mention my or anybody's willingness—to sell this thing on the basis of what you've given me. Do they really have a scenario and the means to carry it out? Or are they bluffing? And what are the consequences of their plan, assuming they have one and can carry it out? How deadly are the consequences, compared with the consequences of our trying to muscle the Arabs? Assuming they're deadly enough for us to act, how about the Soviets? Does the Israeli plan threaten them enough to get them moving? Détente notwithstanding, the Soviets would love to see us belted, and might even be willing to take a punch themselves, if they thought we were being hit harder."

Walking, stopping, speaking, listening, slipping through the summer strollers along Park Avenue on this sunny July day, Bill felt a strange crystallization in his own mind, as he explained the Israeli position and heard his old friend's embryonic presentation of an American answer. More and more he found himself identifying with the Israeli position. More and more he felt the desperate pressure of the ticking clock, the desperate need to convince Pete of the gravity of the Israeli plan—even though he himself didn't know what that plan was.

"But Pete, it's now ten-ten on a Thursday morning. We've got less than twenty-three hours until the deadline at nine tomorrow morning. What are we to do, hold an instant symposium to explore fully the possibilities and options?"

Now Pete was impatient. His dark eyes were narrowed, and he speeded up his pace as if that would hurry the argument. "And what am I supposed to do, Bill, go to the President and say we've got to talk the Russians into helping us muscle the Arabs—overnight, mind you—into giving up a decisive advantage over their hated enemies, and when the President asks why, say I'm not sure; they're threatening something, but I don't quite know what?

"What would you think of those answers if you were the President? Or the Soviet premier?"

Bill looked at his friend, hard. "And suppose someone were to ask you what you did while Israel was being annihilated; how would you answer that?"

"I would say I was waiting for some solid facts on which I could act and Israel wouldn't give me any, and it was typical of the hard-line rigidity that painted them into a corner to begin with."

"And could you live with that answer?" Bill asked.

"I guess we're kind of going around in circles; we're back where we started. Just like our walk." Pete gestured toward the other side of Park Avenue, where the Waldorf stood. They were back at Fiftieth Street.

"Do I take it then that the answer to Shalzar is no, that we shall not act on his list of demands?" Standing on the corner, waiting for the light to change so they could cross, Bill put the question with empty disbelief. Is this it? Is it all over? Do we just wait now for the other shoe to drop? And how does America, the world, begin to deal with this new holocaust?

The light changed; they began walking, Pete smiling to himself and shaking his head slightly. "Your problem is that you're identifying with the Israeli side; it's easy to understand, you're representing them for the moment and so for the moment you're believing only in them. Also there's the touch of annoyance. You're letting on it's because you think I'm hardhearted about the fate of Israel. Maybe, but a good part of it is your taking my skepticism as being skeptical of you.

"Well, Bill, it's nothing of the sort. And I'm *not* saying no."

He's going to work on me, Bill thought. Right here on the corner of Fiftieth and Park. He's starting the sales pitch.

Anyone who had watched Maloney's career or worked with him knew it wasn't his PhD, his grasp of world trade or currency, or his quickness—in negotiations he was an O. J. Simpson—which had won him a board chairmanship at forty and a cabinet post at forty-three. It was his salesmanship; his ability to persuade and, by persuasion, agility, concession on some issues, brute force on others, to prevail. The president of a firm which had been vying with Union Consolidated to buy a Midwestern tool company, and lost, once said to Bill of Pete, "I don't know how else to say it. That man gets what he wants. It's uncanny, the knack he has of getting what he wants."

They had reached the entrance to the Waldorf Towers, but were not yet ready to go in. Pete held Bill's left forearm with his right hand, the grip light enough to be affectionate and strong enough to say: Don't try to get away.

"What I want to do is put the ball back in your court, to get you back playing for us instead of the Israelis. How did you get involved in this? Through Kate, right? Because she goes out with him now, right? That gives her more reason to be co-opted to the Israeli side than it gives you, but I wonder how good a reason it is for either of you.

"What I'm asking of you, I ask of you as an American, as someone anxious to keep the world in one piece, and as a pro-Israeli, which I know you are. I ask you to find out more about the Israeli plan.

Go back to Shalzar, tell him we're anxious to work with him, but we can't on the basis of what we know now. Find out more, right away!"

Now Bill was thrown off stride. He hadn't expected to become a principal in this; he saw himself as a middleman, a high-class messenger. Suddenly he was an actor, he was "involved," and he didn't know if he liked it. "I don't think he'll tell me any more," Bill said. "He said he wouldn't and that man doesn't give ground. He's a fighter."

Pete was still selling. "Look, Bill, if at this moment Shalzar doesn't give ground, he's no fighter, he's a kamikaze pilot, he's a suicide squad. A fighter gives ground whenever he thinks it can help him win."

As Bill knew when he began it, Pete responded to the boxing metaphor. Pete loved fighting; he had been a New York City Golden Gloves runner-up as a middleweight. And though he recognized retreat as a tactic, it was one he had seldom used himself; he preferred nose-to-nose combat and he had a deviated septum to show for it. So rarely did he give ground that if he yielded even an inch, his opponents—in the ring and later in business—deemed it such a major victory they were almost pleased to give away miles in return.

"Shalzar's country is in desperate shape, old boy, and he knows it. Maybe he knows also that part of the blame for it has to be laid at the feet of Israel's own hard-line stand of the past ten years." Pete knew Bill would want to argue that so he raised a peremptory hand. "Let's not. I'm only talking about Shalzar's own perceptions now, not the so-called 'truth' of the situation. My point is merely to sell him on the idea that the more information he gives, the better his chances of getting what he wants. So far, on 'freedom of action,' he can expect nothing. The more we get, the more he gets."

The Secretary had set up his exit and he didn't want it weakened. His arm snapped up in front of him; he looked at his watch. It's ten-twenty-five, and I'm right on schedule." He paused and looked at Brewster. "Bill, I'm reachable all day. I'm not underestimating this situation for a moment. I'm waiting on you now. Work on Shalzar.

"And Bill . . ." Pete hesitated.

"You might see what you can find out in other ways. From other sources. And . . . ah . . . give my best to Kate, will you?" He reached his right hand out to shake Bill's, and with his left, whacked Bill on the shoulder. Then he turned, almost without waiting for Bill to finish saying "Thanks, I shall," and headed for the Towers entrance, the big Secret Service man striding past Bill to catch up to him.

Well, Bill said to himself, standing on the sidewalk, I must concede

Pete has gained somewhat in subtlety. A decade ago he would have punctuated that request, and the "give my best to Kate," with a line like "Do I make myself clear?" He *had* made himself clear. You want me to pump my former lover for information from her current lover, thought Bill. In effect, enlist her as a spy. I got your message. The question is, what do I do with it? Then he realized he was standing on the street, not knowing where to go next.

He took a deep breath. Then he headed for the Towers entrance, strode by the doorman with a wave, and went to the elevators.

"Fifteen this time, Felipe," he said to the elevator man. Swiftly he walked along the fifteenth-floor hallway to his suite, opened the door, and went in. He had two calls to make, to Dov and to Kate. That was easy. Deciding what to say and exactly how was a lot harder. And hardest of all was the decision about enlisting Kate as a spy. It was the kind of decision he would love to talk over with another person and, ironically, the two, the only two, whose advice was important to him, he could not approach, because they were the principals.

First he headed down the hall into his kitchen, where he filled a small kettle and set it to boil. Then he fished in a cabinet for a jar of instant coffee. I've been here nearly two years and I'm still using instant coffee, he thought, and from a tiny jar, too. How's that for permanence? He prepared the coffee, black, no sugar, took a sip and carried the cup into the sitting room. He sat near the phone, trying not to look around; the place depressed him. He had left the decoration up to the hotel, and though they had tried hard to please him, they had, as Kate once put it, "taken a musty, old, impersonal hotel suite and cleverly redone it to look just like a spanking new impersonal hotel suite."

He still felt like a transient. He'd never meant to stay more than a few months. At first he'd delayed because though he hated to admit it now, he had hoped he and Kate would be marrying and there'd been no point moving without planning the step with her. But that hadn't happened, and after it he'd been lethargic, just not interested in making the decisions, taking the time, doing the looking. He didn't care.

The result was a nightly confrontation with this sickly wall-to-wall carpeting and the whorehouse drapes and the overblown satin-covered bastard French provincial sofa. And every night he'd stay out as late as he reasonably could and he'd accept invitations he didn't really care about and use the Southampton house at any excuse.

Now he had to make up his mind. The call to Dov was easy. He'd ask for a brief meeting; he would not lie to get it, would not suggest he had something special to offer. Nor would he say outright that all he wanted was more information. If Shalzar didn't ask why he wanted the meeting, so much the better.

But Kate, that was another matter. First there was the morality of spying, on anyone, let alone someone you loved. And even if he felt it was not immoral, still, could he ask her to do it? Did he have the . . . chutzpah? Suppose someone had asked *him* to spy on *her,* would he refuse out of hand? Not out of hand, he answered; not if the issues were as immense as these. In the end, possibly, refuse, but not out of hand.

He crossed one leg over the other, heard the swish of the satin as his body moved slightly on the sofa. He took another sip of the coffee.

Maybe he was asking himself the wrong question. Suppose he found out that Kate had been asked to spy on him? And had agreed to it? How would he feel? Furious. Tricked. And Kate didn't even love him. He could imagine then how Dov would feel. If he could imagine it, so could Kate. And she would, and that's what he'd have to deal with if he asked her.

And if he didn't ask, he'd have Pete to deal with.

With a sigh, Brewster put down the cup and leaned to the phone. He picked it up, hoping that by meeting Dov he could solve the problem without having to ask Kate to be a spy. Sometimes problems had a way of solving themselves. But he knew this one wouldn't.

Reaching into his pocket he found the slip of paper on which he had written Dov's private number. He dialed it, waited, and then heard Dov's voice on the other end. "Hello?"

"Dov, it's Bill Brewster."

"Yes, Bill. How are you?"

"I'm fine. I'd like to see you again as soon as possible."

"Have you spoken with the Secretary? Do you have something to tell me?" Obviously, Dov was in no mood to be coy; he was cutting right through to the point.

Carefully, Bill answered, following the blend of honesty and optimism he had formulated while sitting there. "Yes, I have spoken with him. I have something to tell you—and something to ask."

There was a pause. Bill was worried. Then Dov spoke. "All right, let's meet. But I don't know how much more I have to say."

Again, following his plan, Bill did not respond to that last sentence at all. He said, "Why don't you come to my suite at the Waldorf, Dov? It's quiet, it's convenient, and it's not bugged."

"I'm afraid not, Bill. Twice in the past ten hours, men have attacked me. The second time we lost a security man and shot three of them. So for now I can't leave the physical and diplomatic protection of this embassy. I'll have to ask you to come here. Is that all right?"

Bill was shaken. He had forgotten about the cloak-and-dagger aspects of this work, forgotten there were times, places, circumstances in which officials and people who worked with them—people like Kate, and himself—were shot.

"Yes, it's fine Dov. But are you all right? Is Kate all right?"

Now it was Dov's turn to be upset. Suddenly he realized that since he sent her off, he'd given almost no thought to her safety. He'd have to do something about that right away.

"Yes," he answered. "I'm all right. She's all right." He hoped he wasn't wrong. "How soon do you want to get here?" he asked Brewster.

Bill checked his watch. 10:45. "Make it eleven-thirty, if that's all right."

"That's fine," the ambassador answered. "Now listen, there is a back entrance to the embassy. On Seventy-third Street. If you go to Madison and Seventy-third and walk along the south side of the street, toward Park, Yehuda—he's the man who was sitting near the entrance to the meeting room at the Unity—will spot you and take you in. And, Bill, I hope we have something to talk about."

"I hope so, too, Dov. See you soon."

Bill put the receiver back on its cradle, then lifted it, dialed his office and spoke to a secretary.

"I won't be reachable for a couple of hours. Take messages, will you, and pick up on the private line. I'll check in with you. Thanks."

Then he phoned Kate at her studio. His timing was perfect. Five minutes sooner she would have been taping. Ten minutes later she would have left. But she was just about to walk off the "Today's Woman" set when the call came through.

"Kate, it's Bill . . . Brewster."

"Oh, that Bill. It's a good thing you told me. Having spoken on the phone with you only 7,312 times, I never would have recognized your voice." Kate was a bit surprised herself that, having just been shot at, been through a wild car chase, seen three men killed, rushed to the studio and done a half hour on "Women and the Courts" for which she'd had absolutely no preparation, she'd have the time or the wish to chide Bill for his formality. It just reminded her of his aloofness, which she'd worked on so hard and, obviously, with so little success.

"Seven thousand, that's nothing," he responded. "I don't really come on strong until ten thousand. But *then* . . ."

Well, maybe she'd had a little success after all, Kate thought. "Has anyone told you lately your answers are getting very show biz?"

"I know, I know," Bill responded. "Next step, black shirts and white ties. Sky Masterson. Listen, if you're willing to settle for the old wardrobe, temporarily, could we meet for a cup of coffee in about an hour? I'm on my way to see Dov . . . ." Just for an instant, he had

124

wanted not to reveal that, and then he decided, no lies, "and I'd like to pick your brain after that, and maybe exploit the world crisis just to have a chat with you." Was there a little lie in there, Bill wondered, a little social inducement to take her mind off the brain-picking? No, there wasn't, he decided. He was anxious to have a few minutes with her.

As Kate listened, another control-room phone rang. A production assistant answered it and gestured to her, his lips forming the words, "It's for you." "Ask him to wait," Kate replied, also soundlessly.

Then she answered Bill. "Okay. Old wardrobe and all, but Bill, please don't let me get caught in the middle. Please. Do you know what I mean? Because I won't stand still for it. If I have to I'll put my head down and charge right out."

Another carefully noncommittal answer from Brewster. "I understand perfectly. Can you meet me here at the Waldorf in ninety minutes?" What he had refrained from saying was, I won't ask anything of you. To his own surprise, he realized he had made a decision in the last few minutes. He would ask Kate what the Secretary wanted him to ask. He'd ask her to spy—*if* it were necessary. He added the conditional to make it easier on himself, although he admitted he knew damn well it would be necessary.

"Good. I'll be there, Bill . . . whatever your name is."

"Wonderful. That'll be twelve-thirty. I'll be looking forward to it." Would he? he asked himself. Yes, as always, but . . . the prospect of "recruiting" her—he had begun to think of it in spy language—dampened the anticipation.

He hung up the phone, took a last sip of the coffee, which was by then tepid, and headed out the door.

In the control room, Kate quickly punched the button to pick up the holding call, knowing who it would be. She was right. Dov.

"Are you all right?" he asked anxiously. Bill's call had made him realize he hadn't given enough thought to Kate. He had taken her through a chase, shooting, killing, and it was Bill who had to remind him to worry about her.

"Well, I'm a little shook, but mostly over it. I hate to admit it, but I don't see men gunned down in Central Park every day, so I'm not as blasé about that as I should be. By the way, who were they?"

"I don't know, although they sure looked like Arabs. And what's more critical, I don't know why they decided to go after me just now. It's almost as if they were tipped off that I was doing something especially important. Those are things I'd love to find out, later, but not now. I'm not setting a foot outside this embassy for that, or any other reason.

"The police are outside right now; we reported the shooting as soon as we got back. They don't know who the men are; they want to ask us, but they can't get in here unless we invite them and we're not inviting them—not before nine a.m. tomorrow. We've got too much to do. What I am doing is dictating a complete statement, which I'll give them. For the moment, I am going to leave your name out of it. You don't have our immunity and they'd be after you for questioning, which I think you can do without for the present.

"Kate, Bill will be here to talk to me in about fifteen minutes . . ." For a moment she hesitated. Should she not tell him she already knew? Should she not tell him she had just been talking with Bill? Once she started hiding things, she realized, she'd never know where she was, what to conceal, what not to; she'd not remember what she had concealed and what she hadn't. She made a quick decision. No tricks.

"Yes, I know, Dov. I was on the phone with him when you called. He told me and he asked me to meet him afterward."

"Oh good, Kate, good."

Kate saw what was coming and dreaded it. She tried to head it off, with a touch of banter. "Here I have the two most attractive men in New York hot on my trail. If only I could believe it were for my charm instead of my services as go-between and counterspy."

But Dov would not be forestalled. "It's essential that we know how seriously we're being taken, Kate. All I'm asking is that you give me your sense of the conversation." He waited for an answer.

Standing in the hallway of the control room, shifting her weight from one foot to the other, Kate realized she was feeling uncomfortable, and not because of the cramped room; it was the narrow space between these two men that was bothering her—and the space was getting tighter and tighter every moment. "I'll either call afterwards, or tell you when I come over for dinner at seven—if that's still on. But Bill will know about it. I'm no good at these kinds of games, Dov."

"That's fine; I understand that and I accept it. Yes, dinner is still on, definitely, but I'd be grateful if you'd call right after you've had the talk anyway. The stakes are high, Kate, but this is no game. This is the real thing. And I don't have to tell you how much we—I—value all that you've done."

Like a canoeist on a river, Kate felt the easy current turning into rapids and her excitement turning into fear. Should she pull for shore now? Could she, even if she decided to, or was it too late?

"I'll call you as soon afterwards as I can. There's almost nothing I wouldn't do for you, Dov. But I won't spy—not for anyone. I will not be a spy."

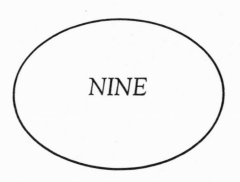

NINE

At one minute after eleven, Mac Seligsohn strode into the library of the Israeli embassy, moving toward Shalzar like a linebacker toward a quarterback, three ambassadorial aides trailing him like failed blockers. Not that Seligsohn was as big as a linebacker; in fact, he was five-foot-seven and a meticulously watched one hundred and forty-five pounds. Not that he was moving fast, for his pace was steady and unrushed. Rather it was that despite his size, despite his speed, Seligsohn emitted waves of irresistibility.

"Tell your associates I'm all right, Dov," he asked in a voice startling big and mellow for a man his size. No, he didn't really ask, he commanded, like someone accustomed to deference. "Mac is the kind of man," his wife had once affectionately said of him, "who, when he puts his arms behind him, expects someone to be holding out his coat. And someone always is."

His irresistibility lay in the serenely regal set of his head and in his cool light gray eyes with their steady signals flashing power. If part of that power came from his personality, another came from the Seligsohn Communications Corporation, of which he was president, board chairman, and owner. A $350-million company, holding a publishing house, newspapers, magazines, and several radio and TV stations, and except for a few token shares held by others, he owned every penny of it.

"It's all right," Shalzar said to the three aides. "This is Mr. Seligsohn." Being young Sabras, they were not quite sure who he was, but his power aura, and the way the ambassador spoke his name, told all they needed to know. The three nodded to the American and left.

"I was just sitting here, going through some material," Dov Shalzar gestured toward a stack of papers on the table near him, "and waiting for them to call and tell me you were here." He found himself in a kind of apology. "Anyway, it's good to see you, Mac."

"That's all right, Dov, I'm sure you've lots of material to look through at this moment." Seligsohn was telling Shalzar his apology was accepted, royally and graciously.

To be on a first-name basis with Seligsohn was, for Israeli politicians, a badge of status, and the publisher had not called them by anything but their first names since David Ben-Gurion, who was "Mr. Prime Minister," and Chaim Weizmann, who was "Mr. President." But back then Mac Seligsohn was just into his thirties and still working on his first $50 million.

In the three decades since the founding of the state, he had raised $500 million for Israel, for which he had been brought to Tel Aviv last year and apotheosized amid trappings he found embarrassing and which a leftwing Israeli commentator pronounced "fit for King Herod." Nearly $30 million of it had come from him personally in gifts and purchases of Israeli bonds; he tried to maintain a million-a-year pace.

Lesser men would have asked leave to enter the room; not Seligsohn. "I hope you have some time," he said, "because I have several things to say, and lots to ask so I can build up more pressure in the old boiler, get some support for you—official, unofficial, all kinds, and get it quickly.

"I *have* time, Mac, please sit down," said Shalzar, simultaneously saying to himself, Goddammit, I *don't* have time. Despite his protestation, the fact was he had forgotten the appointment, and now wished he had never made it.

No, he didn't have the time. Brewster was coming in a half hour and he had to be prepared for a wrestling match; for, barring a miracle, the banker was not visiting to deliver US capitulation to Israeli demands. And Shalzar didn't expect a miracle, although, at this point, he thought, it wouldn't hurt.

And later this afternoon, there was to be the Foreign Minister, Weismann, arriving with the white-glove-inspection attitude he always took on to assert his superiority. He's my boss, and I know it; why does he have to prove it every time, thought Shalzar? Oh hell, I like the guy, he reminded himself, and I've got a lot to talk to him about—starting and ending with the Masada Plan.

Meanwhile, the embassy was taking on the look and the feel of a besieged fortress. Inside, the telexes were pounding out messages and the cryptographer had settled on a stool right at the machines; there was no point in his trying to leave. A half-dozen embassy officials were running around doing—well Shalzar wasn't quite sure what, but he kept thinking of an impending storm, and of the expression "battening down the hatches."

Outside, things were even more frantic; the police were busy both protecting and investigating the Israeli mission. Barricades were up so no one could approach the front of the embassy; in one section of the restricted area the press was confined. By noon there were more than thirty print and broadcast reporters and TV crewmen, staking out the area, watching for entrances and exits, keeping an eye out for demonstrations.

So far there were only a dozen or so demonstrators and six police-men, but a truck with additional barricades was standing by and a sergeant was ready to call the Nineteenth Precinct for help if the crowd got bigger, especially if any pro-Arab groups arrived. Several security men were watching the front of the building, pulling aside the drawn drapes just enough to peek out. On either side of them at the windows were steel shutters that they could close if things got rough. The ambassador had checked the crowds just before Seligsohn arrived. As he stared at the police, the press, and the onlookers, he blamed himself for having urged a visible embassy. And congratulated himself for having had the foresight to build a rear entrance.

Last year, he had been instrumental in the decision to combine the UN mission offices with the ambassador's residence, which until then had been an unidentified Manhattan apartment. Jerusalem had said no; Shalzar had felt the symbolic value of an Israeli presence in New York was worth the risk. He had taken chances before, he told them, he'd be bored without danger. The Foreign Minister had replied, "Don't be funny," but had acquiesced, provided all possible precautions were taken.

The rear entrance had been Shalzar's idea and had been arranged through the good offices of the ubiquitous Seligsohn, who knew the owner of the Seventy-third Street brownstone which backed on the embassy building. In fact, the owner was a wealthy Jewish real estate man who consistently responded to Seligsohn's fund-raising appeals for Israel, and when Seligsohn approached him about access to the rear of the embassy, he was not only delighted to give it and to keep it a secret, he insisted on paying for the construction of the entrance. Since the cost was $50,000 and the embassy was already $170,000 over budget in the overall renovation, Shalzar was delighted to accept the contribution. And so, through part of what had once been a car-riage house and a courtyard, ran a passageway that began with an unobtrusive black door on Seventy-third Street and ended in the kitchen of the Israeli UN mission building on Seventy-second Street.

Returning by taxi from the Central Park shoot-out a couple of hours earlier, Dov Shalzar had used the back entrance, and then at once had told the assistant who generally took on press and public relations functions to phone the local precinct and tell them about the shooting.

"So that's what it was," said the desk sergeant. "The officer on duty in front of your embassy reported the shots and cars there, so we figured you were involved, but we couldn't be sure. Then we heard the shots in the park and found the Audi with the three bodies in it—yeah, they're dead. And the phone has been ringing like crazy all morning, with people telling us what they heard and asking what's been going on. Can we send a couple of officers over to talk to you?"

More foreign embassies and missions lay within the boundaries of the Nineteenth than in all the city's other precincts combined, so the police there were accustomed to the protocol, the prime tenet of which was the immunity of diplomatic and consular personnel and of their headquarters.

The Israeli also knew the protocol and he wanted something in return for their agreement to talk. "Would you tell us who the men were and whom the car belonged to?"

"The three deceased were not carrying any identification," answered the sergeant, sounding as if he were testifying in court. "And the plates were issued to a party named Zohrak. Zohrak, however, has been dead for two years and those plates do not belong to that Audi. All right if we come over?"

"Yes. Provided you understand we shall talk to you only in our front hall, which is Israeli territory and provided that you leave upon our request."

"Yes, we understand," answered the sergeant resignedly. "We'll be right over."

In a transparent attempt at diplomacy, the precinct sent over a lieutenant whose nameplate identified him as Finkelstein. He walked by the patrolman on duty, nodded and rang. After identifying themselves, he and the patrolman with him were buzzed in. They found themselves in a six-by-six foyer entirely lined in steel—including the front door that had snapped shut behind them. Ahead of them was an unwindowed door that looked more like a sliding panel. From one corner of the ceiling they were being watched by a closed-circuit TV camera. Over a speaker, a voice said, "State your names and your business, please."

"I am Lieutenant Finkelstein; this is Officer Jenkins. We're here to talk about the . . . incidents in front of your embassy and in Central Park."

"One moment, please."

In about thirty seconds the steel panel slid open and the two policemen started forward until a voice said, "Stay where you are, please." Then three Israelis stepped into the anteroom and the panel slid shut.

Since the police had entered before Seligsohn arrived, the ambassador had had the time to brief his assistant and Yehuda, and to stand behind the steel door, listening to the conversation as it came over a speaker.

"This is Yehuda, who drove our car. He will tell you everything that happened." The assistant did not identify himself or the third Israeli.

The driver then recounted the episode, fully, omitting only two elements. He did not disclose the identities of the other three in the car, nor did he tell the police Avram had been shot and killed.

"Who were the others in the car?" Lieutenant Finkelstein asked, sensibly. This time the assistant took over the replies. "They were Israeli diplomatic personnel."

"Would you give their names, please?"

"Not at this time."

"Was one of them your ambassador?"

"I told you, we shall not identify them at this time."

Finkelstein knew why he had been chosen for this job, and with his fellow officer standing next to him, felt he had to try to capitalize on his ethnicity. "You know I'm on your side!"

"*Are* you, Lieutenant . . . Finkelstein?" Shalzar, listening, knew the aide had a tendency to get snippy. He also knew there was a lot of anti-American feeling in his delegation.

"Yes, I've got an uncle in Haifa."

"Well, then, have you wired your Congressman, telling him we need an airlift of . . ."

"Stop that!" The ambassador's voice came over the speaker with the snap of a ringmaster's whip. The policemen were startled by its preemptory tone, the Israelis by their recognition of its source.

"Lieutenant Finkelstein," Shalzar went on, "we appreciate your support. But we cannot give you any more information now. Thank you for coming."

Both policemen knew the sound of a superior officer. "Thank you, sir," said the lieutenant, not quite sure where to address it. Then they heard the buzzer sounding on the front door. Finkelstein gave a tight nod to the Israeli aide with whom he'd had the exchange and then the two cops turned and left.

That was just fifteen minutes before Seligsohn's arrival.

"All right now," Seligsohn began. "What kind of shape are you guys in?" Despite his zealous support for Israel, his "we" always meant America and Americans. "You" or "you guys" referred to the Israelis and "they" stood for the Arabs. "They," or just plain "damned-Arabs," said as one word in much the same way some Southerners would say "damnYankees."

"Not good," the ambassador replied.

"All right then, what's to be done at this end?" And before Shalzar could respond to his question, Seligsohn went ahead. "By now," he looked at his gleaming gold wristwatch, "I can guarantee, every one of the fifty senators who is within reach of a phone has been called by at least one person who has contributed to his campaign. Not $5 either. A *big* contributor. I myself have spoken to sixteen senators I know personally. And it's just the beginning. Every senator, every congressman, every state party chairman, every governor: we're going to put pressure on those guys like they've never felt before.

"We're mobilizing. Every Jewish organization in the country is being called. Every religious group. Every labor union. Every veterans group. I've given everyone on two floors of my building the day off so we can get volunteers in there to use the phones.

"Every newspaper in the country is being visited or phoned—and by people who *matter*—advertisers, stockholders, bankers, suppliers. I want to tell you, we are *not* being delicate. We have taken off the velvet glove." Seligsohn held up his hand, his gold watch and manicured fingers catching the light, and he squeezed it into a fist until the knuckles turned white. Despite his watch, his manicure, his size, and his sixty-four years, it was not a fist to be ignored.

"My own twenty-two papers—" he pulled a galley sheet from his pocket and tossed it at them—"are running *this*." It was a long editorial, all in boldface type, with a headline proclaiming: Hitler Rides Again! Shalzar started to look at it and Seligsohn said to him, "Read it later. There's more to talk about." Shalzar put it down. Nobody disobeyed Seligsohn. "We're working up demonstrations," he continued.

"I saw some of them in front of the building," Shalzar began.

Mac Seligsohn was not tolerant of interruptions, especially from someone who didn't understand what he was getting at. His cool eyes turned cold, then he realized you don't talk to the Israeli ambassador as if he were one of your vice-presidents, and his face crinkled into a smile. By God, he almost looks like a kindly old uncle, Shalzar thought.

"No, we wouldn't bother with demonstrators in front of *here*." Seligsohn was still smiling. "We figure you're on the right side already. You are, aren't you?" His smile got wider. Then it stopped.

"No, those jerks out front are just standing around with their fingers up their asses. This is the last place they should be. The only ones who belong here are the damned Arabs!" Seligsohn went off on a tangent. "By the way, you better be ready for some Arab picketing. I'll call the Mayor when I leave—ask for more cops." He pulled out a leather memo book and a gold pen and scribbled a line.

"Oh no," he went on. "*We* should be at the UN, putting the fear of God into all the damned Arab-lovers—oil-lovers, is more like it."

Shalzar was getting a glimpse of ferocity he had never seen in the American before; Seligsohn is a steamroller, Shalzar thought, and if I get in his way I become part of the pavement. He had heard from people in the publishing business how senior executives of the Seligsohn empire were terrified of making mistakes, of seeming stupid, or otherwise awakening the boss's anger. Though he had met the publisher many times, at parties, dinners, conferences, he had never understood why Seligsohn inspired such terror.

Now Shalzar understood. He had seen the laser beams streaming from those eyes in the instant before Seligsohn turned kindly. And he was impressed, he had to admit. He had seen an Egyptian tank column coming across the sand at him, he thought, and not been as impressed.

"But more important than that," said Seligsohn, rolling on, "we've got to put the fear of God into that damned Arab-lover in the White House, and into those shits in the State Department." Shalzar thought he should say a word for Secretary Maloney, who he felt to be the most pro-Israeli of all those close to the President, but as he wondered whether he dared step in the path of the juggernaut, Seligsohn disposed of that issue. "Yeah, I know, Maloney's a hero. I see how much his heroism has done for you guys."

But that was another tangent, and Seligsohn got back on the track. "I drove by the UN on my way over here; there were a couple of thousand demonstrators already, mostly Yeshiva kids, and hundreds more arriving every minute. It's tougher with schools on vacation but when the speeches start—at two, we want them in time for six o'clock news coverage—we'll have 25,000 outside the UN. Let 'em look out their windows at that!

"By the way, we'll expect you at the rally at, say, two-thirty, to make a speech. It won't take long." He didn't wait for a reply; Mac Seligsohn took acquiescence as a privilege of his rank. "But today's rally is just the beginning. Now listen to this. Tomorrow morning, ten o'clock, 100,000 people in Times Square. The cast of every Broadway show—we're going to get some of those actors up earlier than they've been all their lives. Music. Speeches.

"And then," Seligsohn paused to make sure Shalzar was following him because this was big. "We are going to bus every last one of them down to Washington for a huge rally at seven o'clock tomorrow evening. We want it to be covered *live* by the network news shows."

Shalzar felt two emotions, incredulity at the size of the undertaking, and a kind of despair at the thought that all this work was being done for something that would come ten hours after tomorrow morning's nine o'clock deadline for the plan. By seven tomorrow evening, indeed by ten in the morning, the crisis would either be over . . . or . . . The ambassador cut off those thoughts.

"How in the world are you going to get 100,000 people from Times Square to Washington? Do you have any idea how many buses it will take?"

In forty-five years as a businessman, Mac Seligsohn had never been caught on that kind of question. "Somewhere between twenty-two and twenty-three hundred," he replied. "Of course, we don't expect everybody in Times Square to go to Washington. We'll be lucky if we get much more than half of them, so we'll have maybe 1500 buses; they'll be parked in every side street from Thirty-fourth to Fifty-seventh, from Sixth Avenue to Tenth Avenue; traffic'll be blocked off in that whole area; the garment center'll take the day off.

"We'll shake this city up tomorrow; we'll tie it up. We'll show everybody you don't have business as usual while a friend is fighting for his life. And not only this city. All over the country we're throwing together rallies, for today or tomorrow, depending on how fast we can work. And a lot of them will be sending their people on to Washington. Especially from Philadelphia and Baltimore. We want to have over 200,000 in Washington.

"What is it Willy Loman's wife says in *Death of a Salesman?* 'Attention must be paid.' Tomorrow, we'll get the Arab-lover in the White House to pay attention."

But the deadline was nine tomorrow morning, Shalzar thought. He had to say something, but carefully, for Seligsohn was as quick as lightning and he'd pick up on it and want to know more.

"Mac, it's all overwhelming," he said. "I can't imagine how such a project could be put together in so little time. But one thing. Wherever you can push a demonstration ahead from tomorrow, to today, do it. It will help much, *much* more today than tomorrow."

Shalzar's second 'much' had alerted Seligsohn. He was sniffing the wind. "Why much *much* more today?" he asked.

The ambassador backed away slightly. "Oh, just because sooner is better than later."

Seligsohn didn't buy it. "Is that all? I mean, is the fighting going to be over tomorrow?"

"The sooner the better is all I meant, Mac." Then, to get on to something else, Shalzar asked, "And what will the theme be? What action will you be asking the President and Congress to take?"

"The theme I see is 'Airlift Now'; you know, the idea of: Give them the weapons and they'll lick the invaders by themselves. They don't need American boys."

Dov Shalzar nodded and then suggested, "Why not stress ending the fighting instead? The US using its prestige and power to stop the war, rather than supplying armaments. Stop the war before it spreads. Put out the fire in the Middle East."

But Mac Seligsohn, sniffing harder than ever, was on another scent. He had never really pressed his early questioning on the status of the fighting. Now he went back to it.

"You said the fighting was 'not good,' Dov. Just how 'not good' is it?" His eyes were narrowed, his jaw thrust forward. His face said, Don't kid me. " 'Not good' like '73?"

The ambassador and the publisher looked at each other.

"Bad, Mac. Bad." As Shalzar said it, he stood up, paced the room, half trying, by physical activity, to keep the hard-eyed publisher from zeroing in on him, knowing it wouldn't work.

"Don't crap me, Dov." Seligsohn was a well-educated man; he had graduated from Stanford magna cum laude and had a master's degree in English literature from Columbia, but early in his career he got the idea that too much visible education was a handicap in the rough and tumble of business, so he started talking tough, a style he arrived at systematically; short words and lots of profanity, shot out in the staccato tempo of a machine gun. As he grew older, richer, and more powerful, he abandoned the toughness as a regular style and saved it for emphatic occasions—such as this one.

"My phone's been ringing all night. People who want to help. *Big* people, from all over. We're moving. Now don't send us down any blind alleys; I have a feeling you're holding back. Don't fuck with us, not if you're ever gonna need us again."

Are we ever going to need them again? Dov asked himself. His first impulse was to placate Seligsohn with something like: Don't be foolish, Mac, we're not doing anything of the kind. But that wouldn't work. Instead, he said, "Mac, there are things I can't tell you. Please stick with us. Please accept my word that the situation is very *very* grave. Here's what's important to us. That your efforts be directed toward setting up these rallies and demonstrations today, rather than tomorrow. That your pressure on the government be aimed at stopping the fighting rather than sending us arms."

The publisher's eyes were burning into him so hard Shalzar half expected to see his own flesh singed, like when he was a kid and used a magnifying glass to focus the sun's rays and burn a hole in a leaf. For an instant he had thought of hedging the seriousness of the crisis, of making it vaguer. Not with those eyes watching me, he told himself. Besides, with less than twenty-two hours till 9 a.m. tomorrow, this is the time to take chances.

"Israel has never needed you more, Mac, and the crucial time will be the next twenty-four hours, every single hour of it. Pour it on. Don't hold anything back. And do it without asking me any questions. Can we count on you? Will you do it on faith?"

It didn't take much to get a message across to Mac Seligsohn. He could be tough and overriding, but his antennae were fine tuned.

"No more questions. Got you." He paused and then something so dramatic happened in his eyes it was almost like a scene change in a film.

"Faith is something I've never had much of, Dov. I've found more and more that each time I accepted the word of others, took anything on faith, that is, I got screwed. So I've got to where I put everything to the test of my own personal computer," he tapped his temple with a forefinger, "or else it's no deal. And if someone won't give me the data to feed in, it's no deal, either.

"Faith in God I guess I never really had; faith in America—well maybe I've gotten too close to the top, seen too much of the way things work, to have that any more."

Seligsohn was only seventeen years older than he was, Shalzar thought, but he felt himself being talked to like a son.

"The only thing left for me, Dov, the sole repository of my faith, is the state of Israel. I don't mean any particular prime minister. Or any particular ambassador. I mean the state. And I can't tell you how much I *need* an Israel to have faith in."

Seligsohn was about to open up, and Shalzar was listening with a mixture of impatience and intense curiosity; this was the first break he had ever seen in the millionaire's armor. But there was a knock on the door, and no more was to come out.

"Come in," said the ambassador.

An assistant stood at the door. "There is a man named William Brewster at the Seventy-third Street entrance. Says he has an appointment with you at eleven-thirty."

"Give me two minutes, then bring him in," replied Shalzar.

He looked at his watch. 11:34. Seligsohn stood up. Through the last tiny gap in the rapidly resealing armor he said, "You found the one area where faith still gets any results with me. So I'm going to do it the way you want." Then the armor clanged shut.

They shook hands, and the publisher said, "William Brewster, huh? If you've got time to go over your investment portfolio, things can't be so bad." He grinned and waited for Shalzar to tell him something; all he got was a return grin and "Do you know him?"

"Yeah, a little," answered Seligsohn, and he waggled a finger at the ambassador. "Butter wouldn't melt in his mouth."

As Dov walked him toward the Seventy-second Street entrance, so the two Americans wouldn't meet, he thought: In Mac Seligsohn's mouth, butter would turn to frozen cubes—or fry, whichever he wanted.

At the entrance, they shook hands again. Seligsohn said, "I expect to see you at the speakers' platform, Forty-sixth and First at two-thirty."

"If it's humanly possible."

"It's important."

Shalazar had to smile at that. "I know. And thank you."

The American walked out and the ambassador headed back along the thick wine-colored carpeting of the hall to the library. When he walked in, Bill Brewster was standing to his left, looking over the shelves of books that lined the wall.

"Good morning, Bill." He headed toward the taller man as he said it, his hand outstretched. "Sorry to keep you waiting, but as you might imagine, we have so much to do."

Here I am, Shalzar thought, working on an end-of-the-world deadline, but I've got to stay polite at all times. They shook hands and he motioned Brewster to a tan leather easy chair and sat near him in a bentwood rocker.

"No, it's I who am sorry, Dov, to interrupt you this way. I know you have so much to do. I'm trying to help, of course; that's why I'm here." Brewster found himself shading what he said to put himself on the ambassador's side.

Shalzar heard it and decided to test it. "I'd like us to be on the same side."

"Well, we can both wish for an end to the fighting, can't we?" Bill Brewster didn't want to move too far into Dov's camp; gently, he pulled back.

The ambassador spotted that, too. "Of course we can and I hope we do. Would you like something to eat or drink?"

Brewster asked for more coffee.

The ambassador jumped up from his chair, walked to a buzzer near the library door and pressed it. Suddenly he was impatient to start talking. Standing at the door, waiting for someone to respond, he turned to Brewster.

"I must say I am surprised at the speed of your response, and have been spending some time mulling it over. I've decided . . ." There was a knock on the door and when Shalzar opened it, one of his assistants stood there.

"Ask someone to bring us a pot of coffee and two cups. Or bring it yourself. Quickly, please, Shlomo." The young man turned and left; Shalzar walked back to his rocker and sat down.

"I've decided," he continued, "this is just a preliminary response, some way station on the road to a meeting of the minds." He said it lightly, but awaited the reply with breathless seriousness. Brewster did not rush to answer. Shalzar watched, trying not to look too eager.

He had a bit longer to wait, though, for young Shlomo was back with the coffee. "Put it there," Shalzar said, pointing to a low rectangular coffee table between them, this time with noticeable impatience. With a "thank-you," he got the young man out of the room. Then the ambassador stood and poured two cups.

When both men were seated, with their coffee, the American raised his cup and said, "Here's to getting what we want."

"To peace," Dov responded.

"You're quite right about the way station," Brewster began. "I've just been speaking with the Secretary of State; he understands the seriousness of the situation both as it pertains to Israel and as it might pertain to others. He wants to find a way to work with you, a way to talk to the President, as a preliminary to approaching the Soviet Union and the Arabs. But he doesn't have enough specifics . . ."

Bill realized he was sounding like a public service message, so he was surprised not so much at Dov's response as at the promptness and decisiveness of it.

"That's all there is to tell, Bill. That's all."

Dov was all sympathy and kindliness as he said it, almost an older brother explaining to a younger one why he was about to be punished.

Just for the moment, Bill felt like giving up. Then it was the remembrance of his rivalry, not with Dov, but with Pete Maloney, that made him go on. He had to *sell* Dov, the way Pete would.

"Dov, I don't know how much you've heard about Peter Maloney, particularly about Peter Maloney the businessman, but I must tell you, of all his talents, which are myriad, the greatest is his salesmanship. If he starts talking, he can win the President over, maybe even the Soviets—and then the Arabs. *If* he starts talking. But he can't, because he has nothing solid to talk about. Nothing he can get excited about. I need something to give him, Dov. And only you can supply it."

Bill was straining forward. He paused, sipped at his coffee, waited to see what Dov would say.

"And how good a salesman is Bill Brewster?" Dov asked. "Because it's up to him to convince the Secretary of State that when Israel says freedom of action, we mean exactly that, stopping at nothing. It's up to him to convince the Secretary he should take a chance. Risk something, based on his own appraisal of a dangerous situation, an appraisal the Secretary is certainly in a position to make as well."

Now Bill felt he had a talking point. "Take a chance," he replied. "Risk. And how about your risk, Dov? Why won't you take a chance? Open up that portfolio of secret threats and let a little something show, so that the man you need to be your salesman can go out and use his formidable talents." Bill paused for a moment and, with an embarrassed grin, added, "I am referring of course to the Secretary of State, not myself."

We are indeed taking a risk, Shalzar wanted to say but couldn't. Our risk is in *not* disclosing more. With an eye to posterity we are being *very* daring by holding back. It was a daring the ambassador dared not claim.

But Bill had made a strong point and both men knew it. The difference was that Bill expected to gain something from it, and Dov knew there was nothing more he could yield—not then, not there.

And so all he could say was, "My government does not wish to take any more risk than it already has, and I am bound by its wishes, Bill. I can only reemphasize what I said earlier. Freedom of action means we will stop at nothing. And since by now I'm sure you have confirmed our appraisal of our military situation, you know we have nothing to lose."

He was getting nowhere, Bill knew, but he took a final stab at it. He went straight to the point. "The Secretary knows you've got the bombs, Dov. He doesn't think you have the delivery system, so how scared can you expect him to get? Give me something to tell him, Dov!"

For an instant Dov seemed startled. Then he smiled and said, "An interesting point. I wish I could comment on it. However, I cannot."

The ambassador put his cup down and edged forward on his rocking chair as a way of showing he had to get back to other work. But he was also doing it for dramatic effect. Bill's last stab had hit and Dov decided on the spot there was one more thing he could tell, and he wanted to surrender it as an exit line, to give it an impact, perhaps a shade more than it deserved, and to avoid being questioned on it.

Bill saw Dov's movement and understood it. He put his cup down and got to his feet.

"Dov, thank you for the time. I shall tell the Secretary what you've said and what you haven't said. I don't know what's going to happen, but unless he's changed his mind, and I've no reason to think he has, I just cannot be optimistic. Before I go, once again, is there anything, any tidbit, you can give me, any clue to help break the impasse?"

Dov had to smile to himself. Yes, it just happened he had, and Bill couldn't have led to it any better if Dov had written the lines for him.

What Dov said was, "I hope I'll be talking with you soon, Bill." Then he paused for effect, finished shaking Bill's hand, let go, and added, "Yes, there is one more thing I can tell you. We've given our freedom of action—our threat, as you like to call it—a name. Maybe your Israel experts can play with it, for what it's worth. Its name is the Masada Plan."

"Say it again, please," Bill requested.

"The Masada Plan."

Then Dov started for the door. "Let's talk soon, Bill."

Brewster was walking with him. The two men went out of the door, where Yehuda was waiting to escort the banker from the building. Again, they shook hands, this time exchanging only the word "goodbye." They had both said all there was to say at this meeting, and they knew it.

In ninety seconds, Brewster, his long legs striding out, was over to Park Avenue and into a cab. It was noon; he had some time before Kate was to meet him, so when he reached the Towers he went straight up to the Secretary of State's suite rather than his own. He rang the bell, and to a possessive Steve Phelps said, "I need ten minutes with him."

"I'll tell him you're here," was all Phelps said before disappearing.

In a moment, the Secretary was back, looking worried. "Apparently the ambassador was not embroidering the military situation over there. Not by one stitch. The Israelis are being steadily rolled back; they're taking unacceptable casualties; their tank and aircraft losses are so high they're going to be mortally wounded in a day or two. There just doesn't seem to be any chance they can stop the Arabs."

Brewster sat on the sofa and Maloney slumped down next to him. "Well, how does it feel to know that?" Bill asked.

Maloney looked angry. "No. Cut that out. We have a chance to do something; let's work on that. To hell with the old debate. What do you have to tell me?"

With that last sentence, his voice took on an expectancy that reminded Bill of a college boy who had sent a friend out to fix him up with a coed. First time he's ever looked at me with that puppy-dog eagerness, thought Bill, and the banker suddenly felt the misgivings of the friend who had to say: She won't go to the dance with you, buddy.

Brewster went about it circuitously. He leaned back, his suit and shirt as pristine as Pete Maloney's were rumpled, and crossed his left leg over the right, clasping his left knee with both hands.

"First, Pete, the ambassador was attacked by three armed men while driving with Kate after their meeting with me."

Maloney interrupted. Characteristically, he was a step ahead. "Five men, Bill, two in front of the embassy, three in the car following. And Shalzar and his bodyguard knocked off the three in the car. We've heard all about it from the police; they're furious. They want to question the ambassador; they can't. And the Israelis will let them talk only to the bodyguard and only in the embassy lobby.

"We don't know who they are, although they look like Arabs. And we don't know why; that is, whether it's routine hatred or something they know about Shalzar's mission of the moment."

Bill had a rare flash of annoyance at his old friend. All right, all right, he felt like saying, I wasn't trying to get one up on you. I was just trying to supply some background to explain the tone of our meeting. All he actually said was, "Since you know all that, you can understand why it was not a relaxed talk."

"That and the fact that his Foreign Minister, Weismann, is arriving any hour," responded Maloney. Then he realized he had gone one up on Bill again, and to soften it said, "I wish I could have been a fly on the wall when you two got together for your chat." He made a point of showing envy.

Bill only smiled; he had heard the one-upsmanship and then the unspoken apology. He said, "Don't tell me you haven't bugged them?"

Pete put his hand on Bill's shoulder and gave him a look of mock reprimand. "We don't *do* that, old boy, haven't you heard?" Then he grinned and added, "Not in the new embassy, anyway. Not *yet,* anyway."

"In any event," Bill got himself back on the track, "it was rather a short, tense meeting." As he spoke, Bill realized he had been setting up an alibi, as if Pete were his superior, and he hadn't produced all he should have.

"As the expression goes, Shalzar hung tough. I told him you wanted to sell his . . . threat . . . but you didn't have enough to go on, and needed more. He said you should take a chance, trust him that they mean business."

"Yes, but what business is it they mean, that's the question . . ." Pete interrupted quickly, and just as quickly added, "I'm sorry, go ahead."

"Well, Pete, I said pretty much the same thing. I asked *him* to take a chance, to risk telling a little more. He said his government felt it had already taken enough risks, and in any event it was not his decision to make. And he wouldn't say any more."

"I guess that narrows down our range of options." Pete jumped in, only to be stopped by Brewster.

"He wouldn't say any more until the very end. Then he did tell me something, and I think he planned it so that he'd throw it at me on the way out, for dramatic effect, or perhaps to make it seem important.

"In any event," and now Pete was listening, waiting—Bill thought of the expression "hanging on every word" and realized this might be the first time since they had known each other that Pete had been so dependent on him. "As he was walking out, he said he thought it would be all right to give me another piece of information, for what it was worth. And what he told me was the name of this 'freedom of action' or threat, or whatever you want to call it." Bill paused. By God, I am savoring this moment, he thought. "He called it the Masada Plan. Does that mean anything to you?"

"No," Pete answered. "To you?"

"No." Brewster was relieved, he admitted to himself, that Pete hadn't heard of it either.

But the Secretary had the next best thing, access to the information. He jumped to his feet and headed out of the room and down the hall, his bulky body charging rather than merely walking. In sixty seconds he was back, and with him was a pale-looking woman of about forty, average in height, tending toward lankiness, her faded brown hair mixed with gray, her eyes a washed-out hazel. A pale woman altogether, Bill thought. Mousy. An old maid, he said to himself. He'd bet on it.

"This is Linda Janowitz," said the Secretary. "She's on my staff and she's an Israel specialist. And this is William Brewster."

"How do you do, Mrs. Janowitz." Brewster decided on the gallant presumption. They shook hands.

"It's Miss," she responded with a slight smile. "How do you do."

But even before the handshake could finish, Pete was right on the track. "What does the name Masada mean to you?" he asked. "How do you spell that, Bill, do you suppose?"

Miss Janowitz spoke quickly and decisively. "No, the English transliteration is M-A-S-A-D-A and the Hebrew pronunciation is *metz-ah-DAH*. It's the name of a famous fortress where, in A.D. 73, a group of Jewish Zealots, only 960 of them including women and children, held out against thousands of Romans, and then when it was certain they were going to be captured, committed mass suicide, rather than surrender into a life of slavery."

The men looked at each other. The information was both revelatory and puzzling. "I can see," Pete spoke first, "the name given to it as a last-ditch stand. But the suicide? Is that supposed to be a *threat? To us?*"

"There's more to it than that, I'm sure," Bill responded. "Or else, why did Shalzar stress—" and he started to add "nuclear arsenal" but remembered the woman standing there and stopped short. Linda Janowitz stood there, oozing deference but listening and watching intently, then offered more information.

"Masada has come to stand for more than just refusal to surrender, or suicide. 'Masada shall not fall again' has become a shibboleth, an attitude, a determination that the Jewish state never again shall be snuffed out."

Maloney wanted to talk with Brewster, alone, so he turned to the woman. "Linda, thanks. You don't know what a shortcut it is to have someone who knows his—" He stopped short, laughed, and corrected himself. "*Her* subject. Saves so much time. And time is what we need. You'll be nearby, won't you? I wouldn't want to go through this without knowing we can count on you."

Maloney could be imperious and male-chauvinistic but he knew how to make a subordinate feel appreciated, and the pleasure showed in the woman's eyes as she replied, "Of course, Mr. Secretary." To Bill she smiled, nodded and said only, "Mr. Brewster," before turning and walking out of the room.

Pete turned back to Bill and settled deeply into the sofa. "It's something," he said. "But not much. You know where it leaves things, don't you?"

Bill had the strong feeling Pete's question was more for rhetoric than for information and would soon be followed by an answer, one Bill wouldn't like. So although the banker was not quite sure how to reply, he thought he'd try something, "I suppose our fears of the seriousness of the threat are confirmed, and our hopes to learn more are unfulfilled, which leaves us back where we started. Only worse, because time is running out."

As Bill spoke, Pete just looked at him, a patient smile on his face. "And you know what *that* means, don't you?"

Bill smiled back. "Why don't you just tell me, Pete."

"It means, old boy, the ball is still in your court. You are the one who can find out more. And though we're closer to the deadline," Pete looked at his watch, which read 12:20, "in fact, we've got only twenty hours and forty minutes, we're no closer to any hard information. And we still need it."

Now Pete was getting to the part Bill didn't want to hear, and they both knew it. Pete leaned forward, ready to sell. And Bill sat up straight, preparing himself not to buy.

"Kate, because of what she believed to be the most important, the highest values, didn't hesitate to use you—and I don't mean anything evil in that word, *use*—to contact me. You were the one who could do that for her. Now, old boy, she is the one who can lead us to what we need: more information. The time has come to ask her if we can use her. Did you set up that meeting with her?"

Bill nodded. "She'll arrive at my suite downstairs in ten minutes. But asking her, Pete, I don't know. You want me to ask her to be a spy; there's no point in not being blunt about it, and I don't think I can. What am I supposed to do, suggest she sweet-talk Shalzar, run her fingers through his curly hair, and say 'Would the big strong ambassador tell itty-bitty me what he means by freedom of action'?"

Pete shook his head. "International crisis, Armageddon, oblivion, nothing makes man any less vain, especially where so-called love is involved. The idea of promoting intimacy between them is too much for you. Well, rest easy, old boy. I'm asking something completely different. I'm requesting a spy, not a goddamned Delilah. I'm asking that this afternoon, in one hour, she come up here for a crash course in how to use a miniaturized camera; I'm asking her to be rigged with a tape recorder the size of a book of matches." Then he grinned mischievously at Bill. "No, come to think of it. I'm not asking. *You're* asking."

Pete looked to his friend for a reaction. Bill had paled under his tan.

"No, I'm not, Pete. I wouldn't ask anybody to risk her life that way. I wouldn't ask anyone to spy on someone she loved. I wouldn't ask those things singly. And the two of them together? Not a chance."

Maloney stared hard at Brewster. He was ready to pursue this battle, not only because the issues meant a lot to him, but because

143

he relished the contest. "May I take it then, old boy, that you're against spying, that you disapprove of it as a national tactic, that the CIA and the CIC should be disbanded?"

"If you must know, Pete, I have come around to that position. I find the effort more and more useless and dirty and provocative." Actually, Bill felt this only with a number of reservations, but he omitted them, for the moment, to strengthen his position. He knew Pete wasn't ready for his answer. And he was right; Maloney was set back. But he recovered immediately and moved forward, like a fighter willing to take a few punches to corner his opponent and finish him.

"And does Kate agree with your position, old boy?"

"Well, we've never really discussed it, Pete, so I couldn't say."

Pete took on the look of a winning fighter. "I see, and you're not willing to find out if, perhaps, she *doesn't* agree. If perhaps she *is* prepared to—yes, spy—for the sake of her country and the entire world, *including* Israel."

Bill had anticipated Pete on this, though, and had another line of defense. "What you don't understand is that, even if I *did* believe in spying as a tactic, I'd not ask anyone to spy on someone he or she loved. Suppose I asked you to spy on Muffie, would you like it?"

Pete kept charging. "Well, I might like it and I might not. But I can tell you I'd be absolutely furious if, in a matter of great importance—and I think you'll grant the Masada business is that, to put it mildly—you didn't give *me* the chance to decide." Maloney punched his chest with his fist as he emphasized the word 'me.' Then he extended the forefinger of the fist and pointed it at Bill.

"I might say no to you. And dammit, if I thought it was of overriding importance, especially if I thought it was for Muffie's own good, I might say yes. But, hell, I wouldn't want *you* to say it for me."

And continuing to point the finger, Pete took Bill's thrust and turned it back on him. "No, my friend, your decision not to ask is one thing, and one thing only. It is an ego trip, pure and simple. You don't want to risk the personal hurt of a rebuff. You don't want to risk being thought a meanie who'd ask a girl to spy on her boyfriend. You don't want to risk the possibility Kate Colby would, in years to come, tell Dov Shalzar about how Bill Brewster, the bad loser, had asked a nasty thing of her. Bill Brewster, the tender ego, is afraid to take a chance, for fear someone will say no. He hasn't learned that when you ask, someone may say no, but he, or she, may also say yes. Whereas, if you don't ask, you may be *sure* you won't get a yes."

Now Pete was throwing knockout punches.

"Bill Brewster has never faced up to the possibility that Kate Colby might, just *might* have said yes to him a year ago, if he had asked her another question. Just come out and asked 'Will you?' instead of pussyfooting around it. Of course, she might also have said no.

But since he didn't ask for fear of getting a no—what happened? He *got* the no. And Shalzar got the girl. And you can bet that when the ambassador needs Kate Colby—for spying or anything else—*he* asks!"

Brewster sat there on the sofa, motionless, as the attack hit him, his face getting whiter and whiter, lips compressing more and more. And when Maloney finished, even he was appalled by the cuts he had opened. He reached over and squeezed his friend's shoulder.

"Christ, I really gave it to you, Bill. I think I went beyond the line of duty to do it, too. In fact I know I did. I've been planning to say those things to you for a long time; I just never thought this would be the time. I kind of forgot the world crisis for the Bill Brewster crisis. Well, maybe not a crisis, but I've seen it tie you up and cripple you for so long now, I couldn't let it go. I know how rough this was, old boy. I'm sorry."

Bill had not been looking at Pete all this time. Now, by putting more and more pressure on his shoulder with his right hand, Pete forced him to look at him.

"I'm sorry, old boy. But I meant every word of it."

At last Bill spoke. "I guess you're just describing Bill Brewster accurately, Pete, and I guess I just don't like hearing it. And I guess that at forty-seven I'm not a Pete Maloney or a Dov Shalzar. I guess I am I."

Pete took his hand from Bill's shoulder and said, gently, "I guess you are you—and let me tell you, that's a pretty damned fine thing to be, even if once in a while it does inconvenience me."

Then, having seen his fish take the hook, the Secretary of State gave it a final yank to make sure it was embedded.

Pete's voice was almost a whisper. "Kate has *got* to be asked. *I'll* ask her."

Bill felt the hook and didn't even wriggle. He stood up and with a reluctant, admiring smile, answered, "No, you clever son of a bitch. This is one yes-or-no I'll get for myself."

Pete's last words were spoken to Bill's back as he was walking out. "When you get your yes, old boy, bring her up here. We've got a lot of work to do."

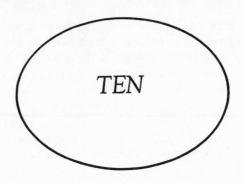

TEN

Back in his suite, three floors and three minutes away from the exhilaration of Pete's challenge, Bill Brewster felt his apprehension
returning. Why am I so nervous, he asked himself, as he took off his
jacket and sagged down on his sofa. What's on the line here, the future of the world? Or my ego? Or have I just had too damned many
cups of coffee?

He reached up and yanked his tie loose. If it's Doomsday or the
coffee, I'm all right, he thought. If it's ego, then I am indeed a handi-
capped person. Crippled by pride. As he sat there, he found, almost
to his surprise, his hands were reaching up automatically to tighten
his tie again, to look presentable. "Presentable," a word from his
childhood. From his proper upbringing. Never attract attention to
yourself by looking outstandingly good or bad. Presentable is beautiful. Fitting in is fine.

Almost angrily, he gave his tie an extra tug to loosen it further,
then put his hands down. Strange debilitating combination, he said
to himself, puritanism and ego. Don't ever be so noticeable anyone
would comment on your appearance. But sit here paralyzed at the
prospect of being turned down by Kate Colby. It won't be the first
rejection, he argued. Yes, but never before has it been so ideological,
so impersonal, he rebutted. Yet you'll take it as personally as a refused
date.

Brewster stood, and savoring every move, took off his tie, unbuttoned his cuffs and rolled up his shirt sleeves. Long-sleeved, broad-
cloth shirts in July, how's that for "presentable?" Then he headed
for the small kitchen and looked through the wine rack, fingering a
Chambertin, sliding it out, pushing it back in. A '67 Chambertin at
12:30 on a summer Thursday, with no food, and one's tie off, is just
not proper; it's showing off, conspicuous consumption.

Conspicuous consumption? For whom to see? The Chambertin. Now.

146

If you're going to break out, start by breaking out the good wine. There was some kind of pun in that, he said to himself, but he didn't pursue it. Instead he pursued the idea of breaking out, feeling a trifle foolish to be worried about molding a new personality right then and there. Forty-seven years, he told himself, I've been enduring this one, and to uncover a new personality and the Masada Plan in one day is too much.

He ran a corkscrew through the cork, pulled it, poured himself a large glass of the Chambertin and sipped it. By God, it was a luxurious wine to taste—with your tie off! He'd have to try it more often. Brewster took the glass and bottle and walked back to the sofa.

No, character renovation was too big a project to begin just now, and the cost was too high. He'd better concentrate on a smaller task, saving the world.

If the Masada Plan was as frightening as it purported to be, and the US would not move on it without more information, and if more information depended on Kate Colby's spying, and if Kate's spying depended on his persuasion . . . well, perhaps he had a right to be nervous.

Why was this little job all tangled up with Kate, who had rejected him? And Dov, who had won her away? And Pete, who always managed to stay a stride ahead of him? Well, Bill, he said to himself, you have certainly put those three hard facts of your life baldly. Putting things baldly was something he hardly ever did, and as he listened to himself this time, he was startled.

"In vino veritas," he said, half aloud, looking down into his wineglass. In fact, the glass was barely touched; the intoxication flowed from the moment, from the task ahead of him, not the Burgundy. Another plain fact was that the very entanglements he was lamenting were the reasons he was involved in the Masada Plan. Without his attachments to Kate and Pete, he wouldn't be faced with the spy recruitment assignment. And that closeness made him all the more determined to go back to Pete with Kate's signature on the dotted line. The metaphor was so businesslike it was depressing, he thought. Then how about Kate's head on a stick? That was horrifying, but closer. Bill drank some more wine; this time almost a gulp.

He was in a classical Walter Mitty situation, and for the first time knew the elation of it. A casual passerby fixing a vital, complicated machine with a nail file while the world marveled, pocketa, pocketa. He was in a unique position to thwart a danger that was—what?—he didn't know, exactly, but was certainly widespread and nuclear, and once you've said that, you were talking about the lives of hundreds of thousands, perhaps millions of people.

Police sirens broke into his reverie. Far below, on Fiftieth Street, squad cars were arriving, looking like Corgi toys. A dozen uniformed policemen were pushing against a crowd of sixty or seventy demonstrators. Under the direction of a sergeant, the cops were trying to confine the crowd to thirty yards of sidewalk on the northeast corner of Fiftieth and Park Avenue. Under the urging of a muscular young man with a fringe of beard and a yarmulke, shouting through a bullhorn, the demonstrators were trying to cross the street and block the Waldorf Towers entrance.

Brewster couldn't make out the chanting, but down on the street it was clear. "Down with Maloney, long live Israel!" was the cry, until their leader switched to "Evict the Nazi from the Waldorf!" Neither slogan was a model of vivid imagery or flawless meter, but considering the haste with which this group had been assembled and come all the way from Borough Park in Brooklyn, it was a logistical wonder they were there at all.

They were a result of the telephoning going on all over two floors of the Seligsohn Communications Building. At ten that morning, one of the calls had reached an Orthodox Jewish Day Camp in Borough Park. Volunteers from among the counselors, staff, and the older campers had been organized, calls made to parents of the younger children. The plan was to meet at eleven at the Day Camp. Meanwhile, in the Arts and Crafts room, signs were being prepared. "Save Israel!" "Send Help Now." "We Demand Action." "Airlift Now!" "Why Are You Waiting, Maloney?"

With the signs, the group marched to the subway, and around noon, surfaced again at Fifty-first Street and Lexington Avenue. Just minutes after Bill Brewster entered the Waldorf Towers, they reached the entrance. At first they were not sure what to do and by the time their leader decided they should inconvenience the Secretary of State's landlord, the Waldorf, by blocking the entrance, enough police had arrived to talk to them and force them across the street.

Only when they were confined to the small corner area did the demonstrators realize they had lost their chance to clog the entrance and lobby. They grew louder and more militant, but, a mixture of young teen-agers and housewives, with a few older men, they were no match for the bulk of the fast-arriving policemen.

As Brewster watched, a truck with barricades pulled up, completing the confinement of the group. But if their intention to obstruct the Towers physically was thwarted, they were succeeding in drawing attention to their message.

As noon passed, lunch-hour crowds were attracted by the signs and the shouting, and soon several patrolmen were assigned to keep the sidewalks clear. Through a gap left by that reassignment, two day-camp counselors, feeling their manhood, made a dash across the street. One was tackled at once and grabbed by two cops. The second almost made it across the street before he was trapped between two limousines parked in front of the Towers. For a few seconds, the youth and the

148

three circling cops had a standoff, then the boy made a dash for the hotel entrance and ran into the arms of a 200-pound black patrolman, who grabbed him in a bear hug. The boy's flailing arms looked like matchsticks to the cop's as they moved together toward a squad car. Oddly, the black man's face seemed red with the exertion and the heat. Soon both boys were in the back of the car and were taken away. They were driven south on Lexington to Forty-third Street, where the cop in the front passenger seat got out, opened the rear door and said to the boys: "OK, get out, get on the subway and go home. If we see you back there we'll arrest you and charge you with assaulting a police officer." Then the car drove off, leaving the teenagers wondering whether they should obey or go back.

Driving the two boys away, giving the impression they were to be arrested, had the desired effect on the demonstrators, who chanted more loudly than ever but made no more tries at storming the hotel. Even as Brewster watched from above, their numbers grew, a greater and greater yield from the steady telephoning.

The reaction of passersby to the crowd, the signs, the chanting, the singing of Hebrew songs was mostly puzzled. Few knew of the gravity of the Middle East war; some, having left for work that morning without having read, heard or seen any news, didn't even know of the fighting; many didn't realize the Secretary of State was at the Waldorf; a few heard and saw the name Maloney without knowing who he was.

One boy, ambling by with an oversized portfolio that had the words JIFFY STAT stenciled on it, raised his fist and shouted "Right on!" not so much to support Israel as to encourage anybody who stood tall against the cops.

Looking down, Brewster reacted to the demonstration with a sense of distance far greater than the fifteen stories separating him from the Borough Park Jews. I hold the key to what they want, he thought, and none of them even knows who I am. I could walk right into their midst and none of them would turn and look at me. And yet if I fail, I'm failing them—among many others.

Almost everyone who knew Bill Brewster would have been astonished to learn he had a keen sense of failure, because there was no way in which he did not seem a thorough success.

He was wealthy, with inherited money to start, but substantially enhanced by his own earnings and investments. His middle name was that of a Dutch patroon forbear, but his lineage was predominantly English. He was tall, handsome, athletic, the president of a major investment house, and a trustee of two museums, four community organizations, and one dance company. He had four teen-aged children, all blonde, all blue-eyed, all beautiful. He was a Coke commercial gone mad, the supposed dream of every American and the actual dream of most.

He could not honestly say he was displeased with his circumstances;

nor did they elate him the way they did the characters in the Coke commercials. The reason was not any specific setback (those had occurred, of course, his divorce, his failure with Kate); but rather a dissatisfaction with himself that he could best express by telling two stories, which he called his "liquid" stories.

The first went back twenty-six years, when he was an undergraduate and home in Westport for a few weeks between a summer climb in the Alps and the fall term at Princeton.

He was sitting in the locker of the tennis club and through the thin wall separating men's and women's sections he overheard the two girls with whom he'd been playing doubles. Guests at the club, they didn't know how thin the walls were.

"Big Bill plays a marvelous game," said one. "And he doesn't even work up a sweat."

"Sweat?" responded the other. "Bill Brewster wouldn't know *how* to sweat. It's déclassé."

Looking back on that locker-room exchange, which Bill did often, he had come to decide he had made a fateful wrong choice. He had been attracted to both girls, but had pursued the one who had commented on his tennis, rather than his inability to sweat. Her name was Penelope Spencer, and he not only pursued her, he caught and married her, although that didn't come until after Princeton, two years in the Navy and the Harvard B School.

Somewhere in the five years between the tennis meeting and the sumptuous Episcopal wedding, Bill came to realize, and was sure Penny did, too, that their match was a mistake. He saw her as the final lock on his haut-bourgeois Westport cage; she saw in him the immature rebel, the eternal child perversely denying a life-style 99 out of 100 Americans would give their eyeteeth to attain.

Her nickname for him, "Big Bill," was gradually joined by "My big boy" and then "My big baby," each more diminutive and more derisive than the last. "My big baby," she'd once said, "thinks it's sinful to be out on the grass swatting tennis balls or sitting around the club pool having a drink when he could be swatting cockroaches in a walkup and splashing around an open fire hydrant in the East Village."

A clear case of reductio ad absurdum, he'd thought; desiring freedom from his cage was a long way from wanting cockroaches. But she used the tactic repeatedly and effectively, especially with his parents, for whose benefit she'd usually add something like, "Of course, I told him to go ahead; he'd always know where to find me. But please, I asked him, on his way back, stop somewhere and have a bath."

Penny pronounced the word almost as if it were "bahth" and almost as if she were English, but then Penny was a Spencer and the Spencers arrived in Greenwich by way of a long line of Boston blue bloods.

150

Very tall and blonde with a full body that was at first voluptuous and then merely heavy, she would have been ideal if Bill's primary purpose in marriage had been to spawn WASP gods and goddesses. However, their emotional pairing was not nearly as felicitous, and the longer their engagement spun out, the clearer their incompatibility became. And the more they felt committed to "going through with it."

Bill knew he was more to blame for that than Penny. She held the honest if benighted hope that her "big boy" would divest himself of those foolish ideas and settle down to loving the manner to which he had been born. He alone knew he didn't want to settle into the plush suburban life, with its daily commute and its cocktail parties and its weekends of tennis and sailing. And he knew Penny couldn't change and he hadn't the courage to confront her with their "problem," because the only solution was to end their engagement. Of course, that was impossible; too many Spencers and Brewsters were counting on them. Their children would be too beautiful.

They were married on a Saturday in June in her church, in Greenwich, both of them knowing the honeymoon had ended even before the ceremony began. Bill had wanted a black friend who had served in the Navy with him to be one of the ushers. Scornfully, Penny demurred. "What are you trying to *prove*, Bill? Does my big boy want to use his own wedding as a showcase for his rebellion? And does he want to use that poor Negro as his puppet? Is it fair to him, to use him that way, to throw him into a situation where he won't *fit in?* And it is fair to your old friends, one of whom will be snubbed merely because he is *our* kind of person and you want to set up a quota system at your own *wedding?*"

Penny could be clever and he could be weak and he had yielded, the first of many times he would yield—and resent it.

One frigid January evening a few years into their marriage, as he dropped into a chair by the fire after spending three hours commuting in the snow, he said to her, "I want to live in Manhattan. Avoid that torture trip five days a week. Have more time in the city where I work. We can spend weekends here, or in Southhampton, or skiing."

Penny hated the idea; it would take her too far from her golf and sailing and tennis and bring her too close to the "dark smelly hordes" she detested. Finally, reluctantly, she agreed that when the children had all gone off to boarding school they could move to New York.

At last, they did, to a twelve-room triplex co-op at Seventieth and Park. That was the beginning of the end of their marriage, for they found a whole new realm of subjects to quarrel about. He wanted to try the New York City Opera occasionally, instead of confining themselves to those stultifying, social Monday nights at the Met. She thought the people who went to the City Opera "tacky." Once in a while, he suggested they visit an ethnic or neighborhood restaurant rather than sticking to their rounds of La Caravelle and La Grenouille and La Goulue—the la-la-la circuit, he began to call them. She called his choices the "creepy-crawlies."

Once in a while, he wanted to spend a weekend in the city and when he did Penny would just throw a suitcase into the car, take whichever of the kids happened to be home for the weekend, and go out to the Westport house without him. This had led, after a year of tugging and pulling, to a kind of limited de facto separation, for soon she was leaving on Friday mornings and returning Monday nights, and as her Connecticut weekends grew longer and longer, his grew rarer and rarer. And then some weeks she just stayed in Connecticut. Bill became a demi-bachelor who found he got along with her much better when they were apart.

Brewster was forty-two years old when he had his first taste of adultery. It was on one of those lonely weekdays when Penny had stayed in Westport between two long weekends. One of the Patton partners invited Bill to make a foursome for dinner with his wife's sister, who was visiting from Nashville.

Bill had often thought of making love to other women, had decided he wanted to, but never would take the initiative. Then came the evening five years ago when circumstances not only made it possible but inevitable.

The evening had begun in a shabby, comfortable family restaurant in Little Italy. When the partner had asked Bill to pick a place to eat, he had chosen this one eagerly, because it was one of those Penny "wouldn't be caught dead at."

Her name was Suzanne. Not Susan; smiling, she had corrected him on that. Now, five years later, he confessed he couldn't remember her last name. What he did remember was that she was twenty-five, with a slim, full-bosomed body and a dark, bony, exquisite face; physically a total contrast to the blonde, tennis-court robustness of his wife. But mostly, he remembered Suzanne's eyes.

For several reasons the first sight of her hit him like a martini on an empty stomach. First, she represented the coalescing of his fantasies. Second, he was literally sex starved; he and Penny were reduced to making love, perfunctorily, once every two or three weeks. Third, she was young, pretty, attentive, and bright—"bright as a Penny" he had later said to himself, and laughed. Fourth were her eyes.

They were dark brown, which made them exotic to a man who couldn't think of a soul in his family—even going out to cousins—with anything other than blue eyes. They were inordinately large for her face. And they were the most expressive eyes he had ever seen. Thinking back on them, as he often did, he would ask himself if perhaps he had overvalued them because of the charged circumstances of the encounter. No, he'd decided he hadn't.

Each time she looked at him, whether listening or speaking, her eyes locked into his, glowing with a luminosity that made him think she was plugged into an outside power source. And they showed so many levels of incandescence. Once, toward the end of the meal, when hearty pasta, veal piccata, and a down-to-earth Valpolicella—Penny would have called it peasant food—had made them all feel relaxed and warm, his partner told a joke, and as they all laughed, her super-heated brown eyes met Bill's cool blue ones, and seemed to tell him: for the moment we're sharing a joke, but there's more, much more.

Never before had a look taken physical hold of him that way—of his heart, of his gut, of his groin. In the twenty-two years he had known Penny, never had he received a signal from her like this one look. All they needed was the opportunity. Within half an hour, they had it.

Bill's partner and his wife lived in Darien. Suzanne was staying at the New York Hilton; she taught American literature at Vanderbilt, and was in town for a teachers' conference, also at the Hilton. Abruptly—so abruptly Bill considered, but dismissed, the possibility it was part of a plan—his partner looked at the wall clock.

"My gosh," he said, "is that the right time? If it is we've got twenty-five minutes to drop Suze at her hotel and catch the last train!"

The girl and Bill tumbled over each other trying to reassure the other two; she that she could look after herself, he that he would see her safely to her hotel.

"Let's all get in a cab," said Bill as they were rushing from the restaurant, "and we'll make Grand Central the first stop, the Hilton the second, and my apartment the third."

Which was indeed the order of the stops, with a substantial interval between the second and third.

On the way to Grand Central, Bill sat up front with the cabby while the other three sat in the back. When they reached the terminal, he jumped out, said goodbye to partner and wife, and watched as they dashed for their train. Then he slid into the back seat with the girl and shut the door.

For all his inexperience and caution, he had no doubt about what would happen next. He moved toward her, she toward him. She reached her hand to the back of his neck, pulling him toward her. They kissed, a long, heated, openmouthed kiss, which they held all the way across Forty-second Street from Park to Sixth Avenue. Not a word was said until they made the turn to head uptown.

"They call you Suze, do they?"

"Yes."

"May I?"

"What?"

"Call you Suze."

"You may do anything you want."

Her voice and her eyes reassured him, as if he were the younger one and she the older. Her eyes had his and held them until they approached the hotel. Then she added, "Will you come up?" There was no, "For a few minutes." Or "For a drink." Just, "Will you come up?"

Bill nodded and smiled. He could not have disengaged his eyes had he wanted to.

"Yes . . . Suze. I'd like to." He almost sighed it.

Fifteen minutes later they were in bed, where they spent the next four hours in the most profound and delicious lovemaking he had experienced in the forty-two years of his life. For Bill, this was not a difficult superlative to claim, for he had been a virgin until he was eighteen, and the dozen or so sexual encounters he had had before his engagement and marriage to Penny had been hurried and clumsy.

Part of the excitement was his first oral sex. Eighteen years of lovemaking with Penny—the best year had been the one before they were married—had given them a kind of routine efficiency, but she made it clear she regarded "sucking and licking" as disgusting. Once, at his suggestion, she had agreed to try, and did for five or six seconds, eyes closed, repugnance on her face. He never suggested it again.

With Suzanne it was delightful, warm, juicy, overpoweringly arousing and—he said to himself with a feeling of insouciance—tasty. At twenty-five, she was the age he had been when he married, so their lovemaking represented for him a kind of turning back the clock, a starting over.

He left her at three in the morning, with a tender, intimate kiss, his heart and mind flowing over with affection for her. He never saw her again, but those four hours in her bed renewed for him the possibilities of passionate sex. After that he made love to a number of women, a few before he was legally separated, most after. None of it was as highly charged as that night with Suzanne, but all of it was freer and richer than the rote performances he and Penny had gone through.

Though a new sex life had opened for him that night, he continued the form of his old married life for two years, deciding to break it after the incident which became the second of his "liquid" stories.

The setting for the second story was similar to that for the first; the men's washroom at Patton and Company. Two young brokers were sizing up the Patton brass, a bit too loudly and carelessly. Again, Bill could hear them without being seen. Soon, the two got to William Schuyler Brewster, who was then executive vice president.

"Yeah, capable as hell," said one, "and a considerate guy to work for. But pisses ice water."

Carefully, Bill stayed out of sight until they left, then he walked back to his office, saying to himself: After two years of what I thought was freeing up, I still piss ice water. And I'm locked into a situation that will keep me pissing it forever.

154

Three months later he told Penny he wanted a divorce. She exploded. She called him an "immature bastard," told him what a lousy lover she thought he was, taunted him with the number of affairs she'd had, threw the names of the men at him. For five months she dragged him through hell, but at the end of it he had a legal separation, and a year later, a divorce.

His new status left him feeling freer and happier than he had in a long time, but with no romantic attachment. Then he met Kate.

The buzzer sounded. Almost as if his daydreaming had cued her appearance, she was at the door of his suite. Trying to snap out of his reverie and concentrate on the job ahead of him, he walked to the door. Bill remembered what Pete had said, "If you don't ask . . . ."

He opened the door; there stood Kate, smiling, looking wary. This will have to be a new Brewster taking her on, he told himself. He saw the wariness; instead of returning it, he stepped forward decisively, put his hands on her shoulders, drew her toward him, kissed her warmly on the cheek.

With an arm around her, he walked her to the sofa and sat her down. "I have no food to speak of," he said, "but the Chambertin is passing good. Let me pour you a glass."

"Thanks, I don't think I want one." Kate was bemused, slightly suspicious, and more than slightly curious about Bill's intentions.

"You can't stop me from pouring," he said, heading for the tiny bar where he had put the open bottle of wine. "All you can do is refuse to drink, and who knows, you may change your mind."

He poured the wine, walked to her, and took a tiny risk. Instead of placing it on the table next to her, he handed her the glass. He'd prevail, he'd make her take it. Of course, she might tell him to put it down, which would be a snub as tiny as the risk, but what the hell.

She took it, smiled, and said, "Thank you." Then she put it on the table. He smiled back, proud he had taken the tiny chance. Their eyes met; she'd realized what had happened. But she took it, he reminded himself, she took it.

Bill walked to a tall armchair, pulled it closer to the sofa so he could be an arm's length away from her, and sat. Kate had on a green, short-sleeved jersey blouse, white linen skirt, and white sandals. Her legs were bare and tanned. He looked at her slim ankles and strong, full calves; he had always admired them and, when she'd complained that they were too muscular, had replied, "You have the legs of a tennis player." To which she'd said, "Maybe Penny would like them; they're wasted on me."

Now he had to ask.

Again he wondered how to start, indeed, whether he could work up the nerve to start at all. To hell with how, he told himself. Just start. He took a deep breath.

"Kate, I want to ask something of you, something that means a lot to many, many people."

Leaning forward, uncrossing her tanned, bare legs, she broke in. "Bill, I'm not sure I want you to; I'm not sure I want to hear it."

He smiled at her, hoping he looked confident. "It's like the wine. You can't stop me from pouring. All you can do is refuse to drink." He stopped, then, almost as if Pete were looking over his shoulder, added, "However, I don't think you will refuse.

"I've told Pete Maloney everything Dov said to me about the Middle East situation and the Israeli threat. He agrees we're all in a deadly serious position. But he doesn't know how serious or what position. And he doesn't know enough to convince the President and the Soviet Union they ought to jawbone the Arabs into a cease-fire and rollback and the other things on the list, which will take muscle and raise serious risks of its own.

"Before they can undertake that, they must know more. I've gone back to Dov to try to get it; he's given me virtually nothing. Which would leave us at a dead end—if there were not one other way out. That way, the only way, involves you."

Damn it, he said to himself, don't take all these dainty little side-steps. You started this with some panache, keep at it. He began to raise his wineglass to his lips. Uh-uh, he thought, do this without help. He lowered the glass.

"That way is for you to go in and see what you can learn."

Bill watched her. She did not look surprised. She lifted her glass and sipped from it. She could use some wine, after all. He was pleased; again it was a tiny thing, but a sign. He had been able to abstain; she'd felt enough pressure to need the taste.

"You want me to spy, Bill. That's it, plain and simple, isn't it?"

"Yes. That's it, plain and simple." Another victory, he said to himself, not so tiny. He had intended a long circuitous reply. At the last instant he junked it in favor of the simple one.

Kate sat shaking her head from side to side. "No way, Bill. No way at all. You want me to go to the Israelis as an invited guest, and abuse their hospitality. To cheat them. That I won't do. You want me to spy on a man I . . . have a great deal of affection for. That I won't do."

The moment had surprises for both of them. When she hesitated before describing her feelings for Dov, she was more upset, more worried about Bill's reaction, than she thought she'd be. She dropped the word love she'd been planning to use. Bill, on the other hand, expecting the word love, was a lot less worried, in the anticipation and the event, than he thought he'd be.

Her upset led her to add a bonus, which made him feel even better. "And, Bill, I wouldn't do it to you, either." As she spoke, it flashed through her mind that she had been asked to do it to him—and by

Dov. Here she was, Ms. Clean, with everyone beating on her door to be dirty. She needed another sip of the wine. By God, he did serve a good wine, considering how lousy the occasion was.

"My main reason is not the abuse of hospitality or the affection; it's that spying on anybody, anytime, for any reason, is just not my thing."

Bill stood and walked to the window, looking down at, without seeing, the anti-Maloney protesters, who now numbered nearly a hundred, but were no longer fighting the police. He was framing an answer. A day ago it would have been a gracious acceptance of her refusal. Now he realized the subject would be closed, unless he could keep it alive; he was determined to refuse the refusal. The time for tiny triumphs was past; he needed a big one. For the world. For him.

He walked to the sofa and sat next to her, aiming every molecule of force, of will, in his body at her. "And do you think asking some-one to spy is *my* thing, Kate? Especially someone I . . . have a great deal of affection for?"

He parodied her pause after the word "I," making his so long it was almost a caricature. Not very subtle for Bill Brewster, he said to him-self, then added, Good for Bill Brewster.

"Let me explain to you," he went on, "why I hope—why I know—you'll agree."

She began to shake her head again, to which he responded, "Just listen." She stopped the shaking; she sipped at her wine and she lis-tened.

"You'll agree with me that what the Israelis hope to do with this plan is not cause widespread destruction among others, but rather prevent their own destruction. As things now stand, they will fail in both. The end result will be a holocaust, in Israel and wherever else their plan is aimed.

"One thing we may be sure of about this Masada Plan: it is not directed merely at the Arabs. If it were, the Israelis would go ahead and carry it out; they would be amply justified by the Arab attack on them. Since they have not, since they have given us elaborate warning, since they make a point of stressing their nuclear capability, I think we may assume there will be devastating repercussions outside the Arab countries, probably in the United States."

She was listening and she was not shaking her head—that much he could see and no more. He grabbed from it what encouragement he could and plowed ahead.

"I could say: Do it for your country, Kate, to save it from a danger we estimate will be horrendous. And I'm not embarrassed to say it. Patriotism is not yet completely out of date, not to me it isn't.

"I'm saying: Do it for your country; I'm also saying a lot more. Do it for all countries, for humanity. Do it for Israel.

"I'm also saying: Do it for Dov Shalzar.

"Though I don't know exactly what the Masada Plan is, I'm sure there is an ambiguity to it; that is, it's both a destructive act of some kind and the threat of that act. And I'm sure there's nothing Dov and his country want more than to have the *threat* work—which would mean stopping the Arabs and granting Israel its demands—so that Israel doesn't have to carry out the *act*.

"Nor do *we* want them to carry out the act, so it follows we'd much prefer the success of the threat. Right now neither of us can have what we both want, because, for reasons known only to Dov and the Israelis, they will not make their threat specific enough to warrant our acting on it."

Sally took another sip of wine. It hadn't occurred to her she'd be forced to take sides in this thing, but if she were, she certainly didn't want to side against her own country. Yes, she was cynical about American society, but by God, she did stand when the flag went by; she laughed at herself as she did. But she stood. And she knew damned well if battle lines were drawn and she had to look across the field and see the American flag on the other side, she'd not like it one bit. Bill had made her think of all that. She was still a long way from accepting a role as an American spy, but a bit closer to it than she had been at the start.

All this occurred to her as he spoke. When he paused for a moment she interjected an objection. "I think you'll grant Dov and the Israelis aren't stupid. If more information is so essential, and you've told them so, why don't they just supply it? If they know it will save them, us, whoever, why aren't they eager to give it?"

"Those are questions you should ask Dov," Bill replied. "I don't know the answers. No, they're not stupid. Maybe they're taking a terrific chance they can get what they want without revealing anything.

"But Kate, make no mistake about this: they have miscalculated. We shall not take any steps to satisfy their demands and meet their deadline based on what they've disclosed thus far. I've told this to Dov. Either he doesn't believe it, or he is bound by orders."

Bill's voice was no longer dégagé and elegant; he was pouring on urgency. "We're on a collision course, Kate, and if what the Israelis are hinting is true, the collision will come with a great big bang. And by the clock it will come in twenty hours, although we probably have less time than that if we are to turn off all the spigots, Arab and Israeli and God knows what other, early enough to make sure there are no fatal drips at deadline time.

"Now perhaps the Israelis think we're bluffing. I can assure you the Secretary of State is not bluffing. The damned problem is that while the two sides circle each other and snarl and probe, time is running out. Something has to change that, now, Kate. Some new input has to break that deadlock. It's like getting stuck halfway through a crossword puzzle: you need fill in only one new word for a realm of additional possibilities to open up."

Bill was looking at her more fiercely than she had ever seen him look before. That's one handsome WASP face, she thought. The only thing it ever lacked was toughness, an edge, and it sure has it now.

"You may be uncomfortable with this news, Kate, but in all this world, we know of only one person who can break the impasse, supply the new word to get us back solving the puzzle again. You. This is the future of the United States we're talking about, and Israel. And the earth, and a lot of innocent little babies thereon. You see, there's nothing I won't say, Kate. And all of it true. And Kate, it's Dov we're talking about, too."

Bill had slowed her, almost to a dead stop; he could see it in her face and he was pleased. But he needed more, so he pressed on.

"How do you think I feel, Kate, asking a woman I love—and you'll have to forgive me if I say that straight out instead of circumlocuting it with my customary dignity—asking a woman I love to spy on the man *she* loves. Talk about a no-win situation! Put yourself in my place for a moment, and think how I must have felt when Pete asked me to 'recruit' you. Well, I want to tell you what went through my mind then, and what should be going through yours now."

Bill grinned at her for an instant. "And if it's not going through, perhaps I can start it."

Kate wasn't sure whether she should call her response to all this hypnotized or paralyzed. She felt like a small, defenseless animal about to be swallowed whole by a snake. And I mean "snake" as a compliment, she thought. Who'd have thought Bill could open his mouth this wide? This is the most determined I've ever seen him look off a tennis court, she said to herself. I should be saying "not a chance" to his offer, and getting up and walking out.

But she sat there. She picked up her glass; it was empty and she'd have loved another sip. But she sat there. Bill jumped up, took the glass, poured her some wine, returned it. Kate could barely break through her spell enough to whisper "Thank you." He resumed.

"Here's what went through my mind. I thought ahead to the end of all this—and there's going to be an end, tomorrow morning at nine o'clock—and I said to myself, Bill old boy, one of two things can happen. First, there's what the strategists like to call the worst possible case; here it would be the world in some kind of nuclear shambles. For the purposes of the discussion, let's say Bill Brewster is a survivor. And he looks around at the ashes and says to himself: I had a chance to do something about this. Just a chance. Can't say it would have worked. But a chance. *And I chose not to take it.* I chose not to try."

Is this what should be going through my mind, she asked herself as she watched and listened to him. Is it? No, no, no. I should be thinking about precisely how I'm going to tell him to fuck off. In fact, I should be telling him. But there was no way she could do it, and she knew that, although she still didn't know whether to call it paralysis or hypnosis. She could not bring herself to utter a word, and he went on.

"Then there's the other outcome. The crisis is averted. The collision course is changed, the explosion does not take place. And I walk into Central Park—let's say it's tomorrow afternoon, and that is so awfully close. It's a beautiful day, clear, even the air in Manhattan seems healthy. And the litter isn't too bad, and there are some mothers with kids, and bicyclists, and a few joggers and a softball game. In one of the playgrounds, I see a young brother and sister on a swing, and I fasten on them maybe because with their towheads and blue eyes they look like my own kids.

"And I say to myself, Maybe, just maybe, they are alive because of me. I may have saved their lives. There was a crisis, and for once I was not out sailing, or playing tennis, or going over my portfolio, or quarreling with my wife or having a martini to forget the quarrel. An opportunity was handed to me—God knows I didn't go looking for it—but it was there, and at least I took it. And more, I did what I had to.

"And there are those kids. No, I can't say for sure I saved them. But I did what I had to, and there they are, alive and swinging."

Bill took a sip of his wine and looked at Kate watching him, her eyes wide and intent. "Want more wine?" he asked. Her glass was empty again. She just shook her head no. He had her. She had stopped running away; she was in a state of perfect equilibrium now; one nudge and she would start tilting toward him.

He went for the nudge.

"I've one more thing to say about my own feelings, which may interest you. I've undertaken all this, and especially this asking you to spy, which is so tough for someone who detests spying as I do, because I am tired of being a sidelines figure in those activities that vitally affect this world and its people. I am tired of sitting in my VIP seat and commenting on what is going on in the arena, and then worrying only about how it will affect the market.

"I keep thinking of it in an egotistical way. I think of writing memoirs. What do I have to put into them that I, or my kids, or anyone could read and conclude: this person *mattered*. He *changed* something.

"How about you, Kate? Isn't the curse of the journalist that she is always reporting actions, without ever really being an actor? Would you be pleased with your diary, if one day in the future you had to pick it up and read a page that said: I had a chance to be an actor in a global drama. And I turned it down. Even stiff old Bill Brewster took the chance. But I turned it down."

Bill watched her breathlessly. And thought, this is the way I should have spoken to her last year at that dinner. On that hot August night.

She had agreed to have dinner with him that August night after putting him off for two weeks. He had been wondering why, although his reticence, his pride, had kept him from asking. Finally he got his answer at a Chinese restaurant on East Forty-eighth Street. He didn't like the place but she had insisted upon it. When he got there he found out why. It was long, narrow, charming, but rather noisy, with small tables. Crowded as they were, shoulder to shoulder, with people at adjoining tables, there was little chance for intimacy. Which is what she had wanted. She wanted to tell him something and the less chance for a rebuttal, the better.

Kate was already there, and having a drink, which surprised him. Later, it became clear she had been setting herself to deliver an unpleasant message. Her smile was strained, not the impulsive reaction to his arrival that he had seen other times. She was wearing white trousers and a pink silk jacket, and looking tanned, athletic, and sensational.

This was the second time around for their affair. A year and a half earlier they had gone out, but never seriously or with great frequency. Then he had started traveling a lot, and when he was in New York, she seemed to be unavailable. They stopped seeing each other. Three months ago, he began spending most of his time in the city again and called Kate for dinner. He knew she had been going out with someone regularly, although he did not know then it was the Israeli ambassador. He also knew that for the first month, she seemed always trying to fit him into a crowded schedule. Then, abruptly, her time was free and she seemed anxious to spend it with him. Again, there was something he did not know, but could accurately guess at. She had broken off with whoever had been taking all her time.

Free of that, though, a strain came into their relationship immediately; it was as if they suddenly realized there were no barriers between them and marriage, and so they began setting some up. Bill, who had felt a growing sense of freedom and relaxation since his divorce, began to tighten up. Kate saw it and reacted to it, and the more she did, the tighter he got. As his attitudes polarized around what she called his "uptightness" she became more outrageous, again reacting without wanting to, asserting her feminism with far more militancy than she really felt.

A wedge found its way between them, and each interaction became a hammer tap, driving it deeper, making the gap wider. Part of it was assertiveness, another part the rigid attempt by each to reshape the other in his or her own image.

Bill, badly wanting her to get on with his business friends, would take her to dinners even he found stuffy. Kate, just as badly wanting him to see how smug and dull these people were, would deliberately take radical positions for the sake of provoking them. She, wanting to strike a contrast, dragged him to show-biz parties so arty and brassy they made her uncomfortable. He, feeling the pressure to be a "swinger," reacted by becoming more proper and pompous.

The wedge went in, tap by tap, deeper and deeper, and their ideological conflict affected their sexual relations, which had started out well—easy and satisfying. Going back to his Waldorf Towers suite after a party at which they had quietly bristled at each other, they found it tough and unnatural to get into bed, the more so because she had to go home to her children eventually and because the suite's airless, fussy decor made it seem a long way from anyone's home.

Bill was much more aware of the growing strain, and of his own role in it than she was. But painted tighter and tighter into his constricted corner he was powerless to change it. Alone, he would resolve to take the situation by the scruff of its neck and shake it loose. He would rehearse speeches in which he'd say things like, "For God's sake, Kate, I'm no longer showing you the real me. I'm a giant step closer to you than I've been letting on, and I know you're a giant step closer to me. Let's take the steps and stop all this retreating." He never delivered them.

His reactions grew schizoid; there began to coexist in his mind two reactions to her. One said, I should marry her and make everything all right; the other said, we'll never get along, we'll never make it, let's be sensible and end this now. For both positions, he'd rehearse speeches, though the only ones he came close to uttering were the marriage suggestions, and these always emerged semi-aborted, and added to the tensions.

Then, for three weeks before the dinner, he'd sensed an imminent split. Twice she had found a reason they could not make love. For two weeks she'd avoided him. Finally, when he called her, she'd asked for the dinner date. Bill sensed the appearance of another man, and he was right.

He leaned across the narrow table and kissed her, then sat down opposite her. To his left sat two fashionable young men talking loudly, with extravagant gestures, about last weekend's party in East Hampton; to his right, a married couple sat, hardly exchanging a word, the woman constantly sneaking glances at the TV star sitting next to her and trying to identify the tall, distinguished man with Kate Colby.

Terrific, Bill thought. On one side, volume to force their own voices up; on the other, two listeners straining for every word. "I hope we're to concentrate on eating rather than talking," he said, trying to sound jocular. "Because the setting is not ideal for conversation."

She would not pick up on his tone. "I'm afraid I have something to say, Bill," was her sober response. She had chosen the restaurant to keep the conversation from getting intimate, but her neighbors-in-dining were too much, so she kept desultory small talk going until the man and woman next to them gave up and left. It was 10:30 by then and the table stayed empty, so they both leaned toward it and Kate, getting right to the point, hit him between the eyes.

"Bill, I'm not going to be able to see you any more."

Bill Brewster had rehearsed the same sentence himself many times and so he was not surprised by it. What amazed him was how much it hurt. Yet the only response he could make was a constipated "I'm sorry to hear that. May I ask why?" God damn it, he thought later, I get bayonetted and I don't have the spontaneity to bleed.

"Because we're grating on each other, Bill. Because I don't seem to be able to please you, or you, me. Because it doesn't show any possibility of improving; on the contrary, it's getting worse. Because, I guess, I want you to be a man you're not and you want me to be a woman I'm not. Sooner or later it's going to tear us apart, and there's no point in prolonging the suffering."

Bill was in pain, yet all he could say was, "I'm not suffering, Kate, although I realize we have a good deal of tension. I had hoped it was something we could work out. Tell me, does the 'sooner' of your 'sooner or later' have anything to do with another man?"

They had been through the lemon chicken and the white wine by then, and Kate was holding a cup of tea in her hand. She looked at Bill long and sadly.

"Yes it does. But only, as you say, the 'sooner or later.' This had to happen."

Bill felt such a sense of bleakness it hardly mattered what he said. "May I ask if the man is the Israeli ambassador?" He could not bring himself to speak Dov's name.

"Does it make any difference?" she asked. Then added, "Yes, it is."

With that he folded, and like a prudent banker began salvaging as much of his emotional investment as he could. Later, he would whip himself for quitting so easily.

"I hope things work out for you, Kate," he said with empty grace. "I had hoped . . ." His voice trailed off. "I hope you get what you want."

"Thank you, Bill," she answered. "I'm sorry."

The rest of the evening had been funereal. Finishing, paying the check, getting up, finding a cab, taking her home, managing a trickle of small talk. At the door of her apartment house, hurt and prim, he put out his hand. She clasped it and leaned forward to kiss him. All she said was, "Oh, Bill."

He said, "Goodbye, Kate."

She held onto his hand. "Let's not lose track of each other."

"All right," he replied stiffly. "Good night." Then he turned and walked off.

That August night he had never fought. He had never really argued his case. Pete Maloney would never have done that, he thought now as he watched her on the sofa. Pete would have "sold" her—just as I'm doing now.

Bill watched her mulling over his last words, "Will you do it?" He was so sure he had started her moving his way, he was disappointed when she responded, "Here's what I will do. I will go to Dov and try to persuade him more information is needed to get the United States and the Soviet Union to act. I'll try to be as persuasive as you are, Bill."

"Why, thank you, ma'am," he answered with a grin. He felt strong and sure. He could convince anyone of anything, and there was more he had to get from her.

"All right, Kate, do this." He was no longer asking, he was telling her, and they both knew it. For him, it was extreme daring, but he jumped into it.

"Go there and do your damnedest to convince him to tell you more. But if he will not, be prepared to find out more any other way you can. We have no time for people to try things and then come back for consultations if they fail. We'll brief you. If he won't volunteer more, find it out."

Kate held her wine goblet in both hands. She looked at him and shook her head slowly. My God, he thought, I've lost.

Finally, still shaking her head, she spoke, "I don't know how good a spy I can be."

A wave of elation surged through him. He had *not* lost.

He could not sit still. To give himself something to do, he leaped to his feet and poured out the rest of the bottle of Chambertin, half in her glass, half in his. She did not say no to it. Something assured him she would say no to nothing right now.

"You'll be terrific," he said, as he was pouring. "Just as you are at everything else."

Kate looked at him. There was a voltage running through him; she could feel it. "Why, thank *you*, sir!" was all she said.

Then she laughed. "Would you believe that Dov asked me, in effect, to spy on *you* for *him?* Well, not quite the same way. To call him and tell him what we said."

He seized her hand. "Please call him! Tell him everything but the spying part. Tell him we asked you to find out more. God knows, if he supplies it, things will be so much simpler for all of us." "Us" was the American side—Bill's and Pete's. Kate had joined it and they both knew it.

"You know, Bill," she said, "all this pursuit makes a girl wonder if you're after her for herself."

164

He squeezed her hand hard. "I'd love to tell you about that, sometime soon, if you'll give me the chance."

Kate just looked at him. She didn't say no.

Bill put his filled glass near hers and said, "I've got to call Pete Maloney; he's been waiting. I can't tell you how grateful he's going to be." Bill picked up the phone and dialed Maloney's number; when he got the Secretary, he said to him, "Kate has agreed to help us."

Then he listened, smiled, and said into the phone, "I'll tell her. And we'll be up in a few minutes." He hung up and headed back to Kate, saying, "Pete wants to know, if he can't get you the Congressional Medal of Honor, what would you like instead?"

"How about James Bond to go to the embassy with me?"

Bill grinned as broadly as she had ever seen him grin. "He's extremely grateful, he'll tell you himself when we go up there for your crash course."

Crash course, she thought, what in hell am I letting myself in for? Well, I'll soon see.

Siting next to her again, Bill raised his wine goblet. "Here's to getting what we want," he said.

"Here's to getting out alive," she replied. And then both took a sip of the wine.

And she asked herself again, What am I letting myself in for? Why have I agreed to spy on the man I love? Will he and the Israelis consider me their enemy now? In Central Park just a few hours ago, she had seen what the Israelis did to their enemies.

Oh, but they wouldn't do that to me, she thought. And then asked herself, Why not?

Upstairs, Maloney hung up on Brewster thinking that possibly they had a shot at it, for twenty minutes earlier, while Brewster and Kate were talking, the Secretary had received another call on his private line.

"Can you help us on this plan?" Maloney had asked.

"Can't get near it. Wouldn't touch it if I could."

"Not even you?"

"Especially not I."

"Frightened at your age?"

"Not frightened. Not crazy either."

"Kate Colby may be going over there to help us. Any point to it?"

"Possibly."

"Can you help her while she's there?"

"Possibly."

"Should I not send her?" Maloney asked, exasperated.

"Send her. Must go now." The phone clicked.

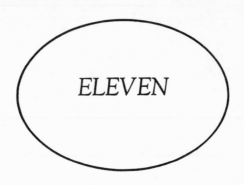

ELEVEN

"Before you take me upstairs to be brainwashed and indoctrinated," Kate said to Bill Brewster, "I've got to call the ambassador."

"Of course," he said, getting up from the sofa. "Why don't you go into the bedroom?"

She stood, too. "It won't take long. I just want to tell him I'm a double agent now." Then she headed for the bedroom. Only for the merest instant was Bill startled. Then he smiled at her back. I'm getting used to that, he thought.

Her reflections were more serious than her quip showed. She realized she had been co-opted by Brewster and Maloney, she was a step away from being an American spy, and she was at a crossroads. Either she would tell Dov, right now, or she'd be concealing information and her position as a spy would be hardening.

As she walked toward the phone, her eyes took in the bedroom. She knew the look of this room well and didn't like it. She never had; there was a leaden quality to its brocade drapes, the patterned tan carpeting, the somber wallpaper. She and Bill had spent time in that bed during the months they had been together last year.

They'd been pleasant hours—elegant, bland. At first she would tell herself they no more represented Bill's ardor than the room represented his taste in decor. She wanted to feel, as he did, there was another Bill Brewster waiting to get free.

After a time she was forced to ask herself, Waiting for what? He was forty-six then and had been divorced for a year. When was that other Brewster going to escape, when was the butterfly going to bust out, all winged and glittery? Confronted with his stiffness and male chauvinism, she began to grow tired of waiting, a process that was speeded up by Dov's decision to seek a legal separation from his wife.

In giving up Bill, she'd lost a lot, but she'd be damned if this room

166

was among it. Of course, she told herself, the time would have come when she could have changed things like furnishings.

She dialed Dov's private number, which rang twice before it was picked up. "Hello," an Israeli-accented voice said.

"This is Kate Colby. May I speak to the ambassador at once, please? He is expecting my call."

"One moment, please."

Phone held loosely to her ear, Kate sat on the side of the bed, looking at the two doors, side by side, which led to the bathroom and the huge walk-in closet. In the closet, she knew, were a couple of dozen suits, all expensive, conservative. "Why do you have so many of them," she'd once asked him, "when they're all gray or blue, and they all look like the same suit? Don't you have even *one* brown one?"

He'd just smiled and replied, "My mother claims she had once pointed to someone and asked *her* mother, 'Who is the gentleman in the brown suit?' and her mother had answered, 'A *gentleman* never wears a brown suit.' " Of course, he was joking, Kate had said to herself. On the other hand, he didn't own a brown suit.

"Mrs. Colby, the ambassador will be on the line in a moment. Will you hold, please."

"Fine."

The delay suited her, because she wasn't sure what to say to Dov, and therefore in no hurry to say it. And she couldn't stall because the first few sentences would be her Rubicon. Right off, she'd either have to tell Dov about spying or not tell him, and if she didn't, she'd be crossing to the other side.

An hour ago, there'd have been no problem. Kate was helping Dov. Dov was confiding in her. There was no question of her allegiance. Now her loyalty was up for grabs. But only for a moment or two; then she'd have to commit herself.

If she spoke to Dov now, without disclosing she had been asked to spy, wouldn't she be hiding something important from him? And what were her choices? First, she could get on the phone and say at once she'd been asked to spy. That would keep her squarely on Dov's side, but it would also close off her options. She could no longer keep open the possibility of spying.

She was groping for a way—without lying to Dov and without being turned against Brewster and the Secretary—to maintain some volition for herself. She wanted to be able to enter this negotiation as a free agent, not as somebody's satellite. For the first time she faced her own discontent at being a go-between, a confidante, at being in somebody's hip pocket, unable to make her own choice and to use that choice to influence the outcome.

In short, was there a course that could keep her from promising in advance to "love, honor, and obey" one side or the other? By the time

Dov got to the phone, she had decided she wanted that course. If she could find it.

"Hello," Dov's voice sounded farther away than Seventy-second Street. "Sorry it took me so long. What can you tell me about the meeting with Bill?"

With a speed and certainty that surprised her, her course of action had crystallized. She knew what she would do, how much she would tell each, how much she would hide.

"Bill says the Secretary of State cannot get you what you want on the strength of the information you've given him so far. He needs to know more, Dov."

Dov sounded weary. "Yes, yes, I know, and I've already made it as clear as I can we have no more to tell. I hope they accept that."

"They don't accept it as a basis for meeting your demands. They won't go ahead." She was no longer the messenger; she was trying to push Dov.

"Nothing more we can give, Kate."

"Look, Dov, they've asked me to find out more. For the sake of getting your demands, why don't you consider giving me something new? Think it over—what you've got to lose versus what you can gain. Then, when I come over for dinner, trying desperately, in my own winning way, to get you to talk, maybe you'll have decided it's to your advantage to tell me something."

"You're beginning to sound just like Bill," he said, trying to make it bantering. "Only much more winning, of course."

"Well, maybe, as a woman, I can see things better than you two nose-to-nose macho men can. Maybe I'm afraid that each of you is so sure the other will give ground, this thing will end up with the clock running out and both sides saying they were sorry—when it's too late. Maybe I'm worried about what the 'too late' is going to be like for all the innocents who are caught between the hard noses of Shalzar and Maloney and who are going to suffer for a decision they're powerless to change. If it were just you two, I'd say go ahead with the brinksmanship, risk your lives, lose them. But how much right do you have to get tough with other people's lives?

"You want to stand up in a bar and yell 'I can whup any man in the joint,' fine. But don't point to some poor guy sitting and minding his own business and yell 'He and I can whup any two men in the joint.' That's not my kind of bravery."

Then she said to herself, easy, don't move too far to Maloney's side; stay in business for yourself. And she veered off. "But then," she told Shalzar, "if I'm too convincing now, we'll have nothing to talk about at dinner, so I'll hope you'll sustain a little sales resistance, to give me something to look forward to." She was being just a bit cunning and manipulative, using their intimacy.

"I'll look forward to it," he replied. "Seven. Use the Seventy-third Street entrance, approach it on foot from Madison. Someone will meet you."

"Fine, see you then."

Kate put down the receiver and sat up straight on the edge of the bed. She felt proud and a little edgy. The time would come, and very soon, she'd have to make a choice—to go for one side or the other, or withdraw entirely. But so far she had kept herself a free agent.

All her early life she'd been conditioned to orbit around a man; as the daughter of conventional upper-middle-class Atlantans, she'd been taught that her schooling, social activities, home life, all were aimed at the single goal of marrying well and becoming a successful wife, mother, and hostess. Her mother's concept of scholarship was to learn to hold up one's end of a conversation about opera or art or current affairs. Her mother's concept of athletics was to be able to play tennis without perspiring, swim without thrashing, and ride without jolting. But never, never, outtalk, outplay, outswim, or outride a man.

Unlike her continuing social education, her parental sex instruction had come entirely from her father and consisted of two sentences.

"Dahlin', every man wants his bride to be a virgin. Ah hope mah little girl will remember that."

She was a virgin when she married, at twenty-one, right out of Randolph-Macon, which she had attended in deference to her parents, rather than trying for one of those northern schools, Radcliffe, Smith, or Bryn Mawr. Edlington Colby III, a Georgia gentleman, disposed of her virginity on their wedding night but advanced her sexual development very little after that.

Ed Colby's attitude toward sex and women was hardly different from Kate's father's, although her husband knew how to coat his male chauvinism with more contemporary explanations. "This is the age of specialization," he liked to point out, "and women are better designed than men for child rearing—which happens to be a function as important as any a man performs." He would make the last part sound very earnest and enlightened, but God help any woman who tried to express herself at the dinner table on politics, or taxes, or the stock market while Ed Colby was there.

When Kate was twenty-six and married for five years, Ed's insurance company transferred him to New York, where he'd have a chance to make vice-president. And in New York, she began to free herself from the subservience she had lived with in her father's house and then her husband's house. But sometimes she wondered if her twenty-six years of serfdom hadn't scarred her forever, if she would ever be truly free.

Even lately she'd been doing either what Dov wanted, or Bill, or

Pete Maloney—until right then, right there sitting on the edge of the bed in the Waldorf Towers suite, she declared a new level of independence.

She stood and walked out of the bedroom. Bill rose from the sofa when she entered the living room. She expected him to look impatient; when he didn't she glanced at her watch. The phone call, daydreaming and all, had lasted only five minutes.

"Is everything all right?"

She smiled. "Shall I tell you what he said about what I said about what you said? And then should I go back and tell him what you said about what I said about what . . . and so on and so on? How far can it go? What's a girl to do?"

Bill answered gravely. "I guess you'll have to do what you think best."

She looked him in the eye and nodded. "I guess I will, Bill. Let's go see the Secretary." And she did something unusual. She didn't wait to see if he would approve and start off; she just headed for the door.

At the Secretary's suite, she, not Brewster, pressed the buzzer. The door opened and Steve Phelps appeared, his face showing deference and urgency; by now he knew they were involved in something significant, no mere time-stealers.

"He's waiting for you. Please sit down in the living room and I'll tell him you're here." Phelps left and within half a minute Maloney arrived. He walked straight to her and said, "Kate, I'm happy you're here." He stuck out his hand and she shook it.

She responded with only, "Hello, Mr. Secretary."

Maloney walked her to the sofa and sat down next to her, swiveling his stocky body so that he faced her, looking straight at her eyes. Bill watched admiringly. Kate braced herself for the hard sell that was about to begin.

"Bill told you," Maloney began, "that we need more information about the Israeli threat. There are several ways you can help us, and we'd like you to be prepared to try them all, if you're willing.

"The first and simplest would be to ask. You are close to the ambassador; he values your opinions, to an extent I'm sure he relies on you. One way you can ask is to tell him, straight out, that we have put you up to it, and that you feel he should tell you, for otherwise we're at an impasse. I'd prefer you do it that way, if I thought it would work, because it's the most direct and honest and it would be the easiest for you to do."

As long as he was beginning this way, Maloney thought he'd try for all the mileage he could get. Disarm her, show her how concerned he was for her. "We do, after all, appreciate how much you're doing, and

170

we don't want to cause any problems for you. That's not our idea of gratitude."

Oh cut it out, she thought. You're on the verge of asking me to spy on Dov. You don't care how I do it; I don't think you'd care if I got bumped off in the attempt, as long as I get what you're after. If the Secretary was waiting for a grateful acknowledgement of his largesse, he was disappointed. He got a blank smile. Curtly, almost rudely, she said, "I think it would be best if you were to lay out all the possibilities first, so I can think about them."

Maloney watched her, paying attention to what she said and what she didn't. He had met her only a few times, and each time he did, thought she seemed a lot softer and more pliant in person than she did on television, where she was kind of cool and tough. Not now, he thought. Now she's every bit as tough as on the tube. She's a big, mean dame who needs a *gentlemanly* type, someone like Bill, maybe like the ambassador, though I don't know him all that well. She'd never be the kind of woman I could get along with, he said to himself. I'm not enough of a gentleman, she'd be throwing things at me in a week.

Kate recognized his look; she had seen it on the faces of many men, enough of whom had then proceeded to explain themselves, so she could correlate the look and the intention: the serene, powerful he-man smile that said, I could tame you, baby, and you'd love it. She knew it was just a guess, she knew she might be unfair to him, but she hated it. She stared back, thinking: that look is gonna cost you a little extra . . . baby.

"Of course, you're right," he answered. "I'll suggest all your options and then we can go over them." He ignored the difference in pronouns. She had said, "*I* can think about all of them." He used "we."

"The other way you can ask is as a confidante, without revealing you are doing it for us and are going to tell us what you learn. That would be spying."

Again, Pete Maloney paused, hoping she'd raise an objection so he could speak to it. He realized they'd just been through a personality collision, which could ruin things; he wanted to get back to issues.

She nodded, said nothing. She'd be damned if she'd react to him, she thought. She'd listen and then tell him what *she* was going to do.

He'd wait her out a bit longer, he decided, push her to react by his silence.

She waited, too, not looking at him, although he was staring at her. Then she said: "Do I take it by your silence there's nothing more you want to ask, that those are the only two options?"

So, he thought, our personalities are still rubbing. No, this wasn't going to be easy; the pussycat was turning tiger. Well, he wasn't unhappy about it. Getting his way too easily had always disappointed him; he liked to fight before he won. Even more important, no pussy-cat could do the job inside the Israeli embassy; she'd need a lot of tiger for that, and he was glad to see she had it. Because, he knew, inside that embassy lay their only chance. Expecting Shalzar to volunteer more now was a pipe dream, and they had been puffing long enough.

"The third way," he went on, as if the battle of personalities were not happening, "is for you to go in and look and listen—to what's intended for your eyes and ears, and what isn't.

"To do that, you'll need help. You may come upon material that is too complicated and scientific for you to understand, or which exists in too great a quantity for you to retain, even if you do understand it. Or which is in Hebrew. You don't know Hebrew, do you?"

She'd been giving him this Sphinx response, Maloney thought, and he wanted to get a rise out of her in some way. He did get a negative shake of the head from her to his question, but her carefully noncommittal attitude remained.

"The help would take the form of auxiliary eyes and ears, a miniature camera, a tape recorder, and a quick recognition course in a few Hebrew words which particularly interest us."

Sending her in with tape recorder and camera was the suggestion at which Pete had expected his first resistance. He looked at her; he got a blank expression in return. She was determined to make him ask. He did.

"Well, there it is. What's your reaction?"

The Secretary of State of the United States of America is waiting on me, she thought. All this salesmanship and power and personality is spinning its wheels while I decide to answer. *He* is dependent on *me*. Can I take this seriously, she asked herself. And then she reminded herself this *was* serious, not just a question of her ego and his supplication. This was a matter of life and death, of many lives and deaths.

"Mr. Secretary, let me tell you what I am willing to do—provided I'm capable of doing it. Let me tell you also what I have already done.

"I've already told the Israeli ambassador you have asked me to pump him for more information, because you don't think their threat concrete enough to grant their demands."

Seldom was Peter Maloney caught by surprise and even more seldom did he show it. This time both seemed to happen and like an angry schoolmaster he looked toward Bill Brewster. For an instant, the carefully papered-over rivalry between the two men seemed to burst through. Then, rarity compounding rarity, to Pete's glare that implied that Bill hadn't done his job, kid, Bill's replied, "Don't push me, I'm not your pupil."

172

Bill resented the suggestion that all the world could be manipulated and the only failures were failures in technique; Kate resented even more the implication that she could be manipulated. She wanted, without being obvious about it, to defend herself and Bill.

"Down in Bill's suite, Mr. Secretary, I was about to say no to any request that I spy, snoop, nose, ask—whatever you want to call it— when Bill came up with the idea that I forthrightly tell the ambassador I had been asked to ask. That gave me something to think about —an honest presentation that just might work and get rid of the whole snooping, spying question.

"While I was chewing on that one, Bill stepped in again to suggest I go in with the honest question up front, and the spying option right behind it. Honestly, I don't know who thought that one up, whether it was part of the game plan, or Bill's improvisation, but whoever's responsible is the one who saved the day, for without it Kate Colby would have gone bye-bye."

Her defense of Bill hadn't been too subtle, she realized, but it made her feel better. She knew Bill would do nothing on his own behalf, beyond that one look of angry disdain, and she wanted to speak for him and to vent some of the hostility she was feeling for this Secretary of State so renowned for cajoling, bullying, selling, manipulating everyone, from the premier of the USSR to his own best friend.

"And to be thoroughly cynical about it," she continued, amplifying the theme, "if I should decide to spy, what could be more disarming than to start the whole thing by telling the Israeli ambassador, See, they asked me to find things out, and here I am telling you about it.

"*If* I decide to spy. Please underline that *if*. If I decide to, Bill has found the only formula under which I could even contemplate it. And that is to go to the dinner with the hope I can persuade the ambassador to volunteer more information; if I get something from him, I'll have to make a quick judgment as to whether it's enough to satisfy you. If I think it is, my problem is solved."

For a moment she felt the headiness of dominance; then as she had to confront the other alternative, its danger and its magnitude sobered her.

"If, on the other hand, I don't get enough for you, I'll have to decide on the spot what to do next. To spy or not to spy."

"To save or not to save the world, that is the question," said Maloney. He was trying to pile guilt on her shoulders, and she didn't like it. The man is a bully, Kate said to herself; he uses different techniques, but all for the same purpose, to push people around.

"Uh, uh. To spy or not to spy. Don't lay the safety of the world on me; I arrived too late on the scene to be blamed for that; you fellas got here first. You live with your responsibility; what I'm worried about is my physical bravery. Will I have the guts, or will my heart be beating so fast and my hands shaking so hard I'll be incapable of opening a door or a briefcase, or snapping a picture?"

For the first time in the last few minutes, Bill Brewster was encouraged. He'd been sitting in an easy chair where he could watch Kate and Maloney on the sofa. He'd seen sparks; while he knew Pete would keep the talk going, he wasn't so sure about Kate. She could dig in her heels and refuse to be pushed another inch. She could also get up and walk out if Pete manhandled her. But when she let herself talk about opening briefcases and snapping pictures, she'd taken the first step toward the deed.

"Expect to be nervous," Bill interjected quickly. "Any human would be. And expect to be able to cope with it. Anyone with your steel would be."

"As the old punch line goes, Bill," she replied, "that's easy for you to say." Nonetheless, she was pleased. Those were Bill's first words since entering Maloney's suite, and while they were manipulative, they were supportive, too. He had not tried to jump in before to help the Secretary push her around.

Kate smiled at Bill, and when she continued, spoke to both men, not just to the Secretary, as she had been doing. "Then, aside from my guts, there's the question of my heart, if I may continue in the anatomical vein. I'm going to have to face a man I care for deeply and when his back is turned for a moment, spy on him. I don't know if I can do it. I can do all the promising here you want, but I won't know until I'm in the embassy face to face."

Bill Brewster was quite right about his friend Pete's feelings never being hurt. Maloney didn't allow himself the anger or the hurt. Seeing an opening, he threw a counterpunch. "Along with your sentiments toward each other, when you're face-to-face in the embassy, I hope you'll feel other sentiments, toward those who, though they may not be in the same room with you, around the same table, are every bit as close."

"Why, Mr. Secretary, I didn't know you cared." She said it with little warmth; it was less a friendly quip than a bit of defiance in the face of his steady hammering. But Maloney would not growl back.

"You bet I care," he replied. "So do Kevin Maloney, age twenty, Pete, Jr., age nineteen, Sheila, age seventeen, and Keith, age fourteen—not to mention Muffie, age forty-five. And so do the Colby children—how old are they, eight and ten?—and the Shalzar children in Israel, whatever their number, names, and ages. And the Brewster children, too numerous to list."

For the first time, Kate voiced her hostility. "Mr. Secretary, I consider that unfair, unnecessary, and cheap."

Maloney would not be drawn into a fight. "And I consider it none

174

of the above," he said, intensely, with no animosity. "But even if it were all of them, I would use it when confronted with a display of pure ego, at a time when the world is . . ." and he looked at his watch dramatically, "nineteen hours and ten minutes away from God knows what."

"Fright I can understand—although my money says you've got courage to spare." The Secretary would make points wherever he could, even in passing. "Worrying about looking your lover in the eye is an ego trip, and it's a hell of a lot harder to understand at this moment, under these circumstances."

The heat of her anger turned to ice. She stood and walked away from the sofa toward the window, parted the draperies to look out, seeing nothing but her own cold rage. She turned and started back. "Mr. Secretary, it's too bad you are reduced to dealing with a weak, egotistical woman rather than the brilliant, selfless states*men* whose grandness of spirit and Olympian overview have thus far so admirably brought the world to the brink of the—utopia—at which we now find ourselves."

Maloney smiled, but it was a tight smile. "If I were defensive I could easily call that a cheap shot—female chauvinism to boot."

Kate, still on her feet, spoke quickly. "But you're above that, I know, I know. However, since it is this bundle of feminine weakness with whom you must deal, you'd better listen to my conditions. And I'm not finished giving them to you.

"In addition to my problems with my guts and my heart, there's a third consideration. Should I decide against spying, I'd then have the option of disclosing to the ambassador that I'd been recruited and wired for sound and picture."

Bill Brewster was startled. "You're not seriously suggesting you may tell Dov we sent you in as a spy—are you?"

Kate sat on the sofa again, but this time far forward, her body telling the men, I'm ready to get up and go anytime.

"Bill, I'm not suggesting it, I'm stating it—as one option."

"Do you realize," the Secretary broke in, "what such a disclosure might do to our talks?"

One part of Kate's hostility toward Maloney came from the way the Secretary's administration had treated Israel, and she now had a chance to express it. "If the Israelis are still talking to you, after what you've done to them over the past couple of years, a little thing like this won't stop them." Her Southern accent, usually hidden, grew more noticeable as she grew more angry.

"That, however, is not the point. I am telling you the conditions under which, in about five hours, I am willing to go in there. And I'll tell you both something else. I think I'm being brave as hell to go in there at all, because I am scared to death. If my conditions are too onerous, get someone else. Strap the damned devices on and go in there yourself. Believe me, if you were to take me off the case, I'd be mighty relieved."

She didn't care how provocative she was being. But Brewster did, and he knew Pete had a temper, controlled but there. Pete had once called it getting his "Italo-Irish up." "If an Italian Irishman isn't entitled to a temper, who is?" he had said. Bill also knew if you caught the Secretary when he was hot, you got a fire. But it didn't take long for Maloney to cool, and Brewster had to give him that time.

"Kate," Bill said, "you are not merely the *best* game in town, you are the *only* one. We need you—to move us toward a result *all* of us want. All of us, not just the American side. So we shall abide by your brains, your courage, and your decisions in there."

Maloney had the breather he needed. The anger was drained from his face. When his friend looked at him, he nodded. To Kate he said only, "We'd like to brief you now. After that it's up to you."

He was a killer, Kate thought, as she looked at the Secretary, but she had to concede he knew how to handle himself. And she also had to concede her own ego had been running loose since she'd entered Maloney's suite. The attention paid, the terms listened to—and she'd enjoyed it more than she should.

She looked at Bill, then at the Secretary. "Please don't think I won't do my damnedest to make the right choices and carry them out competently. I know how important it could be and, also, I want to do well. There's ego in that, I admit it. I want to be able to look back at this and be proud of myself."

Then, roughly the same thought occurred to the three of them: I hope we can look back without horror. I hope we can look back at all. None of them said it. When Maloney spoke, it was to move on to the details.

"I'm not worried for you." He said it with a smile and he meant it. Then he jumped up from the sofa and left the room. Ninety seconds later he was back with a man and a woman.

"Kate Colby, William Brewster. Linda Janowitz and Stuart Waddell." Then Maloney turned to Kate and Bill. "Ms. Janowitz is an expert on Israel. Stu Waddell is a surveillance specialist." Waddell, with his crew cut, rimless glasses, and calloused hands, looked like a shop teacher.

Maloney motioned the woman to a chair and Waddell to the place he had been sitting in. He said, "Stu, you take over."

Waddell seldom had the chance to teach a TV star, so he began somewhat pedantically. "Miss Colby, I want to familiarize you with two pieces of equipment." With each hand he reached into a pocket of his brown jacket. When he withdrew them, each was closed into a large fist.

First he opened his left. In it was an object about the size of a thick, stubby pocket flashlight, except that it was rectangular rather than cylindrical. "I'll skip the name and model number, because they're not important. This is one of the newest, smallest, most precise cameras in the world. It's from Japan."

Then he opened his right, revealing what seemed to be an oversized book of matches. "And this is a tape recorder, entirely self-contained." He closed that hand again, and put it back in his pocket.

"I'm going to teach you to operate both pieces of equipment. This will not be hard and you will not need much time to learn. Suppose we start with the camera."

He held it between his thick thumb and forefinger. "You need not worry about loading and unloading this instrument; you will be given one with a new roll of film in it, and you will shoot pictures until all twenty exposures, or as many as you wish, are used. The film is black and white, and is so fast you may assume anything your eye can see, it will register.

"Picture-taking is simple; you need make no adjustments in shutter speed or size of the diaphragm opening. You merely look through the viewfinder . . ." Waddell put the tiny camera to his right eye, and squeezed his left shut . . . "and you push this button to snap the picture. To take the next picture, you grasp the camera and pull it out as if to stretch it. And then push it back. That advances the film. You're now ready to take another picture.

"Only one variable is within your control, and that is the distance between the camera and the object you are photographing. Since this camera was designed to take pictures of printed material, not sunsets . . ." Waddell smiled. It was his standard quip at this point in the lecture, and he waited for appreciation. Mechanically, Kate smiled back. He continued, "It must be employed at close range. For most accurate results, it should be no less than eighteen inches and no farther than thirty-six inches from the object you are shooting. That is between a foot and a half and three feet away from the object, which gives you a depth of field of eighteen inches, or a foot and a half."

Waddell had delivered all this in the pedantic tones of a teacher speaking to a willing but retarded pupil, and she reacted as if she were one. She was getting more nervous. "I have never been able to take a snapshot with a Brownie without blurring it or making it too dark or too light." As she said it she looked first at Waddell and then around the room.

Waddell was used to that reaction, and he handled it with smiling, superior tolerance. "This instrument is a lot better than a Brownie, Miss Colby, and a heck of a lot more expensive." Another of his sprinkles of wit, and she gave him the smile he expected. "The shutter speed is so fast and the diaphragm opening so small, you couldn't blur a picture or expose it badly—that means make it too dark or too light—if you tried. In fact, we are going to let you try in a few minutes.

"There are just four things to do. One is to advance the film, pulling out the camera and pushing in after each picture you take, so that you don't expose the same piece of film twice—in other words take one picture over another.

"The second is to make sure the camera is no less than eighteen inches and no more than three feet from the material being shot.

"The third is to see, through the viewfinder, the picture you wish to take. To aim the camera, in other words.

"The fourth is to click the little button that takes the picture.

"The first and fourth are merely a question of remembering. The second and third take a little practice, but they are, I assure you, very little harder than the first and fourth. Let's start with the distance of the camera from the object. What you should try to do is set up a measuring device for yourself to estimate the critical distance. To be safe, you should try to place the object midway in the depth of field, that is, halfway between eighteen and thirty-six inches, or at twenty-seven inches. The question is how to measure twenty-seven inches."

Waddell paused and looked at Kate. He always did that at his point, to allow the brighter pupils to venture a suggestion. When she sat there looking blank, he went on, pleased that the TV star had to have everything spelled out.

He reached into his pocket and pulled out a tape measure. "Miss Colby, will you please sit up straight and then stretch your arm directly out in front of you." Like a good pupil she did. Waddell held one end of the tape to her extended fingertips and stretched the other end to the space between her eyes. He showed her the distance. It was twenty-five inches. He smiled at her, as if to say, you see how simple it is. "Now, Miss Colby, were you to rotate your arm downward, the distance would increase slightly, so that when you reached your knee with your fingertips, the measurement would increase to about twenty-seven inches." She stretched her hand to her knee, and he measured it. Twenty-seven inches.

"To approach a table of ordinary height, and reach your arm to it, would increase the distance even further, because of the different angle. Would you try it, please, there?"

He pointed to a rococo wooden table near the window. She walked over, reached her arm to its surface, having to bend slightly to touch it. He was alongside, stretching out the tape. "A shade short of twenty-nine inches."

Waddell's smile was a shade short of triumphant. "You see, Miss Colby, your arm is your guide. And material on most tables will be about twenty-nine inches from your eyes, well within the depth of field, which is why the camera was designed this way." The two walked back to the sofa together, Waddell unable to resist shooting out a confident look to the Secretary that said, Please notice the way I know my job.

"Oh those Japanese!" was all Kate could think of to say, although she knew it was not properly respectful.

"Actually," Waddell replied, "they designed it to our specification. Because they are substantially shorter, their model is slightly different."

"Oh, Mr. Waddell, you people think of everything."

He grinned, but was a little puzzled, not sure if it was admiration or mockery he was hearing. Then he went on.

"Now for point three, which is looking through the viewfinder to frame the material you're photographing. At twenty-seven to thirty inches, holding the camera vertically, that's up and down, you should be able to get an entire eight-by-ten page in a single shot. If you cannot quite do it, you might move the camera back a couple of inches, but not too much. We'd rather have a page of clear material, with its fringes cut off, than an entire page, all of which is blurred.

"If the material is far too large, then turn the camera horizontal, that's sideways, and shoot the page in two sections, first the top part and then the bottom, making sure to allow an ample overlap.

"So there are the four points. Advance the film, check the distance, frame the material, press the button. Are there any questions about any of them?"

Waddell paused and looked around, again the lecturer who has just said his last word and is anticipating the approval to follow, pretending he doesn't want it.

"Mr. Waddell, that was a very clear and simple presentation," Kate told him. "Even I could understand it." He beamed at her. Too bad, he thought, he couldn't tell his neighbors out in Hempstead he had tutored the famous Kate Colby. But he was accustomed to secrecy and thoroughly conditioned to it.

"My only problem," she added, "is trying to remember them and make them work. I am helpless with mechanical things. When I put a hand on them they either freeze into immobility or fall apart."

Waddell was miffed with this, not because he couldn't handle it, but because it weakened his finale. He got up again, grabbed a copy of *Time* magazine from the coffee table in front of the sofa, carried it to the table near the window, and spread it open.

"Now," he said to Kate, "why don't you come here, take the camera, and practice the four steps." Obediently, she walked toward him.

He reached out and handed her the camera. "You know how to advance the film," he said. "Of course, for this first shot you don't have to." He pointed with a calloused forefinger. "And there is the button

to open the shutter and take the picture. The one that goes click."
He was now presuming nothing about her comprehension. Kate smiled
at him, wanting to say it's my mechanical aptitude that's faulty, not
my English. But she didn't.

"Now, stand right up to the table and measure your distance." Obediently, she did. With the camera in her left hand, she extended her
right arm to find the desired proper distance. Then she waited,
thoroughly docile.

"Remembering where the button is, hold the camera to your eye,
vertically, up and down, and frame the left-hand page of the magazine." Again, she obeyed.

"Does it fill the frame?"

"Not quite."

"Do you mean it's slightly too big or too small for the frame?"

"Too small."

"Well, that's all right then. If it were slightly too big, you could
move the camera back a couple of inches, remembering always not to
get farther away than thirty-six inches. All right, then shoot the picture."

She pressed the button, took the camera away from her eye, and
looked at him, triumphantly.

Waddell rewarded her with a "Good!" and she looked over at the
Secretary and Brewster. "Do you suppose," she asked, "Margaret
Bourke-White is getting a little nervous up there in shutterbug
heaven?"

"Not till you shoot the roll and it's developed and printed," said
Maloney, with a grin. He wasn't sure she'd intended that for him, but
he replied anyway, as a truce offering.

With exaggerated casualness, Kate flipped a couple of pages of the
magazine, measured the distance, held the camera to her eye, moved it
an inch or so closer to show how confident she was and pressed the
button. Nothing happened.

She looked up in consternation. "What's wrong?"

Maloney and Brewster were grinning. Waddell did not allow himself
that luxury; he felt a teacher should never show amusement at a
pupil's mistake. "Have you forgotten something?" he asked gently.

Now she was flustered. "What?"

"You didn't advance the film. Step number one."

"Oh dammit," she said, "supposing this happens when Mr. Waddell
is not around?" Suddenly there flowed over her a wave of fright. What
am I getting into? she asked herself. I must be crazy to consider doing
this.

Maloney got to his feet. "It won't happen," he said, walking to her,
"because you're going to practice with the whole roll of film, remembering the four simple steps. Advance. Distance. Framing. Click. Just

go ahead and practice." He smiled to encourage her. Pete knew that just as a setback with the camera had made her despair of the whole project—he had seen that in her face—increased involvement with it would draw her deeper and deeper into the whole scheme, draw her closer and closer to their side. At the same time she learned the technique of using the camera she was learning the *idea* of using it, too.

Kate ceremoniously moved the arm on the camera and began measuring off the distance when Waddell interrupted.

"May I make a suggestion, Miss Colby?"

"You mean you think there's something I still have to learn about photography, Mr. Waddell?" When he seemed unsure about her quip, she added, "Please do make suggestions, and forgive my bad jokes; I use them to cover up my ineptitude."

He was relieved that she had resumed her humility and in a spirit of noblesse oblige, said, "Miss Colby, I assure you I'd be a lot worse on television than you are with a camera."

"Oh, Mr. Waddell," she said, half teasing, "do you think that's possible?"

"Oh yes!" was all he could manage, for he was now blushing, and tongue-tied and she realized she had carried the banter too far. So she hurried to extricate him. "Mr. Waddell, please help me in any way you can."

"May I suggest that when you are shooting several pages of documents of the same size, once you have determined that, at let's say twenty-eight inches in this case, the page fills the frame, you need not remeasure distance for every shot. Merely fill the frame with the page and you'll know you're at the proper distance."

"Of course," she said. "So simple and so right. In order to get the right framing I'd *have* to be twenty-eight inches away! Why, it will save time, and wear and tear on my measuring arm! Thank you so much."

"Miss Colby, let me say it's a pleasure to be able to help someone my family and I have enjoyed so often on television."

"Why, thank you!"

Maloney was chafing at the time being wasted in banter, but since he didn't want to antagonize Kate, and since he realized she was more and more accepting the camera and the role it implied, he chafed in silence. Brewster correctly interpreted the impatient look on Maloney's face but he mistook Kate's chatter as a sign of ease. Actually, she was using the talk to cover fright and misgivings.

Kate had turned and was snapping pictures of the pages of *Time* magazine, this time not omitting any steps. After several snaps, Waddell replaced the magazine with a large book from a nearby shelf. It was a picture history of the life and career of Van Gogh, and when she measured the distance and tried to frame a page, she saw it was too big, so she first shot the top half of the page, then the bottom.

"And I left plenty of overlap," she said, looking up at Waddell. "How's that, professor?" Then she lifted the camera and took a shot of him. "I know, I know, you're more than thirty-six inches away."

In the next few minutes she shot the entire roll, using several kinds of printed material—paperback books, typewritten pages, anything they could pick up quickly.

When she was finished, Waddell took the camera and said, "Now we have to get this processed to see how you did." He started out of the room.

She couldn't resist calling after him. "If you take it to the drugstore at Sixty-fifth and Madison, they'll have the prints back to you by Monday."

At first he was startled, but he was getting used to her humor. He shook his head and said, "We can do better than that right here."

He walked down the hall into the suite's second bathroom, which had been fitted out as an impromptu darkroom. Waiting there was a technician who, like Waddell, was on around-the-clock duty for the next day. Waddell opened the tiny camera under an ultraviolet lamp and removed the film. He replaced it with a new roll, closed the camera and clicked off a couple of shots to make sure the film was moving. Then he handed the first roll to the technician.

"I hear Kate Colby's out there. How'd she do?"

"OK. She cracks a lot of jokes. But her hands are shaking."

Waddell walked out with the reloaded camera in his hand, and he turned it over to Kate solemnly. "Good luck. It's a terrific little piece of equipment and if you use it the way you just did, it won't let you down. Of course, we won't know for sure until we check the negatives, but you did fine."

"Why, thanks, professor. This feels just like graduation day at Randolph-Macon." She grinned at him and he looked grateful. Then he got back to business.

"The question now is how are you going to carry it with you, Miss Colby. Will you have a purse?"

"I could."

"Could you keep the purse with you all evening?"

"I suppose, if I use a small evening purse on a long chain and wear it on my shoulder. Of course, it would be too dressy for the occasion, and I hate to do that." Kate looked at Maloney and Brewster. "I might, though, if the Secretary writes a note of explanation to *Women's Wear Daily*. This was to have been my year to make the best-dressed list."

Waddell waited patiently for her to stop. He noticed the hand that held the camera was unsteady. Then he said, "Good, the purse will solve it."

By now a lot more confident and expansive with the TV star, Waddell began his new course. He reached into his pocket for the tape recorder. "Here is my second little marvel." Slightly disappointed that the simplicity of the instrument left him little room for teaching, he made the most of what he had.

"It's hard to believe, but this little thing holds forty-five mintes' worth of a recording tape that's half the width and two-thirds the thickness of any developed before. That's a lot of tape, but not nearly enough for a whole evening, so you must decide when you want it running and when you want it turned off.

"To turn on or off, you move this little switch, right here. The only real problem is deciding where to carry it so that it's hidden, yet open enough to record conversations and accessible enough to reach the switch."

Waddell hesitated and his face reddened as he began the next sentence. "Without wanting to be fresh, Miss Colby, we have found that on a woman, one of the best locations for the recorder is in the bra, where, because of its small size, it can be safely hidden."

God, this is intrusive, she said to herself, I almost feel as if I'm being handled. Already embarrassed by having to talk about such intimate things, Waddell misunderstood her questioning look.

"When I said small size, I was referring to the tape recorder, of course, Miss Colby." He was blushing again.

Hardly concentrating on what he had just said, she answered, mechanically, "Of course." Then it registered and she added, "Why Mr. Waddell, what else could you have meant?" His redness deepened; she smiled at him to ease his discomfort, and then told him, "Your idea is a good one, Mr. Waddell, but suppose the woman doesn't wear a bra?"

Waddell was speechless, Brewster mortified; Linda Janowitz sat in her chair and looked at her lap. Maloney was simply impatient.

"She could wear one, though, couldn't she?" Maloney asked.

"Why, yes, she could."

"Fine, Kate, terrific. Stu, just tell her where to put it."

For Waddell, things kept getting worse. "Well, Mr. Secretary, it's just a case of fitting it in the cup so it won't show and is comfortable, and, ideally, where the wearer could reach a finger in to move the switch."

Maloney wanted this thing ended. "OK, Stu, you did a hell of a job. Is she all set now?"

"I guess so, Mr. Secretary."

Despite his embarrassment, Waddell was sorry it was over. Kate realized he hated to have his big scene end, and that she had given him a tougher time than she need have. "Mr. Waddell, you were a marvelous instructor, and I'm sorry I made it more difficult than it need have been. Thank you so much for your help." She reached out her hand and shook his.

"Miss Colby, it's a pleasure to have met you and much as my wife and I enjoy you on TV, you're even nicer in person."

"Oh, thank you. And please tell your wife hello for me. If she ever wants to watch my show being taped, just have her call my office, will you?"

"Thank you," he said, beaming. "It was my pleasure."

Then it was Linda Janowitz's turn. She took from a small briefcase a piece of paper. Kate watched her as she did it. This woman is barely three or four years older than I am, she thought. But look at the difference. She has no makeup on, hair in a bun, lots of gray in it. She looks like an ascetic, Kate told herself. And she disapproves of me, I'll bet. I'm too flashy for her.

And indeed the Israel scholar did disapprove. But she was all business. "Here is a list of words Secretary Maloney asked me to make up. Next to them are their Hebrew translations, in print and script. We'll go over them so that you can recognize and identify them.

"But first, do you know that Hebrew words and lines read from right to left, and Hebrew books, newspapers, and documents begin on what we consider the last page?"

Unlike Waddell, for whom Kate had felt a certain warmth, this woman aroused resistance in her; she looked at the older woman innocently and said, "Miss Janowitz, don't you know the joke about the reporter on the Jewish newspaper who got a scoop and ran into the city room shouting, 'Hold the back page!' ?"

Miss Janowitz managed a polite smile and replied, "Mrs. Colby, can you imagine that the same joke might be told in Hebrew about an English-language newspaper reporter? Well, it is. However, I'm glad you know of the difference; it will help you look for the title pages of books and documents.

"Now, let's have a look at this list. The most important words are on top." Kate took the list; the paper felt unusual, flimsy, and crinkly. There, heading the list, was the word Masada, and its transliteration. Her eye ran down the Hebrew list; all the words looked alike to her.

"At first," the other woman said to her, "all the words will look alike to you, but as we go over them, in this little drill, you'll begin to tell them apart." She reached into her briefcase.

"Oh no!" Kate almost shouted, "not flash cards! You're not going to test me with flash cards?"

"They're not exactly cards, just pieces of paper," the other woman said, "but then our supplies are limited. Aside from that, yes, you're absolutely right."

For twenty minutes, while Brewster and Maloney whispered in a corner, the two women went over the words, until finally Linda

Janowitz put them down and said, "Very good, Mrs. Colby, I think it's safe to say you're as good a Hebrew student as you are a photographer."

Kate let out a snorting laugh. "Wow! Thanks. I think." For a pedant, this woman can sting, she said to herself.

"The list is for you to keep," said Miss Janowitz, handing her the paper, "so that you can look it over and carry it with you in your purse. "This may sound overly dramatic, but it's rice paper, so you can chew it and swallow it, if necessary.

"In fact—" and she fished in her briefcase again—"I brought an extra so you can taste it just to see how pleasant it is." She handed the paper to Kate, who looked at it and fingered it, keeping it moving to hide the fact that her hands were still shaking badly. "I don't think I'll try it just now, thanks, unless you've got some soy sauce to put on it. Or is that what the ink's made of?"

She was being too damned clever, she knew, but somehow she felt more vulnerable in front of this woman than with anyone else, and she did not want her to see how nervous she was. Kate said, "If I have to, I'll just chew and swallow. I don't think I want to practice right now. However, if I don't have a chance to get a sandwich soon, I may change my mind." Kate took both pieces of paper and as quickly as she could, to hide the trembling, put them in her purse, along with the camera and tape recorder.

The woman rose. "Good luck, Mrs. Colby. I'm sure you'll be fine." I hope she doesn't try to shake hands, Kate thought; mine are so clammy I'm ashamed. But when Kate said, "I hope so; thank you for your help," the other woman just smiled at her and turned and walked out.

Clearly both men had been keeping an eye on her progress, because as soon as Miss Janowitz left, they came over and resumed their seats.

"Well?" Maloney said.

"I'm not sure if I'm supposed to know how to say 'depth of field' in Hebrew, or whether the camera works from left to right or right to left. And I'm scared. My hands are shaking, my feet are cold as ice. Be prepared for failure. If you try to strap a pistol on me, I'll collapse."

"There's no pistol," Maloney told her. "There are no requirements, only that you do as much as you can. Stay loose, keep your sense of humor, see what happens. For whatever you can do, we're grateful. If you fail, we'll understand."

Maloney pushed and prodded right to the very last word; he never gave up, and he usually scored his points. She knew what he was doing, being a nice guy, but stirring up her competitive instincts, suggesting, gently, that as a woman she wouldn't be held to the same standard of spying as a man. She knew what he was doing—yet she did not want to fail. And by saying he would understand, he was making it all the harder for her to fail.

"I *hope* you'll understand, because the way I feel now I'm not going to get the first spoonful of soup up to my mouth without spilling it all over myself. Can soup gum up a tape recorder?

"I sure hope I can talk the ambassador out of some more information, because if I can't we're all in a spot. Especially me."

Kate looked at her watch. Past three; she had been here nearly two hours. In less than four hours she had to be at the embassy.

She stood. "Well," she said brightly, "think I'll go home, have a bottle of Valium and try to catch a nap before dinner. If the camera and the tape recorder and the rice paper come back by messenger, I hope you get the message. Look at these hands."

Kate held out her long, tanned fingers. They were bouncing around; she could not steady them.

The Secretary didn't mind her talking of her fear as long as it was with the assumption she was going ahead. Talk about return of the camera disturbed him because it questioned the assumption. He didn't want her to leave that way.

"Before we let you go, Kate," he said, taking one of her outstretched hands in his, holding it tight to warm and steady it, "I'm going to go out on a limb and tell you this. We have a man inside the Israeli Embassy. I won't disclose his identity; that would be too much of a burden on you and him. He won't reveal himself to you. What he will try to do is help you in any way he can—to locate material, to get you out of there, if you need it. Only don't try to find out who he is."

Maloney had said all this in one steady stream, deliberately giving her no chance to stop him. And he had been right. Kate wished she could make him take it all back. The more he confided in her, the more he welded her to his side.

She was angry, but she had already been through so much jockeying, shoving, sidestepping, she couldn't work up much heat. She stood up to go, noticing as she did, her linen skirt looked as if she had slept in it. And that's the way all of me feels, she thought. Wilted.

"Mr. Secretary, you *know* that not only did I not wish to be burdened with the identity of your agent in the embassy, I didn't want to be burdened with the knowledge of him at all. Why did you tell me? Was it to warn me that if I turned on you in there and revealed my spy apparatus I could expect to be shot on the spot, or have my dinner poisoned?

"Or was it to pile so much guilty knowledge on me I'd be stuck to your side? Well, let me tell you what I think of both possibilities.

"If it was to frighten me, you made a bad mistake. I'm scared enough already. One more fright and I won't trust my hands to hold a camera or my voice to ask a question.

"If it's the guilty knowledge, let me assure you you could give me the key to your nuclear arsenal and I would still not be signed, sealed, and delivered in advance. All you're doing is getting my temper up. After all, God damn it, I have agreed to go in there, do something for you and consider doing a lot more. Why do you keep pushing?"

Maloney and Brewster both stood. The Secretary knew she had caught him; he had been trying to wrap her up. Now he'd have to back off.

"Believe it or not, Kate, my only thought was to let you know you had a friend in there who'd try to help if you needed it. I wasn't trying to push."

"First of all, Mr. Secretary, I *have* a friend in the embassy, and his name is Dov Shalzar. Remember? How long he'll be my friend is another matter. Second of all, if you have an agent in there, why not let him do your snooping instead of depending on a novice like me?"

Maloney looked chastened. "I know Shalzar is your friend, and you are risking a lot. I also know you have a good idea of why you are taking the risk. What the issues are. I don't have to remind you. As for our agent, if he could do it, do you think I'd invite you to take the risk? He's done things for us before, but this one he won't get close to. This one's got to come from outside. It's all up to you now, Kate. We'll be grateful for any favors. Think it over carefully."

His humility did not soften her. "That I can promise. And I also promise to let you know the results, a complete report."

"Good afternoon, Mr. Secretary. Good afternoon, Bill." She turned to start for the door, when Bill Brewster spoke for the first time in many minutes. He was worried about the friction between Kate and Maloney.

"Kate, don't let side issues make you forget the magnitude of this thing, the vast numbers of people involved. I know you'll want to do the right thing."

She smiled warmly at him, then looked at both men. "You fellas know the Pirates of Penzance, when they're sending the cowardly policemen off to capture the pirates, and the girls sing, 'Go ye heroes, go to glory/though ye die in combat gory/ye shall live in song and story. . . .' Well, fellas, I'm too scared for glory, and living in song and story just ain't my idea of living. See you, fellas."

She headed for the door; Brewster took four long strides to catch her and open it for her. As he did, he said softly, "Take care of yourself." And she answered, "Thanks." Then she was gone down the hall.

Brewster closed the door, turned and walked back toward Maloney, who had resumed his seat on the sofa.

The Secretary looked at his friend and said, "Well?"

"Considering you two had a fair amount of hostility crackling between you, I'd say you did a good job, Pete. Tactically, you were moving her the way you wanted to. Emotionally, you got her back up; emotionally, she left here committed to being a free agent. I'd say the only thing you can be sure of is getting your equipment back. Until you told her about the agent in the embassy, I should also have said you could be certain she'd pump the ambassador for information, if nothing more. Now I'm not even sure of that. Why did you tell her?"

"It was a risk, old boy, no question. But I say she'll do it—and knowing about the agent will help. The more baggage we saddle her with, the harder it is for her to move to their side. Besides, I want her ready if someone drops clues for her; I want her to accept them, trust them.

"And, of course, I want her to relax as much as possible in there, thinking she'll get help if she's in trouble."

"I must say," Brewster responded, "it relaxes me, too, knowing someone will bail her out if she needs it."

The Secretary stared at his old friend, hard. "Don't feel too relaxed about it, old boy. She will get no protection from inside. Our man will not blow his cover to save her. That place is on a wartime basis; chances are even if our man tried to help, they'd make short work of him. In this business you learn to prepare for the end of the world —and then worry about what you'll do for an encore. If we know she has information crucial to us, we'll do anything to get her out—blow his cover, or blow up the embassy walls. But we won't lose our man in there unless we know she has got what we want. I'm very much concerned with saving human life—many, many human lives. And Kate's life is only one. Remember the Masada Plan, Bill? Are you going to blame me more for merely suggesting one life could possibly be in danger—and I don't think it is, by the way—than you blame the Israelis for threatening who knows how many lives?"

Brewster didn't like that. "I find it strange for a Secretary of State who sits by while the Arabs overrun and destroy Israel, to blame Israel for anything. But this is not the time to debate that. I'm worried about one particular life right now, Kate Colby's.

"After all the talk about the agent, what you're doing is throwing a total amateur in to spy, carrying incriminating equipment. And you're telling me once she gets in there she's on her own."

The Secretary didn't look so much tough as tired. "Yes," he said. "That's what I'm telling you."

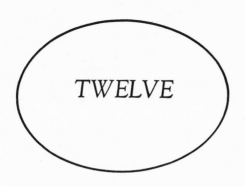

TWELVE

A tall man in a brown striped suit sat reading a newspaper in the narrow lobby of the Waldorf Towers as Kate walked through on her way out to Fiftieth Street. That she didn't notice him was due partly to her preoccupations and partly to his ordinariness. Out on the street, Kate spent a minute or so finding a cab; the man in the brown suit watched her from just outside the revolving door. When she entered the cab, he walked quickly to a black, four-door sedan and got in the front seat next to a man who looked and dressed very much like him. The sedan followed Kate's cab.

Behind them another cab fell into line. In it was a single passenger who could have been a cousin to the other two. His suit was non-descript and baggy like theirs, but not an American cut. He was following Kate, knew that the pair in the sedan were also, and estimated, correctly, they were American Secret Service agents. They, on the other hand, were not aware of him; had they been they would not have been worried, for all three had the same assignment: to keep an eye on Kate Colby, the two on behalf of the Secretary of State, the single man on orders of the Israeli Ambassador to the United Nations.

Again, Kate didn't notice them; they were skillful at their jobs, but she would not have noticed them had they been riding in red fire engines with the sirens on. All her attention, thoughts, fears, were focused on the objects in her purse and the use she might have to make of them. Five times during the short ride to her apartment on East Sixty-fourth Street she opened the purse to look at them.

Each time, the camera took on a look of greater and greater complexity, the tape recorder seemed more and more foreign an object for the inside of her bra, the rice paper with the translations seemed to rattle louder and louder in the purse. What I am considering seems crazier and crazier, she told herself: not only exploiting a friendship, double-crossing someone I love, but jumping in as the lowest of amateurs, to a game played by professionals. And I am scared.

Almost as soon as she sat back in the cab she thought of an easy way out: she would simply leave the camera, recorder, and list at home, and end for herself the possibility of using them inside the embassy. Afterwards she could either admit it, or merely say she found nothing to shoot or tape. Why don't I just decide on that, she said to herself, and pacify my weary mind?

But she wouldn't, and she knew it and knew why.

First because she'd feel silly having gone through all that instruction just to keep her options open, and then close them off before she got into the embassy.

But more important, Kate Colby was a fear junkie. The more frightened she became, the more she asked herself, why am I doing this, the more she was propelled toward the danger. She had seen it operate her very first day as a radio reporter.

She'd been assigned to cover a demonstration by welfare recipients protesting a cut in their payments, and she'd been standing in front of City Hall, tape recorder slung over her shoulder, notebook in hand, when the fighting started. Suddenly the pickets' signs were waving violently, a policeman's hat flew in the air, mounted police moved in, bodies began surging like a swift current around the pilings of a bridge.

Her first reaction was to go with the flow of those fleeing the violence. But that was momentary, then she felt herself pushing in the opposite direction, toward the melee, saying to herself, get the hell away from here, moving all the while toward the center of the action. And that contradiction, the battle between fear and exhilaration for control of her, was to take over many times.

She wasn't hurt at the City Hall demonstration. Perhaps if she had been, she'd thought later, it would have cured her. At any rate, although she barely knew how to cover a story then, she got some surprisingly good interviews. On the bus home afterwards, she'd tried to understand her feelings and her move toward the danger. She hadn't succeeded, then or subsequently. But as time went on she'd gotten to know the feeling well, and so when it coursed through her now, on her way home from the Waldorf, she treated it like an old friend who visits too often.

This was a little more complicated than a question of bravery, though. She had problems to solve before seven. Which flag should she be waving when she walked into the embassy? To preserve her allegiance to Dov, she'd have to show him the equipment at once, tell him what Maloney and Brewster had asked, and then ask him, what do *we* do now? Anything less would be a step away from him. But if she did that, she would probably get no information from him, and she would certainly forfeit her role as a free agent.

After that? Well, probably neither side would trust her fully, surely neither side would make any further use of her. In short, with the deadline for the **Big Boom** only hours away, she would have thrown away her chance to help stop it. She was in a new situation. Watching a crisis, reporting on it, unable to affect the outcome, was one thing. She was used to that. Now something else was expected of her. Suppose she failed to produce for Maloney and Brewster? What would they think of her? Suppose she were caught by Dov? What would he do to her?

Israel came first; she knew that about him. And there was no second. And in the past when she was rattled and hurt at his priority he'd told her not to compare apples and oranges. But if she were caught spying against Israel, with a camera and tape recorder, *he* might have to compare apples and oranges. And make juice of the orange, or sauce of the apple—whichever she was.

All right, she told herself as she reached into her purse to pay the cabby, don't get melodramatic, you're not juice or sauce yet, you haven't even decided to walk into the embassy with your purse and your bra loaded. She saw her billfold in there; she also saw the camera and recorder. Their presence was a kind of commitment already, wasn't it?

As her cab stopped, the Secret Service car glided slowly by it, this time with only one agent in it, the other having gotten out at the corner of Sixty-fourth and Madison and stationed himself so he could keep an eye on her building while pretending to look in a shop window. And as the Israeli agent had seen the car ahead of his cab slow down to let the American agent out, he'd told his driver, "Stop here, please." Then he'd paid, gotten out and crossed Madison Avenue purposefully, headed straight for a phone booth where he could watch the window-shopping American agent and the entrance to Kate's building. He picked up the receiver; anyone wanting to use that phone would be confronted by an Israeli holding an endless conversation with a dial tone.

In her apartment, Kate tried to nap, exhausted because she'd been up since 3 a.m., after two hours of sleep, yet unable to drop off, wanting to take a Valium, yet fearing if she did she'd sleep too long. So in her robe, she lay on her bed, tossing, turning, thinking, closing her eyes, at one point actually falling asleep only to be awakened by a dream in which she was running from someone or something that kept gaining on her.

Finally at about 5:30, restless, afraid of another dream, she got up to shower and begin the deliberately drawn-out process of dressing for dinner. How do you dress for spying at the Israeli embassy, she asked herself.

Two accessories were her starting points: the beaded evening purse for the camera, a brassiere for the tape recorder. She should have a dress that would go with the purse, and require a bra. The long white summer knit would do for both, dressy enough to suit the beaded purse, revealing enough to demand a bra—unless you were sixteen, as she had commented when she bought it. She looked at her naked body in the full-length mirror. Not bad, she said, but not sixteen. She found a light, opaque bra and put it on.

Then the tape recorder. But which side of the bra? And which side of the recorder out? And which side up?

She had a moment of acute panic. Easy now, she told herself; in the privacy of her bedroom, saying it almost aloud. The heart's on the left. No it isn't, she contradicted herself; it's in the center, facing left. Well, either way, she thought, put the instrument on the right, just to be safe. After all, *nobody* says the heart's on the right. And put the side with the switch up, so you can reach it with a finger. But which side out and which next to the skin? She looked at the recorder. The circle of tiny perforations, she guessed, marked the location of the speaker. That side away from the skin—unless they wanted a recording of her tremulous chest cavity; she thought of the Robert Burns line, "O, what a panic's in thy breastie!" How would a panicky breast sound on tape?

She fitted the recorder into her bra, trying to tuck it under her breast so it was riding just above the band. With the index finger of her left hand she reached in and felt the switch. In the Off position it was to the right; with her finger she moved it to the left. That was on. Left—On. Right—Off. Left—On. She moved it to the right again. Off. Too bad it wasn't Right—On, she thought. And then: cut it out. You've got too much unavoidable confusion to bother about inventing any.

In bra and panties, she went to her closet for the white knit, and slipped it on. Yes, decidedly, she told herself, as she gazed in the mirror, this dress demands a bra. No one will question that. She looked with satisfaction at the gathers along the neckline, which covered the guilty part of the bra as if it had been made to hide spy equipment. She bent over, she twisted; the instrument didn't show. It's OK, she thought. He won't know it's there unless I stand on my head and it drops out or unless he puts a hand in my bra, and I don't anticipate either this evening.

From a shelf in her closet she pulled down a bin full of purses, and began rummaging through it for the beaded one. It wasn't there! Of course not, what made her think it would be? After all it was the one she needed. A second moment of panic. Which could she use instead? None for this dress, which meant she'd have to change, but into what? And when would she have a chance to comb out her hair?

With all that time, why had she waited so damned long, she asked herself.

Frantically she grabbed the bin and turned it upside down over her bed, dumping all the purses. One by one, she picked up each and put it back in the bin. No! It still wasn't there! Yes. It was. There was the gold chain, sticking out of the big brown leather Gucci bag. She fished the beaded one out, began putting just a few things from her other purse into it. On top of them she carefully placed the little camera. Then she closed her purse and opened it, at if she were sitting at dinner with Dov and the Foreign Minister and casually reaching for a Kleenex. The camera was all too visible, so she dug with her hand and made a space for it at the bottom of the purse. No, she thought, too far down, she'd never get to it when she needed it. *If she needed it,* she edited herself.

She'd put it on top, cover it with a couple of Kleenexes and remember not to blow her nose more than once.

Do I have everything now, she asked herself. Camera. Tape recorder. Right. No. Forgot the rice-paper Hebrew vocabulary list. She grabbed for it in the purse she'd used earlier, and in doing so also found the blank sheet for test chewing. Should she try it? What the hell, she'd be trying lots more soon, why not?

Disdaining the option of tasting a piece, she wadded the entire sheet into her mouth and began chewing, expecting it to crumble and melt like a butter cookie. But it was like a soda cracker, only more resistant and more elastic. It was not crumbling and not melting, and stubbornly, desperately, she tried swallowing the unyielding wad. It wouldn't go; for one terrifying moment it lodged in her throat, bringing on a flash of screaming panic that made the earlier two seem mere whispers. She leaned over the bathroom sink and retched. Out it came.

Well, she thought, if I have to swallow that list it had better be a word at a time. Then, squeamish but stubborn, she reached for the pulpy mass in the sink and tore from it a soggy piece the size of her thumbnail. She put it in her mouth and swallowed. Down it went, easily. "There," she said to the mirror.

Her bedroom digital clock registered 6:35. She no longer had time to spare, so she combed her hair, put on a pair of white shoes, and left. In the elevator mirror, she gave herself the customary inspection, only this time for an extra reason. She focused on her right breast. No sign of the recorder. Reflexively she felt for the camera in her purse; her fingers could make out its shape. Well, she thought, I haven't left them upstairs, so I'm a step closer to using them. It's open, she added, I don't *have* to. But I'm getting closer all the time.

She headed west on Sixty-fourth Street, covering the few yards to the corner of Madison and then standing on the southeast corner. Directly north of her stood the American agent, completing a three-hour inspection of a window full of women's sandals; diagonally across from her the Israeli agent was working on his one-way marathon call, during which he had survived the dirty looks of a half-dozen would-be telephoners.

Kate looked at her gold Tiffany wristwatch, the gift from Brewster. She reminded herself that originally she had recruited him to help Dov, and now she had enlisted on his side against Dov. Then she corrected herself: not his side, the American side. And was it against Dov? Or for him, too? Her watch read 6:40; she had the time to walk the nine blocks up Madison to Seventy-third. Maybe on the way she could decide what to say to Dov when she first walked in the door; that would be the moment for "Look what they've rigged me with." Every moment after that would make it harder and harder to speak up.

She started up the east side of Madison, passing close enough to the Secret Service man to reach out and touch him, never noticing he was the same man who had been sitting in the lobby of the Waldorf Towers three and a half hours ago. He let her get all the way to Sixty-fifth Street before following her, knowing his colleague in the sedan would be looping around the block and then following them slowly uptown. The Israeli let them both get a head start before casually walking up the west side of Madison. He was not unhappy with the presence of the Americans; they were doing his work for him, while he relaxed in the role of standby.

As she had been instructed to do, Kate went to Seventy-third, where she turned right and walked twenty-five yards before being met by Yehuda, Dov Shalzar's driver and bodyguard. The American agent had speeded up when she made the turn, so as not to lose sight of her, and as he came around the corner he saw the burly Israeli approaching her. Quickly he moved forward, anticipating trouble, when he saw by the relaxed set of Kate's body and her greeting that she was expecting this meeting. By then the American was quite close to them, so, smoothly, he took on the role of a confused out-of-towner looking for an address. He peered at house numbers, consulted his watch, shook his head in annoyance and then, apparently having spotted his destination, crossed Seventy-third Street, heading for an apartment house in the middle of the block.

The Israeli who had been tailing both of them was, in turn, startled when he saw the American move quickly toward Kate and Yehuda. For a moment he questioned his assumption that the American was an agent, and he feared an attack on Kate, so he began closing the gap between himself and the others. Then he saw the American agent cross the street, and not wanting to be spotted, he turned into the nearest brownstone as if he had been headed there all along.

Using a key, Yehuda led Kate through the first of the double doors of the rear entrance. As in the front, they were in a small, windowless lobby scanned by a closed-circuit TV camera. But this time there was no spoken challenge; Yehuda used another key to let them into the passageway leading to the embassy proper. In it sat a security man who had been reading a newspaper but looked up at them as they entered. He and Yehuda exchanged brief, muttered greetings. Amazing, Kate thought, how cops the world over look like cops.

The two of them went through the embassy kitchen before reaching the large sitting room, in front of which stood another security man, with thick neck, thick wrists, and jacket too big for him.

"The ambassador will be right here," Yehuda said. "Please have a seat."

She sat on the sofa. Well, she said to herself, now is the time. If I'm going to tell him, it's got to be now. She was having a little trouble breathing, she realized. She waited.

Three hours earlier, the Foreign Minister of Israel, Itzhak Weismann, had also been brought in through the Seventy-third Street entrance, and the ambassador had been spending all the time since with him. Weismann had no sooner entered the embassy and rested his attaché case, than he wanted to be "put in the picture." Shalzar had to smile when he was reminded how British Weismann was. British and aristocratic, and in the early days of the UN when Israel was not yet a pariah, Weismann had established a formidable reputation as the new nation's eloquent spokesman. He had become a hero in New York and in the media; ironically the geographic weak spot in his prestige had always been Israel. His relentless pursuit of the Prime Ministership had never been successful, and even his appointment as Foreign Minister was in response to his value abroad, not at home. Privately, the powerhouses of Israeli politics felt the shiny superstructure of Weismann's verbal brilliance sat on a shaky foundation; he was indecisive, an issue-straddler.

The Prime Minister shared this view. Once when an American correspondent, praising Weismann's talents, said to the Old Man, "But he speaks seven languages!" the Prime Minister replied, "So let him be a waiter at the King David Hotel." The story got out; Weissmann was furious. The PM denied it, but it sounded so much like him and made such good telling, it gained wide circulation. At the same time, the Prime Minister knew Weismann had value—in ways not even his Cabinet knew about.

Dov Shalzar liked Weismann. Behind the orotundity, he found honest idealism, behind the indecision, a talent for analysis that, if sometimes Byzantine, nevertheless contributed substantially to the decisions reached by firmer minds. He was totally ignorant of the clandestine use to which the PM put his Foreign Minister.

One characteristic of Weismann that Shalzar felt a blessing at the moment was his fervent preference for speaking to listening. Although he had wanted to be "put in the picture," Shalzar had hardly begun briefing him when, at his first chance, he launched into a vivid re-creation of the early morning meeting in Jerusalem at which the Masada Plan decision had been made. His telling of it exemplified his strengths and weaknesses.

"All I could do, given the exigencies of the moment," he said, "was try for a moment's breathing spell, a moment of contemplation before the headlong race to oblivion began." Weismann leaned back on the sofa, sipping a glass of sherry, still the image of the Oxonian he had been in the late thirties. He was of medium height but seemed taller because he was so lean and hawk-faced. Except for the years he was actively seeking the Prime Ministership and wore Israeli clothing, he always had his suits tailored in London.

At once Shalzar understood Weismann was trying to rationalize the weakness of his protest against the plan; Shalzar also knew that at least the protest had been there. Weismann's abhorrence of violence had resisted the fevered chauvinism that had captured so many others. At least that was how Shalzar would describe it. Others would perceive the same phenomenon as a failure of nerve. But then others were ready to see a failure of nerve in the Foreign Minister at the drop of a gauntlet, for the fact was, Weismann could never live down his lack of a combat record. Although he had given up a promising academic career as a medieval historian to move to Palestine in 1938, he had been through five wars without having been a combat warrior in any of them.

There were publicly known reasons, and secret reasons, all of them impeccable. But he hadn't fought, and in Israel if you were neither bloodied nor a kibbutznik, your political chances were so circum-scribed, it was a tribute to Weismann's talents that he had come as far as he had.

Shalzar could imagine his friend trying to stand up against the majority at that meeting, and felt a surge of sympathy for him. "That you could even try for a moment of contemplation in the face of that steamroller, Itzhak, is a tribute to your strong-mindedness, perhaps even foolhardiness." Shalzar was toying with a glass of sherry as he spoke. He seldom touched alcohol before dinnertime, and never drank sherry at any time, but he knew Weismann tended to read a rebuff into every gesture, and would take the ambassador's abstinence as a reprimand to his anglophilia. So Shalzar could not refuse.

Shalzar knew, too, Weissmann would take the word foolhardiness as a compliment; seldom did anyone charge him with daring, and he liked it. He gave a pleased smile and then offered a modest disclaimer. "Throughout the discussion, I felt I was speaking on your behalf as well as my own; I felt you would wish me to represent your sentiments as I did my own."

Realizing Weismann could play the self-congratulatory motif at great length and with infinite variations, the ambassador wanted to move away from the meeting to the plan and the business at hand. "It's odd, isn't it, Itzhak," he said, "that of all the hawks available, we two reluctant ones are the ones here to effectuate the plan." Shalzar was amused to note he was beginning to take on a touch of the Foreign Minister's floweriness; it always happened, and he always recovered. Without pausing, he went on, "You have the actual documents to show me, don't you?"

"Yes, I have," answered Weismann, his voice lowered to a nervous whisper. "Right here." And he patted the attaché case, which only then Shalzar noticed he had kept on his lap since he sat down. Reverently, the Foreign Minister placed his case on the sofa between them, then he worked the combination lock on the case to open it, failing the first time, starting again, and succeeding. The case was slim, of beautifully tooled leather; in it were two sets of mimeographed sheets. Each had a title sheet in Hebrew. On one was the word "Masada" and the words "New York"; on the other, the word "Masada" and the word "Summary"; on both were the Hebrew words giving them the highest of security classifications. They were the only papers in the Foreign Minister's attaché case.

For a moment Weismann grew even more pompous as he said, "I am enjoined to caution you, Dov, you must first read the instructions for destroying these documents; they are just inside the title page."

"Of course," Shalzar responded, holding out his hand.

The Foreign Minister picked up one set and handed it to Shalzar. "This is your New York set," he said. "There are, of course, equivalent sets for the other locations involved. Read the instruction page first, please!"

Shalzar did. When he looked up, Weismann said, "Dov, please read the document now; it has only eleven pages and I have been instructed never to let it out of my possession." He seemed a bit embarrassed to say it, as if cloak-and-dagger work were not congenial to him, and he feared Shalzar might be insulted by the precautions being taken.

But again the ambassador said merely, "Of course." And he began reading. Although there were only eleven pages of text, they were single-spaced and he read carefully, and so it was nearly five before he finished. He handed it back to the Foreign Minister and started to speak, but Weismann said, "Here, read this one, it's the summary document, then we'll talk."

Carefully, painstakingly, Shalzar perused the twenty-two pages of text, plus the accompanying maps; it took him nearly an hour, throughout which time Weismann sat motionless on the sofa. When Shalzar finally finished and handed it back to Weismann, the time was almost seven.

Neither had been watching the time and both were startled when there was a knock on the door. An assistant opened it and said, "Miss Colby is here."

"Good God," said Shalzar. "Is it that late?" Then he checked his watch and saw it was. "Itzhak, why don't you take the material into the library." He motioned toward a door at the far end of the living room. Flustered, Weismann picked up the open case and carried it in two hands to the library door, where he stood, indecisively, unable to turn the knob, until Shalzar, who had been right behind him, reached out to open the door. The ambassador shut the door behind Weismann, and then turned to the aide. "Please show her in," he said.

The entire exit had taken about fifty seconds, but to Kate standing in the hallway it seemed an hour. Her tension had made her breathing a conscious act.

When the young assistant turned to her and said, "Please go in," she jumped so visibly, he grew startled. Then, trying to seem calm, she said softly, "Thank you," and entered the living room. Shalzar stood up and walked toward her. A fine-looking man, she told herself, the man I love, and I've got to start lying to him—unless I tell him right now.

The words—a disclosure of what was in her purse, her bra and her mind—were in her throat. If she was to say them, now was the time. Shalzar held out his hands. "You, in that dress, are the calm in the eye of this hurricane. And a touch of beauty just when I need one."

Now, she told herself. Now, I must tell him. Or lose my chance. She spoke, but only to respond to his compliment. The moment for confession came and went.

"Why thank you," she said. "And you certainly are dazzling this evening, Mr. Ambassador. One would think you didn't have a thing on your mind besides looking and acting like Cary Grant." If for a moment he had forgotten the news from Israel and the contents of Weismann's briefcase, her words reminded him. He tried to hold a smile, but his look darkened.

"Each message we get from Israel makes the picture look worse. We're apparently in trouble everywhere, and we're taking such heavy losses, there's no prospect for things changing. I wonder what Cary Grant would do in a spot like this?"

She looked at him lovingly. Just what he needs right now, she said to herself, another enemy, a new spy in his own embassy. Then she thought, hoping it wasn't a rationalization, what he needs is to bring the United States and Russia in to stop this war. And he may not believe it, but they won't help if I can't learn more about the plan.

Maybe I can convince him to tell me. If not—if not, then what? she asked herself. Then we'll see, she thought. We'll see how my hands shake when I try to eat the soup.

To Shalzar she said, "Cary Grant would probably say to himself—at least he would if *I* were writing the script: What has my country got to lose now? What harm would it do if I told the American Secretary of State more about the Masada Plan? After all, wouldn't I rather get what I want and stop the plan than go ahead and use it?"

Shalzar's return smile was grim. "Stop for a few moments," he said. "As long as you're going to begin your—what did you call them, winning ways?—you may as well wait until the Foreign Minister is with us. That way you can try to win two for the price of one."

He took her arm and started her toward the library door. "Let me introduce you to Weismann, or Don Itzhak, as his friendly detractors—of whom there are many—like to call him."

Shalzar opened the door to the library a crack, knocked and opened it farther. Kate could see the thin, sharp-featured Foreign Minister seated at a desk, looking into an open attaché case. He seemed startled by the knock, but recovered quickly, smiling toward them, then looking down and replacing papers. He tried to snap the lock shut and failed. Then he rose as the other two came closer.

"Itzhak," Shalzar began, "may I present the distinguished American television journalist, and my dear friend, Kate Colby. Kate, may I present our Foreign Minister, Itzhak Weismann."

They moved toward Weismann as Shalzar spoke, and the Foreign Minister, standing, tried twice more to close the lock. Then, because they were almost at the desk, he stepped around in front of it and extended his hand to Kate.

"Miss Colby," he said, his British accent thoroughly scrubbed up, "I am delighted to meet you, at last. Among those who follow American journalism, your work is highly respected."

Usually Kate's inner response to a line like that was: cut the crap. But this man, she had to admit, did it beautifully. She shook his hand saying, "And I am delighted to meet you, Mr. Minister. Among those who follow diplomacy, your charm is even more respected than my journalism, and for better reason."

Shalzar sensed the touch of a sting to her remark, and to blunt it, he added, "We three are meeting for dinner under circumstances that draw us very close to one another. We share knowledge of an impending deadline, at which time the world could be changed. We are three of the very few people on earth who know of this deadline, so it's fitting that we dine together while waiting for word from the other side, word which we hope will restore peace and sanity to the world."

Kate had never heard a speech so pompous from Dov under such informal circumstances. She wondered if he had made it for her benefit or the Foreign Minister's. And she was struck by his phrase "the other side." What makes you think, she asked the ambassador, silently, that I'm not on the other side? But she didn't ask it aloud.

"May I suggest," said Shalzar, "that rather than having a drink in the sitting room, we go straight into the dining room and have some wine while we are eating?" He smiled. "You see, unless you count the excellent coffee at the Unity Club this morning at eight, I have had nothing to eat since dinner yesterday. And I shouldn't be surprised if that were true of you, too, Kate."

She thought of the rice paper. "Well, virtually nothing," she said.

"And you know what airlines food is like, even if you are the only passenger," added Weismann in a humorous, yet slightly grandiose allusion to the fact that he and two security men had been the only passengers aboard the El Al jet that had flown them to New York.

"So we are unanimous," said Shalzar, leading them to tall double doors on the far end of the library where it adjoined a large dining room. He opened one of the double doors and let them walk ahead of him. Three places had been set at one end of the long table, which could seat fourteen.

"Since I am playing host," Shalzar said, "why don't I sit at the head, with Itzhak, our newly arrived guest, on my right and Kate on my left." They took their places, Shalzar helping Kate with her chair.

In front of them stood an uncorked bottle of red wine. Without looking at its label, Shalzar took it in his hand and asked, "Will this do, or would someone prefer a drink of whiskey or something else?"

"This is fine," said Kate.

"A 1964 Haut Brion will always do," answered Weismann. He had already noticed the wine and its vintage, something to which the ambassador was oblivious.

"Then you must approve it for us, Itzhak," said Shalzar, pouring some into the Foreign Minister's glass. Weismann went through the tasting ritual, and said, "Perfect."

"Some day, at our leisure, Itzhak, you must drill into me the connoisseurship that will keep me from seizing a bottle like a barbarian and pouring, without even looking at the label." Then Shalzar poured wine into Kate's glass before going back to Weismann's and then his own.

All three raised their glasses and Weismann proposed a toast. "To the day and the leisure of which Dov spoke, when, with easy minds and joyous hearts, we shall be able to dwell on the delights of good wine and good company."

They sipped from their glasses. Then Shalzar raised his and said, "To 9 a.m.—may it come and go quietly." To which Kate and the Foreign Minister added, "Amen."

200

Shalzar turned to his Foreign Minister. "I should tell you, to begin, Itzhak, how valuable Kate has been in putting us through, informally, to the Secretary of State. She knows of the Masada Plan, and she has heard the list of demands I have transmitted to the Secretary of State."

The ambassador swiveled his head from Weismann to her and continued. "Kate, I've told Itzhak that the Secretary and Bill Brewster have asked you to come here and find out more about the plan. Why don't you pick it up from there. How are you going to go about it?"

Shalzar was joking, yet putting her on the spot. "Well," she replied, "I thought I'd start by just asking, before I get to the serious stuff like the bamboo splinters under the fingernails." To herself she said, If only he would tell me something so I don't have to do any more!

"What can you say that Bill Brewster hasn't already said?" Shalzar asked her.

"I can try to assure you the Secretary wants to stop the Arabs, but can't go ahead until you tell him more. I can try to assure you he has not changed his mind about that. Perhaps you'll believe me because I'm not the Secretary's close friend, as Bill Brewster is. Perhaps you'll believe me because hours have gone by since your demands were first presented to the Secretary and he has not taken any step to meet them."

She could take in both Israelis at the same time. Both looked back at her. They'd not give in, she could see it.

"What have you got to lose by telling more?" she asked almost desperately. "Why not?"

"Maybe we're afraid he wants to know more about the plan for the purpose of thwarting it," Shalzar began. "Maybe it's just a battle of wills, which we've got to win to get us by this crisis and keep us in position for the ones to follow. Maybe, personally, I just don't want to be pushed around by Maloney. He's great for doing that, you know. Maybe I'm bound by my orders, and unable to disclose any more even if I wanted to. Which is not to say I want to. And maybe it's all four —and there's a five, six, and seven, too. At any rate there's nothing more we are going to disclose, and the sooner the Secretary realizes that, the sooner he'll decide to act. There are only fourteen hours left. Slightly less, actually."

The ambassador looked up from his watch and stared at Kate. "The best thing you can do, Kate, is assure Maloney no more is forthcoming. If you lead him to believe anything else, you're doing him and all of us a disservice." His face showed no softness, no suggestion he regretted not being able to offer more.

"Well, so much for my winning ways," she said, looking at both men and lifting her wineglass to her lips.

Weismann spoke. "I hope you are not discouraged, Kate. I hope this will not dissuade you from continuing to bend your best efforts toward a resolution of this matter. We need and appreciate your help. Please continue to give it to us."

Maybe I'm pushing everything through the filter of my own nerves, she thought, maybe I'm just imagining this, but if I didn't know better, I'd swear Weismann was deliberately encouraging me to go ahead and—do what? Of course, I'm being ridiculous, she told herself. Then she remembered what Maloney had told her about his having a man in the embassy. Cool down, she said to herself. Here she was on her first spying assignment and she was trying to mastermind the situation. No, she thought, no. It's not my first spying assignment. Not yet.

To Weismann she replied, "Well, I am trying, Mr. Minister. Doing my best, and Mr. Hard Liner over there stops me cold. Why don't you give him written permission to open up a little so we can stop this foolishness, the three of us, and then march up together, hand in hand, to collect our Nobel Peace prizes?"

She suspected Dov wouldn't like this tentative move to split them. And she was right; his hard look at her became a glower. But hell, she thought, I've nothing to lose by taking a chance, before having to decide whether to go on to something he'd like even less. As it turned out, she had antagonized Shalzar for nothing. Her hope that Weismann would be more malleable was mistaken. The Foreign Minister stopped her short. His style was rococo, but he stopped her.

"Alas, Kate, ours not to reason why," he began. "We, like the Light Brigade—and the analogy may be all too fitting—are sent forth, perhaps insufficiently armed, perhaps in insufficient force, but with our weapons specified and our options numbered. And however high we may stand in the chain of command, we nonetheless remain a part of it and subject to its hierarchical discipline. As an individual I could deny you nothing, as a soldier in the ranks I can yield you nothing. I am chagrined to have to say it, and I'm sure my chagrin is as nothing to Dov's."

Wow, had he made all that up right then, she asked herself, or did he compose speeches like that in advance and commit them to memory, to be trotted out when needed? She lifted her glass and tipped it to him in recognition of the velvet glove treatment. Dov Shalzar just watched and listened. Kate thought he had seemed worried at first about the Foreign Minister's giving something away and had relaxed only when he heard Weismann holding the line.

Now she had to face a dead-end sign in her own path. Her earlier ruminations had been eased by the possibility Dov would volunteer something. She may never have believed it, but there was always the possibility, in which unlikely instance she could leave her tape recorder unswitched in her bra, the camera untouched in her purse, and the whole spying alternative an unrealized horror about which to tell her grandchildren. Now the possibility was no more.

She just refused to believe it. Desperate to keep it alive, she turned to the ambassador for a final try and, as she did, wondered why she persisted. Was she really hoping for an eleventh-hour commutation of sentence? Or was she just laying a psychological groundwork for spying, trying to demonstrate to herself that she had tried her best, before believing that the next step was inevitable? She didn't know which, but either way she'd give it one last try.

"Mr. Minister, Mr. Ambassador, are you so bound by orders you have no room for improvisation? Doesn't every soldier have a certain leeway with which to meet extraordinary circumstances? And doesn't that flexibility mean the difference between a force that can respond quickly and imaginatively and one that is slow and rigid? Like the difference between a panzer attack and the Maginot Line?"

The very danger of that analogy spurred her on to another. She almost began it with "And speaking of panzer attack." But she didn't have the nerve. Instead, she said, "And going back to the Minister's talk of 'ours not to reason why,' why it sounds so much like 'I was just following orders,' I'm amazed that anyone, let alone any Jew, would use it. May I assume from what you said before, Mr. Minister, you have reservations about the Masada Plan? I *know* the ambassador does. Shouldn't you be reasoning why, instead of offering up to me a hunk of warmed-over Tennyson that tried to glamorize one of the major botches of nineteenth-century warfare? Shouldn't someone have reasoned why at Balaclava? Wouldn't that have saved those poor slobs of the Light Brigade from getting cut to ribbons?" Kate put her hand to her side as she spoke and she brushed the purse with the camera in it. The reminder gave her a jolt, and she dug in harder.

"Of course I assume the damage to the Light Brigade resembles the Masada Plan the way a hangnail resembles terminal cancer. So I'm asking, when do you two start reasoning why?"

Shalzar was furious. "I'm *amazed*," he said, attacking the word, she thought, as if he wished it were she, "at the effrontery of so many Gentiles in using Nazi comparisons when speaking to or about Israel. Why do you do that? Do you think you'll score more points that way? Do you seriously believe there is an analogy between the Foreign Minister, or me, and Adolf Eichmann? Every time the Israelis attack an Arab terrorist camp that has been bleeding us white, we're like Nazis. Why not, for the sake of a fresh metaphor, compare us to the US Army at Wounded Knee, or the US Army at My Lai, or the New York state troopers at Attica, or the Chicago police at the '68 Democratic convention? What's the matter, don't you think they were brutal enough?

"I always thought we Jews would get into the habit of calling Gentiles Nazis any time they displeased us. As it turns out, it happens more often in reverse. Well, let me tell you, you haven't earned the right to do that. For a Jew to see a Nazi under every Gentile bed is regrettable but historically comprehensible. For a Gentile to cry Nazi every time a Jewish floorboard creaks is cheap sensationalism and lousy imagery to boot."

Kate was devastated by the ferocity of Shalzar's reaction. White faced, she could only begin to answer, "Sorry, I didn't mean . . ." He refused to acknowledge she had tried to speak, and rode right through.

"But lumping us with Eichmann and the Light Brigade is not merely cheap sensationalism and lousy imagery, it is dangerous because one of those stands for immorality and the other for mere stupidity, a substantially lesser charge.

"If obeying one's orders conflicts with one's sense of morality, and the issue is important, one should not obey. If I believed the Masada Plan was immoral I would have resigned rather than have any part in it. So would the Foreign Minister. In fact, I could have refused for any reason whatever. I expressed my reservations, and chose to go ahead. So much for lumping us with Eichmann.

"In the case of the Light Brigade, someone had blundered, yes; it would have been preferable had wiser heads prevailed. Should a soldier disobey orders that are merely stupid, as opposed to immoral? Of course not. The remedy lies in wise orders, not disobedience. One can always find some soldiers who consider any single order stupid. If they were free to disobey merely because they thought they knew better, nothing would ever get done. So the men of the Light Brigade *should* have obeyed; they should *not* have reasoned why.

"Now let me stress that, whatever my, and the Foreign Minister's, reservations may have been, may *be,* they are based *neither* on immorality nor stupidity."

Shalzar had cooled as he spoke, and realized he'd spoken, urged by raw nerves. "That leaves one other point you made, and it doesn't make me nearly as angry as the first two—you'll be pleased to learn." He smiled at her.

"Yes, a good soldier is supposed to be ready with 'field expedients,' improvisations to respond to the unexpected, what you call 'extraordinary circumstances.' What you don't understand, Kate, is that so far there *are* no extraordinary circumstances. The American response to the plan was expected and our reply worked out in advance. Nothing you've done or said so far is a surprise.

"Now, if you walked in here with a gun in that purse . . ." Kate jumped, she hoped not visibly. Did he know? Was he playing with her? She tried to hold steady as he went on. "And tried to kidnap us, *that* would be extraordinary, and we would not have to phone Jerusalem for orders on whether to put up our hands or tackle you."

The shock had made Kate forget her indignation at Dov's Eichmann speech, and as she answered she just tried to disguise her fright. "I'm not going to ask which of those you'd do."

"That's all right," said the ambassador. "I don't know the answer. I suppose it would depend on how quick on the draw we thought you were, and how the Foreign Minister's old Rugby knee was holding up."

Recovered, Kate felt for a moment like returning to the Eichmann argument, but decided against it. She remembered her mission. "But thirteen and a half hours from Doomsday and a 'No' from the Americans is not extraordinary enough for you?"

Weismann spoke, "Perhaps the very desperation of the situation and the imminent deadline are what should make you Americans change your minds rather than we ours."

"And suppose neither side does?"

Shalzar wanted to stop this; he didn't want Kate to think she was going to get anything from them. "Listen," he said. "If the Lord parted the Red Sea for us, what's a little thing like getting a Secretary of State to change his mind?"

She had run out of road, Kate saw that; now she'd have to turn off, and she didn't like her new direction. "Are we going to be able to eat a meal now, do you think," she asked. And is it to be our Last Supper? If it is, I'd like . . ."

An explosion, nearby, powerful, yet muted, interrupted her. The table seemed to rise from the floor and settle with a bang. Silverware rattled. Wineglasses toppled, the claret reddening the white tablecloth. Most frightening to her was the feeling of concussion. The air seemed to expand with a bang, pressing on her eardrums, her eyes, her scalp. Then it was over; in the hall outside men were shouting; the door to the dining room opened quickly, a young man with a mustache stuck his head in and yelled something in Hebrew. Weismann yelled at Shalzar, also in Hebrew, and Shalzar leaped to his feet and ran from the room.

The Foreign Minister was on his feet, too, staring around. He seemed bewildered. He, too, started out of the room, saying, "Wait here!"

Oh no, don't leave me! she wanted to shout, but there was no one to shout it to. On the table in front of her, the red of the spilled wine had spread over the white cloth like blood, and the sight of it stunned her. She stood, looked around, when another alarm stabbed through her.

I am alone, she told herself. My first hope was they'd tell me something. That's gone. My second was they'd never leave me alone, never give me the chance to spy. That's gone.

In the hall outside, footsteps, confusion.

How do I spy? she asked herself. Where do I look? Not in a dining room, that's crazy. Her heart was thudding, her eyes scanning the room wildly, not knowing what to focus on, when she heard the snap of a door being opened. She looked toward the sound; the door connecting to the library was now slightly ajar. Quickly she walked toward it. How had that happened? Someone had done it, it was no accident—a door can swing open by itself, but someone had to turn the knob to open the latch, and she had heard the quiet snap of the latch.

And as she reached it and looked through, in that instant she saw the door leading from the library to the hall close. Her imagination? No, again she heard the click of the spring latch. Someone had opened the library door for her. She remembered Maloney's words, "We have a man in the embassy."

Then, almost against her will, her eyes moved from the door to the desk where the Foreign Minister had been sitting. There, still on it, stood the attaché case, with which Weismann had been fumbling when she walked over to meet him.

There it is, no excuse now, she said. I can't, she answered herself. They might walk in any second. Then lock the doors. The bomb, being left alone—perfect excuses. She could hear police sirens outside. They're too busy to be thinking of me, she thought.

Turning, face hot and flushed, hand in an icy sweat as it gripped the purse hanging from her right shoulder, Kate ran to the door connecting the dining room with the hall. She found a new barrier. If it can't lock, no go, she decided. There was a lock; she turned it shut, and ran back toward the door to the library; she opened it and went in; it too had a lock that she snapped. To the far end of the library and the sitting room door. Same kind of lock. She closed it. One more door, the one to the hall, which the "man in the embassy" had just used. She locked that one, too. She was now locked in the library.

On her way to the desk she told herself, the attaché case will be locked and that will be it. The adventure will be over.

The case was open. Weismann, by moving one of the tumblers while the combination lock was disengaged had kept himself from snapping it shut.

Suppose someone walks in? The fear ran like a mild electric current, through her body, uncomfortable more because it was there than because it hurt. Even as she felt it, she was lifting the lid of the attaché case. Her brain answered her body: the three doors to the library are locked. As soon as I hear someone trying one door, I go out one of the others. No matter where I go, the explosion gives me a reason for being there.

She saw two sets of papers. Each one the size of *Time* magazine, she told herself. Vertical framing. One page at a time. Simultaneously she tried to make her eyes focus on the cover of one set and her hand open her purse to reach for the camera. She could manage neither. I'm not going to make it, she told herself; I'm not going to be able to function. Do one thing at a time. Just one.

She stopped fumbling with the purse and stared at the title page of one of the two documents. The Hebrew letters were a jumble, they would not come into focus. Concentrate, she told herself. She tried. Then she heard voices just outside the hall door, and without thinking started back toward the dining room. But the voices did not stop at the door; they continued along the hall and receded.

Kate wheeled back toward the attaché case. Again she stared at the print. There was the word Masada on one title page. No question. And on the other document, there it was, too. That's enough, she told herself. How much do you need? Take the pictures. Quickly. Quickly.

One seemed to have about twenty or so pages, she estimated, the other somewhat less. What should she do? Take the first ten pages of each. Yes.

With both hands she clutched her purse. First she had to open the snap; it had never been so hard to work, her slippery fingers could not open it. Yes, they could, at last. Move the Kleenex aside, pick up the camera. Easy. But hurry.

Now it was actually out of the purse. Measure the distance from your eye to the table. With your arm. She did. Perfect for *Time* magazine—and for these sheets of paper. But her purse slipped off her shoulder as she was measuring, the strap sliding down her arm, the purse hitting the desk with a noise that seemed to her louder than the explosion. For an instant she froze, and listened. Outside the vague, confused noises continued, remote and unthreatening.

Kate slid the purse strap up over her shoulder and moved the camera to her eye. Frame the title page. Click. Turn it. It won't stay down. Frantically she looked around. Then thought, my purse. Without taking the strap off her shoulder, she used the bag as a weight for the turned title page. Again she aimed the camera, looked through the viewfinder, pushed the button. No click.

An instant of panic. Then—remember to advance the film, dummy. She pulled the camera at its ends, then pushed it back. Put the camera to her eye. Click. Two down, eighteen to go. Turn the page, tuck it under purse. Advance the film. Aim the camera. Click. Advance the film. Turn the page. Under the purse.

Wait a minute. Footsteps, headed for the hall door. Go by, please go by. The footsteps did.

Aim, frame, click, advance. Four. Sixteen to go. Turn the page. Shoot it. Five. Turn the page, shoot it. Six. Turn it, shoot it. Seven.

But wait, seven was no longer text. A map, with concentric circles on it. Even in her fevered condition, she recognized the map. New York City.

Eight. Shoot it. Another map. And nine and ten. Now she should go to the other set of papers. But wait, if there were more maps, shouldn't she go on? She turned to the eleventh page. Another map. She shot it. And twelve, thirteen, fourteen, fifteen. Nine maps in all, fifteen shots used. Or was it eight and fourteen? It doesn't matter, she told herself, it doesn't matter, go on to the other and shoot the roll.

She lifted her purse, put the second set of sheets on top of the first, and shot the title page. She went on: seventeen, eighteen, nineteen, twenty. Still not sure of the count, but she took three or four more just to make certain she had used every exposure.

Thank God, she said, it's done. Can't get caught now. She put the first document back on top of the second, closed the case. Is this the way I found it? she asked herself. Think so. Anyway, it stays this way.

Put the camera back in the purse. Close it. It would be crazy to get caught now. The control she'd been able to impose on her shaky hands while shooting gave way. They were not merely unsteady, they were vibrating.

Get out of this room. Get the hell out. She started toward the dining room, when she remembered she had to unlock the other two doors. Quickly she reversed direction. Then stopped. Why did she have to? Who'd notice, and if they did, who'd know she did it? Again she did an about-face, made for the dining room, unlocked the connecting door, stepped in, and closed the door behind her.

What do I do now? she wondered. Wipe the sweat off my face. Instinctively, she opened her purse and pulled out a Kleenex. With it came the camera, dropping to the floor onto the thick carpeting. Thank God for the carpet, she said, bending over to pick up the camera and seeing it had not come open. But just suppose I had done that with Dov in the room. The bend had sent the blood rushing to her face; it had also spilled her compact, comb, wallet, keys, lipstick out of her open purse.

This is almost a comedy, she thought as she furiously stuffed the things back in. Then the knob of the hall door was being turned.

"Kate, are you all right?" Shalzar's voice from the hall.

"Yes, yes," she shouted, "I'll be right there." She hoped she hadn't sounded too loud or too nervous. Snapping her purse shut, she ran toward the door, when she realized she was still holding something. The one object she had not returned to her purse was the camera! Two steps away from the door, she stopped, and trying to sound calm, said, "Coming! Coming!" She opened the purse, pushed in the camera and continued.

When she opened the door, she saw Shalzar and Weismann, their faces pale with anguish. "With all the fuss and shouting," she told them, immediately setting up a defense, "I thought I'd lock the door." When she saw the two were not only not suspicious but paying her no attention, she asked "What happened, what was it?"

"One of our men was killed," Shalzar replied. He said nothing else, walking by her and patting her arm without even looking at her. He walked to his place at the table, slumped in his chair, righted his overturned wine goblet, poured himself more of the Haut Brion and swallowed some.

Kate and the Foreign Minister resumed their places, too.

"Twenty-five years old," Shalzar added. "Married a year and a half. Has a newborn daughter. He was a lieutenant in a tank unit, that's why I picked him. Fought on the Golan Heights the whole Yom Kippur War without a scratch. And he got killed on East Seventy-second Street, in the Israeli embassy, by a bomb. How'd you like to have to tell that to his wife?"

The pressure is off me, she told herself. Then was ashamed. A young man had been killed, and she was thinking of her own nerves. "A soldier goes where he's assigned, Dov. Without knowing where the danger might come from. Yours not to reason why. At Balaclava or East Seventy-second Street. What was his name?"

"Moshe Aroni. North African. Smart boy. Would have gotten places."

"Where did the bomb go off?" she asked. "Whose bomb? What happened?"

"It was planted in our outer lobby, we don't know by whom," the ambassador replied. "It would have blown out the entire downstairs, including us, if we hadn't built those walls a foot thick. Thank God for that."

Weismann sagged in his chair, elbows on the table, hands supporting his head. "He wasn't supposed to be in there," he said. "We told them to . . ."

Kate was startled by the speed and rudeness with which Dov broke in on his superior. "We told them to use the Seventy-third Street entrance while the crowds were out front," he added in a strong voice, looking at Weismann and not at her as he spoke. "You're right, Itzhak."

Weismann looked up, and, again to her surprise, was not offended by Shalzar's interruption. In fact he seemed subdued as he added, unnecessarily, she thought, "Of course, Dov."

The ambassador took another drink of his wine. "Kate," he said, looking at her guardedly, "don't tell them anything about the explosion, will you? They'll know there was one; it knocked two cops off their feet out front; but they won't know any of the things I've just told you. Keep those to yourself, will you?"

He's looking at me as if I were on the other side, Kate said to herself. And I guess he's right; all he'd have to do would be to look in my purse for the evidence of that. People have been executed for less. To him, she said, "Oh, Dov, of course not, I . . ." She wanted to say she was still on his side, but he'd wonder what she meant. And, moreover, she'd be lying. She completed the sentence lamely. "I won't say a word."

Whatever he thinks of me at the moment, she thought—and he is looking at me strangely—whatever suspicions he has, they're justified. In fact they're modest compared to what I've done. For just an instant she felt a powerful impulse to open her purse, grab the camera, and hand it to him. Here, she'd say, this is what I've done for them. I was on the other side, but I'm back on yours now.

No, she reminded herself, the American Secretary of State is not the other side, the Arabs are the other side. What I must do for Dov is *not* give him the film. What I must do is something he can't or won't do for himself: give the Secretary of State the film, and with that he may have enough to stop the *real* other side. Luckily, she thought, I don't owe a soldier's devotion to either side. Mine *is* to reason why.

"May I, Dov?" Kate extended her wineglass to him. "Of course," he responded, as he poured her the little wine left in the bottle. She began raising the glass to her lips, when suddenly she said to Shalzar, "He died for his country, just as if he'd been killed on the Golan Heights."

"Yes," the ambassador replied, but his look was doubtful.

And here, Kate told herself, his death gave me the time to take the pictures that may save his entire country.

The ambassador looked at his watch—eight o'clock. He hadn't eaten all day, yet he was no longer hungry. Nonetheless he suggested food to Kate. Her response was the same as his. "I don't think I could put a spoonful of anything into my mouth. I may as well go back and tell Maloney everything you wouldn't tell me." God, what a double entendre, she thought. Why do I do things like that? "Unless," she added, "you want to change your mind. I want to help. Dov, that's why I'm doing this." Then, to explain her desire to leave, she added, "I've hardly ever been around death, and I can't get used to it."

Shalzar looked at her. "I've been around it a lot and *I* can't get used to it!"

"Doesn't it change anything?" she asked.

The Foreign Minister spoke up. "We were in a critical situation before the boy's death and we remain in one. In Israel right now, many, many boys and girls are dying."

And Shalzar shook his head. "Our answer remains the same as it was before. The sooner and the more unequivocally they accept that, the better."

"So what happens now?" she asked.

"We sit and we watch the clock—thirteen hours to go—and we wait for the Americans to say something to us," the ambassador answered.

"Dov," Kate said, "I'm sitting here right now and even with the help of an explosion I find it impossible to imagine what the world will be like at dinnertime tomorrow. Madison Avenue looked too calm, and this wine is too gentle and the silverware too well polished, and we're sitting here talking too sensibly. I can't believe we're on the brink of—God knows what—a holocaust."

Shalzar smiled grimly. "Expecting you to imagine a holocaust is like expecting a blind man to understand Rembrandt, or a deaf man Bach. That is, you can all absorb secondhand impressions, but the primary stimulus is denied your eyes, or your ears, or, in the case of you Americans and a holocaust, all your senses.

"Sure, it's impossible for Americans to imagine their homes leveled, their loved ones dead on the streets, their country overrun by alien soldiers. You haven't experienced that since the Civil War. But we Israelis have seen the colors—the dark red of blood, the orange of fire, the dismal gray of smoke and ruins. We've heard the sound of bombs, the grinding of tanks, the moans of the wounded.

"We've seen enough of that kind of Rembrandt, heard enough of that kind of Bach. For us, it's not impossible to imagine. And though for our sake I wish you—Maloney, Brewster, you, all of you—knew it better, you must believe me when I tell you, that kind of Rembrandt, and Bach, you should make a point of missing."

Kate's remorse grew almost unbearable. Once more she wanted to throw the camera at him and shout: Here, darling. I'm sick of sitting here and lying by keeping quiet. I want to be on your side. And again the answer came to her. I'm trying to stop the Masada Plan. I'm trying to win for all of us.

But, she told herself, I'd better get me and my camera the hell out of here before I do something melodramatic and stupid. She stood and said, "Well, I'm on my way."

Weismann and Shalzar both got to their feet. "Mr. Minister," she said to Weismann. "I hope we all come out of this alive and well, and that we have a chance to have dinner—really have dinner—under less explosive circumstances."

"Seconded," Weismann responded, shaking her hand, "devoutly seconded. And I assure you, however much we may differ on strategy, we are grateful for all you're doing."

She smiled at him and walked toward the door, Dov with her. For just an instant Weismann's words made her ask a second time: is he the "man in the embassy"? Then she wiped the question away.

She and Dov walked down the hall together. In the area where the bomb had exploded, plaster and glass still lay on the floor—for despite the thick concrete reinforcement, damage had been done to the inner hall. They headed away from it, toward the rear entrance. Neither spoke. Finally Dov said, "Hope I see you very soon."

Warmly and honestly she answered, "So do I." To herself she said: Last chance to tell him. Now. He put his hands on her back to press her toward him in an embrace, and she suddenly remembered the tape recorder in her bra, the tape recorder she had forgotten to turn on all evening. Surely he would feel the hard metal if their bodies touched. Quickly she raised her hands to his cheeks, placing her arms between the two of them as they kissed. Her last chance was gone.

"Sorry about the dinner," he said with a sad smile.

"I am so dreadfully sorry about the young man," she said.

"How will you get to the Waldorf?" he asked.

"Oh, I'll get a cab," she answered. "It's only a little after eight."

Knowing an Israeli security man would pick her up and follow her, Shalzar wasn't concerned. He said, "Good night, dear." And she answered, "Good night." Then she started slowly toward the corner.

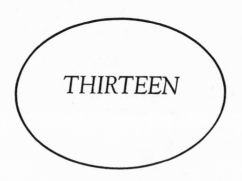

THIRTEEN

New York is a target. Well, hold it, Kate told herself, you don't know that, you couldn't read any of the Hebrew; there might be another, more rational explanation. Name one, she challenged herself. Then, Thank God my kids are up in Maine—I hope it's far enough away.

For a moment she stood on Seventy-third Street and looked up at the sky. All this couldn't be happening, not on an evening like this one. The air was too clear; the sky, darkened by approaching sunset, too blue; the humidity too low. This was an evening to be walking to the Mall for a band concert, or ambling up Madison to the Carlyle for a drink, an evening to be thinking about what she'd be taking out to Long Island tomorrow to the weekend house she'd rented.

Her eyes moved from the sky to Park Avenue, to see if a cab was coming along Seventy-third. There was none, so she turned toward Park, to find one that could take her the twenty-three blocks south to the Waldorf. Oddly, although she had been in a shoot-out that morning, although a bomb had exploded in the embassy a half hour ago, although around the corner police squad cars and emergency vehicles were clustered in front of the embassy and the entire street was closed off by police barricades, Kate felt no apprehension, no fear anyone would be after her.

Nor did she have any idea circumstances had combined to strip her of the protection of two-thirds of her three-man escort. When the explosion sounded, one of the two Secret Service men got out of their car and headed around the corner, looking for its source. He felt safe in doing it because his fellow agent remained behind and because there was little chance Kate would finish dinner and leave so soon. The Israeli agent also heard the blast, and was worried about it because he thought the embassy might be involved, and so he, too, took

213

off for the front entrance on Seventy-second Street, knowing the second American remained on watch.

But by then there were others watching for her. Four Arabs, sitting in their Chrysler, had seen her arrive just before seven, and had quickly phoned their superior; they were told what to do, and settled in to wait for her. Not knowing her plans included dinner and not caring what the explosion meant to the embassy, the Arabs did not budge. They double-parked on Seventy-third near Park, ten to twelve cars behind the American sedan with its lone agent, prepared to move when the woman left the embassy and headed toward Madison Avenue. To the Arabs' surprise, she went toward Park, which meant she'd go right past them.

The American agent was astonished when Kate emerged so early and turned east toward Park. He was in a predicament; his car was headed the wrong way—west on a westbound street, so he could not drive after her. He'd have to get out and walk. Quickly he turned on the two-way radio to warn his office, and almost as quickly he realized he'd be getting his buddy in trouble. So he switched it off and climbed out of the car, saying under his breath, "Goddammit, John, where are you?" and started after Kate, who was by this time a hundred yards ahead of him.

On the lookout for an empty cab, Kate hardly noticed the two short, dark men get out of the Chrysler ahead of her and disappear around the corner. Nor was she disturbed when they reappeared in front of her as she got near the intersection. What first bothered her was the way they stared at her; she set her no-autographs-please look, then almost at once realized this was something else. These men were not interested in her for autographs; fear that was close to a physical pain stabbed through her, far different from the shakiness she had felt in the embassy. Despite it, for a moment she had a shatteringly clear picture of the two Arabs. Short men, and slender, both of them wearing suits with narrow lapels, made of shiny fabrics. The one on the left wore a white shirt with no tie and the collar outside his jacket, the one on the right, more formal, wore a light Panama hat and a black string tie on a shocking yellow shirt.

But her overriding impression was how small they were. She, nearly five ten in sensible heels, was decisively taller than either and probably as heavy. And that physical matchup, so apparent to her, had a decisive effect on what was to happen in the next thirty seconds. The men had not given any ground, so quickly she turned to look behind her; there stood the third passenger from the Chrysler, not taller than the others, but extremely broad-shouldered and much heavier.

Even before she could fully turn to the front again, the man in the hat spoke to her. "You must come with us, Miss Colby." The Arabic accent was unmistakable.

Somehow the effontery of it, coming from these little men, dulled the pain of her fright, and instead of shrinking back or moving to the side as the men expected, she answered, "Oh no, I mustn't!" and headed straight at the tieless one, arms in front of her. He was unprepared for the charge and for the momentum a 130-pound ex-field hockey player could work up, and he was pushed back two or three steps before the man alongside him and the heavy man could each grab one of her arms and start shoving her toward the open door of the double-parked Chrysler.

All this happened while the American agent was still seventy yards away, and though he started running toward them, it was likely they'd have forced her into the car before he could stop them—shooting was out of the question with the four of them so closely bunched —had not a lucky coincidence saved her. After looking over the front of the embassy, and chatting surreptitiously with one of his countrymen for a while, the Israeli agent started back to his assigned post. But instead of returning the way he had come, along Madison Avenue, he decided to go the other way, up Park, so that he could have a better look at the American agent in his car.

He saw the woman being shoved by the three Arabs; by this time they had managed to wedge her between two parked cars and near the door of the Chrysler. But she was still fighting strongly, shouting, "Stop it! Stop it!" digging in her heels, trying to hold on to the car's open door. The American agent, seeing he wasn't going to make it, shouted, "Hold it!" The Arabs turned and, as they did, the Israeli charged into the four of them. He seized one of the slender Arabs, pulling him off Kate. As he did, the tieless Arab leaped on the Israeli's back, carrying him to the ground.

Desperately, Kate seized the open car door, knowing she'd be saved if she could just hold on. The heavy Arab grabbed her around the waist and tried to carry her into the car. Meanwhile the Israeli had got to his feet and, with one Arab around his neck and the other trying to hold his arms, was moving toward the car. But the Arab driver had come around the car to help and he and the powerful one were just wedging Kate into the rear seat, when the American plunged into the space between the parked cars. He got one arm around Kate's shoulders and with the other straight-armed the driver; as he did, the heavyset Arab suddenly let go of Kate and she and the Secret Service man tumbled back onto the sidewalk. The heavy Arab rolled over into the front seat, started the car and drove off, with the driver lying on the floor of the rear seat and the back door still open. When the two who had been battling the Israeli heard the car start, they disengaged themselves and started running.

Both the Israeli and the American having been charged with guarding Kate Colby, and both having come perilously close to failing, neither was anxious to leave her and pursue the Arabs.

Kate didn't know who any of the six men were, and lying half on the sidewalk, half in the gutter, with a large man she had never seen before, she was only slightly less apprehensive than when she had been in the clutches of the Arabs. The American helped her to her feet, and had no sooner done so when he pulled a snub-nosed revolver, pointed it at the Israeli, and said, "Put your hands up," which the Israeli did, looking none too pleased about it.

Kate started brushing herself off, when she hit her purse with her hand, and had a new moment of fright, when she realized she could have lost the camera during the scuffle. But she hadn't; she could feel its shape in her purse.

"Who are you?" the American asked the Israeli, but before he could answer, Kate spoke up. "Yes, who is he? And who are you? And who were they?" For a moment, the American agent was angered and puzzled. He wanted his question answered first, but then Kate Colby was important and in view of the way he had almost lost her, he decided not to risk antagonizing her.

"I am a Secret Service agent, Miss Colby, assigned by the State Department to look after you."

"And I, Miss Colby," said the Israeli, "am a cultural attaché at the Israeli Mission to the United Nations, assigned to look after you." He said it with a British-Israeli accent and a slight smile, because all security men at the embassy were called cultural attachés. Then his smile widened and he said to the American agent, "And here comes your associate."

The American looked around quickly; there, loping down the street, was the Secret Service man who had gone off to look at the explosion scene.

"What's happening?" asked the late arrival.

"I'll tell you later, John," said the man with the gun. "Will you check that guy's papers and see if he's connected to the Israeli Mission, like he says he is."

"Will you get my wallet, or shall I?" asked the Israeli.

"Hold still," John warned. And he patted the Israeli all over his body, first finding and removing an automatic pistol and then coming across the man's wallet. He opened it, looked at the ID card, and turned to the other American. "His name is Chaim Ben Zion," the American said, anglicizing the Hebrew pronunciation of the first and last names, "and he works for the Israeli United Nations Mission."

"And he kept me from being carried off while you guys were showing up," Kate added, just a touch accusingly.

Not quite sure how to answer, the agent with the gun said, "Are you all right, Miss Colby?"

"Yes, I'm all right," she answered. "My dress will never come clean. But I'm all right." A silly answer, she thought, but she was so relieved to have escaped, for just a moment she forgot the spy mess and the Masada deadline and was giddy. But not for long, for then the agent said, "As long as our presence is no longer a secret, Miss Colby, we'll be happy to drive you wherever you're going. It would be safer and simpler."

"All right," she replied, "may as well. I am going to the Waldorf Towers, Fiftieth and Park." And she remembered why she was going, and what she had in her purse and how she had gotten it.

"But before I go," and she walked over to the Israeli, "Mr. Ben Zion," she said, pronouncing the name correctly, "thank you for helping me. Thank you very much."

"You are most welcome, Miss Colby, and may I make a suggestion? While I am here, I think you should ask to see these men's credentials, although I am confident they are genuine."

Kate hadn't thought of that, and she said, "Of course! Gentlemen?"

The two Americans looked furious, but reached into their hip pockets and produced small billfolds, which they showed her. She could not make the print come into focus, but she nodded, coolly, she hoped. "Thank you, gentlemen," she said. "Shall we go?"

"Thanks again," she said to the Israeli. "By the way, who were they?"

"Who do you think? Arabs."

"Yes, but which Arabs? And who sent them? And why?"

The Israeli smiled and shrugged. "To us the word 'Arab' is the same as the word 'enemy.' It's all we have to know."

She wanted to ask more, but knew it was useless. "Well, thanks," she said.

"Take good care," he said, "and before you go, may I have my weapon, please?" He turned to the agent who had pocketed his pistol. The Secret Service man looked at his partner and got a nod in return. He handed it over.

"Glad to help," said the Israeli.

Suddenly the American with the gun smiled, for the first time. "Thanks," he said to the Israeli. Kate and Ben Zion exchanged smiles, and then she and the two Americans walked toward their car.

On the way downtown Kate first opened her purse and looked at the camera. Still in one piece. She patted it, closed the purse, then looked ahead. She noticed the driver was checking his rearview mirror every ten or fifteen seconds.

"The Israeli still there?" she asked.

"Yes he is, Miss Colby."

"Bet you were glad to have him there a few minutes ago."

The Americans had been out of position, they had come close to losing their charge, and all three of them knew it. The driver offered a defense.

"When John heard the explosion, he ran around to see what had happened while I covered the back. Then, when he saw the bomb had gone off in the embassy, he tried to find out about your safety. Meanwhile, you came out a lot earlier than we had anticipated."

Kate was a bit annoyed at their refusal to credit the Israeli. "You would have lost me if it hadn't been for him, wouldn't you?"

The driver, who had been the first of the two to run up, shook his head. "Don't think so. Don't think they would have had you in the car before I could get to them. And if they had, I'd have shot out their tires. They couldn't have gone too far."

Why am I getting into this debate? she asked herself. But she wouldn't let go. "Far enough to have the time to shoot me."

"Oh, Miss Colby," said the one who had gone around the block, "if they wanted to shoot you they could have done it as you walked out of the embassy or at any point between then and the time you reached the corner. They could do it when you get to the hotel. We can only protect you up to a certain point; after that it's armored limousines and plastic bubbles and bulletproof vests." He said it noncommittally, like a mechanic explaining how much an engine tuning could help your car and how much it couldn't.

"Thanks," she said, "for putting my mind at ease. Do you think they'll try at the hotel?" They had reached Fifty-third Street; on the Seagram Building plaza she could see an abstract sculpture, with huge petals of red and white and patinaed steel. The evening was clear, at 8:30 the sky halfway to darkness. The Waldorf was only three blocks away.

"Probably not," answered the agent in the passenger's seat. "If they didn't try it at Seventy-third. Of course, since they weren't able to grab you uptown, they might . . ." He didn't finish. Instead he said, "Don't worry, we'll be right alongside you walking in; we won't give them much to shoot at."

"You going to put your bodies in the line of the bullets? Why do you want to do that?'

"That's what they pay us for, Miss Colby. Besides, nothing much ever happens."

"But I would worry about it all the time," said Kate.

This time the driver answered. "So does my wife."

They had made the left turn onto Fiftieth Street and pulled into the interior driveway. Both agents jumped out and came around to her door, enveloping her as she walked out. One was six one and the other an inch or two taller; between them, she felt cut off from everything around her. And somehow next to her, they realized their conversational moment had ended. She was a celebrity, they, two anonymous agents assigned to protect her. In silence they rode to the eighteenth floor, Kate more and more forgetting the fright of the past hour and a half and looking ahead to the film and what was on it, assuming she had succeeded in taking the pictures properly and the camera had remained operative and the film unexposed to outside light.

Well, she'd soon know; they were at the door to the Secretary's suite. She turned to the agents. "Thank you," she said, shaking the hand of each of them. "You're brave men. Your wives must be brave women."

"Thank you, Miss Colby," said the one who had driven the car. "It's a pleasure meeting you."

"A pleasure," echoed the other.

Inside the Secretary's suite Pete Maloney and Bill Brewster spent the hours after Kate's departure waiting, speculating, talking. During those hours they got reports on the ambush in Central Park, and later on the bomb blast at the Israeli embassy. When Maloney hung up after the first report on the park incident, he turned to Brewster: "Well, they *think* it's Arabs,"—isn't that great intelligence work? I would have bet it was Liechtensteiners, or Icelanders. Or maybe New Zealanders. They don't *know* a damned thing."

"Even *I* think it's Arabs," the Secretary went on. "What I'd like to know is why now? Given the Arabs' abiding hatred of the Israelis, I'd expect it any time, but least of all now, when they have reason to believe they're close to the extermination of the Zionist nemesis."

During those hours Maloney drank, or rather fidgeted with, several highballs. He gesticulated with his tall glass as he said, "Why now? *Unless* they think the Israeli ambassador is doing something that's gotta be stopped, something that could screw them up so seriously, it's worth risking an incident with the United States to stop.

"Now it seems to me, if I were an Arab, the only thing I'd want to stop is something that might get in the way of my march to the sea. Something like a Masada Plan."

He sipped his Scotch. He was tired and looked it, the boyishness giving way to the face of an old bulldog, pouchy around the mouth, baggy under the eyes, saggy along the jawline.

"Of course, the Arab motives are just my calculations, without the help of an intelligence army. Sometimes I wonder about those guys. Anyway, two of them are keeping an eye on Kate; I figure they can handle that OK."

Most of their waiting time, however, was spent conjecturing—"making book" as Maloney put it—as to what Kate was doing in the embassy and what she would come back with. "Let's first predict," he suggested, "which side of the fence she'll come down on, and then what information, if any, she'll come back with."

"All right," Brewster replied. "The first question is whose side will she end up on: totally his, somewhere in the middle, or totally yours."

"Why not say totally *ours*, old boy," Malony responded. "Or how about totally yours?"

The blood rushed to the surface of Brewster's fair skin, but he tried to sound clinical. "No, if there is a singular pronoun, it would refer to the Israeli ambassador. The other side is decidedly *ours*. *Mine* plays no part in this whatever."

A twenty-five-year friendship gave Maloney the right to answer brutally. "Couldn't be yours, huh? Of course not. Pure chance has thrown Bill Brewster right back into the race, but don't let him stay there. Get him the hell out!"

Elaborately, Brewster ignored that. "In the middle there are infinite gradations, that can be put into two classifications: their side with reservations, or ours with reservations."

And then, having heard his own pedantry, Brewster mocked it by exaggeration as he went on, "But her allegiance is only one variable to be considered in predicting the results. We might call it willingness; the other two are capability and availability. Do I make myself clear?"

"Would you mind explaining that further, professor?" said Maloney.

"Yes," said Brewster. "To use simpler language, something I have heretofore avoided on the grounds my hearers might understand it, Kate has to *want* to help us; she has to be up to it, physically, when the time comes; and she has to find the material, at an opportune moment. All three are of interest to us."

"Wrong, professor," said Maloney. "Right now the only thing of interest to us is number four, What will she bring us? None of the other stuff is worth a damn, except for her memoirs, and that's for her literary agent to worry about."

Maloney took a token sip of his Scotch, and without putting it down, stood up and paced the room, as he was to do many times in the hours they waited for Kate. With his jacket off, his tie loosened, and his sleeves rolled up to show his thick, hairy forearms, he looked to Brewster more like a trucking foreman sweating out a late shipment or a line coach going over game films than a Secretary of State facing . . . what? Brewster had more and more begun thinking of the impending cataclysm by its Israeli name, the Masada Plan. Somehow it was more comforting than contemplating actual possibilities and the pictures of destruction they evoked.

The Secretary stopped briefly and looked at Brewster, who remained sitting on the sofa, jacket and tie still in the perfect order he had placed them in while on his way from his suite to the Secretary's hours before.

"Want to make any bets, old boy?"

"On what?" Brewster asked. "On what Kate brings back, or on what happens at 9 a.m. tomorrow?"

"The odds on 9 a.m. tomorrow," said Maloney. "I don't think about. You see, I have to go along on the assumption we are somehow going to call off Doomsday."

"And when, sir," said Brewster, looking startled and amused, "did you put on the rose-colored glasses? Didn't know you owned a pair.

This doesn't sound like your hardheaded, pragmatic Pete Maloney, considering it all seems to be riding on the exploits of one amateur spy of uncertain loyalty, minimal talent, and raging hormonal imbalance.

"Suppose she comes back empty-handed, Pete? Do we all head for the bomb shelters?"

Brewster thought for a moment and corrected himself. "We don't *all* head for them, do we? Let's see, you're way up there on the list of those who get in to the shelters, aren't you? Can you sneak me in, Pete? And Muffie and the kids—do they go with you? Or do they face the blinding flash with the rest of us?"

The Secretary had stood listening, and for an instant Brewster couldn't be sure that burly form wasn't going to charge across the room at him. In fact, for an instant Maloney felt like it. Instead he settled for another pseudo-sip from his drink, during which no liquid passed down his throat. He went back to the beginning of what his friend had said.

"Pragmatic Pete. I like that. Maybe I'll use it when I run for President on the Let's Clear Up the Rubble ticket."

Maloney balled his left hand into a meaty fist, and shook it. "If we get nothing from Kate, we try something else."

"For example?" prompted Brewster.

"Well . . . maybe we drop a couple of airborne brigades in the center of Jerusalem, take the whole Israeli government hostage, put a gun to their heads and say, 'Take your finger off the button.' "

"The government might be in Tel Aviv by then."

"Don't quibble. Then it'll be Tel Aviv. We'll know. Know how long it'll take?"

"No, I don't," said Brewster, by now curious.

Maloney became guarded. "Not long," he answered. "We've got carriers in the eastern Mediterranean. You know that. And they're moving closer every minute."

"And you've already alerted them; they're ready to go, aren't they?"

"Just a phone call," the Secretary answered. Brewster looked at him with such alarm, Maloney added, "You wanted to hear a couple of alternatives, didn't you?"

"Yes," said Brewster, "but . . ."

"Well, what the hell did you think I'd suggest, that we strew olive branches all over the Middle East?"

"No," said Brewster, "but . . ."

"All right then. And here's another maybe. Maybe I go up to Seventy-second Street in the middle of the night and grab that . . . Israeli son of a bitch by his pajama tops and beat some more information out of him."

Brewster could almost hear the Secretary thinking the word "Jew" as he said "Israeli." But the personal bluster made him smile; it took the sting out of the earlier threat. He grinned at Maloney as he answered.

"I think those are just terrific ideas, Pete, both of the 'hold my coat' school. Of the two, I think I prefer the second, because then I really could go up and hold your coat."

Maloney had started grinning, too. "Big guy like you," he answered, "should be up there throwing punches, not holding coats."

"What?" said Brewster. "Pete Maloney needing help?" Then he changed his tack. "The more I hear of your alternatives, Pete, the more I pray Kate walks in here with something. But I don't see how she can; the Israelis are too smart, and they're bound to be too careful."

"Yeah, they're both. But you see, they're like anyone else in that all their brains and precautions are aimed in certain directions and not in others, aimed at certain people and not others. Tell me, Bill, when you went in there today, were you searched?"

"No."

"So you could have gone in there with some plastique around your body or in a briefcase and blown the place up."

This conversation had taken place before the explosion at the embassy, and hours later when they heard about it they would both comment on Maloney's prescience.

"Surely a stranger," continued the Secretary, "had he been let in at all, would have been searched carefully. In other words, they trust you past the point of explosives. But I'll bet, if you had tried snooping around for documents, you'd have been stopped pretty damned quick. Because they don't trust you *that* far.

"Now let's take Kate. To begin with, I'd guess most of their security apparatus is dismantled as it relates to her, because they knew of her relationship with the ambassador."

Maloney had thundered right through, intent on making the point, forgetting its effect on his friend, until he heard the words coming out of his own mouth. Then he stopped short. And stared at his friend.

Brewster stared back and said quickly, "Yes, I heard, and, yes, it hurts. Go on."

The Secretary went on. "And because anybody on the embassy staff would probably figure, I'm not going to be the one to keep an eye on her and risk making her—or my boss—angry. Let *him* do it himself. So my guess is their guard is down past the point of snooping as far as she is concerned.

"Then, of course, they know she doesn't speak Hebrew. So that's a plus for our side. And I imagine things are pretty hectic at the embassy now, with their Foreign Minister just arriving, and demonstrators out front, their country fighting for its life. All of them,

222

loopholes in their defense for her to sneak through. And Kate is a slim woman."

"Not that slim," answered Brewster. "I'd say it's more likely she'd prevail upon Shalzar to volunteer information than that she'd get it by spying."

Maloney shook his head. "You think a mere slip of a girl could get from him what the likes of Bill Brewster could not? Never!" Maloney smiled. "If he wanted to disclose more, he would have done it; he wouldn't be waiting for another request, he's not bashful."

"True, but she's very persuasive—and very close to him," replied Brewster, trying to make it sound detached, and not doing very well.

"I know what makes you ache, Bill, and I feel for you, although I must admit, being married for twenty-two years, if I felt a pain in the heart I'd know it was angina, not romance. What you mustn't do is let your pain distort your sense of proportion. With a guy like Shalzar, a love affair . . ." Maloney had started to say "an affair" and thought better of it . . . "just could not get in the way of his job. He would not tell Kate word one without a tactical reason for it."

"You're arguing this both ways, Pete," Brewster said. "You say he wouldn't give her any information for romantic reasons. A minute ago you said she'd have a better chance to spy because they were so close."

"Yeah," Maloney answered, "but not because he *let* her spy. Because his guard might be down. What I said was, being human, he's probably learned to expect danger from certain directions and to guard against them—and not to fear other directions, and therefore not to guard against them, not as carefully, anyway."

"But the heart never dominates, right, Pete? Not with you big guys anyway."

"Listen," answered the Secretary, "be assured the Israeli ambassador to the UN won't get carried away by cupid. I hesitate to say this, but we've got a dossier on this guy. Bill, he's had a girl in every port. Nice, clean, nothing messy, nothing freaky; heartfelt, I'm sure. But in every port. He's learned how to handle them."

Brewster was quietly furious. His face grew red under its tan and his eyes came as close to ferocity as his friend had ever seen them. He stood up, saying nothing, and walked to the bar. It was about seven; he had eaten nothing all day, and had drunk some wine in his suite hours ago. He put a few cubes of ice in a glass and poured some Scotch over them. He took a sip, then walked to an easy chair near the sofa, and slumped on the upholstered arm. Then he was ready to say something.

"That being the case," he asked Maloney, "how tough do you think he'd be on her if he caught her snooping?" The Secretary looked at him and shrugged.

It was a long afternoon of waiting for Maloney and Brewster, and they spent it fidgetting with drinks, looking at their watches, talking, and for long stretches, in silence. For both, the most pressing concern was: How is Kate doing? But for the Secretary, there was another problem. How was "our man in the embassy" doing? Had he been able to help her? Why could he not—or would he not—touch the plan himself? Maloney could only wait—for Kate's return, to get some of the answer, and for God knows what, and God knows when, to get the rest of it. "Our man" had sounded as if he might be able to help Kate; at any rate, Maloney was counting on him. Why should I? the Secretary asked himself. And his answer was, What the hell else do I have to count on?

Just before eight they got word of an explosion at the Israeli UN mission. The police quoted the Israelis as reporting no one injured. Frantically, the Secretary checked the police and could learn nothing more. One of the Secret Service men assigned to Kate phoned in and also reported the explosion. No one was hurt, he was told.

"I'm going up there," Brewster said, and in fact had just stood up, when the doorbell rang. And there was Kate, looking pale under her tan.

Brewster grabbed her by the shoulders. Maloney burst out with "Come on, sit down, have a drink?"

"Thanks," she said in response to the chair, throwing herself into it. "No thanks," was her answer to the drink.

The two men resumed their old places on the sofa and sat staring at her, worriedly.

She tried another smile. "Boy," she said, "if looks could X-ray, you too would be seeing the tape recorder in my bra." And suddenly she remembered. "The tape recorder I did not turn on all evening."

For an instant, Maloney's face sagged. Brewster did not react to her statement. "Are you all right? Were you hurt?" he asked.

"Well," she replied, "the bomb didn't get me and the Israeli counterespionage didn't get me and the food sure as hell didn't get me, 'cause I didn't get to eat anything. Which reminds me, could you send out for a corned beef sandwich or something? I'm starved."

"Of course," said Maloney, but made no move to do anything about it. He sat there, and with his mouth tight, asked, "You didn't turn it on, huh?"

Kate shrugged. "Never used it, maybe you can get your money back on it." This was a big moment for her and she wanted to taste it some more before she took a gulp and it was gone.

"You won't be able to get your money back on the camera, though."

The Secretary was on his feet and moving toward her. Were it not for his smile she would have feared he was going to attack her. "You did it," he shouted. "Good girl. Good *girl!* Where's the camera?"

He stuck his hand out as he reached her. His personality had taken such a manic turn, she slowed down in protest. She unsnapped her purse, reached in and came out with the camera. Before the movement from her purse could become a movement toward him, Maloney snatched it from her.

"Steve!" he shouted, "Steve!" When Phelps appeared, the Secretary yelled, "Get me Waddell, quick, and get Ms. Colby a corned beef sandwich. In fact get us *all* corned beef sandwiches!"

Phelps disappeared and within twenty seconds the technician strode in. By then Maloney was almost in the hall, on his way to meet him.

"Take this camera," he ordered Waddell. "Process the film; don't bother to print it; call us as soon as we can read the negative. Fast as you can, and for Christ's sake, be careful!"

Waddell tried to look past the Secretary; he wanted to see Kate, to ask her how she had done. But Maloney had a fierce grip on his arm just above the elbow, and as soon as the technician had the camera and his instructions, the Secretary half guided him, half spun him in the reverse direction, and sent him back down the hall. "Call me the instant it's ready, Stu," he shouted to the man's back.

"Yes, sir!" answered Waddell over his shoulder. By then Maloney was back in the living room, on his way to his seat on the sofa.

In the few seconds it had taken the Secretary to get the film processing begun, Bill Brewster had sat looking at Kate. He could see she was tired, frightened, wrung out; behind the façade of flippancy, she looked like a lost child suddenly returned to her parents: glad it was over, only half believing she was safe, exhausted by the experience.

Now Maloney was back on the sofa. "Tell us everything that happened—start to finish. What about the explosion? You must have been terrified."

Suddenly Kate realized she had been terrified. Not only by the explosion, but the whole episode. She did not want to cry, and for the first time felt she couldn't control it. "Me terrified? Ridiculous! Cool as a cucumber. Nerves of steel. Ice water in veins. In total command . . ." Her lips were quivering. "Oh, shit, get me a little Scotch, somebody, will you?"

For another moment or so she tried to control herself, then gave up, lowered her head and covered her eyes with her hands.

Brewster leaped up and covered the width of the room with the speed of a quarter-miler, threw three ice cubes in a glass, splashed Scotch on them, wheeled around, strode back, and handed her the glass. She took a sip and looked up.

"Sorry," she said. "Won't happen again. Wild Bill Donovan of the OSS didn't cry, did he? Nathan Hale didn't cry—and they *caught* him. Name some of your other really outstanding spies, and tell me who cried. I mean how can we women ever get to be equal until we learn to spy without tears . . ."

"Oh, cut it out, Kate," said Maloney. "You did a great job. Without knowing—without caring—what's on that film and what it will change, I tell you you did a great job. If you can tell us, we'd like to hear what happened, in any order you want to give it to us."

"OK, Mr. Secretary, OK, Mr. Brewster, I'm ashamed to have to cry, no kidding. And I wished I hadn't. That's all that was about. Now, I'll tell you what went on, with the kidnaping attempt by some Arabs to start with, or I should say to finish with, because it happened as I was leaving."

Kate took another sip of Scotch, started to pat her hair in place, and withdrew her hand guiltily, hoping it hadn't been noticed. That's a woman's tic, too, she told herself. No man would bother to fix his hair at a time like this.

Then she recounted the attempt at kidnaping as fully as she could, altering only a few details so as to play down the late arrival of the American agents.

From there she backtracked to her attempts to talk the ambassador into disclosing more, and to her decision to move when the explosion distracted them.

"You knew of the explosion?" she asked. "Yes, we did," the Secretary answered. "But we don't know the cause, or who did it. We heard no one was hurt."

She almost blundered into revealing the death Dov had asked her to conceal. On the brink of saying it, she held back. And then told herself, Why am I not spilling it all? I've already done the worst of it. But that I did for *Dov,* she tried to convince herself, for what seemed like the hundredth time in the past few hours. The death of the young Israeli was not something she had to reveal; Dov had asked her not to, and she wouldn't.

"I got the impression," she replied, "that they didn't know too much themselves. At any rate, they didn't tell me and I didn't ask. You see, when they walked back into the dining room, I had just done the guilty deed and barely made it back into the room myself. My only thought was, What are they going to ask me? Are they suspicious? Do they see how nervous I am? And I tell you, I was shaking. It took me a couple of minutes even to realize they were upset themselves, and when I did, I embraced it as a gift, delighted to have it take the pressure off me. And I tell you I was not about to question or disturb their preoccupation in any way. When the ambassador said he didn't feel like eating, I grabbed at that, too; agreed, happily, so I could get the hell out as soon as possible. The camera was becoming so hot I could almost feel it burning a hole in my purse."

My God, she thought as her explanation went on and on, you are overtalking this one. Shut up already.

When she stopped, Maloney said, "Of course, you didn't go there to get an exclusive on a bomb exploding. Tell us about the photography, where you found the material, how you shot it, what made you think it was usable. Whatever you think is pertinent."

Kate tried to answer that as fully as she could, beginning with her entrance into the library, and Weismann's attempts to close his attaché case.

"I got the distinct feeling that the Foreign Minister is a bumbler—brilliant, eloquent, but when it comes down to things like closing the briefcase, inept. The kind of man whose finger you wouldn't want on the button, not so much because he'd push it when he wasn't supposed to as because he couldn't when he *was* supposed to."

She described her reaction when the bomb went off, the mysterious opening of the library door, her nervous entry, the locking of doors, the discovery of the material.

"Why did you shoot that material?" Maloney asked.

"Simple, there were only two sets of papers in the briefcase, one with about twenty pages, the other with about a dozen. Both had the word Masada in Hebrew on their back pages—ha, ha—I mean their front pages. At least I think it was the word Masada. Once again, and I feel silly repeating this, because it doesn't seem so important now that I'm sitting here safe and calm, I was too scared to concentrate. I wanted to shoot the roll and get out. I think if anyone had walked in, the punishment of the Israeli terrible swift sword would have been rendered academic by the immediate and total failure of my heart.

"I decided to take ten pages of each but when, on the fatter sheaf, I ran across some maps, I shot all of them, rather than stopping at ten pages. So on the first set, I took about fifteen shots, I think, six pages and nine maps, and on the second I shot the remaining five."

"Did you recognize any of the maps?" the Secretary asked.

Kate took another sip of her Scotch, more to stall than because she wanted the alcohol. She didn't want to tell him what she had seen—or what she *thought* she had seen, because knowing the shape she had been in earlier, she wasn't prepared to take an oath on any of her recollections. Yes, it had been New York she was quite sure, and the concentric circles, she was sure of those, too. Yet she couldn't bring herself to tell him all that. Why not, she asked herself. The answer forced itself through to her: the map with the circles was too damned incriminating. She didn't want to be the messenger. So she compromised.

"Well," she said slowly, playing up the tentative quality of her answer, "you've got to remember I was having a lot of trouble focusing on anything, and I was concentrating much harder on snapping the picture than on what I was taking, but it seemed to me one of the maps was of New York City. At least I think it was." The last she

227

threw in as an added emphasis of her uncertainty. And she said nothing about superimposed circles.

"Why a picture of New York, do you suppose?" Brewster asked.

"I don't know," Kate answered, to get herself on the record, although what she did know, and damned well, was that Bill had put the question to Maloney.

"Well, let's see," said Maloney. "They sent their Foreign Minister over in a commandeered El Al jet, with a Doomsday deadline breathing hot on our necks, so he could deliver a transit map of the city to the embassy employees. Tell me, Kate, did it show the IND subway stop on Roosevelt Island? I want to see how up-to-date their intelligence is. Come on, what the hell else can it mean but that they want to attack the place? Why don't the two of you stop pussyfooting around? Unless you can suggest another explanation!"

Maloney waited. Neither said anything.

"Well?" he asked. Still neither spoke.

"I don't blame you," the Secretary said. " 'cause if you can't provide an alternative, then you're forced to concede the target possibility. And if you are, then you have to ask what the other maps could be. Podunk, Iowa? Outer Mongolia? Beautiful Samoa? No. Maybe London, or Berlin, or Moscow, or Tokyo, or Rome. Or LA?" Maloney nodded his head.

"They're not kidding are they, those . . . Israeli bastards. Threatening the world to save their skins."

Kate forgot her fragility and got angry. "Yes, despicable, isn't it? Almost as bad as letting a little country die to protect your Middle East investments, to save your Sunday drivers from inconvenience. What the hell should rule the world, anyway: concern for life? Or for oil—and money?"

As Secretary of State, Secretary of the Treasury, chairman of the board of Union Consolidated, Peter Maloney had not often been spoken to with that effrontery and he had forgotten how to handle it. The aggressive juices in him reached the overflow level; he began to move out of his place on the sofa, not quite sure where he was going, what physical action he was going to take, but knowing he had to do something. Brewster saw the move and he, too, was unsure where or how it would end, and while he never really thought Kate was in any danger, his friend's energy level had risen so violently, Brewster was alarmed and started to move to intercept him.

But the Secretary seized control of himself again, turned the movement into a trip to the bar so he could refill his glass, which actually needed no refilling. He added an ice cube, a drop of Scotch, a dash of soda water, using the time and the motion to cool down. He cooled, but not much.

"There is a limit to what is acceptable as a tactic," he said, not

228

looking at Kate, but directing the comment at her. "I don't care what the situation. *This* country recognizes that."

Kate had seen the possibility that Maloney had risen to threaten her and it awakened memories of physical intimidation that raised her anger to a white heat. "*This* country recognizes that, does it? Tell that to the Vietnamese. Tell it to the Cambodians. Tell it to the citizens of Hiroshima and Nagasaki. What you mean is *this* country recognizes limitations on tactics used *against* it. *This* country is great at dishing it out. When's the last time it had one of its cities leveled, or armies pouring over its borders? Of all the goddamned sanctimonious bullshit!"

Brewster saw he had to take charge, before this thing fell apart. He stood and stood tall; he knew sometimes size could be intimidating and he stretched to all his six three and a half. Then he did something he was rarely heard to do. He raised his voice.

"How in hell can you two egomaniacs concern yourselves with this disputation while we're all on the brink of . . . disaster! As for you, Pete, this sensational amateur spy . . ." and he jabbed a finger toward Kate as he said it, "did some dangerous work, with incredible results, and you've barely worked up one percent of the sweat thanking her that you have fighting her. With the world—Americans, Russians, Arabs, Jews—waiting on her, she came through. And she did it at the behest of the Secretary of State. To thank her for it, the Secretary proceeds to lecture her on international morality—from an extremely shaky position, I might add, but I have no intention of joining in the debate."

Maloney had long since realized he'd have to control his temper if he were not to be victimized by it. Determined though he was to hold back—even at the expense of a coronary or an ulcer, he had told his wife—he had never succeeded in killing it. What he had done was develop a mechanism for turning it off quickly after the first outburst. Which is what he did now, a process showing itself first in the relaxation around the mouth, then in the widening of the eyes, then in the fading of the angry red from his face. He walked toward Kate again but this time there was no threat in his advance. He stuck out his hand.

"Kate, Bill is right, as always. That's why I love him." As his right hand gently shook Kate's, his left reached over and lovingly pinched Brewster's cheek.

"Frankly, Kate, you did better, you got more—assuming the pictures come out, and if they don't I'll regrade you—than I expected or even hoped for. You went in under tough, dangerous circumstances, did a job you'd never trained for or even dreamed of, and you did one hell of a job. It may sound corny, but if the world gets out of this one, we all ought to line up on your doorstep, all three billion of us, to shake your hand and thank you. Just like I'm doing now. The Nineteenth Precinct would have a hell of a job with the crowds, but we ought to. Thanks, Kate."

Kate was less adept at turning off her anger than Maloney was, and she was just calming down. She smiled at him, a little tightly, and said, "You're welcome, Pete. Glad to help save the world, anytime."

Despite the handshake, Brewster knew the debate could flare up again at any moment, at the smallest sign of disputation. He was worrying about how to keep the talk cool, when his problem was solved by the arrival of Phelps.

"The film is ready, Mr. Secretary."

Maloney was halfway out of the room before Phelps had finished speaking and almost all the way out before he turned and said to the two of them on the sofa, "Stay right there. I'll be back as soon as I can and tell you about it."

Then he wheeled and said to Phelps, "Get Linda Janowitz in there, too." And they were gone.

"I was frightened for you, Kate." Brewster said it with his arm still around her, before his reticence took over and he realized that with the reason for the protectiveness now removed, the arm should be, too. Slowly he withdrew it, not because he wanted to but because he couldn't think of a reason for keeping it there.

She looked at him warmly, trying to show him she hadn't minded the arm. "I was more afraid of Maloney than the Israelis." She smiled. "Seriously, I *was* frightened for myself. But actually we were both being silly. There's no way I could have been harmed. I was really worried about failing, of not showing grace under pressure. But I can't imagine I would have been harmed. The ambassador doesn't do that kind of thing." As she said it, there flashed through her mind a picture of Dov in Central Park, holding a smoking pistol. And she wondered, but not aloud.

"Speaking of fear," she said to Brewster, "I'm really beginning to be frightened for my children, and yours, and all of those three billion the Secretary wants to line up to shake my hand. What did that kid say to the crooked baseball player? 'Say it ain't so, Joe'? Say it ain't so, Bill."

"Certainly, I can say, based on what we know, it ain't *necessarily* so, Kate." Brewster grinned at his inadvertent song title. "I'll tell you the name of the crooked baseball player: Shoeless Joe Jackson. If you'll tell me the name of the lyricist."

"Ira Gershwin," she said. "It's a lot easier than Shoeless Joe Jackson."

"Certainly," he went on with his answer, "there are possible explanations of the maps that fall between the target theory and the transit-map theory."

"Ah, Bill," she said, "there's something I didn't tell Maloney. I couldn't bring myself to; I wanted him to see for himself. Which is probably what he's doing at this very moment, so there's no reason I shouldn't tell you. There's more than just a map of New York City, and eight other maps." She paused. "Every one of the nine maps had a series of concentric circles on it. You know, like a target. Unless you want to suggest the circles indicate bus-fare zones—public transit seems to be popular lately."

Brewster was looking at her grimly and though she stopped to give him a chance to speak, he remained silent.

"And you know where the center circle on the New York map was, Bill? Right in midtown Manhattan. We're in it now. So is my apartment. The center circle. That's ground zero, isn't it, Bill?"

When again he didn't speak, Kate began to grow frantic.

"For Christ's sake, tell me something, Brewster, will you? A map with target circles on it. What else could it be? A hostility dart board?" She laughed at her own joke; the laugh close to being out of control. "What a dart board! What hostility! What *darts!*"

Brewster was worried about her. The tension she'd been under was oozing through the protective cover of her wisecracks. People had started asking things of her at three-thirty in the morning and, in the nineteen hours since, the demands and the strain had grown. She'd had no sleep, nothing to eat, crisis upon crisis. Now for the first time, her personal trial by ordeal was over; all she could do was sit back while the world went through its trial. Sit back and grow lightheaded with relief and release—and a new kind of terror. He reached an arm around her again and squeezed to comfort her, realizing only after he'd done it that he hadn't been embarrassed or self-conscious at all.

"You've been through more in a day," he told her, "and performed better than most women—or men, for that matter, glad I caught that . . ." he smiled as he said it, "have in a lifetime. Thanks to you, we've got a chance to wipe the circles off those maps. Why don't you take a deep, well-deserved bow, and bask in that for a few minutes before you go on to the hostility dart boards?"

"Is there time to wipe the circles off the maps, Bill? Twelve hours? Is that enough?"

Brewster looked at her and shook his head. "I don't know, Kate; it would be so easy to reassure you. But how can I know? Nothing like this has ever happened before. Considering what there is to do before nine tomorrow morning, I'd be stupid to guarantee it. This much I *am* sure of: our chances of success would be immeasurably less, were it not for you."

He held his glass up to her. "And may I say your success doesn't surprise me? If I had to pick one woman—or man—to send into the lion's den, I can't think who I'd pick ahead of you. Well . . ." He shrugged and smiled, "maybe Pete Maloney. It'd be a toss-up. Either one would be great—provided you didn't tear each other to pieces before you had your chance at the lion."

She looked at him, and then leaned forward and kissed him lightly on the lips. "You make me feel good, Bill, do you know that? You know just how to be comforting and supportive. Aside from that, you are one hell of a classy guy. You are so good at saying the right thing with the right tone at the right time. Who writes your stuff for you? Huh?"

She meant it affectionately and was surprised to see how bitter Bill's reaction was. "How ironic," he said, "that the very person who congratulates me on my deftness is the one person in the world to whom I have *not* been able to say the right thing at the right time." And as he said it, he withdrew his arm. The size of his wound, after all this time, surprised her. She linked her arm with him.

"I'm sorry." She almost whispered it. "It's easy to underestimate someone else's pain, when it doesn't hurt you at all. I just didn't know . . ."

He stopped her, ashamed at letting so much of the wound show; it was not like him. "Amazing how egocentric a person can be; how an affair of the heart can make one forget the end of the world. It merely proves what you just suggested: that no one else's pain hurts like one's own."

"I'd much rather be talking about the ache in my ego right now than about the Masada Plan, wouldn't you?"

"Do we have that choice?" he asked.

"You don't understand, Bill," she replied. "What I'm trying to say is that personal pain is the only pain strong enough to compete with the sinking feeling of cosmic doom. You know what I was chewing over when you so nobly distracted me with your egocentricity? I was thinking what I should do about my kids. They're away at camp in Maine, Belgrade Lakes. Is that far enough away, Bill? That's what I was worrying about. Should I try to get them up into northern Canada? How many more of those concentric circles are there that don't fit on the map? Were you worried about your kids, Bill? Or is it a peculiarly female form of egocentricity, to think of one's own when everyone is in danger?"

"Both my boys are at a mountain camp in Wyoming," Bill answered. "Penny and the younger girl are visiting Penny's sister in Seattle. The older girl was living at home in Westport and teaching tennis at the club. Seven hours ago I sent a car to get her and take her to La Guardia for a flight to Seattle. The plane took off . . ." he looked at his watch, "three hours and twenty minutes ago. Does that answer the question about your peculiarly female form of egocentricity?"

She nodded.

"And, Kate, Belgrade Lakes is way up there. What is it, three hundred miles, something like that, from New York? That's a long way. You're lucky."

Then something registered in his eyes. "Kate."

"Yes."

"Why don't you use my car to take you out to the airport and catch a flight to Augusta or Lewiston or Portland? Then rent a car and spend a long weekend with your kids? If anything happens, you ought to be up there holding their hands."

"You mean I ought to save my ass, Bill?"

That was exactly what he had meant, but he wouldn't admit it. "Kate, only a very few people know all you know about the Masada Plan and everything that's happened with it in New York. If the worst eventuality occurs, and . . . well, I think it would be a damned good idea for somebody to be able to write about it afterward—particularly somebody with a lucid prose style."

"Mr. Brewster," she answered, "I must concede that the second try was much better than the stuff about holding my kids' hands up in Maine. Both tries, however, Mr. Brewster, are devastating me. They are not what I want to hear from you, for God's sake. Tell me I'm hysterical and hallucinating, that nothing's going to happen to New York or anyplace else. Tell me the target circles I saw were round blood vessels on my fevered eyeballs and will never show up on the film. Tell me there's some mistake."

"There's no goddamn mistake."

They both jumped when they heard Maloney's voice and turned toward it. He was standing at the entrance looking like the Angel of Death, as if a makeup man had darkened the pouchy flesh under his eyes and traced the lines from the sides of his pug nose to the corners of his mouth.

"What?" asked Kate, foolishly, because she had heard him clearly.

"There's no mistake. They weren't transit maps. I'll give it to you fast, 'cause I've got a lot to do.

"The goddamn Jews have pulled the hijacking of all time. They've taken the world as hostage." The Secretary of State's fists were clenched, his arms bent as he spoke. He wanted to punch somebody.

He spoke again.

"Nine maps. Nine cities. Nine big booms, if we don't give in by nine tomorrow morning. At least it's rational. New York. Los Angeles. Moscow. Leningrad. They know who they want to scare most. London. Paris. Berlin. Cairo. Jerusalem."

"Jerusalem?" Kate was not sure why she had picked that to question. Maybe, she thought, because the rest was too stupefying.

"That's the Masada part. You see, they go, too," Maloney was apparently angry she didn't see that at once, actually just angry and ready to pounce at everything. "We're all in this together. Get it?"

"Nasty, if they could deliver." Brewster said it so tentatively he made it more a question than a statement. "But if they don't have the rocketry system to knock out the Arabs in a radius of a couple of hundred miles, how in hell are they going to sell us on delivery to New York? What's that, 6,000 miles? Let alone Los Angeles, which is more like 9,000."

The bleakness, the anger on the Secretary's face never lightened. "You don't understand," he said. "They don't need a delivery system; they've already *made* delivery."

"How?"

"Simple and old-fashioned. A crate shipped in wherever Israeli products are sold. A suitcase or a trunk carried in wherever Israeli diplomats enter with immune status."

"An atomic bomb in a suitcase?" It had become a ghastly quiz session, each question asked by Brewster or Kate with the frenetic hope of finding a valid objection and with the growing horror of the certainty they wouldn't succeed.

Maloney tried a laugh, grim and forced. "Are you kidding? An atomic bomb the size of a *grapefruit!* A half dozen in a suitcase and, judging by the radii of those concentric circles, it'd have to be a few. Unless it's a hydrogen bomb, which would be a little bigger but not much. And they'd only need one. Let me tell you something; we've got some small enough to . . ." And Maloney clammed up.

"Anyway, we don't think they have the technology to put together thermonuclear devices. Mind you, I'm not writing it off; the point is they could do this with what we *know* they've got. And the beauty of it . . ." Maloney laughed at his word, "the *beauty* of it is the damned things could be sitting in the attic of the embassy building on Seventy-second Street . . ."

"We could raid the place, now." Brewster's interruption was uncharacteristically warlike.

"Yeah," continued the Secretary, "and they could also be in the apartment of some JDLer in Brooklyn. Or in a hotel room off Times Square. Or, better still, in the trunk of a car—in the trunks of cars—you could drive anywhere you wanted."

"How do you suppose they got them into Moscow and Leningrad? And Cairo?" Kate wondered why she was curious about that. New York was good enough.

"The Israeli intelligence arm, Mossad, has always been fanatic about placing people in foreign embassies, or recruiting people who are already there. It wouldn't be easy for them to get into Moscow and Leningrad and Cairo, but given a few years, which is how long I gather they've been setting this up, they could probably do it through embassy personnel. My guess is European personnel, but hell, it could be American.

"You see," the Secretary explained, "these are not technical docu-

234

ments. One is apparently designed only for the eyes of a few highest level officials. The other is one of nine detailing the plans for the individual locations. But you don't have any specifics on the kind of devices, the means of detonation—or their exact locations. There are certain conjectures we can make, though. For example, we can estimate the immediate casualties would be numbered in the millions, maybe something more than four million and less than ten million. Conjecturing from the circles, several millions more would die within days or weeks. Again, the fallout would depend on the kind of weapon, but the circles lead us to guess these are not particularly clean bombs. After all, why should the Israelis bother about that?

"The bastards!"

Maloney had made his way into the room, and stopped at a mirrored mantelpeice across from the sofa where the other two sat. As he spoke the last two words, the brought the hard, heavy palm of his right hand down on the mantelpiece with a loud slap. Then he turned and repeated the words more quietly.

"The bastards."

"Do you believe them?" Brewster asked.

"To answer that," the Secretary said, "I'd ask myself, Do they have the means? Do they have the reason? Do they have the nerve?"

"And what are the answers?" Brewster asked it when Maloney seemed to hesitate after he had put forward the questions. Two answers were easy for Maloney. The means, sure. He knew Jews were smart. The reason, yes. Israel was about to be wiped off the face of the earth and Maloney didn't kid himself about Arab mercy. But the third gave him a problem. Pete Maloney had been raised as a poor, tough kid of Italian and Irish background in Brooklyn, and with that upbringing went a set of attitudes toward Jews. It was with those feelings he had to deal now.

"The answer to all three questions is yes," he said, finally. "They are a bunch of nervy bastards; I gotta give 'em that." He said it reluctantly, then explained. "I grew up with the idea that Jews weren't fighters; that was accepted street wisdom, on our streets, anyway. If we lost out to a Jew in brains, broads, jobs, power, money—anything—we always had it in reserve that physically, we could beat the hell out of him. We could fight and Jews couldn't. To have that feeling of unassailable superiority in one area was comforting. And I guess I never really unloaded it from my mind, not even when the Israelis trounced the Arabs. I guess I always felt that I could out-tough them. And I guess to answer 'yes' to the third question was to leave the toughness up for grabs, to give up that comforting superiority."

Ignoring the full glass of Scotch he had left behind in the room a few minutes earlier, Maloney fixed himself another, and sipped from it. "My first impulse when we got the sense of the documents was to walk straight to the phone and tell Shalzar to turn off the Masada Plan at once, or we'd wipe his country off the globe. Nobody out-toughs Maloney, you see. But one of the things I've learned since I was a hard-nosed kid is, before you make a threat, think how the opponent might answer it. So I made up an answer for Shalzar, and the answer was: You'll wipe us off the face of the earth? The Arabs are doing that right now!"

Maloney walked to an easy chair, glass in hand, and sat down. "Now, mind you, I hadn't picked up the phone, let alone dialed. Actually, though, my hand was on it, while all this was going on. Well, then I formulated another threat. We'll notify the nine cities, find the bombs, evacuate the populations, and the only place that'll really be ruined is Jerusalem. Of course, his answer to that was easier: Find the bombs? Maybe more than one per city? In twelve hours? How? Evacuate cities, with millions of people? In twelve hours? How?

"So I dropped that. With my hand still on the phone, I planned another speech, an appeal to conscience: How can you do a thing like this? Again, I could hear his answer: How could you let us get to the point where we have to do it? All you have to do to stop it is . . .

"So before I ever got to pick up the phone, I realized I couldn't muscle him, I couldn't bluff him and I couldn't sweet-talk him. The only thing I could do to stop the Masada Plan was to give them what they wanted, to do what they wanted me to.

"And it made me furious." Maloney smiled grimly. "As Bill knows, I don't like to do what others want. I like them to do what I want. I was boiling but I took my hand off the phone and came in here."

"What happens next?" Kate asked.

"What choice do I have?" answered the Secretary with a shrug. "I'm going to do what they want. Or try. Talk to the President; talk to the Soviets; talk to the Arabs; try to show them they've got to do what the Israelis want. Then talk to Shalzar. All in twelve hours."

He stood and came toward Kate. "One thing I must admit. I've been saying we didn't have enough to go on. Well, we've got plenty now." He looked down at Kate. "Thanks to you. You got it for us; you've done one hell of a job." He leaned forward and kissed her on the top of the head. "Remember what Linda Janowitz said about a Masada medal being struck in Israel? Well by God, beautiful . . ." Kate hated that form of address, along with "girl" and "doll," but she didn't tell him so, "if we get out of this, I'm going to buy one and have engraved on it: Masada Plan Canceled, July 13, 1979, on account of Kate Colby."

As she listened, Kate had three reactions. The first was satisfaction at having been able to do the job. The second was new terror at the deadliness of the Masada Plan. The third was: How do I face Dov now?

"I'm proud I was able to do it, and damned glad it's over," she began. "I'll accept the medal and give it a place of honor among my trophies, but there's something you can do I'd like much more."

"What is it?" asked the Secretary of State.

"You can write me a script I can use the next time I face Dov Shalzar. What do I say, I've been a naughty girl?"

"No," answered Maloney. "Just say, you're welcome. That's right after he says, 'thank you.' Unless he's become unhinged by the events of the past day—and God knows that would be understandable— thank you is what he's going to say to you for what you've done."

"For what I've done," Kate said. "And what is that? Turn traitor on him. Lie to him. Spy on him. Steal from him. And you think he should thank me? I'm thinking about a personal relationship, not a CIA assignment. He trusted me and I turned on him. Tell me, Mr. Secretary, how would you like it if I had done that to you?"

"I'd give you a medal," Maloney answered immediately. "A Masada medal with the words: Masada Plan Cancelled, etc., on it. Does that answer your question?"

"But would you ever trust me again?" she asked.

Maloney stood up and smiled, patiently, his way of showing he was impatient. "Don't have time for another circle on this merry-go-round right now. If the world doesn't end, we'll have dinner sometime soon and worry this at length. On me. You name the restaurant. We may even let him come." Maloney nodded his head toward Brewster, then started out of the room, only to stop short and turn.

"I'd rather you didn't go home, Kate. You'd be a lot safer here, where we can watch you. We'll get a suite for you, we usually book an extra on this floor. With security protection. For tonight, anyway. All right?"

"All right," she said. "I'd be phoning you every five minutes any-way to find out the latest developments. I'd just as soon stay nearby. But promise to use rank to get me that corned beef sandwich."

"Coming up!" Maloney answered, and walked out.

There was another reason to stay. It would delay the chance of a meeting with Dov. And she couldn't face that until she decided what to say. Should she confess it all and tell him she did it for his own good? Should she keep it a secret and tell *herself* she did it for his good? She remembered she had a glass of Scotch and she took a sip. And wondered.

What in hell should she tell Dov?

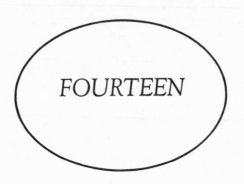

FOURTEEN

I've got four deals to put through, Maloney told himself as he walked into the small private study at the rear of his suite. That's all they are, deals, salesmanship. Get on that phone and convince four people they should do what I want.

Actually, the phone was six phones, four at his desk and two at the desk of his assistant, Steve Phelps. One of the Secretary's phones was a standard instrument with buttons and three outside lines. The other three were hot lines, to the White House, the Kremlin, and the State Department in Washington. That distinction aside, the office was modest, almost shabby, barely large enough for two desks, an easy chair, a small filing cabinet, and a floor-to-ceiling bookshelf along one wall.

The telephone circuits were about to be heated up. Over and over Maloney kept using the word "deal" as he thought of his job; he must not become overawed by its magnitude. It's just like any other business transaction, he told himself. I have to sell someone on the idea that the course of action I offer will benefit him. This time, if my customers have any sense, the selling shouldn't be that hard. I've sold tougher, he thought.

But never bigger. Never higher stakes, and, therefore, never scarier. Had he lost the Southern Steel merger five years ago, his firm, Union Consolidated, would be half the size it was now. Had he lost the African oil-fields lease four years ago, dividends would have been off twelve cents a share. If I lose this one, he said to himself . . . and let it drop. That's just the kind of thinking that'll freeze me up, Maloney thought. Cut it out. Just do the selling job.

Four deals, each a problem, each compounded by the ticking clock.

First the President. Talk him into buying the Israeli conditions, decide with him if there is any they should refuse. Get his OK to approach the USSR and the Arabs.

Then the Soviet Premier. Sell him. Convince him to pressure the Arabs. Reconcile any differences in position between Russia and America.

Next, the Arabs. Here Maloney was lucky. Only eight months before, in late 1978, the new, militant Egyptian government had pushed through a joint military command for the Arab forces, and their President dominated it, so by persuading only one man, Maloney could stop the attack. But here he knew salesmanship alone would not be enough. It would take muscle, too—the carrot and the stick. Bribe them and beat them. He was ready for both.

Finally, the Israelis. Two problems here: getting them to accept terms short of their total list of demands, and getting them to be patient if the talks, or the turnoff of the Arab attack, went beyond the deadline.

He sat down in the swivel chair at his desk and fixed on the White House phone as if trying to mesmerize it. Then he picked it up, waited for the click at the other end, and spoke: "This is Pete Maloney. I'm at the Waldorf. I've got to talk to the President right away."

The voice at the other end said, "One moment, please," and then the President's personal counselor, Fred Goode, was on the line. "Hey, Pete, how are you?"

"I'm pretty fair, Goody, and I'll be a lot better when I can talk to him. No kidding."

"Peter, old buddy, the boss is wining, dining, and wooing six Senators, committee chairmen every one, and all major committees. These guys had him nailed up on the cross all spring, and one of the places a nail went through was your very own foreign aid request. When they come back in session, he intends to climb down. Rise again. Got it, old buddy?"

"Who the hell am I talking to, the White House or the Vatican? This is *important!*" Maloney's temper was heating up.

"Anything short of the end of the world, Pete, don't expect him to get back to you before midnight. For the end of the world, maybe eleven forty-five."

Very funny, you asshole, Maloney said under his breath. And supposing I told you it was the end of the world. But he knew how to handle Goode, and when he spoke it was more a snarl.

"Listen to me, Goody. I want you to hang up this phone, walk into that dining room and get the President out and on the line. Now. Because if you don't, when he finds out what I wanted, and that you kept me away from him, somebody will be nailed to the cross, but it won't be the President and he won't be climbing down in the fall and he will never *never* rise again—except maybe to work in a very small law office in some place like Juneau, Alaska. Got it, old buddy?"

The President valued Fred Goode because he guarded his time like a petulant watchdog, but the counselor's camaraderie and bluster were both sham; under pressure he turned hostile and cowardly. "I think you better tell me what it's about, old buddy," he said, his voice an officious whine, "because the President has entrusted me . . ."

Maloney broke in. "You get your ego out of earshot, and your ass into that dining room! Or else, in addition to the President losing you your job, I personally will lose you your teeth." Maloney slammed down the receiver.

Four deals, and that sure as hell wasn't the world's smoothest start. But I can do it if the stakes don't make me clutch, he told himself. Just like trying to sink a two-foot putt, he thought. Ordinarily a cinch; with the US Open riding on it, suddenly a lot tougher. And made tougher still by the clock. The easy way to handle the four would be ad seriatim, one at a time, with, of course, a return to each when any one of them suggested changing an element. That would take, perhaps, a week, maybe ten days. He had, and he checked his watch, eleven hours and twenty-five minutes, or little more than one hour for each day's work.

No, I can't ask one and sit around waiting for an answer, hoping it's a yes, so I can go on to the next, he thought. That was a luxury, too expensive. Percolating in his head even before he slumped into his swivel chair and called the President was an alternative, and by the time he hung up on Fred Goode, Maloney was prepared to use it if he had to.

It was a desperate scheme, but hell, he told himself, if this was not the time to take chances, the time would never come. And it was as simple as it was desperate. If he had to, he'd call each of the four and tell him the other three had already agreed, that only *his* approval stood in the way of a solution, and world peace.

Risky enough under any circumstances, sure, but what made it double risky was another decision Maloney had come to. And that was to reject one of the Israeli demands. There would be no accession to the international hostage community, with the provision for Israel's holding leading citizens and priceless art and artifacts from all over the globe. First, Maloney realized he couldn't commit numbers of nations without their approval. Nor could he attempt to get that approval in the time remaining. Second, the Secretary felt a hostage community would be a festering reminder of Israel's blackmail, and therefore a threat to ignite a new war at any time.

So he would compound risk with risk. And on the seventh day I shall rest, he said to himself. What the hell, he thought, as long as Pete Maloney is playing God, he may as well go all the way. And what are my qualifications for the role? he asked. Pete Maloney, from Bay Ridge, Brooklyn, son of an Irish longshoreman—who am I to be deciding how to save the world? Why should this responsibility be mine? Let this cup pass from me.

Suppose I fail? Suppose those bombs go off and millions upon millions are killed, maimed, disfigured—he remembered the Hiroshima photographs. And suppose the Metropolitan Museum is blown to ashes, and Westminster Abbey and Notre Dame, and the Church of the Holy Sepulchre and the Statue of Liberty? And Disneyland! That's right, God, keep your sense of humor.

Why should it all depend on me? I don't want to be lying in rubble somewhere, asking myself what I did wrong. Don't worry, God, he thought, if it hits, and those circles are right, you'll be spared the self-doubt; it'll be a real test of your immortality. I'm the wrong casting for God, he said to himself. God shouldn't look like an Irish bulldog. My face is too round; it's not bearded, not ascetic, not otherworldly, not . . . godlike.

He didn't want the job; could he give it back? Why not? he asked himself. It's the job of one person, but why does it have to be me? Why not call the President and drop it in his lap? Let him take it the rest of the way. Or the Vice-President; he's got all those international pretensions. Or the Soviet Premier. Why me? He thought of that two-foot putt with everything riding on it. It's a no-win situation. If I do it, no one will credit me with a miracle. If I blow it, everything blows—and it's my fault. It's a job that goes with the Presidency. Or the Premiership. Not mine.

If he rejected the roles of God, President, and Premier, he did not reject the role of Pete Maloney, and there ran through his head a characteristic Maloney thought, mistaken by some for immodesty: since it's got to be one man, who can do it best? The President? The Premier? No, dammit, no one can do it better than I can.

He had been sitting with his head in his hands, mulling all this over. Now he looked up and let out a shout, "Steve, get in here!"

The young assistant came dashing in and Maloney barked at him, "Call Shalzar on Seventy-second Street, tell him I want to meet with him in . . ." Maloney looked at his watch again, 9:50, "make it twelve-thirty. And be nice, don't make it seem like I'm issuing orders. Tell him I'll go up there if he wants."

Phelps started to sit at his own desk to make the call, and the Secretary surprised him by snapping, "No, not there; go into one of the other rooms." The aide looked up, startled and hurt, and Maloney softened. "I've got a couple of other calls to make, Steve, and I may do some shouting." He waved the young man away, smiling as he did. Phelps smiled back, said, "Sure," and walked out.

Yeah, I've got a couple of calls to make, he said to himself. Just Moscow and Cairo. He felt a strange, heady sensation; he was going to get on the phone with two heads of state and say listen, Vassily, or listen, Karim—as every news watcher, or reader, knew, he was on a first-name basis with both, which certainly wouldn't hurt—listen, I need your help in saving the world.

Maloney had given himself two and a half hours to win over the President, the Russians, and the Arabs, which was goddamned impossible, he told himself. Two and a half hours before going up to see Shalzar. If he didn't have the three lined up by then? "Negative thinking," he told himself. "Bad. It's in all the salesmanship books. Spend your effort doing it, not talking it down," he said. Right now all he could do was sit there and wait for the President to call back; until then he couldn't put in the call to the Kremlin. Should he be on the line with the Soviets when the President called, he'd have some explaining to do.

Phelps rapped at the door, and as soon as the Secretary barked "come in," stuck his head in. "You're on for twelve-thirty at the embassy. You've got to go in a special entrance; I've got the details. Want me to go with you?"

"Yeah, Steve, sure," he answered, only half hearing him. "But right now, get through to the Soviet Union and set up a call to the Premier in . . . forty-five minutes, that'll be ten forty-five." Phelps stood and waited. "That's it," said the Secretary. "Thanks." The aide left.

Maloney was working on a timetable. The President would call—any minute, he hoped—which would give them nearly forty-five minutes before the call to Moscow was put through. Another forty-five minutes and he'd call Cairo; then he'd head uptown to talk with Shalzar. By then it would be 12:30, eight and a half hours away from the deadline. Assuming the Israelis took, let's say, two or three hours to give him an OK—and it would surely take that long, what with the hostage community knocked out—he'd still have five or six hours to iron out any differences with the other three. Not much of a cushion, he thought. And he knew the Israelis would need time to contact their Masada teams in nine cities, and take their fingers off the buttons.

But it could work, he told himself. If only the others would run by his timetable. He sat staring at the white phone, willing it to ring, blaming its silence on perversity. That's what I need now, he thought, a goddamned phone that won't obey orders. And a goddamned President who's kissing senatorial asses when he should be saving the world.

Of course, Maloney conceded, the President didn't know the world needed saving. The President knew nothing of the Masada Plan; that's what his Secretary of State was calling to tell him about. Which offered Maloney a choice of tactics. Suppose he didn't mention the Masada Plan? Just urge the President to join with the Soviet Union and pressure the Arabs to stop their invasion of Israel on the grounds it was a threat to world peace, which it sure as hell was. If he didn't disclose the plan, the President would refuse to act to stop the fighting. In fact, he already had refused Israeli pleas to intervene.

And if Maloney did reveal the plan? The danger there was that the President might get his back up, start waving the flag, and spewing out careful analyses like "millions for defense but not one cent for tribute." Behind the President's détentist façade, lay the gut reactions of a hawk.

The choice didn't take long. Flag-waving or not, Maloney would have to disclose the plan to the President. What decided him was the realization that there was no hiding the Masada Plan from the Soviet Premier, and if he told the Premier, he could hardly not tell his own President. Maloney's timing was perfect, for just as he made the decision, the white phone gave one short ring. He grabbed it.

"Hello, Pete Maloney."

Fred Goode's voice came over, yielding no hint that Maloney had just pissed all over him. "I've managed to get the President away from his dinner for a few moments, Pete."

"Thanks. Put him on." Then the President was on.

"Hello, Pete, I just told my guests who was interrupting our dinner. It'll probably cost you a quarter of a billion out of your foreign aid request. But I know it's worth it to you." The President was not a witty man, but in private he kept trying to be, probably to counteract his stolid public image. With his flat voice and his briskly rolled "r," he always sounded to Maloney like a bad imitation of Herb Shriner.

Maloney knew he had to shake the President right at the start. "Mr. President," he said, "I've never exaggerated, you know that; so when I tell you I'm calling about the most important mission either of us has ever had to handle, I hope you'll believe me."

Occasionally, the President came out with an expletive that made Maloney wince, and he managed one now. "Great crested grebes!" he said. "What a beginning. How are you going to live up to it?"

"The easiest thing in the world, Mr. President. We are less than eleven hours away from a global series of nuclear explosions that could destroy a substantial hunk of our world and make an even bigger hunk of it unfit to live in. Major cities are involved. So are millions upon millions of lives. And it's up to you to take the first step in preventing it."

For a moment, there was no reply. I don't blame him, thought Maloney; after all, what do you say to that? Finally, the President managed, "Pete, what is this? What are you talking about?"

And Maloney told him—about the imminent Israeli defeat, and the Masada Plan. He listed the Israeli conditions, and deferentially explained why he thought the hostage community should be rejected. Maloney never made it sound as if he were telling the President what to do. Finally he let it be known they got the details of the plan through intelligence sources; he didn't reveal who their spy had been.

Then he waited.

Again there was no immediate answer. Then the President said, "You're not suggesting, are you Pete, that you believe this plan? And that we should knuckle under to it?"

Oh, oh, Maloney said to himself. Careful now.

"The answer to the first part is yes, I do believe it. We know they're capable of it, they're desperate enough to do it. And we have hard evidence of the plan's existence." Now comes the tricky part, Maloney thought.

"But as for knuckling under, that's the wrong way to put it. I wouldn't call it that at all. It's up to us—to you, Mr. President—to take the lead in saving the world from a catastrophe, to shove aside a desperate threat and give ourselves the time to resolve the Middle East crisis without a gun at our heads." Let's see how that works, Maloney thought.

The President answered his question quickly. "Stop the crap, Pete. I said knuckle under, and you're saying knuckle under."

Well, I am trying to crap him, Maloney thought. And I'll keep it up. And by God, I'll win him over. I'll say whatever I have to: Damn the Israelis, call the Arabs living saints, promise him a Nobel Peace Prize. Even laugh at his jokes. I'll do what I have to.

"Look, Mr. President, someone's got a gun at our heads. The reasons for it are, at the moment, immaterial. The only question is do we stop him from pulling the trigger, or do we let him, just to show how brave we are? And I'm not talking about personal bravery. If either of us could challenge the Israeli Prime Minister to a duel—pistols, swords, knives, name it—I'd battle you for the privilege of taking him on. This is not your own life you're risking. Or mine. It's the lives of millions—kids, women, old people. Millions in New York and Los Angeles will die; millions more will be mutilated; California and the Northeast corridor will be under radioactive blankets.

"Do we have a right to risk their lives? Do we want that on our heads, Mr. President, assuming we have any heads left?" Maloney was a boxer throwing combination punches; he had to get them all in there.

"What's real bravery here? I'm just brave enough to deflect that gun and deal with the gunman later, when he's not armed to kill. And believe me, Mr. President, I've never been one to back away from a fight, you know that."

The Secretary felt the muscles in his right forearm cramping from the fervor with which he was squeezing the phone. Just one more, he said to himself, and I'll stop. Dammit, he thought, I wish I had the man face-to-face, instead of this way. Into the phone he said, "Give me the chance to shove that gun aside. If you do, we'll not only save lives, we'll be in a helluva spot to settle the Mideast situation once and for all. It'll put you in the history books, and maybe get you a Nobel Peace Prize, too, I promise you."

More crap, Maloney told himself. He waited.

"You're a persuasive son of a bitch, Pete; you managed to work your way out of a straight no. At least I'll agree to kick it around for a couple of hours."

"A couple of hours?" Maloney half shouted it into the phone. "We don't have a couple of hours!" With his left foot he kicked out at the desk. Goddammit, he said to himself, what does he think this is, the selection of a local postmaster?

"Mr. President, it's nearly ten-thirty. At nine tomorrow morning our time is up, which gives us ten and a half hours to pull off three tricky negotiations. I was counting on being able to begin at once."

The President's voice began to sound annoyed. "No way I'm going to OK it off the cuff, Pete. Consider it a compliment; it's not an outright no. When I said I'd have to kick it around, that's just what I meant. Maybe talk it over with some people. Why did you wait so long to get started?"

Suddenly the Secretary was glad his chief executive wasn't in the room with him. Why did I wait so long? What in hell does he think I've been doing down here? The hora? Political ass-kissing? I was sending a defenseless amateur spy out to risk her neck to get the material we needed!

"I called the moment we learned what the plan was, Mr. President. The instant. If I don't get a go-ahead right away, we won't have the physical ability to turn the thing off before the deadline, even if we all want to!"

Another pause. It's so tough not to see the man's face, Maloney thought, not to see if I'm getting anywhere. But surely the hesitation had to be good, it had to mean he was thinking about a yes. Maloney tried nudging him. "If nothing else can do it, would it help to ask you to say yes on faith? Would you say yes because you trust me? Because I have never, *never* steered you wrong? Because my sense of the situation tells me we must move—immediately?"

Almost detached from his own voice, Maloney looked at his left hand and watched himself cross his fingers.

"I appreciate all that, Pete, but . . ." Well, there was the answer, in the word 'but,' Maloney told himself. "But I'm not as lucky as you are. You've only got to report to me. I've got a country to answer to, and a Congress, and a party. But I'll tell you what. I'll make it *one* hour. At eleven-thirty, I'll be back to you with an answer."

Shit, Maloney said to himself. To the President, "Promise me two things. Let me hear your answer from you, not anyone else. And not a moment later than eleven-thirty, or the answer may turn out to be academic."

"Personally," said the President. "At eleven-thirty."

"All right, Mr. President. Thank you. Goodbye."

Inches away from slamming the receiver down, Maloney reined himself in and lowered it gently. There goes my timetable, he said to himself. What in hell do I do now? In ten minutes I'm supposed to talk to the Soviets, then the Arabs, then the Israelis—and without the President's approval, I've got nothing to tell any of them.

He stood and took a couple of steps, but there was no room in the tiny study. The walls seemed to be closing in. No room. A perfect setting for the spot I'm in, he thought. The walls closing in.

I let myself in for this, he thought. I could be finishing dinner now at Park and Seventieth, after a day's work in the chairman's office at Union Consolidated—an office big enough for ten of these, with a view of the East River, and no walls closing in. Someone else could be here in this padded cell, waiting for the world to blow up in his face. And I've got to *act,* instead of just sitting here, or it will blow up in my face. Like Kevin and the grenade.

Ever since the Korean War, whenever Maloney thought of indecisiveness, one image burned in his mind. He had served as a lieutenant in the Marine Corps, and struck up a friendship with Kevin Dougherty. "He's from Brooklyn, like me," Maloney had written to his parents about Kevin. "And he's Irish, like me." And then Maloney had thought of his mother's reaction, and added: "Like half of me, anyway."

He had met Dougherty on the troop ship going overseas, and again and again they were assigned to the same units, until finally they were platoon commanders in the same company. One morning, their company was assigned to take a hill a few miles below the 38th Parallel. Side by side, Kevin's platoon and his moved up over rocky ground, with lots of cover for the North Koreans, and the Marines began taking heavy small arms fire, backed by a few mortars and grenade launchers. Crouching, using boulders for protection whenever he could, Maloney ran over to Kevin to talk to him about getting behind the mortar emplacement that was hurting them. He was five yards from his friend, behind a rock, when someone yelled, "Grenade!" He looked up, and there it was against a blue sky, floating through the air, as if in slow motion. Maloney dove behind the rock, hit the ground, face to one side, and as he did, got a perfect view of Kevin Dougherty.

The grenade hit the ground and, almost in slow motion, bounced right at the young lieutenant. For a couple of seconds, Kevin froze, unable to decide whether to hit the dirt or grab the grenade and throw it away. Had he done either right away, he might have made it, but the momentary indecision cost him his life. And Maloney saw it all: Kevin standing there, frozen, hands out in front of him. The grenade five feet from him, bouncing, going off. Kevin's hands blown away, his face a disintegrating red horror. Kevin dead when he hit the ground.

Maloney got a piece of shrapnel in his left buttock, which took a lot of explaining in later years, but which got him out of the Corps ten months early. When he got home, Maloney went to see the Doughertys in Red Hook, but never gave them the graphic details of that bloody picture. In fact, he never told anyone. Nor did he ever forget it. More and more it became for him a metaphor for indecision.

And right now the grenade was about to go off, and he hadn't decided whether to go for it or bug out. Standing there in the cramped study, he suddenly realized the fantasies about his old office, his old job, were just a wish to get the hell behind a rock. Then he asked himself, If I bug out, who goes for the grenade? And if no one goes for it, is there any safety behind a rock?

Partly his decision came from the honest (and justified) belief he could handle the grenade better than anyone else. The importance of this belief would have startled Maloney-watchers who attributed his ambition to lust for power or fame or money; of course, that lust was there, but overrated. Much stronger was his drive to take on assignments just because he knew he could handle them so well.

Partly his decision came from the sudden realization, as he questioned himself, that he didn't have the options poor Kevin did. If there was no safety behind the rock, why bother?

As he ruminated, Pete Maloney found himself standing with his hands out, arms bent, in a morbid, unthinking imitation of Kevin Dougherty's last pose. Every time he thought of the scene, it happened. He looked down at his hands. They're still on, he thought. Then he looked up, startled, when Steve Phelps stuck his head in the door. "I knocked three times," Phelps said. "We've got the call to the Kremlin set up; the Premier and his interpreter are ready at the other end; our interpreter is ready to pick up in Washington. You get on, and then the Premier will."

Now the Secretary of State had to do one of two things: postpone the call until he heard from the President, or get on the phone and lie—say the President had agreed, and try to get the Soviet Premier to go along, hoping the President would say yes later. It was one thing to contemplate the lie as a possibility; it was another to get on the phone as someone who served the President, and actually lie— misrepresent the President in the gravest decision he'd ever make.

Maloney was staring at his outstretched hands; so was Phelps. Maybe he'd have bugged out if he could think of a way, he told himself. No way. And he couldn't just stand there—like Kevin.

He went for the grenade.

"OK, Steve, I'm ready for him." If the President would not say yes in time for this call, his Secretary of State would do it for him.

Maloney took two steps back to his desk and sat down. Only then did he break the fixed position of his arms to pick up the red phone.

Then followed a forty-minute conversation that was the most astounding Maloney had ever taken part in. Mechanically, it was cumbersome, speaking in short bursts and then waiting for the translations —although he knew damned well the Premier understood English.

Getting the Russian to agree to the Israeli demands, however, was incredibly easy.

And during the translations, Maloney had a chance to try to figure out why.

First, he was astonished by the Premier's lack of surprise. Nothing startled him: not the progress of the fighting, not the outlining of the Masada Plan, not the listing of the conditions. All along, his responses were, "I understand" and "I see." And Maloney remembered his own reaction to the plan, and tried to come up with a reason for the Soviet's equanimity.

More and more, he began saying to himself, the Russian knows. I'm not telling him anything he hasn't heard before. But how? Well, he answered himself, we found out, why not they? They've got spies, too. Sure, there are no copies of the document in Moscow or Leningrad. But there are in Jerusalem. And in New York—in Israeli hands and in ours. And presumably there are in London, Paris, and Berlin. Leaks. Could be anywhere, including right in this suite.

And if they knew, Maloney thought, that might explain the ambush attempts. Why shouldn't the Russians tell their friends the Arabs, who might then try to thwart the plan by getting to Shalzar, or Kate— or maybe to me, Maloney thought. If the ambushes succeeded, the Arabs would be grateful to the Russians, of course. And if they didn't? Then, of course, the Soviets could always refuse to go along with Maloney in meeting Israeli demands. Without Soviet agreement, the US could not possibly stop the Arabs, not with the threat of a full-scale American-Soviet war in the offing.

So beyond the lack of Russian surprise, Maloney, as the conversation progressed, became astounded by the easy Russian acquiescence. And again, he asked himself, why?

Part of an answer came to him at once. The Soviet Union did not *want* the Arabs to wipe out Israel, because if they did, they would no longer need the Soviets.

The other part was suggested in two conditions the Soviet Premier laid down for his approval.

"How do you intend to stop the Arabs?" he asked. Without evasion, the Secretary answered, "The bottom line is the use of force. The next to last line is the threat of force."

"Whose force?" asked the Premier.

"Ours," answered Maloney, deliberately ambiguous.

248

"Does 'ours' mean both of ours, or just yours?" the Premier wanted to know. Even before Maloney could reply, the Russian added quickly: "The Soviet Union will not threaten its Arab friends."

Maloney waited. The Premier added nothing.

"And if *we* threaten force?" the Secretary asked.

"We deplore it," answered the Premier, pompously, "but we are not adventurers, like you. We will not risk a nuclear war."

Oh ho, I've got it, you clever bastard, Maloney thought. Let us be the bad guys, worm your way back in, make up all the ground you've lost with the Arabs over the past four or five years. But Maloney accepted, because he had to, and because he didn't think the Arabs would be taken in by the Soviet hands-off attitude.

"We are glad you will not intervene, should we have to move to keep the peace. Shall I assure the President, then, we have an understanding on that point?"

"Yes, although we deplore it," answered the Premier.

Then came his second condition. "We wish to be the first to speak to the Egyptian president about this matter," said the Russian.

Squeezing the last drop of blood out of us on this one, aren't you, Maloney thought. He could almost write the script for the Premier's speech to the Arabs: The imperialists are going to club you into stopping your holy war against the Zionists. We've done everything we could to stop them, but to allow a nuclear holocaust would accomplish nothing for either of us. So let us bide our time; we will stick together and win. Just remember who is stopping you. And who your friends are.

That's what the Russian would say, thought Maloney. But he accepted the second condition, too, again because he had to, and again because the Russians wouldn't gain as much as they anticipated; nothing Maloney couldn't counter in a session with the Egyptian president. Besides, the Secretary said to himself, if I'm right about their already knowing the Masada Plan, then they've already spoken to the Egyptians about it. So I'll give away a little ice in the winter. He promised he'd give the Premier two hours before he called Cairo.

"My dear friend Vassily," he said to the Russian. "I had hoped I could count on Soviet statesmanship in this crisis, and I was not disappointed."

The Premier replied, "We want to make it clear we deplore the threat of force in the Middle East."

"The United States deplores the threat of force and the *use* of force in the Middle East or anywhere, and we want to cooperate in keeping the peace everywhere." Then, laboriously, Maloney managed "Goodbye, my friend," in Russian.

Effortlessly, the Premier returned it in English.

Four receivers were hung up.

He's a fox, thought the Premier, but this time we got the better of him.

He's a wolf, thought Maloney, but he ripped off a lot less raw meat than he thinks.

Now Maloney had the Soviet Union. He still needed the Arabs, but that seemed a bit easier, thanks to the Russians. He also needed the Israelis, to go along with the rejection of one demand. And he needed the President. If I don't get him, thought Maloney, none of the others counts.

He also needed a new timetable. Because of his promise to the Premier, he couldn't call Cairo until 1:20. He could hold to the schedule for the President's call, which would come in soon, and for his visit to the Israeli ambassador at 12:30. If I'm not shot or kidnapped, that is, Maloney said to himself.

He was now taking the major gamble of going to Shalzar and making *two* promises he couldn't yet deliver on: the agreement of the Arabs and of the President of the United States. Still, Maloney thought, leaning back in his swivel chair, and taking a deep breath, a bit of the pressure is off. We've got a good shot at it now; I can see the light at the end of the tunnel. Then he thought, that's what they said about Vietnam.

He looked at his watch; ten minutes till the President's call. Well, he wasn't going to spend it in this cubbyhole. He jumped up and headed for the living room, slowing down at the room Phelps was using to shout: "Steve, I'll be out there, call me when the President phones."

While Maloney was on the phone, in his study, Kate Colby and Bill Brewster had been sitting on the sofa making cautious conversation, mainly about their careers. Bill was reticent because he didn't want to use this crisis to push a personal cause; Kate because she was preoccupied with thoughts of her next meeting with Dov. But as they tried to pass the time, both felt their thoughts going, again and again, to their children, who were out of the city, out of the target circles. And to the many children not out of the circles. From there their minds took them down the hall into Maloney's office, where the Secretary was trying to erase those circles. At every sound, one or both would look toward the doorway, expecting to see the stocky figure come through.

When at last he arrived, all they could do was stare—and wait. But Pete Maloney first walked to the bar to make still another Scotch and soda he would not drink. Glass in hand, he sat on the arm of the sofa.

"No calls tonight, to anybody, from either of you. OK?"

"Not about this," Kate answered.

"Not about anything. To anybody." He punched out the words. "OK?"

"OK," said Kate. "OK," echoed Brewster.

"Oh, and everything off the record, before, now, and later. OK?" Maloney again looked at both, but longer and harder at Kate.

Why does he look at me that way, Kate asked herself. Because I'm a journalist or because I'm a spy? The juxtaposition of the two gave her a pang, because she suddenly remembered the way the CIA had recruited newspeople. And now I'm one of those, she told herself. How do I get my purity back? Let's hope it's not by radiation, she thought. Then she realized Maloney and Brewster were looking at her, waiting for her to say something. Maloney spoke, "I know what you're thinking, Kate, and as soon as we can, you and I will have a talk about what's off the record and what isn't. We owe you a hell of a lot, and I'm going to give you as much as I can."

No, you don't know what I'm thinking, she said to herself. To Maloney she just said, "OK," and smiled.

Pete sipped from his glass, let out a deep breath, and said, "One down, three to go."

"The President," Brewster volunteered.

"Wrong," answered the Secretary. "Want to try another?"

"What do you mean, wrong?" Brewster asked. "How can you have anyone else's approval—how can you even ask anyone else—without the President's approval?"

"How can I?" said Maloney, making a noise that was a cross between a laugh and a snort. "A good question. So is: How can I send a female amateur in to spy on an ambassador? And how can I give back to the Russians the toehold they've lost in the Middle East in the last five years? And how can I threaten the Arabs with an airborne assault and God knows what else, if they don't stop fighting. Those are all things I've either done or will do very soon.

"How can I? The answer is . . ." and he looked from one to the other, "in the next nine and a half hours, I can do anything I damn please if I think it will take the finger off the button."

Brewster was both fascinated and offended by this eleventh-hour anarchy. "Since the one-down is not the President, it must be the Russians, the Arabs, or the Israelis. In any case it is, in effect, an international agreement, made without the approval of the President. And, of course, the Senate knows nothing about it. So you've taken the reins yourself, Maloney."

"Yeah," answered the Secretary, smiling but pugnacious. "The reins. The helm. The bull by the horns. The tiger by the tail. Want 'em? Go on, grab. They're red hot, and me wearing nothing but my velvet gloves."

"No," answered Brewster. "It's not the particular set of hands I object to; its the presence of only one set."

"For Christ's sake," said the Secretary. "We've got nine and a half hours to go and the man wants me to organize a task force, call a meeting."

"It's the same excuse every strong man has ever used," replied Brewster.

"Jesus, a goddamned civics lesson," said Maloney. "First I thought I was gonna be lumped with Metternich and Kissinger. Now I see it's gonna be—who? Franco? Stalin? Who?"

Brewster smiled, but he was getting angry. "You've got the soul of an autocrat, Pete, and the chief symptom of one, too, which is you'd love to let others share your power—*if* you could just find anyone as smart as you are. But you just can't seem to. Now I'll admit it's hard, but that's not the way we run things in this country."

Maloney turned serious. "No, there you're wrong, old boy. There are enough smarter than I am. You're one of them, Bill. What I've got more of than you is plain old nerve. Why, with your brains and my balls, we could rule the world."

"Why include me, Pete?" Brewster asked. "You're doing it alone with your balls and *your* brains."

"Bill, my oldest and dearest friend, what I'm getting from you now is a quick character analysis to go with your history-civics course. What I need from you—both of you—is your ideas and your support and, if an old blasphemer dare suggest it, your prayers."

Brewster laughed. "Pete Maloney asking for prayers. Now I've heard it all. You think I was calling you a Metternich, a Kissinger, a Franco, a Stalin. All right. All of those. And do you know what else you are? You're a con man!"

The Secretary of State nodded his head. "A con man. You don't know how right you are. I had an uncle who really was a con man. Luigi. On my mother's side, but you probably figured that out." Maloney grinned. "I'm not sure what he was, a bookie, a numbers man; my father would say he was a small-time Mafia operator, which would make my mother furious. All I know is he was always on the phone, involved in long conversations in which he was trying to talk somebody into something. Never once did I ever hear anyone trying to talk *him* into anything. He would do the conning, always punctuating his spiels with 'see?' and 'get my meaning?' Penny ante stuff, of course, but he was amazingly successful, and never because of subtlety or cleverness, both of which he was notably short on. What he had was persistence; he was inexhaustible; he wouldn't take no for an answer; he'd keep at whomever he was talking to, with his 'see?' and 'get my meaning?' and his Damon Runyon accent—only authentic—until he wore down the opposition.

"Yeah, in a way, this is a con job I'm doing, and whenever I think of a con man, I think of Uncle Luigi and the way he would do it, because he was the best." Maloney took on the raspy voice and accent of his uncle as he continued.

"This is the way I do it. I call the chief, see, and I tell him we gotta get our asses in gear, get movin' like a Marine on leave chasin' a piece of poon tang. And all the chief's gotta do is give me the high sign, and I'll do the rest. Get my meaning? But he ain't havin' no part of it, see. Says he's gotta swim it around the old think tank first. Which means I gotta twiddle my thumbs." Maloney gave an extravagant pause before going on.

"So I say to myself, what if? What if I just wait for the OK from the boss, before I go ahead to the others of the fearsome foursome? And I'm doin' great, see, *only I run out of time*. I could do it all, clinch the deal, but instead it all falls apart. Only because of time. Wouldn't that burn me up? Me and maybe a few others, too. Get my meaning?

"Then I say to myself, what if, on the other hand, I just make believe I got the nod from the chief, and go after the other biggies. That gives me maybe an extra two hours that I woulda spent waitin'; the worst I could get from the boss is a slap on the wrist 'cause I broke early from the starting gate."

Then the Secretary concluded, still with the same impersonation but with the smile gone. "And if I go through all this and then the chief does not give me an OK, so what does it hurt, since alles is kaput anyway, if you get my meaning. The worse could befall me is I get angry phone calls from certain gents in Moscow, Jerusalem, and Cairo who claim I'm a welsher. But even that's a long shot, see, because odds are, by then the telephone lines in said burgs, not to mention right here in the Big Apple, will most likely be *fused,* if you get my meaning."

Then the Secretary dropped the accent and said to Brewster, softly and soberly, "Give me one reason, other than rigidity, for waiting. Let's say your mother warns you *never* to leave the house in the morning without brushing your teeth, which is a fine rule. One morning you wake up and your house is burning down. Should you stop to brush your teeth?"

Brewster nodded at his friend. Maloney was right, of course. And Brewster thought, I would have waited; it would never have occurred to me *not* to wait.

"So we got the Russians." The Secretary went ahead as if his friend had never challenged him. "I had to give them some Middle East Brownie points, but not near as many as they imagine. In a couple of minutes the President will be calling, I hope with an OK; it damn well better be. Then I run uptown and talk the Israelis into giving up the international hostage community, and with three lined up, I put the screws to the Arabs. And then we break out the champagne."

Maloney leaned back on the sofa and brushed his hands together, saying, ironically, "There, that wasn't too hard, was it?"

Kate pursued the irony. "And to think for a while I was worried." Then, more seriously, "The Russians sound like a miracle, but you don't really think you're going to get what you want from all those others in the time you have left, do you?"

Maloney didn't want to show a confidence he didn't feel. "Put it this way," he said. "We're closer to it now then when we had no OKs, and not as close as we will be when we have two."

If Kate was hoping for comfort, she hadn't gotten it. She asked another question. "Would you say, Mr. Secretary, that the specific information I got made a lot of difference in your decision to go on?"

"Not a *lot* of difference," he answered, "*all* the difference."

"In that case," she asked, "why didn't the Israelis just present you with the Masada Plan, instead of concealing it and risking failure the way they did?"

"I've been asking myself the same question," Bill Brewster added.

"Which makes three of us," added Maloney. "One answer I come up with is that the plan is so deadly, the Israelis never wanted it stated, directly or indirectly, officially or unofficially. They want it off the history books, and so they took the desperate gamble they could make us buy it sight unseen—a pig in a poke, to put it in unkosher terms."

He shrugged. "And come to think of it, they won their gamble, didn't they? We never heard it from their lips. We happened to uncover it, *grace à* Kate Colby. But they can always say we're nuts."

"Except for one thing," said Brewster. "The film. We have the film."

The Secretary nodded his head. "That's right, by God. We have the film."

Phelps burst in at the end of Maloney's sentence, to tell him the President was on the line. Maloney leaped to his feet, muttered "Now we'll see" to Brewster and Kate Colby and hurried from the living room.

In his study he slammed the door, sat at the desk and lifted the white receiver. "Pete Maloney here," he said, when he heard the click at the other end. The voice from the White House was not Fred Goode's. He had had enough of Maloney. An aide whose voice the Secretary didn't recognize said, "Yes, Mr. Secretary. Here is the President."

"Pete," the President began. "I've been sitting and talking with my old colleague Tom Holloway about the Israeli situation . . ."

Oh shit, said Maloney to himself. Not Holloway, not that missile-

254

totin' machismo corn-belt blowhard! Nothing scared Senator Holloway —he was too gaddamned dumb, Maloney thought. He was also an old friend of the President's from Congressional days and he brought out all that was stupid, reactionary, bigoted and xenophobic in the President. In short, the President felt comfortable and nostalgic with him, and listened to him.

It was for reasons like Holloway that Pete Maloney almost didn't take the Cabinet job. Like many top East Coast executives, Maloney was a moderate liberal on foreign policy and somewhat more conservative domestically. He found the enlightened side of the President very compatible and when associates asked why he wanted to join "the Holloway gang," Maloney replied, "If Holloway were running him, would he be asking me to be his Secretary of State?" A good answer, convincing to others, and sometimes even to himself.

The President continually startled Maloney, not because of his politics but because he was far and away the most political man Maloney had ever encountered. A political writer had once told Maloney, "If the President's wife were drowning, as he jumped in to save her, he'd be wondering: what'll it do to my chances in the next election? Not a bad guy, mind you, just totally conditioned to political responses. The difference between him and Holloway is, even if it hurt politically, the President would still save his wife. Holloway would let *his* drown."

So Maloney knew, if the President was listening to Tom Holloway, he was being fed a mixture of flag waving, chest thumping, and animal cunning, the end product of which would be the Marines landing on the beaches of Haifa. It would help him in the polls, Holloway would guarantee—even if the next polls were taken on flat stones with flint knives by men in animals skins.

"I've been talking with Tom," the President was saying, "and he feels it's a dangerous thing to do . . ."

"Tell the Senator I agree with him," the Secretary barked into the phone. "It's the most dangerous game in town. Except for all the others."

Either the President didn't understand the answer, or he ignored it. "Tom thinks there may be a better answer than surrender."

Here it comes, the Secretary thought, and me without the strength to fight this American he-man bullshit. "The Senator is worried about the Israelis coming off tougher than we are, right Mr. President? Well, tell him that all Jews are hysterical cowards, OK? But right now they've got their greasy finger on the button, and we have got to be calm and heroic and slide that finger off. And then we'll have them put away—you know, barbed wire, striped uniforms, numbers on the arm, and everything. I think he'll buy that."

No, it was not the smartest response, Maloney knew that. But effrontery had worked with the President before. And he was too exhausted to be tactful. And he loathed Holloway, who was anti-Semitic, anti-Catholic, anti-black, a walking compendium of every Know-Nothing strain that had ever soiled American history.

"Now, Pete," the President's voice was harder, "there's nothing to be gained by being derisive." The man always comes up with little homilies like this to coat his waffling, Maloney thought. And for it he gets a reputation for "fairness."

"I'm not saying I go along with Tom," he went on, "but he has made me think we're not spending enough time exploring our options. Tom thinks . . ."

"Screw Tom!" It burst out of the Secretary. Fresher, calmer, he would have swallowed it. But he didn't regret saying it. He'd reached the end of his rope. "Holloway doesn't know what's going on. I've been in this up to my ears and I tell you there's no sensible alternative to be found, even if we had the time to look for one, which we don't. Believe me, Mr. President, I've been going through the options, every one Holloway can come up with and then some. We have no more time to play around!"

"And I tell you," answered the President, his voice resolute, as if delivering a speech, "you're letting yourself get psyched out by the Israelis. You're ignoring the advice of a respected and knowledgeable Senator . . ." Oh, now I get it, Maloney said to himself. Holloway is sitting next to the President, and the ole political prexy is putting on a show for him. Keeping his fences mended, no matter that in a few hours they might be blown into the ionosphere. He doesn't have the imagination to believe in disaster!

"You've given up on finding another solution," the President went on. "Now what I want, Pete, is for you to take a couple of hours to mastermind this and come up with some new initiatives. We'll be doing the same at our end. Two hours. Not before. I'll make a decision then. Is that absolutely clear?"

Tired, angry, despairing, Maloney still managed to stifle the expletive that came surging up from his gut. Two hours. 2:10 a.m. Less than seven hours from the deadline, and from the sound of the man, it was damned likely he'd say no even then. But the Secretary knew there was no point arguing any more at the moment, not with Holloway there.

"Yes, sir," he said quietly. What the hell, he thought, soon the world may end with a bang, so I can end my conversation with a whimper. And gently he put down the receiver.

In a little while he'd have to be at the Israeli embassy. How amusing, he told himself, that my original timetable had me going there with all three approvals in my pocket. Instead, I don't have the President's and I haven't even spoken to Cairo. How amusing, he thought, that the only one on my side is the Soviet Premier. What should I do, call him and tell him it's all off? Or ask him for a job? Not, of course, in Moscow or Leningrad. For the first time, he thought, Siberia is the place to be.

He got up and walked into the living room. Kate and Brewster looked at him. At first he said nothing. The three other glasses he had filled with Scotch, ice and soda, and then barely touched had all been taken away, so he made himself another, walked to the easy chair and sat down.

"I've got a couple of minutes before I head for the Israeli embassy."

"And the President?" Brewster asked.

"Well, the President is kind of against it. He wants me to put some more thought into it, and he's promised to do the same, with the enlightened, cerebral assistance of Senator Thomas Holloway, who, if I am Metternich, stands squarely in the fur boots of Attila the Hun. Senator Tom has warned our leader if we get another yellow stain on our escutcheon, every Jewish bully on the block will start picking on us."

"Then what are you going to tell the Israelis?" Kate asked.

"Well, I'll begin by warning them if they don't drop the Masada Plan at once, Senator Holloway will come by personally and thrash them soundly." Maloney was too low and tired to squeeze the full sarcasm out of the statement. "Then, if that doesn't work, I'll just go on and try to get another of my four deals out of the way."

"What good will that do?" Brewster asked, "if you get a no from the President?"

The Secretary of State looked at his watch, and slowly stood. "I've got fifteen minutes to get to the embassy. Eight hours and forty-five minutes to the deadline. If in two hours, the President should by chance say yes, it'll be better to have two down than one. Or better still, three down."

"If he says no . . ." Maloney shrugged. "We'll still have six and three-quarters hours. In the State Department helicopter, we can be way up in Canada by then."

The Secretary smiled weakly, waved his hand, turned, and walked out.

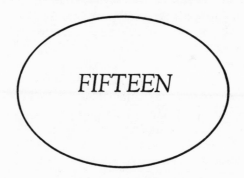

FIFTEEN

It was 11:50 and Shalzar had forty minutes to wait before the Secretary of State was due, so he was startled when there was a knock on the library door and a security man stuck his head in.

"There's an American outside who says he must see you." My God, Shalzar thought, Maloney so early? "Who is he?" he asked.

"His name is Seligsohn. He says he doesn't have an appointment but that you'd see him. We figured that since he knew the Seventy-third Street entrance, he might be someone you'd want to know about."

Suddenly, the ambassador remembered: The rally at UN Plaza this afternoon! 2:30. He was supposed to have been there to speak. Damn! He didn't want to see Seligsohn, but it didn't matter. Either the button was pressed at 9 tomorrow morning, or it wasn't. What could Seligsohn do?

Shalzar ran his fingers along the soft brown leather of the library easy chair. This was one of the newer pieces, picked by him when they moved into the new embassy a year earlier and it was his favorite chair in all the building. He wondered if he'd be sitting in it tomorrow. And then thought: You always had to prepare as if there were going to be a tomorrow, a next week and a next year; and he might be needing Seligsohn.

"Yes, of course, send Mr. Seligsohn here." Shalzar knew the tone he took would be picked up by the security men in dealing with the publisher and he wanted it to be respectful.

Within a minute, Mac Seligsohn was in the room, and Shalzar waited for the frontal assault. Instead, Seligsohn just grinned at him and said:

"The rally was nine hours ago, better hurry or you'll be late."

Clever son of a gun, thought the ambassador; rather than haranguing him and getting a heated answer, Seligsohn just introduced the subject mildly and let the apology flow freely.

"Mac, I'm sorry. I could tell you I was waiting for the imminent arrival of the Foreign Minister. I could tell you the situation here is so critical I couldn't get away. Both of those would be true. But the fact is, with the pressure of both of them, and a dozen other things, I just forgot, and I'm sorry."

With no one to argue against, Seligsohn in turn could not stay combative. "How is Weismann, by the way?" he asked.

"Fine. In his room, tired from the trip, from being up all the night before it."

"Are you going to ask me how the rally went?" Seligsohn was amused at himself as he put the question. His ego was visible and he knew it.

Shalzar smiled briefly. "Believe it or not, and why should you, I was just about to ask."

"We wanted 35,000, we needed 25, we expected 15. We got 40,000," said the publisher proudly.

"How'd you do it, Mac?" Shalzar asked, without really caring.

"All the telephoning I told you about; radio and TV spots all morning, rammed in there at the last minute. You know what it takes to get those spots at the last minute?"

"It can't be easy, Mac."

"It can't be *done*, Dov. It's *impossible!* Unless you're holding some mightly valuable IOUs. And there are a group of us who have cashed in a few of our biggest. That's how much this crisis worries us. I wish we could take it as calmly as you do, Mr. Ambassador. Maybe we cashed them in for nothing. Maybe you knew better than we, that we shouldn't worry. How come you don't seem to give a damn, Dov?

"Did you see the network news?" Seligsohn went on, "did you see the half-hour specials two of the networks did right afterwards? Do you know the last time any network put a *live* news special on at seven-thirty? Well, they did it to cover our White House demonstration. And you know who spoke? Six senators, five Nobel Prize-winners and Paul Newman *and* Robert Redford, who flew down from New York by chartered helicopter after they spoke at the UN Plaza rally— where they replaced *you!*"

"That's fantastic, Mac. I don't know how you do it."

"Of course, Newman and Redford couldn't match your sex appeal, Dov. But after all, there were two of them. And *they* showed up!"

"For fill-ins, I'm sure they were passable," said the ambassador. Then he looked at the American, hard. "Mac, you're too smart to have come here just for a thank-you. What are you after?"

"I'm also too smart to think you'd miss the rally, and you'd be so damned blasé about everything I've told you, if you thought any of it mattered." Until then, Seligsohn had been standing. With his last words, he sat on the edge of the sofa. "What have you got up your sleeve, Dov? What do you know that makes you so damned uninterested in everything we've been doing?"

How much should he tell? Shalzar asked himself. Not all of it, he decided, but some couldn't hurt. "Things are more critical than you think, Mac. Our best hope is to get the President to step in, and frankly all of my energy has been aimed in that direction."

"Hell," Seligsohn said. "If this were only ten years ago, I'd have a pipeline. But look, what's the harm of my calling the President just to tighten the screws a little?"

The ambassador thought about it. Would a call throw Maloney off? Shalzar didn't know and couldn't take any chances. "Can't risk it now, Mac," he replied. "That may change any moment, and if it should, and you can help, I'll get right to you. Right now, though, we're doing some careful talking, which could make things a lot better by tomorrow morning—if it works."

Shalzar had no intention of telling him about the Masada Plan. "And if doesn't work?"

"Then things could get a lot worse." With that, Shalzar stopped talking.

Seligsohn waited. Then, "Do I take it by your silence you're not going to tell me any more?"

"Yes."

"May I ask a few leading questions?"

"No, Mac, please. No more."

Seligsohn was an aggressive man, also a very smart one, who knew that if his hurtling body met a stone wall, all his determination wouldn't hurt the wall, or help his head. He knew when to stop.

He got to his feet; Shalzar rose to walk him out. "Besides leaving," he said, "is there anything I can do to help?"

"Yeah, Mac," said the ambassador as the two walked to the exit. "Stick with us. We don't have too many friends left."

Seligsohn clenched his fist and shook it. "All the way!" He said it softly and fiercely.

And then, "You know me, I'm a pusher. Allow me one more question, which you can refuse to answer if you want." And he waited.

I owe it to him, Shalzar thought. "Go ahead."

"What time tomorrow morning will you know?"

"Between us, Mac?"

"Of course!"

"Nine o'clock."

"And after it, how can I know whether to breathe easier or not?"

The ambassador smiled a mirthless smile. "You'll know, Mac, you'll know."

And again Seligsohn clenched his fist and said, "All the way, Dov. All the way." And he left.

At about the same time he walked out on Seventy-third Street and into his waiting Fleetwood limousine with its MS-1 license plate, the

Secretary of State was walking toward the black sedan parked in front of the Towers entrance, to take the short ride to meet with Ambassador Shalzar.

He stepped into the back. Up front were two agents, and in a car behind them, two more, the same two who had been guarding Kate Colby.

Starting late and racing out of his suite, Maloney had forgotten his aide, Phelps, and by the time he remembered, the cars were on their way up Park Avenue. It was too late to turn around and get him, and Phelps was the only one who knew the Secretary was supposed to enter the embassy at Seventy-third Street, not Seventy-second.

Sitting back in the car, the Secretary asked himself, Why don't the Arabs try kidnaping me? That would solve all the problems, all the juggling. I could drop all the balls and sit back and watch someone else try to pick them up—before they blew up in his face. His face—not mine. But even as he tasted the possibility, he knew he was fantasizing. The balls were up in the air, and he was trying his damnedest to keep them there. He. Not anyone else. And if they dropped and exploded, it would be in his face. But not just his. Everyone else's, too.

When Maloney said to the driver, "You know we're going to Seventy-second between Park and Madison," the agent didn't question him; he merely made the left turn at Seventy-second. Had one of the two agents who'd guarded Kate been driving, he'd have suggested the rear entrance. But those two were in the car behind, and when the lead car turned on Seventy-second, they followed.

Israeli security men, on the other hand, were expecting the Secretary at Seventy-third, because that had been specified. Those at the Seventy-second Street entrance were alert, suspicious, and angry because their security system had been damaged by the blast and one of their men killed. And they were expecting no one.

At 12:30, two dark autos drove up and three bulky men jumped out, two of them agents, and the third, Maloney, with his thick neck, broad shoulders, and boxer's face, looking like an agent. The Israelis thought they were being attacked.

Maloney and his escort anticipated a welcome; instead, as they approached, they saw the two men in front of the entrance whip out pistols. Each side had a reason to fear an attack, the Israelis because of the bombing, the war, and their garrison mentality, the Americans because of the plan and the attacks on Shalzar and Kate Colby. Instinctively, the American agents began to go for their guns. Had they continued the move, the three Americans would have been shot.

But the Secretary of State raised a hand imperiously. "Hold it! Hold it!" he shouted. "I am the Secretary of State! I have an appointment with Ambassador Shalzar! What is this?"

The Israelis' stance changed from hostility to puzzlement. Although they understood English, what impressed them more than Maloney's words was his aura of aggrieved officialdom. That they recognized in any language.

The man on Maloney's left asked in a heavy accent, "What is your name and what do you want here?" He was slightly taller than Maloney and as heavy but without the pudginess. He had a pale, broad, powerful, Slavic face, brown eyes, and a broken nose. That, said Maloney to himself, is the meanest Israeli I've ever seen. Hearing the accent, he answered slowly, clearly, and at the top of his voice, "My name is Peter Maloney. I am American Secretary of State. I have appointment with ambassador, Dov Shalzar. You understand?"

"Yes, yes, I understand," replied the Israeli, irritated at being patronized and shouted at. "But we should have been instructed, if visitors were expected by the ambassador. Stand there. Do not move."

During this exchange the two Secret Service men from the second car were coming up, and the Israeli's last words were addressed to them as well as the three in front.

"Don't move!" The Secretary shouted the words as he looked around and saw the other two Americans. He knew that if they pulled their guns, the Israelis would fire. To the American agents, yielding so meekly was a humiliation, but they knew the Israelis had the drop on them, and it was the Secretary's life they'd be risking if they tried to draw. They stood motionless.

Then the Israeli next to the one with the broken nose recognized the two agents who'd been with Kate; he, too, had been assigned to her. He turned to his colleague and spoke to him in Hebrew. Broken Nose seemed almost disappointed; there was to be no fight. The other Israeli put his weapon back in its shoulder holster; reluctantly, Broken Nose followed. With a key the other man opened the outer door and started into the small lobby.

Two of the American agents would remain outside, the other two would go in with Maloney. With one Israeli holding the door, the Secretary started in. Broken Nose moved to follow him, so did one of the Secret Service men, and the two tried to step through at the same time, the American slightly ahead. The Israeli, who was as hostile as he looked, reached a stubby-fingered hand to the Secret Service man's arm, seized it, and tried to move him aside. He wanted to be right behind Maloney; so did the American. And the American, four inches taller, slightly heavier, would not be moved. He wrenched his arm from the grasp of Broken Nose and shoved at the Israeli.

Maloney saw the Israeli's hand moving toward his holster; he knew that in another couple of seconds shots would be fired—from distances so close it would be impossible to miss. He bent his knees slightly, pivoted his body, and brought his right fist around in a short, tight hook that caught the Israeli on the left cheekbone and spun him clockwise. Maloney felt something snap in his hand. As the man

262

turned, the American agent stepped forward and clutched him in a bear hug, pinning his arms to his sides. The other American reached into Broken Nose's jacket and plucked the gun from its holster. Holding it by the barrel, he handed it toward the Israeli at the door.

"Here," said the Secret Service man. "You'd better hold onto this; your friend seems to think we're Arabs. We're not." The Israeli nodded his head, took the pistol, turned toward Broken Nose and started shouting at him in Hebrew. He paused for a moment to pound the inner door with his flat hand; the buzzer and closed-circuit TV camera had been destroyed by the blast. A muffled voice shouted from the other side; the Israeli security man shouted back.

In less than a minute the door was opened. There stood two more Israeli agents with drawn pistols; between them was Dov Shalzar. He stepped forward, smiled, extended his hand to Maloney. "We have been known to give better welcomes than this, Mr. Secretary." They shook hands and the vague pain in Maloney's right hand turned immediate and sharp as Shalzar squeezed. He knew the feeling; he had a broken knuckle, maybe worse. Just what I needed, he thought.

Shalzar saw the pain register on his face. "What happened?" he asked. Briefly, the Secretary explained.

"I'm sorry," the ambassador said, "this is a hell of a way to start a meeting. But I must say in our defense, your assistant was told clearly to enter by way of Seventy-third Street, not Seventy-second."

"I forgot him," said Maloney, smiling. Then he noticed, for the first time, they were standing where the bomb had gone off. He said, "Quite a blast, I heard. Anybody hurt?" Shalzar, knowing Kate had been told of the death and then had gone off to see Maloney, watched the Secretary closely as he answered. "No, just a few scratches; we were lucky. Someone could have gotten killed." He saw no surprise in Maloney's face. Then he added, "Well, come on in."

As the two of them walked along the hall, the Secretary looked at Shalzar. He had met the Israeli briefly on several occasions and rather liked him; they were contemporaries and New Yorkers. They had probably waited in line together at the Garden to buy basketball tickets, maybe sat side by side in the main reading room of the Forty-second Street library. He felt at home with Shalzar; he had to remind himself that this man was responsible for carrying out the Masada Plan.

"I know you're going to think we've got a lot to learn about hospitality," said Shalzar. "Anyway, no matter how rough the entrance and how strained the circumstances, welcome to this little bit of Israeli soil in New York. How's your hand?"

"It feels broken," replied Maloney, "and it hurts like hell. But a little Scotch, administered internally, should help, and, besides, I'm not going to have to punch again for a while. At least I *hope* not."

He smiled at the Israeli as they entered the large sitting room. "You know," he said, taking the easy chair Shalzar motioned him to, "on my way up here, I was daydreaming about being kidnaped as a solution to all my responsibilities. But I can tell you, when I saw those guns pointed at me and thought it was about to happen, the thrill was gone."

"I *am* sorry," Shalzar said, as he poured a Scotch for the Secretary. "Especially about your hand. Shall I call a doctor?"

"No," answered Maloney. "Just put a little soda and ice in that Scotch, and put it in my hand—my *left* hand. Good thing I'm a two-fisted drinker." As always, Maloney fostered the image of himself as an Irish drinker, letting the other person think he could pour the booze and loosen up the Secretary.

Shalzar made himself a drink, the same as the guest's, as he always tried to do, and sat in a red-and-black striped wing chair, looking across at the Secretary. He. too, felt close to the other man; he, too, was aware of their common background.

With their closeness, though, came a danger, for they tended to know each other more as types than as individuals, and each tended to attribute stereotypes to the other.

Maloney, for example, went into this meeting with his group's accepted wisdom that you could always out-tough a Jew in the crunch. The Israeli knew it, and worried about it, because he feared Maloney might go over the brink with it, tough—and mistaken—to the end.

Shalzar's own arrogance, based on *his* group's wisdom, was that goyim could be outwitted, that Irish and Italian kids were so obsessed with head-on charges to prove their manhood, they could be out-maneuvered by Jewish boys with good brains, cool nerves, and fancy footwork.

When the ambassador was seated and looking at him, Maloney raised his glass. "Will you think I'm patronizing you if I say: To life, l'chaim?"

"Nothing could be more appropriate," answered Shalzar. "L'chaim. To Life." Neither man was a drinker. Both sipped, Maloney perhaps a bit more than usual, because his right hand, now swollen, was throbbing.

He welcomed the delay, not only because the Scotch might help his hand but because he had two decisions to make. First, should he tell Shalzar he knew all about the Masada Plan? No, he decided, there was no advantage to it, and he could get Kate into trouble. Second, should he tell him he hadn't yet gotten the approval of the President and the Arabs to the Israeli demands? Again, no. Shalzar would be more likely to give in on the hostage community if he thought the deal were ready to be consummated; if he knew two others were not yet committed, why should he concede anything?

So Maloney would conceal two important facts—unless something changed that made it advantageous to reveal them.

Shalzar spoke first. "Mr. Secretary, I hope you've come with the word that can stop the ticking clock. We have so little time."

"Your Excellency," replied Maloney, "with so little time and such short names as Dov and Pete available to us, would it be possible to stop the Mr. Ambassador and Mr. Secretary?"

"Possible, and welcome, Pete," answered Shalzar with a grin.

Then Maloney began selling. "Yes, Dov, I do think I have word that will stop the clock. Although the specifics of the plan are unknown to us, we perceive it to involve nuclear power and to be extremely dangerous." As he spoke, he realized he was keeping his fingers crossed; silly, but ever since he was a kid he did that when he told a lie. Then, suddenly, he uncrossed them; for a moment he feared that Shalzar, a New York boy, might spot them and know what they meant.

When he had to cross them again, which was almost at once, he did it surreptitiously. "The proposal I am about to make," he went on, "has the endorsement of the United States and the Soviet Union, and the acquiescence of the Arabs will be forthcoming momentarily. Just a question of mechanics." Maloney watched the Israeli; there were two catches in his statement and he could tell from Shalzar's narrowed eyes the ambassador had heard both. The "proposal" Maloney spoke of was not the same as acceptance of the Israeli demands; it meant there was a counteroffer. And the "forthcoming momentarily" meant the Arabs hadn't said yes.

Cautiously, Shalzar asked, "Which would you rather talk about first, your proposal or the Arab acquiescence—or lack of it?"

"Thanks for the choice," answered Maloney, trying to keep the talk easy, recognizing he wouldn't succeed, that the ambassador was tense and guarded. "Let's talk about the Arabs first; let me explain that their failure to say yes up to now doesn't mean a thing. Because of the joint command, the Egyptian President has to go through the motions of consultation. The yes will come."

"What makes you so sure?"

"There is a simple answer," said Maloney, "provided I don't have to make it as a diplomat. In plain language, we're so sure because we and the Soviet Union will do what we have to to get the yes. Bribe them. Coerce them. Whatever we have to. Plain enough?"

"And suppose they tell you to go to hell?" Shalzar asked and then he almost added something, barely stifled it, and was startled to hear Maloney say it for him. "You mean, the way you have?"

The Israeli relaxed and smiled. "Yes, the way we have."

But Maloney didn't smile back when he continued. "The US and the Soviet Union, for many reasons—some identical, some different— do not want to be told by the Arabs to go to hell. No point going into the reasons now, we don't have the time, and some I'm sure you can figure out. You've set a deadline and we're prepared to meet it. OK?"

Shalzar hated to drop the subject, but he said, "OK."

"Then," said the Secretary, "shall I go on to our proposal?"

"One thing first," the ambassador responded. "Might one of the 'bribes' to the Arabs be a promise to supply advanced nuclear arms and delivery systems? So next time Israel can be wiped out before mention of a Masada Plan can escape from our lips?" Shalzar looked at Maloney and shrugged. "After all," he went on, "think how inconvenient our plan is for the Arabs. Another few days and they'd have pushed us into the sea."

Though he spoke jovially, Shalzar wasn't joking and Maloney knew it and didn't like it. He was supposed to be softening the Israeli up to settle for less, not the other way around. The Secretary rose abruptly and headed for the bar. "Mind if I freshen up my drink?" he asked as he went.

As usual, most of the drink remained, but he went through the motions. As he raised his right hand to the Scotch bottle, he knew the hand wouldn't function; it had been throbbing since he sat down, but now as he looked at it, he was alarmed. The area around the fourth and fifth knuckles had swollen so that he thought the skin would burst; the fingers looked like knockwurst; he could not move the last three; merely making contact with the bottle sent a pain shooting up through his hand, wrist, and forearm.

Grimacing, he put his glass down and used his left hand to handle Scotch, ice, and water. He picked up the glass and walked back. Shalzar had been watching him and asked, "Want a doctor?"

"Tomorrow," answered Maloney. "Tomorrow. And I'll send you the bill."

Shalzar nodded. "And we'll send you one for our man's cheekbone."

"Your man doesn't have cheekbones," answered the Secretary. "He's got poured concrete."

"Yes," said Shalzar. "He's rugged and he's an angry, deadly man. Great for dealing with Arabs; not so good for Secretaries of State."

Maloney had had a pause to think. No, he couldn't guarantee which promises they'd make to the Arabs and which they wouldn't make. God knows he was winging this, and they'd certainly owe the Arabs a lot, if they could turn off the attack. "Now, Dov," he said, "I know the conditions; Bill Brewster told them to me and he's got an infallible memory—and mine isn't bad either. And I don't recall any condition limiting inducements to the Arabs. Did I miss one somewhere?"

Seeing Shalzar about to jump in, he resumed quickly. "Of course, I am aware of the condition that would guarantee Israel weapons parity with the Arabs. That's not the same thing."

For a moment Maloney almost added, Don't tell me you'd settle for mere nuclear parity with the Arabs. You've got the advantage now—and we know what you're planning to use it for. But he held back. Instead he said, "We have never considered supplying nuclear weapons to any nation at any time for any reason. I cannot envision that policy ever changing. As for other inducements to the Arabs, who knows, we might find some that are painless to Israel. Suppose, for example, the Arabs were dying to learn the formula for a good egg cream. You wouldn't mind if we supplied that, would you?"

"You know Kate Colby, don't you?"

Shalzar said it suddenly and Maloney's left hand holding his drink jerked—not noticeably, he hoped—as he heard it.

"Yes, of course. Not very well. I do know she contacted Bill Brewster about the Masada Plan. And that she had dinner with you here tonight. As you're aware, I've spoken with her in connection with the Masada Plan." Maloney paused for a moment, but he didn't know how much to say or when to stop. He kept going.

"We've probably met only three or four times, although I suppose I feel I know her better because I've seen her on television so often. Bill introduced us, perhaps a year or so ago. They're good friends—as you know."

Amused by the reaction his innocent question had drawn, Shalzar said, "The only reason I asked is that your egg cream remark sounded as if it were written by her—a small witticism that generalizes, invalidly, from the parochial folkways of the New York Jew. Would it surprise you to learn that ninety percent of Israelis wouldn't know an egg cream from a two-cents plain?"

Maloney was relieved, and now sorry he had gone on so; he hoped his answer hadn't given too much away. "I meant it only as an example of an inducement not dreamt of in your philosophy. Who said that? Hamlet?"

"If you mean the philosophy part, yes, Hamlet," Shalzar answered laughing. "If you mean the inducement part, I think it was Kissinger."

Maloney laughed back. "I thought today's Israelis were losing the sense of humor the Eastern European pioneers had."

"Ah ha!" said the ambassador. "You've been reading up! But you skipped the chapter about how Dov Shalzar was raised as a bourgeois-but-honest boy on the wise-ass West Side of Manhattan and then spent the last two years back in the Big Apple, honing his Jewish wit to its old razor-sharp edge."

Then Shalzar turned brisk. "All right, let's put the egg creams and the stand-up routines aside and talk about what you call your 'proposal' and what I call either your acceptance of our conditions or your rejection of them."

Maloney went right at the issue. "We accept each of your conditions. Except one. This the President, the Premier, and I are agreed upon. And that one is the international hostage community. We cannot accept it for several reasons. One is we have no authority to commit other nations to it and see no point in trying to jawbone them, even if we had the time. Another is we have no authority to order our own citizens into such a situation. Remember the flap we had over two hundred technicians for the Sinai, and they were volunteers, and circumstances were much calmer back in '75. Another is, the precious objects requirement is out of the question. The Soviet Union may be able to command the Hermitage, but we can't order the Metropolitan Museum to send a Rubens, or the Modern to send a Picasso.

"And if we ever get to the point where Willie Mays's glove gets crated and shipped, we face a violent overthrow of the government.

"But the most important reason . . . ," and Maloney was pouring it on, "is one that stands to benefit your country more than any other. This community, while it may have some hostage value, will stand as a continuing reminder to all the world that Israel is blackmailing them. Those few who knew of the Masada Plan will feel their noses rubbed in it, steadily, strongly, and unpleasantly. The many others, unaware of the plan, will see Israel in a new and threatening light.

"Why prolong the threat? Why advertise it? It's for your good and ours that we refuse the one condition."

Shalzar was serene as he answered. "I'm not going to say your reasoning doesn't impress me, Pete. I am going to say it is irrelevant, because I have no leeway in this."

The Israeli was being tough, turning down what anyone would admit was a very good deal, and he knew it, and was tense doing it. He stood, his long fingers squeezing the glass he held until the fingers were white at the tips. He walked to the bar, putting another cube of ice and some more soda water in his glass—but no more Scotch. Then he turned and walked to the wall, where a map of Israel hung in a dark wood frame. He jabbed a finger at it.

"You know," the ambassador said, in an apparent tangent, "I just pointed my finger at the seat of government, Jerusalem, forgetting for the moment our government may right now be moving—or trying to move—to Tel Aviv. That's how bad the situation is. Did you know that?" Shalzar looked at Maloney. He hadn't intended to take the tangent this far, but realized it would have dramatic effect.

The Secretary shook his head no.

"So I realized I had pointed to the wrong place," Shalzar continued. "But then I also realized that Israel is such a small country, a finger pointed at Jerusalem also hits Tel Aviv . . . and that distance is the entire width of the country."

He let his voice fall away, then went on. "At any rate, my government, whichever part of the finger hits it, has given me strict instructions on this, and they are that the conditions are neither separable nor negotiable. However persuasive your reasoning, I have no authority to change that. It is fixed.

"Maybe it's good protection for me," Shalzar added, pleasantly, "for if what I've heard—and what I've witnessed in the past fifteen minutes—is true, you'd probably be able to talk me into giving up the Masada Plan for a case of M-1's and a year's supply of lox. How's that for New York Jewish?"

The Secretary no longer wanted to play games. He got to his feet, walked up to the map, jabbed his finger in the general direction of Tel Aviv, and pointed his face straight at the Israeli's, no more than two feet away from it. They were a strong contrast, those two faces, Maloney's florid, with pug nose, well fleshed, Shalzar's darker, nose bony, far leaner. Maloney, being a few inches shorter was looking up at Shalzar, which not only seemed no disadvantage but gave him an angle that turned him ferocious, the more so because of the grimace of pain that flashed across his face every time his swollen right hand moved.

"What you've got to do, Dov, is contact your government and tell them you have been offered one hell of a deal, missing only *one* of many desired ingredients, and offering all the major ones—the Arab rollback, the peace-keeping force, the guarantees of arms, finances, and energy. You've got to give them a chance to reconsider."

Shalzar didn't like the physical bullying Maloney seemed to be trying. Just as the Secretary had boyhood street impressions of the New York Jew and what he was supposed to be like, the ambassador had his own recollections of street contact with the Gentile kids—and one of those was their threatening physicality. And so his temper, as well as his instructions, played a part in his answer.

His face said, Don't push me around. His voice said, "My government has specifically weighed the possibility of reconsidering and has specifically negated it. We insist that every condition we have set down be accepted, or else we consider the response a refusal. That's what I'm to say. Nothing else."

Temper spoke in the final words of his response, "And nothing I've said should suggest I am opposed to our official position."

If one of Maloney's faults was his aggressiveness, a virtue that made up for it was his quick sense of when he had overstepped, and his ability to change tone. He was thus not only able to soften the effects of his toughness; he could often, by a sudden reversal, capitalize on it by making his adversary grateful for the sudden switch to amiability.

The Secretary knew this about himself, and had once described it. "When detectives question a subject," he had said, "they often work in pairs. One is the bad guy, who threatens physical force, long jail terms, whatever he has to. The other is the nice guy, who tells the suspect he is his friend, and will keep the bad guy off his back, if only the suspect will open up and tell all.

"Well," Maloney had said, "I do the same thing. Only I play both roles myself."

And seeing that the bad guy wasn't doing too well, he quickly introduced the good guy. He sighed and walked away from Shalzar, throwing himself back into his easy chair with a weariness that was only a slight overstatement of his fatigue and pain.

"I know I sounded as if I were trying to get you to disown your official position, Dov, and I'm sorry. I didn't mean to. I know you believe in it, and very much identify with it."

He picked up his glass and sipped at his drink, more for the pause than for the Scotch. "I also know," he went on, "how difficult a spot you're in. Making nuclear threats is repugnant to any civilized person or society, and of course you and your country must feel deeply the gravity of what you're doing.

"I in my turn," and he said this, his eyes following the Israeli from the map back to the chair, "feel the responsibility the United States and others must assume for letting Israel become so isolated and friendless it would have to resort to the tactic it's now using. And I want you to know . . ."

The ambassador interrupted him angrily. "No, you don't feel it. You're looking at all this on a chessboard, which, strategically, may be valid. But chessboards don't show on them the wreckage of communities we built out of the deserts and the swamps. Chessboards don't show the farmland, roads, irrigation systems blown to bits. Chess figures don't bleed. That's what's happening to Israel right now. The pawns are all bleeding, some of them dying, some of them dead. And pawns are all we are in your game of power and energy and money. You're dealing with us now only because we've shocked you into realizing you'd better pay more attention to us."

Gesturing with his glass, Shalzar raced on, cutting Maloney off when he tried to speak, which was no small achievement. "Even if you should decide to meet all our conditions—*all*, because that's what it will take—and even if the firing stops on schedule, which is less than eight hours away, much of Israel will be a bleeding pile of rubble.

"If one thing is clear, it is that the very tactics you're using to stop the Arabs now, you could have used before the attack started. Which means the death and destruction were needless. We had to threaten you to get you to do what you should have done by yourselves—and earlier. And not only the United States, the Soviet Union, and all the other bystanders.

"Do you know what that means?" the ambassador was leaning forward as he put the question, but he was not expecting an answer. "It means," he replied to his own question, "that our blood is on your hands. Yes, we have threatened you, and you don't like it, as you keep saying. Yes, the world, or as much of it as knows of our plan—however vaguely—will think of us as dangerous characters.

"Well, just consider for a moment what we dangerous characters have inflicted on you. Nothing. And if our threat works perfectly, nothing is what it will continue to be. Not an American scratched, not a Russian, by these dangerous characters. Whereas you are responsible for—God, I hate to think of how many deaths."

Through the last part of the Israeli's tirade, Maloney sat nodding his head. When he got the chance, he jumped in.

"You'd be amazed at how much of what you say I agree with—speaking privately, not officially. That's why I am willing to improvise, wing it, play it by ear, however you like to say it, even playing fast and loose with my instructions, in order to stop what I assume to be the cataclysm awaiting us at 9 a.m.

"Where I strongly disagree with you—and let's put it bluntly, where I think you're nuts, is in the inflexibility you're showing in response to our proposal.

"To threaten some sort of nuclear action is extremely serious, but to prevent the extinction of your country, such a threat may be justified. Let me say personally, I might do the same thing; maybe a risky remark, but hell, this is a day of bigger risks than that."

Maloney's fervor—and the throbbing agony of his hand—drew him to his feet. He started pacing the room as he spoke.

"Now let me tell you where you lose me. When you are offered everything you've asked, minus one, and that one, however ingenious, a goddamned piddling gimmick, if you'll pardon me for saying so—and you say no because of a remote blueprint created maybe one, two, three years ago, then you lose me.

"When you refuse even to go back to your government, and say Christ—pardon me, I get carried away, you wouldn't say that, would you?" Shalzar smiled in spite of himself. Maloney returned the smile. Then he reached his right forefinger to his soaking shirt collar, and the pain in his hand forced a gasp out of him. "And tell your government—good God, the blood is flowing. In seven and a half hours, much, much more will flow. This is no longer a goddamned piece of paper, let's look it over again. We've won, we're getting almost everything we want. So *screw* the hostage community.

"When you not only refuse to change your mind, but *single-handedly* deny your government a chance to change *its* mind, you lose me.

"Are you going to blow up . . . ." Maloney thought he'd better watch out, and not, in the heat of argument, give too much away, "whatever the hell it is you're going to blow up, but plenty, right, for the sake of a hostage community? Ask yourself that. Because that's what it's come to, fella. No more to save Israel from extinction. Anybody could understand that, and a lot of people would go along with it.

"But nuclear detonation for the sake of a gimmick? Lives lost, the war goes on, the Arabs overrun Israel. How would you defend that in the eyes of the Israeli people? In the eyes of the world? Of history? But most of all, in your own eyes?"

Now Maloney figured he'd thrown enough punches; he'd wait to see if his opponent had any fight left.

The ambassador looked at him calmly, almost with amusement. "If it is, as you say, a meaningless gimmick, and if it is, as you say, the obligation of a negotiator not always to follow orders but sometimes to take initiatives, then why don't you take it on yourself to go back and ask that the Israelis be given this meaningless gimmick, which they happen to think essential to their preservation?"

The Secretary was hoping the Israeli wouldn't ask him that. The plain fact was he couldn't go back with a change of plan simply because the President hadn't yet approved the first plan. The President would want to know why he was changing his mind about the hostage community. If he said it was merely a feeling, the President would probably say, Why not let the Israelis turn down the first offer before we make them a better one? Then Maloney would have to admit he had already approached the Israelis. To which the President would probably reply, What? Without my approval? After which the President would probably climb up into the attic, break out his old combat fatigues, dig in his heels and yell "Fix bayonets!" And everything would fall apart.

But Shalzar *had* asked him, and to answer it, he tossed his battle plan out the window—the same window out of which he had earlier thrown his neat timetable.

"This negotiator," he confessed, "cannot go back to his President and urge him to approve the hostage community, because *not* being a good soldier, and being an initiator and an improviser, he has offered you and the Soviets a deal without the approval of his President. His President has not authorized him to offer you a goddamn thing, not a single soldier, a single cent, a single gun, a single barrel of oil, a single ounce of muscle."

Maloney had kept pacing while talking, trying to keep control, to maintain his energy level, but he was losing ground. He was tired, tense, frustrated, light-headed from not having eaten all day, worn down from battling—with the President, the Soviet Premier, Kate Colby, Bill Brewster, Shalzar—and the Arabs still to come. And his hand, now a mottled, frightening-looking mixture of purple and red, no longer merely throbbed, the pain was steady, and almost unbearable every time he moved it suddenly or tried to touch something. He sagged into his easy chair, lifting the glass of Scotch to his lips with his left hand.

Shalzar saw all this, and was surprised. He also saw Maloney sip his Scotch, not gulp it. The Secretary was hurting, but still in control.

"This negotiator," Maloney went on, "is cutting all the corners, with the President, the Russians, with you. When the time comes, with the Arabs. And he's doing it to keep the fucking world from falling apart." Maloney slammed his drink down, sloshing some on the table.

"And sometimes he wonders if he is the only one trying. You guys have your backs to the wall, so you're interested in saving yourself. OK. The President has one of his goddamned hawks whispering in his ear, so he's worried about looking like a weakling and an anti-Arab in the eyes of the tough guys and the oil guys. OK. The Soviet Premier is a Sphinx, and when you can convince him they'll come back strong in the Middle East he does you the favor of a yes. OK. The Arabs just want to overrun Israel and they'll stop only when they see they won't get away with it. OK.

"In the middle is Pete Maloney like a one-armed juggler with four balls in the air asking himself how the hell he got there.

"Look, you guys have asked for the world, and I am taking it on myself to offer you the world minus Bismarck, North Dakota. It's not enough. OK. You don't even want to see if your people will change their minds! OK, I give up. That makes it easy. I'll go back to the President and confess I've been a naughty boy, and didn't even succeed at it. And I'll quit."

Maloney had his head back and his eyes closed. "And by God, I'll call all the media in the middle of the fucking night—especially those that can give me some coverage before the deadline, because after that, there'll be a bigger story. I'll phone my friend Barbara Walters. I'll get on all the networks.

"You know what I'll say? I'll say the Israelis are pressing some kind of nuclear button at 9 a.m. because we are denying them Bismarck, North Dakota. So it'll be all over for them, and for a lot of others, too. And for those left, the name of Israel will be blackened forever.

"And for what?" Pete stood up. "And how come, of all the people who could have done something about it, nobody gave a shit but me?"

The Secretary of State stood, this time holding his right hand up with a bent elbow because it hurt slightly less that way, and started toward the door. Shalzar stood with him, puzzled. Maybe with the pain and everything else, the man is coming apart, he thought.

Then Maloney whirled. "And you know, Dov, considering I was running the frigging thing alone, I came pretty damned close. In fact, I might have done it. Until I was stopped right here. By the people who need it most of all." He pointed his left forefinger straight at Shalzar.

The Israeli's jaw muscles clenched and unclenched. Then, slowly, he responded. "I will contact my government and see if they're willing to give up Bismarck, North Dakota."

Through Maloney's pain and tension came a weak smile; he shook his head. Suddenly he clapped his good hand on the ambassador's shoulder with such force, Shalzar was shocked.

"No, Dov, for God's sake, don't *see* if they're willing. *Tell* them to be willing. Don't let me carry this thing alone. It's getting too heavy; I don't know how long I can hold on. Help me save us."

"It would have been an easy job for you over the last couple of years," Shalzar answered. "It wouldn't have taken much. But you people just stood there and did nothing."

The two were walking along the hall toward the rear entrance. "Maybe," said Maloney, his left hand still on the ambassador's shoulder, "but we can't roll that back. All we can do is start again, after 9 A.M.—if there's anything left to start with." He looked at Shalzar. "Dov, tell them, they've *got* to be willing."

"Pete, I shall *ask*."

Maloney acted as if he hadn't heard that. "I'm going after the President now," he said. "And I'll have faith you can deliver your people. My next step will be the Arabs."

"Pete, I'm going to *ask*. An ambassador proposes; Jerusalem disposes." Shalzar's face turned grim. "Or Tel Aviv."

They were at the door. The Secretary said, "Before it's too late, Dov." Then with a lighter tone, "If you don't come through, it means I'll have spent the night getting a couple of OKs it turns out were useless. What the hell! Maybe I can catch up on my sleep tomorrow night. Think so, Dov?" Outside the open door, the American agents, who had been sent around to the rear entrance, waited.

Framed in the doorway, the Israeli smiled at Maloney and shrugged. "I hope so. Anyway, for you, it will be with your hand in a cast."

Maloney carried the right hand up at his chest, and though this position helped drain the blood, it still ached and throbbed. "I gotta great left hook, too, Dov."

Shalzar smiled. "Well, don't try it on my people, Pete."

"No, actually it's the Arabs and the President I'm after," Maloney answered. "You go after Jerusalem—or Tel Aviv. And you've got two good hands to do it with." The Secretary clenched his left fist and shook it at Shalzar. Suddenly, he no longer seemed tired, or worn down or in pain; suddenly, with the shaking fist he looked like a winning football coach going into the final two minutes with a lead and exhorting his team to put the game away. With a final shake and a smile, Maloney turned and walked briskly to his car.

Shalzar was smiling, too, and he kept smiling as he watched the stocky American bounce toward the black sedan. He was amused because he realized his fears for Maloney's control had been ridiculous. Maloney had been about as out of control as Horowitz in the middle of a sonata, Nureyev in the middle of a solo variation, Muhammad Ali in the middle of a fight. Sure, the Secretary had been tired, tense, and in pain—and he had used all those to build the feeling of doom he wanted. Maloney was a method actor and the purpose of his act had been to bring Shalzar around.

And it had worked.

Yes, it had been an act, but never had a method actor more material to work with, and as he sat in the sedan for the ride down to the hotel, Maloney, buoyed though he was, wondered how much longer he could have gone on. What do you mean 'have gone on'? he asked himself. It's not over; it's still going on and don't kid yourself on what you've just accomplished.

The best he could claim was he'd just got Shalzar to agree not to say no, which was a long way from saying yes. And there were still the President and the Arabs. Of the two, oddly, he was more confident of the Arabs. Presumably, the Soviets have been softening them up; they're going to be a carrot-and-stick operation and God knows we've got the carrots and the sticks and know how to use them.

But the President was something else, he thought. The man's my boss; him, I've got to persuade. If he's still got that bloody troglodyte Holloway with him, and the two of them start measuring biceps—and cocks—then I've had it, Maloney told himself.

And if I don't do something about this hand soon, I've had it, too, he thought. I should go straight to New York Hospital and get a shot of painkiller and an X ray and have the thing set. Yeah, he answered himself, and then who's going to talk to the President and the Egyptian, not to mention Shalzar, if there's any trouble there? And why shouldn't there be? Nothing's coming easily.

He put his head back on the upholstery and smiled to himself. Of the four deals, the only one I've got firm is the Russians, and they would have been my choice for last place of the four. After all, he told himself, the President is supposed to listen to his Svengali; the Israelis are getting an offer they shouldn't refuse; and the Arabs can be bribed and muscled. The Russians should have been toughest, and I've got them. Right now, my number one problem seems to be my Trilby, the President. Too bad I can't give him the carrot-and-stick treatment, like the Arabs.

Suddenly, Maloney sat upright, a pain stabbing through his hand as he switched positions. Why not? He uttered it half aloud. I mean who the hell is he? Just the President. Does that make him immune?

Yeah. Maloney nodded and leaned back again. He smiled to himself. Machiavelli, Metternich, and Maloney. Should he throw in Kissinger? No, not enough of a powerhouse. And his name didn't even start with an M.

The black sedan turned into the Waldorf Towers driveway, and as soon as it came to a stop, Maloney, fatigue, broken hand and all, leaped out, the agents scurrying to catch him. In the elevator, he looked at his watch. Five after two. My God, he thought, I didn't realize I'd used so much time up on Seventy-second Street. Seventy-third Street, he corrected himself. If I'd known that I wouldn't have this. Again, he looked at his hand; it now looked less like a hand than a swollen udder, the fingers a row of teats. Carefully, he pressed it with the forefinger of his left hand. There was no place on it not painful to the touch. Left alone, the hand was a generalized mass of pain, the injured knuckles and bones no worse than the rest.

Less than seven hours. Well, he'd now rearrange his order. Next would come the Arabs, with the President, formerly his number-one boy, last. And he had made up his mind: he'd carrot-and-stick the President, just as he would the Arabs.

Maybe I won't have to, he thought, as he walked along the eighteenth floor to his suite, two agents with him. Maybe he'll give me the OK all on his own. I hope so. Under seven hours, he told himself, actually less than that, for he knew—he had read it in the Israeli documents—that the explosions would be automatically triggered at 9 A.M. in the absence of further instructions. In other words, the nine teams would push their buttons *unless they were called off*. And Maloney would sure as hell like to sew up the deal early enough to give Jerusalem—or Tel Aviv—the time to contact the nine cities. It'd be ironic, Maloney thought, if he did it all and then a bomb went off because the Israelis hadn't been able to call and say, Don't do it, boys.

Maloney pushed hard with his left index finger on the buzzer of his suite. A worried Steve Phelps opened the door; Maloney just nodded at him and then, turning to the agents said, "Thanks, fellas, see you later." He walked into the suite and closed the door.

"I know, I know, I forgot you," Maloney barked before Phelps could say anything. "And I paid for it; went to Seventy-second instead of Seventy-third, had a showdown at the OK Corral, and I got this for it." The Secretary held up his right hand. Phelps blanched.

"Does it hurt?" he asked, rhetorically.

"What?" said Maloney. "Oh, the hand? Let me see now." He started toward his little office, Phelps trailing him. "Yeah, it hurts. Something's broken. What I need is a painkiller that won't make me sleepy. Not to mention a doctor. Later."

"How did it happen?" Phelps asked.

"Later," Maloney repeated, by now at the door to his office. "For now, get on that phone and get me my buddy Karim in Cairo. 'My Buddy Karim in Cairo' sounds like a song title, doesn't it?

"That'll take about—how long? a half hour?—to set up, Steve. When you've got that under way, call the White House and say I'll be phoning the President sometime after three on the same matter, and it's absolutely highest priority. OK? I should be calling him right about now, but my carrots and sticks aren't ready."

He fell down in his battered old easy chair, and looked toward his aide who was standing in the doorway, staring at him. "Your what aren't ready?" Phelps asked.

The Secretary gave him a tired smile, and cradled his right arm in his left. "Never mind. This hand is making me delirious."

"My first call should be to a doctor," Phelps said.

"Uh uh, do as I say. First Cairo. Then the President. Then a doctor. Unless the Israelis sneak in ahead of him. Besides, once the pain stops I'll fall right asleep. Go on, Steve. And next time remind me never to go anywhere without you."

"How about a doctor, just to give you a shot?" Phelps asked.

"Guarantee it won't blunt my razor-sharp mind?"

"He'll give you an upper with it; you'll be so sharp you can slice the President down the middle and leave him in two parts without his feeling a thing."

"Steve, I was born ten years too soon for that. I was a late-forties-early-fifties youth—'dull and drug free' was our motto. The old dog would rather take the pain than try a new trick at this late date. Go make the calls. Leave me to suffer."

Phelps shook his head and left, closing the door behind him.

Leave me to suffer. Let's face it, old boy, he told himself, you are trying to squeeze your fat form into the Christ mold. You not only want to redeem mankind, you want to feel a little pain while doing it. Not a little pain, he corrected himself, a lot of pain. Again he put a finger of his left hand delicately to the swollen skin of his right; it hurt to the touch. Quixotically, he tried to clench his right fist: the pain became excruciating. Without thinking, he put his left hand to his head and squeezed, trying to pinch off the pain. It didn't work. In squeezing, he felt the new sparseness on the crown of his head. Losing some more every year, he thought. This'll finish me off. He had to laugh at that. Yeah, finish me off, one way or the other.

And I'm working on a new way now. If the bombs don't get me, or the Arabs and the Israelis, the President might. Wouldn't it be funny if I got everybody lined up—except him? Why, that would mean I'd be negotiating as an unauthorized agent! Hell, I *am* negotiating as an unauthorized agent right now. The only question is, Am I gonna be legitimatized after the fact? Will they get married just to give the little bastard a name?

And if they don't want to, do I have the shotgun to make them? Well goddammit, if I have to, I am gonna point something at that man in the White House and it better look like a shotgun. I can see getting wiped out by outsiders, enemies, but I'll be damned if I'm gonna go because of the one man who's supposed to be on my side!

Despite the pain, he fell into a half sleep, thinking about his kids, and the thought became a dream in which he was walking frantically across leveled city blocks, searching, hearing them but unable to get close to their voices. The terrain resembled the empty lots he had known as a kid near the Brooklyn waterfront, where old buildings had been demolished, or fallen apart, leaving a rubble of bricks and glass, with an occasional beam sticking through and a crater that became a pond after heavy rain. In the dream he was both a father and a young child; searching for his kids, yet wanting to turn and go back. Back to what? Yes, he saw it, back to his old semidetached house in Bay Ridge, where he'd come home from school and head straight for the warm kitchen, have a glass of milk with a piece of the pastry his mother always baked. Pastry, mother's pastry. Milk, mother's milk. Warm. Safe. Home.

Phelps had to say "Mr. Secretary" three times before Maloney heard him. He jumped, the hand moved, pain shot up to the elbow.

"What?"

"The Egyptian is ready to talk to you. Are you awake? Want a minute?"

"No, No, I'm ready. Boy that was fast, Steve; what time is it?" He looked at his watch. After three. Not so fast; he'd been asleep for nearly an hour.

Phelps picked up one of Maloney's phones and punched a button. He spoke into the instrument. "I'm putting the Secretary of State on."

To Maloney, he said, "You get on first, Mr. Secretary, the President won't until you do."

"Of course," Maloney said, and, unthinking, reached his right hand for the phone. The sudden pain stopped him; he returned the hand to the bent position at his chest and took the phone in his left.

"This is Peter Maloney. I'm ready whenever the President is."

The voice at the other end said, "Very good, sir. One moment, please, sir."

Thirty seconds later, Karim Rasad, the President of Egypt and the commander in chief of the Combined Arab Forces, got on the line. And the Arabs fell into Maloney's lap. He was amazed at how easy it was. The Egyptian began with one word: Peter. Only it was more like "Peetah." He had studied at the London School of Economics, and the precision and elegance of his English made the American Secretary of State feel like an immigrant just off the boat.

"Peetah," he said, "why are you doing this thing to us, Peetah?" There was bitterness and resignation in his voice, the tone of a friend who has been turned against. Maloney could hear there wouldn't be much of a struggle; the Russians had done his work for him, they had pulled the plug on the Arabs, and the Egyptian knew he couldn't fight them.

Maloney could almost write the speech the Soviet Premier had made: the Israelis, as usual, are unscrupulous warmongers, ready to

278

blow up the world. The Americans, as usual, are interested only in themselves and their own aggrandizement. The Soviet Union, in a spirit of global responsibility and solidarity with its Arab brothers, has tried to dissuade the Americans, to no avail. The Soviet Union will not risk a world nuclear war. So although it will do nothing to assist the United States, nor will it stop them. Too bad the Egyptians saw fit to expel the Soviet military advisers from their country several years earlier. If it hadn't . . .

The Egyptians wouldn't fall for that, Maloney knew. On the other hand, it would be clear to them the Americans, not the Soviets, were the prime movers and therefore the prime villains. Maloney still had to be persuasive enough so he wouldn't appear to be rubbing Rasad's face in his humiliation, so the damage to America and the advantage to the USSR were minimized. Most of all, he had to make the Egyptian look good to his Arab colleagues and rivals.

"Listen to me, Karim," he began, leaning forward as if the Egyptian were in the room with him. "If ever there were a situation we were all in together—all of us, the United States, the Arab nations, the Soviet Union, indeed, the world—this is it." Carefully, he explained the Masada Plan and the Israeli demands. "You see, Karim, if the Soviets told you we were interested in saving only American cities, I tell you your city, too, is in danger. And the Soviets', and more. And who knows what the first explosions might trigger?

"One alternative would be to risk that destruction; another would be to turn to a clean new page in the Middle East. Now let me tell you the first things to be inscribed on that new page. One will be the admiration and sympathy of the entire world for Arab statesmanship in stopping the war. Another will be a pledge from the United States—and I hereby make it—that our support for the Arab nations will take second place to no one's. We will have no closer friends than the Arab nations. *None.* You will, by your action, create an unbreakable bond with America, its government and its people. A bond you have never had before."

What the hell am I promising? he asked himself. The Israel lobby is gonna love me for this. Well, I'll worry about that later—after nine tomorrow.

Rasad remained unhappy, but he knew he was dealing with a *fait accompli* and the best he could do was get as much for his people, and himself, as possible. "And this is promised by your government?" he asked.

Maloney crossed his fingers, and made his answer as ambiguous as he could. "Would I undertake such a pledge on my own?"

The Egyptian ignored the ambiguity; he was depressed. The great Arab victory was being aborted and despite the consultations among all the Arab leaders, he would bear a heavy part of the blame. "Peetah, what am I to say to my Arab brothers about American pledges, after this?"

"That there is a gun to our heads, Karim. Ours, and yours. And the Soviets'. I don't have to tell you they feel the same as we and are merely letting us do their dirty work."

"Do you think I shall be a hero in the Arab world if I recommend the course you are asking?"

This is a game we're playing, Maloney thought, just a game, because there's no way he'll say no—not after the Russians. And I'm too tired, and I hurt too much to be playing games at three-thirty in the morning—five and a half to go, he suddenly remembered— but I've got to play.

"If the attack continues, Karim, Cairo will be destroyed. Not Damascus, not Beirut, not Amman, not Baghdad. Perhaps that will make you a hero in other parts of the Arab world. But how about at home? Will you be a hero there? Or will your enemies sharpen their swords—and call you the man who destroyed Cairo?"

"And supposing we are willing to take the risk, and continue our attack, will you then interfere?" Rasad knew the answer to that; he wanted it on the record.

"The gun is at our heads, Karim. And at the Russians. And yours."

"You leave us no choice, do you?" asked the Egyptian. Again, Maloney knew what he wanted. As much as possible, he wanted to be taken off the hook. The Secretary accommodated him.

"No. Because we have none ourselves. We can bring on the holocaust, or prevent it. I don't call that a choice."

Still, the Egyptian President was not finished with his maneuvers. "Aside from internal Arab politics and my future, what do you think the Arab attitude toward America will be after this, which we will come to regard as our Pearl Harbor?"

"We hope," he told Rasad, "that you'll come to see we took the lead in preventing a nuclear tragedy, and used that initiative to then bring about a real peace in the Middle East. Karim, if we are lucky, this crisis could be a blessing in disguise; it may shock us into a solution we've never been able to manage before."

The Egyption was silent. There was no getting around the American stand; yet he wished to say nothing that would imply his assent. Maloney felt the time had come to stop persuading, to stop asking for a yes, and just assume he'd gotten one.

"Karim," he said, "I know how difficult a position this is for you and let me assure you, it is no easier for me. Some day, perhaps we may sit down together at our leisure and talk this over more fully and personally. For now, though, we have all sorts of technical and logistical questions to work out; I shall have a personal representative call your office soon to set up a staff liaison.

"Karim, I want to say how fortunate we are to have you to work with; we know we can count on you. And, though you may not believe this now, some day your countrymen and all your Arab brothers will come to look upon you as a hero."

Maloney concluded, "I thank you, personally, as a friend. And I want you to know I am always at your service. We shall meet soon, Karim. Until then, goodbye. Thank you."

Then Maloney held his breath, and waited. Finally, Rasad said, "I shall delegate a senior staff person to work with you. There's not much time. Goodbye, Peetah. I send you my personal salutations."

The Secretary let out his breath in a long sigh. No "thank-yous" there, he thought, but no "noes" either. He stood up, the pain in his right hand building and building. But he felt an elation anyway; he had knocked off another. He'd have to put the Israelis down as a probable, and the President was his next target. He was getting there, and a good thing, too, because his hand wouldn't let him go on much longer. He stuck his head out the door of his office and shouted, "Phelps, get in here!"

"Next stop, the White House," he began saying, "We're on our . . ." A look at Phelps's face told him something was wrong.

"What is it, Steve?"

"The White House just called. Ten minutes ago. Fred Goode. The President's answer is no. Definitely no."

"No?" Maloney shrieked. "No!"

Instantaneously, the no, playing on Maloney's pain, exhaustion, tension, drove him to fury. Unthinkingly, he lashed out at the panel of his office door with his right hand. Somewhere, as the punch shot forward toward the unyielding wood, he realized what he was doing and tried to pull it. But it was too late.

The stretched skin split and spurted like a balloon filled with water, except that the liquids gushing out were blood and lymphatic fluid. The broken fifth knuckle was shattered, a piece of bone breaking through the skin; the fourth knuckle was now fractured, too.

The pain crossed the threshold of human endurance. Clutching his bleeding hand to his belly, the Secretary of State doubled over, writing in agony.

Phelps leaned to him and then turned, shouting, "Get in here! We've got to get the Secretary to a hospital!"

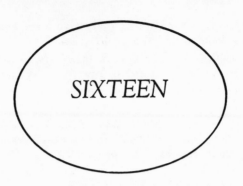

SIXTEEN

Nearly three and a half hours passed between Maloney's departure for the Israeli embassy and Phelps's frantic shout, "Get in here!" Kate Colby and Bill Brewster spent that time sitting in the living room of the Secretary's suite, talking, brooding, getting a little drunk. They had been through the future of the world, Kate's feminism, Bill's personality defects and a half-dozen other subjects, and were talking about Pete Maloney as a Presidential candidate, when they heard Phelps.

"We've got to get the Secretary to a hospital!"

Both of them leaped up, Brewster for once not yielding to her, but racing ahead. In the hall outside the study, he saw Maloney bent over in pain, clutching his right hand to his spattered shirt, his face contorted.

"What happened?" Brewster asked Phelps, who was leaning over the Secretary, not sure how to help.

"He hurt his hand at the Israeli embassy," the aide replied, "and then hit it again just now, on the door." Phelps paused for a moment. "The President just said 'no'."

Brewster turned to Kate. "Get a clean towel, dampen it in warm water. Let's wrap that hand. Then call the Secret Service man from the hall. Mr. Phelps, you stay with him. I've got a call to make." He looked around for a phone, spotted several on Maloney's desk, walked over and reached for the white one.

"No, not that one!" Phelps shouted. And then, more calmly, "Try the black one with the buttons; press down the second button."

Brewster, who was on the board of New York Hospital, dialed the number of the hospital's president, John Hastings. He looked at his watch as he waited for an answer; 3:40, he said to himself, not a decent hour to be phoning. Oh, well. A sleepy voice answered.

"John, this is Bill Brewster. The Secretary of State, Peter Maloney, has just been seriously injured and I'm on my way to the hospital with him. He's going to need . . ." pause, "It's his hand, John. Not critical but looks awful. Yes, an orthopedic surgeon, X rays, anesthesia. Get it all. And John, he's got to be able to function again right away. This is absolutely top priority! Please, do what you can, John, at once! Good. Thank you. I know you will."

Brewster strode back to Maloney, who by this time had straightened up somewhat, but still clutched his hand to his chest. Kate stood there with the towel, unable to reach the hand. The Secret Service man and Phelps stood waiting to be told what to do.

For a second or two, the only sound was Maloney's repeated "Goddammit, goddammit," spoken to his hand and to the President of the United States.

Then Brewster grabbed his friend's left arm above the elbow. "Pete," he said, "listen to me. We've got to take you to a hospital . . ."

"No, goddammit, no!" Maloney's fierceness turned on his friend.

"Otherwise," Brewster went on, as if the Secretary hadn't spoken, "you're going to be out of action entirely."

"No time," Maloney hissed. "The goddamn President . . ."

This time the tall banker interrupted. "You're not functional now, Pete. Not with that pain. We'll have you back here in no time, and in shape to work again. Come on."

He tightened his grip on Maloney's arm and began walking, Kate, Phelps, and the agent falling in behind. At the door they paused, and Brewster suddenly noticed the towel Kate held. "Pete," he said gently, "it'll be better if we cover that hand. Let go of it." He pulled Maloney's left hand away from his right, and they saw for the first time, amid the blood and swelling, a tiny piece of bone sticking through the skin. Forcing herself to look, Kate wrapped the towel around Maloney's hand. As soon as she was finished, the Secretary again held his left hand to the towel, protectively.

"You stay here," Brewster ordered Phelps. "Stand by for the President. In fact, call him, tell him what's happened and that the Secretary must talk with him in an hour or so."

Maloney nodded his head. "Yeah, yeah, right," he muttered in a thick, distorted voice.

"Now let's go," said Brewster, and they headed for the elevator, the tall banker in the lead, the agent and the Secretary next, with Kate off to the side, helping to hold the towel in place.

In the lobby, they found another agent, who raced out to get the car. Six minutes later they were at the emergency entrance to New York Hospital. Waiting for them were the senior resident on duty, an anesthesiologist, a nurse, and two orderlies with a wheelchair.

The resident took one look at Maloney's face and turned to the anesthesiologist. "You'd better put him out."

The energy of Maloney's response astounded them. He began to wrench away and said, in as close to a shout as he could manage, "No! No! A local! Nothing but a local! Bill, make sure! Stick with me! Don't go away!"

"Don't worry, I'm right here," Brewster responded.

Ordinarily, he would have considered pulling rank indelicate, but right then he had no time for delicacy. "I'm William Brewster, doctor; I'm a trustee of the hospital, and I'm the one who called John Hastings. As you probably know, this man is Secretary of State Peter Maloney. He has critical business to transact as soon as he is able to. That's why he cannot be given a general; it's got to be a local. And I want to stay alongside him." Brewster was not asking; he was ordering.

The resident looked at the anesthesiologist, who returned it with an expression that said, If that's what they want . . .

"All right," said the resident, "you come with us, Mr. Brewster." Then he looked at Kate and the agent. "If you two will have a seat in the waiting room . . . There's a coffee machine right over there," and he gestured down the hall.

"They've got to be immediately outside the room where we are, that's essential," said Brewster.

"All right," said the doctor again. "Emergency surgery is down the hall and to the . . . Miss Hollings," and he nodded toward the nurse, "will show you the waiting room just outside it. We'll go to X-ray and be at surgery in ten minutes; the surgeon should have arrived by then, too."

Maloney got on the stretcher and they all started down the hall; then the orderlies wheeled the Secretary straight ahead, with the doctors and Brewster following, while the nurse led Kate and the agent to the right. Kate paused for a moment, grabbed Maloney's left shoulder. "Hang in there, Mr. Secretary. We need you back in the game."

He managed a smile. "Don't worry, kid. I can't let a mere girl show me up."

Then he was wheeled off. The nurse led the two of them to the waiting room. In it were three wooden chairs, a small, upholstered armchair and a long black vinyl sofa. Kate headed for the sofa and collapsed onto it. The nurse walked off and she was left alone with the Secret Service man, who had taken the armchair. They looked at each other; Kate, exhausted, told herself, my God, I've got to carry on a polite conversation. And not about the Secretary or his injuries.

"What in the world ever made you want to become a Secret Service man?" she asked, thinking: It's not one of my best openers, but who'll ever know?

"I guess I always used to admire policemen when I was a kid, and when I got to college . . ." The agent went on for about three minutes before he realized she was asleep. And she stayed that way for nearly an hour, until she was roused by a gentle shaking of her shoulder, and Brewster's voice saying, "Kate, Kate."

"What?" She jumped awake and saw Bill Brewster standing alongside Maloney, who was in a wheelchair, jacketless, his right hand in a cast, the arm held by a sling. His face was pale and tired, but gone was the pain she had seen earlier. Behind the chair stood an orderly; next to him, a man with a black bag, obviously a doctor. Behind them was the agent whose life story she had never gotten to hear.

Wearily, she got to her feet. "You're looking a lot better, Mr. Secretary. How do you feel?"

"Feeling a lot better, Kate," he said with a wan smile. "And they're sending the good Dr. Stein here with me to make sure I stay that way."

She smiled at the doctor and he at her and they headed for the sedan outside the emergency entrance. The Secretary was helped into the front seat next to the driver, and to give him room, the other four squeezed into the back, Kate on Bill Brewster's lap.

"Am I too heavy?" she asked.

"Unbearable," he replied.

For the first time since she had fallen asleep, Kate looked at her watch; five minutes before five. Four hours to go, and she knew the President had said no, but they couldn't talk about it here. Instead, they listened as the physician explained the injury. Maloney had a simple fracture of the head of the fourth metacarpal and a compound comminuted fracture of the head of the fifth metacarpal. Luckily, he said, the bone had barely pierced the skin, but even so, the decision to work on the Secretary so quickly and release him was extraordinary. He'd have to return later and have the hand reset properly.

"Later," Maloney said with a laugh. "Yeah, later. If I have the chance, If *we* have the chance."

When they returned to the suite, the agent remained outside the door; the doctor was given a bedroom to nap in. Kate and Bill Brewster resumed their seats, their brandy sipping, and their conversation, and Maloney, groggy and not fully recovered from the shock he had been in, went back to work.

His first business was with the President. He picked up the white phone. "Hello, this is the Secretary of State, Peter Maloney. Get me the President, please."

"Just a moment, please."

It was more like two minutes before the sleepy voice of Fred Goode was heard. "For Chrissake, didn't you get the President's message?"

"I've got to talk to him. Right now!"

"Out of the question."

This man can stop me, thought Maloney. This ass can fuck up the whole world. "You tell him I'm calling about my resignation and my press conference tomorrow morning. I'm sitting right at this phone and waiting." And he slammed down the phone.

Three minutes later it gave a short ring. Maloney picked it us. "Is this the Secretary?" the operator asked. "Yes," he said. He could hear the voice say, "Go ahead, sir, he is on the line."

Then the President spoke. "What the hell is this, Pete?"

"This is to say that I've done the thinking you asked me to, and I find no alternative to the one I suggested, none that makes sense, anyway. We must accept the Israeli conditions, minus the one I mentioned before, get the Soviets and Arabs to go along, and then use the crisis to bang out a comprehensive settlement in the Middle East."

"Pete," the President replied, "heard about your hand and I'm sorry. Weren't you told the plan is out of the question?"

"Why, Mr. President. Why?"

"Because," he replied, "even if the Soviet Union and the Arab nations were to go along with it, which I doubt, I will not agree to blackmail. Nor will the Senate. Not everyone is as sure as you there's backbone behind that bluster."

Oh Christ, thought Maloney, I really should tell him the story of the Masada. I should get him up here to look Shalzar right in the eye. Then he'd know. But the Secretary knew there was no time. He'd have to break out the stick.

The first thing he did was to drop the "Mr. President." "Jack," he began, "there's no doubt in my mind the others will agree, because while you've been thinking it over, I've been talking with the Soviets, the Israelis, and the Arab joint command. They were reluctant, but they will go along. You're the only holdout, Jack." Then he waited, but not for long.

"Let me get this straight, Pete! Do you mean to say you approached them without my approval?"

"If I waited, Jack," the Secretary replied, "there would be no time to do it all. I was confident you would approve, and decided to go ahead on that basis."

The President's voice rose to a roar. "Well now, goddammit, you can call them back, tell them you made a big mistake when you thought this President would knuckle under, and all signals are off. Got that?"

When Maloney didn't answer, the President roared again. "Got it?"

Well, here I go, thought Maloney, stepping up into the world-class Machiavelli League. "Listen to me, Jack," he said to the President. "What I've done is going to save the world from nuclear devastation, and it will assure your immortality as a Solomon and a peacemaker."

Then Maloney added. "I'm not going to call anyone back. If you want them called, you'll have to do it yourself."

286

"The hell I will," the President shouted. "You'll do it or else! You will take orders from me! I am your superior! You are my subordinate!"

"That will change at seven-thirty, Jack, when I hold a press conference to announce I'm resigning. I'll tell the world about the imminent explosion—how the Russians, Arabs, Israelis, and I had it all turned off, only to have you turn it on again. Then I'll go on the network morning news shows to say it all over again. Live! The world will know whose finger pushed the button."

Maloney paused. "Or, Jack, I can call mine off, and you can call one for 9 a.m., to announce you have restored peace to the Middle East. You will, of course, not detail the Masada Plan, so none of your Holloway faction can publicly accuse you of knuckling under.

"Which would you rather be in three and a half hours, Jack: the President who has been the peacemaker, the Solomon, or the President responsible for nine major nuclear explosions—two of them in your own country's largest cities?"

"You bastard!" Maloney had never heard the man so furious. "You suckered me. They warned me about you . . . you . . . New York *finaglers!* But I trusted you and you screwed me. You've got me, haven't you? I can't get out of this, can I? I can't let the world think that the President of the United States isn't running his own foreign policy. Can I? Well, you hear this. As soon as we get through this, I'm going to destroy you, you son of a bitch! Destroy you! You're a marked man, Maloney. A marked man!"

Sitting in his swivel chair, phone to his ear, right hand, in cast, held to his chest by the sling, Maloney gave a big grin.

He had done it.

Well, not quite; he still had to hear from Shalzar. Light was streaming through the end of the tunnel. He looked to his window. There it was, at 5:33, the sun low over the East River. Like a light at the end of a tunnel.

"Mr. President." He went back to polite usage; he could afford to now. "Did you ever see the photograph of the Japanese soldier silhouetted against a brick wall at Hiroshima by radioactivity? That's my idea of a marked man."

"You're not even going to have a silhouette left when I'm through with you, Maloney. I'm going to destroy you!" The President was screaming now.

"If you don't decide to thank me instead." Maloney was feeling positively benign. "The crisis is over, Mr. President. You have saved the world. Now it's just a question of working out details, which is what I've got to do now. I'll keep you informed, sir."

"You've had it! You've had it!" The President screamed and then hung up.

Grinning, Maloney got up and shouted, "Steve, come on in here." When Phelps arrived, he said, "Call Shalzar's people. Tell them we've got three out of four yesses. We're waiting only on them. Come out and tell me what happens." Maloney squeezed Phelps's neck and shoulder so hard, the aide looked at him and said, "Ow!" But the Secretary just grinned and squeezed harder. "We may make it yet, Stevie boy, we may make it yet."

Slowly, he walked to the living room, smiling.

To Kate and Brewster, Maloney looked the winner of a tough fight, too bruised to be cocky, too happy to show the pain.

"Take one foot out of the bomb shelters," Maloney said. "Not both. I've got the President. He's not smiling." Maloney smiled as he said it. "But I've got him. And we should have the Israelis soon. I don't think they'll blow up the world for Bismarck, North Dakota."

"Bismarck, North Dakota?" Kate repeated, mystified.

The Secretary laughed. "Never mind. It doesn't matter. For the first time since all this started, it looks as if we may get out the far end. We may see that sun go down tonight." He looked out the window, then turned back to them and said, "It looks like we're gonna get a beautiful day."

For a couple of seconds, the three remained in place, beaming at each other. Then Brewster got up, walked to the Secretary, shook his friend's good hand, and gently cuffed him on the cheek. Kate came over, forming a tight circle, one hand on Brewster's waist, one on Maloney's, and leaned to Maloney, then Brewster, and kissed each on the cheek. For another few seconds they stood, smiling.

Then, for some reason, Kate started to cry. She broke away, went back to sit down, took a sip from her glass, and tried to stop.

"Want something to drink?" Brewster asked Maloney.

"Uh uh," he answered, still grinning. "I don't drink this early in the morning. I'm too full of stuff anyway, uppers, downers, siders, the doctor warned me not to. You see, you two old folks don't know it but I'm now a member of the drug generation."

Kate wiped her eyes and raised her snifter. "Permit me to thank you for allowing all us old folks—and our young folks—to grow older. L'chaim!" She sipped. So did Brewster. Maloney just grinned. Then she added, "It means 'To Life.'"

"I know, I know," said Maloney exuberantly. "I'm half Irish and half Italian. And half Jewish."

"After what you've done," said Brewster, "three halves is a conservative estimate. Here's to you, Pete." And the two of them sipped again. The Secretary kept grinning.

"I hope, Mr. Secretary," Kate said, "you're going to tell us how you shaped your miracles. The precise language, the nuances, the details, the actual words God whispered in your ear, what His hand really felt like on your shoulder."

Maloney never got to answer because Phelps walked into the room looking worried. "Mr. Secretary," he said.

"Yes, yes," answered Maloney, impatiently.

Phelps looked at Kate and Bill Brewster doubtfully.

"It's all right," said the Secretary, even more impatiently.

"The proposition has been put to the Israeli government, but as yet no answer has been received." Phelps waited.

"Please get back on the line and ask them to urge Jerusalem to hurry."

"Well, that's part of the problem, Mr. Secretary. The government is being moved to Tel Aviv, and they're having trouble reestablishing communication."

The smile disappeared from Maloney's face. "My God, wouldn't that be the final irony," he said. "To have it all go up in smoke because the line was busy. Ask if we can help."

"I've already suggested that," Phelps replied. "They say there's nothing we can do; they've got to solve it alone. They're working on it and hope to reestablish contact within an hour."

"That'll make it nearly seven," Maloney said. "Keep with it, Steve. Get back on the line, tell them we're ready to assist. Tell them the President is ready to fly over with a message tied to his leg. No, don't tell them that."

Phelps nodded and left. Maloney stared at the other two, no longer pleased. "There goes Cloud Nine," he said. "We'd better grab for Cloud Six and hold on for dear life, so we don't drop any lower."

"That's a lot of problem to solve in a short time," said Brewster.

"Just a few hours ago," answered the Secretary, "or was it a few years?—I told myself nothing was coming easy. Why should this be any different? They seem optimistic about the communications, though. And let's face it, we *have* made them an offer they can't refuse, not unless they're nuts. Well, all we can do is wait."

"We'd still like to be filled in on the details," Kate said. "We're all ears."

Maloney hesitated, looked down at his right hand in its cast. When this was over, assuming it ended well, he'd encounter a new set of problems. The President would be after him, surely force him out of the Cabinet and probably pursue a vendetta beyond that. I'm going to have to present my case, he thought. I'm going to be judged in many ways, not the least of which is by history. I've got to make sure my story is on record, and these are two people who can tell it in important places, when I'm ready.

The Secretary smiled at her, but with none of the joy he had shown a few minutes earlier. "It's not the ears I'm worried about," he said, "it's the mouths and typewriters. Look, you two, some day I may want this story told, fully. Until then, this, and everything else, is off the record. And only I can change that. If I die without changing it, the story dies, too. Is it a deal?"

Brewster nodded immediately. Kate thought about it. If I agree, she thought, the more he tells me the more gets locked away. Where could I hear it *on* the record? Dov. But how, after an evening of spying, could she ask him anything? In fact, she wondered, how could she face him at all?

There seemed no better way. "It's a deal," she told Maloney. "But I want to ask one thing of you."

Maloney looked wary. "It'd be hard to turn you down on anything, Kate, so be gentle."

"I want to get a head start on the cease-fire story. As soon as you know, I'd like to do it on our morning news, which is on from seven to nine. I'll limit myself to the statement you give me for the record. I won't go a word beyond it."

The Secretary of State sat, staring at her for a few moments. Then he nodded. "Believe it or not," he said, "the one thing that bothers me most is jinxing our chances by assuming it's a fait accompli before it actually is. But we'll underline that it's conditional right now and let that satisfy my superstitiousness.

"My statement only. Right?" he asked.

"Right," she replied.

"Not for attribution or quotation. Right?"

"Right."

"For use when I say so. Right?"

"Right!" she exclaimed, and then added, "Would you give me the statement now, so when I get the OK, I can shoot over to the studio?"

"Yes," he answered.

"And can I phone them now to warn them I may have something important?"

"Absolutely not," he said.

"I know, I know. I'm just greedy," she told Maloney, with a smile. And she reached into her purse for a small pad and a ballpoint pen. "OK."

"Israel and the Arabs have agreed to a cease-fire, to go into effect at 9 a.m. today. It was arranged through the good offices of the United States and the USSR." The Secretary thought for a moment, then said, "That's it."

Kate looked up from her notebook, startled. "What do you mean, that's it?"

"That's all I can give you, Kate. That's what I mean."

"How about the rollback? And the peacekeeping force? And the guarantees to Israel?"

"And how about the nuclear bombs in the nine cities?" he asked. "Would you like that, too? And the address of the house with the New York bomb, if we knew it? I hasten to add, we don't."

He looked at her, hard. "Kate, that's all at the moment. Just what I gave you. The fact, the time, the good offices. That's all. Period. No more. Understand?" She could see he was finished playing around but she took a chance anyway.

"Would you go on the air with me, live, this morning?"

"Absolutely not!"

"How about this evening—seven o'clock?"

"I see you didn't get where you have on looks, Kate. I don't know. Depends on whether it's to announce my resignation, explain my firing or extol the international vision of my President. We'll see. Seven p.m. is so damned far away."

"Yes, I'm nervy," Kate said. "Also grateful. Thank you for this. I'll add to it wire copy on the latest developments in the fighting. That OK?"

"Sure," Maloney replied. "Anyway, you didn't get that from me, so I couldn't tell you not to, even if I wanted to."

"Great," Kate said. "Now, back off the record."

Because he wanted everything known, and because he had to keep his mind occupied while waiting for word from Shalzar, Maloney told the story fully, beginning with the encounter at the embassy, to which Kate replied, "Even *I* know about Seventy-third Street. It could have saved you a lot of pain." He told of his talk with Shalzar, and the Egyptian. He told of the President's refusal, of Holloway's influence, and finally of the way he had coerced the President.

"He promised to get me for it," Maloney added.

"What he should get you for it is a medal," Kate said.

Maloney's detailed narrative took nearly forty minutes and as he recited it, he looked at his watch more and more frequently, more and more nervously watching the minute hand move toward the twelve, the hour hand creep toward the seven.

Where was Phelps? Where was Shalzar? By having Phelps make the call for him, he was hoping to give the impression to the Israelis he regarded their acceptance as routine. Now he was close to giving in and phoning himself, although he knew there was no point to it.

The story over, he began making conversation, about his hand, about technical arrangements, trying not to show them how apprehensive he was. God, I could use a brandy, he thought. But he knew he mustn't.

Their conversation became more and more intermittent; their euphoria of an hour ago was drained, so was their energy, by the long hours, the lack of food, the tension, the alcohol, Maloney's by the hand injury and the drugs.

When, finally, at 7:10, Phelps walked in, they were sitting in silence and they turned to read his face for a clue.

His face and his words were disappointing. Instead of excitement, he registered a somber neutrality; instead of saying, "The Israelis are going along," he said merely, "Ambassador Shalzar wants to speak with you. He is holding."

With a burst of energy Maloney rose and headed for his office, thinking: If Shalzar wanted to say yes, he would have said it to Phelps. Which means he has something disturbing to say. Then Maloney thought, Why do I say that? Maybe he wants to ask a question first. Maybe he wants to . . . No, Maloney decided, none of it is worth anything. Wait and see.

He reached his office, breathless, lunged for the phone, punched the lighted button and snapped, "Hello, this is Pete Maloney. Dov?"

An accented voice said: "One moment, please. I have the ambassador here."

Then the Israeli ambassador spoke. "Hello, Pete. How are you? How's your hand?"

My God, thought Maloney, has he called to ask about my health? "I'm fine, Dov. Hand's OK. What can I do for you?"

"Do I understand correctly," Shalzar asked, "that you have the acquiescence of all the other parties to your counterproposal of several hours ago? Is that so?"

Maloney held his breath. He dared not think it, but he might be getting a yes. "That is so," he answered.

"In that case," said the ambassador, "my government has decided we can do without Bismarck, North Dakota. We acquiesce . . ."

Maloney let out his breath like a steam engine; its sound almost obscuring the end of the sentence, "and our staff people will be in touch with yours at once to make sure the terms are carried out on both sides."

"And may we be assured," said Maloney, "that the consequences of the Masada Plan, whatever they may be, have been cancelled and will not occur?"

"You may be assured, Pete. We hereby assure you of that."

Maloney slumped to a sitting position on his desk. He didn't know what to say. The anguish was draining out of him so fast he began to worry. It had been the starch that had held him up over the last day. Without it, he feared he'd sink to the floor like a soft rag. Finally he managed, "We are very pleased, Dov. I know you must be, too." Then he paused and added, "I guess I've got to congratulate you. You outmuscled the big guys."

292

"We are pleased, too," Shalzar answered. "We were trying to save our lives, Pete, and for the moment it looks as if we've succeeded. But you are the one to be congratulated. You saved it all. You did an incredible job. I know of no one else who could have done it."

Somehow Maloney couldn't work up any elation at the compliment. He was still trying to digest the fact that the crisis was over. After another pause, he spoke, not responding to Shalzar's compliment.

"Dov," he said. "I'd like to meet with you. As soon as you can. Just the two of us on a man-to-man basis. It'd mean a lot to me. I'll come up there, if you like. To *Seventy-third* Street, that is."

"When?" asked Shalzar.

"About eight?"

"About eight. Perfect for breakfast," the Israeli said.

"Good," said Maloney. "See you then. And congratulations."

"To both of us," said Shalzar.

"And Dov," Maloney said.

"Yes," said the Israeli.

"The finger is off the button? No danger?"

"No danger," said Shalzar.

"Good. Goodbye."

"Goodbye."

Maloney put his phone down. He started toward the living room, smiling. But exhausted, he realized, with the pain coming back in his hand. The false ending an hour ago had robbed some of the orgasmic explosion from the real one.

He stood in the doorway, Brewster and Kate staring at him.

"It's OK," he said. "It's all OK. We've got it.

"The Masada Plan has been called off. Or, to put it another way, the Masada Plan has worked."

One person in the suite had no time for the jubilation of the moment. Down the hall, Linda Janowitz, the State Department Israeli expert, quietly stepped into the impromptu darkroom and closed the door behind her. Quickly she reached for a bottle and poured some of its contents into a shallow pan. Then she took the film Kate had shot, put it into the solution, and watched as the only hard evidence of the Masada Plan in non-Israeli hands faded away.

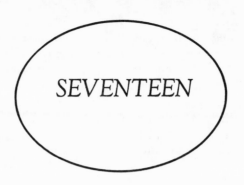

SEVENTEEN

At 7:15 on the morning of Friday, July 13, 1979, with an hour and three-quarters to spare, the ticking clock of the Masada Plan was turned off. For one day, the plan had glued together Kate Colby, Dov Shalzar, Bill Brewster, and Pete Maloney. The moment it ended, the four began to come unstuck, each knowing their relationships could never resume earlier shapes.

Kate's thoughts turned to her scoop and to Shalzar; Shalzar's to the cease-fire and to Kate; Brewster's to Kate and to his future; Maloney's to Shalzar and to the President. Of the three who had only an hour before stood in a tight circle in Maloney's suite, Kate was the first to move away. She began by phoning the producer of the morning news to warn him she had a big story; they decided she'd be on the second hour with it; she'd get to the newsroom as soon as she could to write it.

Maloney offered her a ride in his car. "With the crisis turned off," he said, "I don't think there'll be any more danger of ambush. The word'll be sent out PDQ to lay off. But let's just play it safe, take the car and an agent. Besides, I won't need it for a half hour or so."

Brewster got up. "I'll go with her," he said. Then he turned to the window and saw the brilliant morning sun in the east. He smiled. "We can walk off into the sunrise together."

"Why, Bill," Kate said, smiling. "How genuinely droll!"

"I'm trying to be the new, light, insouciant Bill Brewster," he responded. "But how can a man take off and fly when there's someone waiting to deride the first flutterings of his fledgling's wings?"

"Come on," she said, seizing his hand. "Let's flutter off."

"Steve," the Secretary shouted. When Phelps arrived, he said, "Phone downstairs and ask someone to drive these two to Ms. Colby's office, and then have him come back to pick me up."

"OK," said the aide, and left.

All three felt the glue giving and all regretted it. Kate and Brewster hated to walk out; Maloney hated to see them go. "Are you going on the air in your spy dress?" he asked.

She looked down. She was still wearing the long white gown she had put on for dinner at the embassy, messy from her wrestling match on Seventy-third Street and still clutching to her side the purse that had held the camera. She had been a spy. Long, long ago.

"I have a change of clothes at the office," she said.

Maloney took her hand. "I've said it before, Kate, and I'll say it again, many times, to your face, I hope. It couldn't have happened without you. You made it happen."

"I gave you something to fiddle with, Mr. Secretary. That's all. You were the Heifetz."

"You gave me a Stradivarius, kid, a Stradivarius." And he put his left arm around her and kissed her on the lips. He teetered almost on the edge of tears, then pulled back.

"I'll be watching after eight," he said, switching to mock severity. "Don't make any mistakes, or I'll do to you what I did to that door in there." And he waved his hand in its sling.

Then the Secretary turned to Brewster, looking up at him. "As for you, you son-of-a-bitch, the world's tallest éminence grise, thanks for being here, not to mention for knowing the right people." He tilted his head toward Kate as he said it.

"I'll be in town for the next couple of days, at least. When we've caught up on our sleep, and you can take a few hours off from ruining the economy, we'll have dinner."

Then Maloney suddenly had another thought. "And, Bill, if I need you for this Middle East thing, can I count on you? Shalzar trusts you, and right now there aren't too many non-Israelis they do trust."

Brewster's automatic first reaction was to say no, but he swallowed it. If he was to try to change anything, this was the time, this was day number one.

"Yes," he said. "Count on me. It'll be good for me. And if it helps you, I'll do anything. The world may never learn what it owes you, Pete, but I know. I don't know if anyone else could have done it."

"You could have, Bill," Maloney said. "Don't kid yourself."

"I don't kid myself," Brewster answered with a smile. "Goodbye, Bill."

"Goodbye," Kate echoed.

Clearly, Maloney was prolonging the departure. "This has made us Siamese triplets—if there is such a thing," he said. "We can never be separated, you know."

"Then we're going to have to stretch some flesh," she answered, laughing. "Because I've got to be at the office right away! Goodbye!"

And with Maloney watching, the two of them turned and left.

Settled in the back seat of the car, Kate turned to Brewster and said, "Do you know how I feel right now?"

"Let me take a guess," he answered. "Let down. You've just been on top of a mountain. Very dangerous and very exciting. Now you're at the bottom again. Safe. But you miss the thrill."

"Yes!" she said. "Exactly! Isn't it awful? I mean I should be as high as a kite over the story I've got but I can't get up there. Having been a doer, a shaker, a mover, I'm not finding the kick I should in being a reporter."

"If you think that's short on kicks," he replied, "you should try being an investment banker."

She turned to him and put a hand on his arm. "If I run for the Senate, will you be my chief fund-raiser?" She was joking, at least she thought she was.

"What? Haven't you heard? I may drop out, run off to a pueblo, teach Navajo kids how to sell short? You want fund-raising from me? It may have to be in wampum."

"Best offer I've had so far," she replied. "You notice I didn't say 'how droll'?" She held on to his arm. "What I really want from you, Bill, is not wampum, it's advice. What do I do about Dov?"

He tightened up. She saw it. "I've got two answers, and I don't know which to give first. One is, What do you mean, *do* about Dov? The other is, That's a hell of a question to ask *me!*"

"I know it is, Bill, and I suppose I shouldn't have. I'll withdraw it if you want."

"No, don't," he answered stiffly. "It's too late, anyway."

"All right, then, dear Bill. What I mean is, do I go to Dov and confess that when I was a dinner guest in his house—my God, it was only twelve hours ago, and it seems like a week—I violated his hospitality, his trust and his . . . feelings, by spying on him? If I tell him that, how will he ever trust me again? And if I *don't*, how will he ever trust me again? And either way, how can I face him? So there you are, Solomon."

He relaxed a bit. "Don't face him. Write him a letter, and then run away with me to the Navajo reservation. You can teach broadcast journalism, while I'm handling the high finance, and we can combine our talents in a syndicated TV series called 'Know Your Bond Market,' which might sweep the country like wildfire. And might not."

Kate knew he was kidding—yet serious, and, for him, daring. What surprised her was how little she minded hearing it. "Let me kick your Navajo proposition around for a while; if you think it's a bad way to go, you're crazy. Of course," she added, "I don't know if I could become hooked on rugs—instead of scolding me for that atrocious pun, please give me some serious advice. Put yourself in Dov's shoes; what would you expect?"

What Bill Brewster had expected, in his own shoes, was to be taken less seriously than he had been, and the new turn made him even more daring. "In his shoes, as in my own, I'd want the truth," Brewster answered. "And when it came I'd be angry and hurt. Then I'd probably put my arms around you and forgive you. But I'd forgive you almost anything . . . if I were in his shoes."

Kate found herself in deeper waters than she had anticipated. Again, she was surprised at how little she minded, and she began asking herself why that was, not really wanting to face any new complication at the moment. So she was grateful when she noticed they were only half a block from her office. She turned to Brewster, and he thought he spotted an intensity he hadn't seen directed at him in a long time, perhaps never before. She was taking him seriously, he thought. Or hoped.

"We're almost there," she said, "for which I thank God, because the talk is getting a little heavy, for the moment, anyway. Right now, I've got to concentrate on my ethical dilemma, Bill."

"I'll wait," he said. "When do you expect to confront Dov?"

"Just as soon as I can. After I get off the air I'll phone and try to see him sometime today."

"Well," he said, "after the seven o'clock news this evening, if you're too wound up to go to sleep right away, and have no one better to have a drink or a meal with, I'm available."

The sedan came to a stop in front of the studio entrance. "Saved by the bell," he said, smiling.

She grabbed his hand and squeezed. "Have you gathered," she told him, "that I am not at all displeased by your availability? As for having no one better, a better man would be hard to find, as the song almost goes." She leaned over and kissed him on the lips. Then she jumped out of the car and turned to him.

"Let's see how we both feel later, Bill. Let's talk."

"Let's," he answered. She ran off.

"Can I drop you somewhere?" the driver asked.

"No," Brewster replied. "I'm going to walk from here. Why don't you just go back and wait for the Secretary? I've got nowhere special to go." And he climbed out of the car and slammed the door.

It was not yet eight, and the sun was hanging brightly above Queens, its rays directly in his eyes as he slowly walked east along Fifty-sixth Street. He had nowhere special to go and he found it a joy to be able to amble.

Later, the temperature would be near ninety, with the humidity intolerable, one of those July days in New York, but right now it was still clear and in the seventies, a scintillating morning. Brewster

297

opened his jacket, loosened his silk paisley tie and then took it off. He jammed it into his pocket, put both hands in his pockets. William Brewster never walked in the street with his tie off, his jacket open, and his hands in his pockets.

After a dozen or so strides, his hands came out of his pockets and he broke into a trot, headed for the next parking meter. It was an unusually high one, but with a leap and a thrust of his arms, the forty-seven-year-old president of Patton and Co. vaulted it as easily as a teenager.

He grinned at a plate-glass window, contemplating his reflection and his euphoria as he walked. Why did he feel so good? Because the city wasn't going to be blown up; because Kate had kissed him on the lips; because, for the moment anyway, he was on the high ground alongside the rut in which he usually traveled, and the view was majestic. And he had time to enjoy it. He had nowhere special to go.

Pete Maloney, back at the Waldorf, had to be at the Israeli UN mission in half an hour and until then had no time to look at the view, for he must begin setting up the machinery to assure the Israelis of their demands, putting together a peacekeeping force, assuaging the Arabs, and seeing to it no one reneged on promises.

He thrust seven separate assignments on Phelps, alerted key State Department people at their homes around Washington, spoke to the American ambassadors in Tel Aviv and Cairo, put calls in to embassies in Moscow, Amman, and Damascus. As he reviewed the scope of the guarantees to Israeli, he saw months of unrelenting work, with crises cropping up all the time, and he began to wish he could count on the President's firing him—soon.

But he started doubting that. Sure, the man hated him, but the President was, above all, political, and might postpone his vendetta if it seemed expedient. Maybe I should quit, Maloney thought. And if I do, who'll finish this job? To dump it on someone else right now would be cruel and unusual punishment. Here we go again, he told himself. I haven't contemplated my own divinity for more than two hours. How did I hold out so long? He stood from his desk and walked into the bathroom for a quick shower.

He showered carefully, keeping the cast dry. Drying himself, he looked in the mirror and whacked his belly. What I can use, he thought, is another few days of fasting. Or a real diet. Between crises, I've gotta lose twenty-five pounds. He faced another fact about himself. My problem is not that I'm afraid someone else *can't* handle the crisis; it's that I'm afraid someone else *can*. And I'll be on the sidelines.

He found a short-sleeved shirt that would fit over the cast; his jacket would not, so he carried it. Well, I'm not sidelined yet, he thought, as he headed downstairs and climbed into the car. So for now, how do I handle the Israeli? Nice guy, or tough?

At Seventieth Street and Park Avenue, Maloney said, with exaggerated emphasis, "The Seventy-third Street entrance, *please!*" The driver, who had been one of the agents at the earlier confrontation, laughed and said, "Yessir!"

This time their entrance was as smooth and gracious as the earlier one had been hostile. Shalzar was waiting for Maloney in the hall and they greeted each other as if they had been through a war together —which they had.

"How keen is your appetite for breakfast?" Shalzar asked. "Coffee, milk, two lumps of sugar," answered the Secretary. Then, remembering the gut he had seen in the bathroom mirror, said, "Make it one lump."

"Coffee for me, too," said the ambassador to an aide. The two went into the same sitting room, took the same chairs they had been in earlier. They smiled at each other, then Maloney spoke, his tactic suddenly decided upon. Frontal assault.

"Now that you guys got what you want," he began, "how can we be sure you're getting those things out of those cities?"

If he was waiting for the Israeli to be startled he was disappointed. Shalzar's face was blank, except, possibly, for a touch of a smile, as he answered, "What things? What cities?" It was a pro forma expression of surprise, said as if it were expected of him.

Maloney had to smile in return. Only his was not happy. With the crisis now averted, he felt a growing resentment at being outmuscled.

"The things are nuclear devices. The cities are New York, Los Angeles, Moscow, Leningrad, London, Paris, Berlin, Cairo, Jerusalem. Do I have that right?" He was angry; he looked straight at the ambassador, who replied in a voice totally without expression, "Where did you get that information?" With one inflection, the question could have meant: You're ridiculous. With another: How did you find out? As said, it was carefully ambiguous.

"Very reliable sources," said the Secretary. To himself he said, There's no point in trying to get the son of a bitch to admit anything, may as well just go along on the assumption that we both know. "There's no question I know what the Masada Plan is; the only question is, since we paid one hell of a price, what are we buying for it? Are we buying the end of the threat? Or a couple of days' breather? Suppose someone gives you a dirty look next month? Do you put your finger back on the trigger?"

At this, Shalzar got angry. "Where do you come off suggesting we would make a threat for a 'dirty look'? Was the Arab invasion your idea of a dirty look? How dare you suggest we have been so capricious?"

The vehemence caught Maloney by surprise. "And how long would you say it's fair for the United States to live with an Israeli nuclear gun at its head?"

Shalzar got angrier and quieter. "If you'll forgive the Jewish trait of answering a question with another question, I'll ask you: How long would you say it's fair for the United States to live with a Russian nuclear gun at its head? Or the Soviets to live with an American gun at its head? Or for that matter, the world, the bystanders, to live with an American-Soviet nuclear gun at *its* head? Twenty-five years? Because that's how long it's been—so far!"

"Look, Dov, you know as well as I that it's the Soviet and American guns at each others' heads that keep the peace in the world." The Secretary was impatient with the ingenuousness and presumption of the Israeli's comparison.

"Keep the peace?" asked Shalzar. "For whom? Not for Israel they didn't keep the peace. What would the big two peacekeepers have done if there had been no Masada Plan? Fished a few Torahs from the rubble for the Jewish Museum?"

Maloney's reply was pure chest-thumping, and he knew it. "You expect us to sit still while you tell us the installations might stay right where they are and while you tell us you might use them anytime? Well, now I'll tell you something. We can find the goddamned things—don't think we can't. And if I tell the others—they're gonna go looking, too, and they'll do some finding. And then a lot of people will feel we don't owe you anything, and all our pledges will be off. Then where will you be?"

The Israeli shrugged. He knew it was bluster and it didn't bother him; in fact, he was reassured. If the Secretary of State had nothing more to threaten with than that, he didn't have much. "You're going to search for it, are you? Go ahead. Where will you start? With the two million Jews around New York? In their basements and attics and stores and warehouses and offices? And what makes you think a Jew would be hiding it? You think there are no blacks that would? No Ukrainians? Cubans? Puerto Ricans? Not to mention uncounted others? How about, for irony, if it were in some Arab's house? There's almost nothing you can't buy, you know."

"I'm not talking about breaking and entering, Dov. Our technology has gone way beyond that." It was bluff, and not Pete Maloney at his best. Shalzar spotted it and could not risk being just a touch derisive.

"Pete, either you know little about the technology of detection, or you think I do. In fact, I don't know much, but I have been briefed on the possibility you're suggesting, and let me tell you there's

no way you could find such an installation without a fine-tooth comb—
I mean a physical fine-tooth comb, not an electronic one—not heat-
sensitive, not radioactivity-sensitive, not any kind of sensitive. It's
just too easy to protect against that."

Slowly Maloney was becoming furious. He was supposed to be
able to handle this kind of guy. This kind was not supposed to out-
muscle or outbluff him. He found it tough to take. "Do you know
what this continued threat is going to do to Israel in the eyes of
the world? What the Soviets will think? Has it occurred to you, Dov,
what its effect will be on anti-Semitism?"

"Ah ha!" said the ambassador. "Bad for the Jews, right? An
American finger, OK. A Russian finger, OK. But a Jewish finger on
the trigger of a Jewish gun—we really should be more careful, shouldn't
we! Pushy, isn't it? Who invited us into the club, anyway?

"Well, my friend, we may be doing you a favor, by being your
DEW line, your early warning that the nuclear club has been broken
into through the front door, back door, windows, and basement. That
someone may put a finger on the trigger for a hell of a lot less reason
than we did. And it may not even be a nation. Suppose it's just some
group that's desperate—or crazy? You want to trust a nuclear weapon
to the hands of the IRA? Or the Black Septembrists? How about
those Zebra killers in California a few years ago? Suppose they had
had access to a small atom bomb?"

"Yeah," answered Maloney, "a roster of bogeymen, but so far no
one has done anything—but you."

"Done? What have we done? The Arabs started a war that, so
far, has killed thousands; the rest of you watched them and didn't
lift a finger. And we merely threatened, with a plan that killed no
one and is going to kill no one. What we did was quite the opposite.
We *stopped* the killing—or, at least, I assume it will stop.

"And, mind you, we would not even have threatened had we not
found ourselves in extremis."

"Are you saying then," Pete asked, "that you think it's justifiable
to threaten the world as you have? That more and more countries,
and political groups, and God knows, maybe disappointed soccer
teams, and rejected artists, and liberated women—will be doing it,
and we should understand it?"

"It's strange," replied Dov, "that you should choose women and
soccer players and artists as your hypothetical villains, when the death
instrument is the United States' gift to the world. It's strange that
you should be lecturing anyone on responsibility, when the only one
—and that includes soccer players and the whole list—ever to use a
nuclear weapon is the United States. And may I point out to you
that it did not do so under any such exigency as Israel has just been
facing. I don't want to get into the morality of the bombs on Hiro-

shima and Nagasaki, so, even accepting your explanation that you dropped them to shorten the war and save lives, you certainly didn't do it to save yourself from extinction!"

Maloney tried to say something, but Shalzar, on a full head of steam, rode right through. "You know, you remind me of a bit of Shakespeare—it *would* be Shylock, wouldn't it? 'This villainy you teach me, I will execute.' Only we haven't 'bettered the instruction.' You're still the champs.

"You—actually, in 1945, for me it was still 'we'—gave us the bomb, and showed us how to use it. That was the villainy you taught us. Now find a way to take it back, or make sure no one will use it. That's the only way to get a *real* guarantee."

The Secretary took his first sip of coffee; it was cold by then. His hand was shaking with anger. "That's one hell of an assurance. That's more like a kind of running blackmail. How long do you people think you will last doing that?"

"That's mighty threatening," answered Shalzar, "but somehow I'm not scared, because the answer is easy: Longer than we would have without it.

"What puzzles me," the Israeli went on, "is what kind of guarantee you think you've 'bought,' as you put it. What you bought, and you obviously think it was worth the price, was the stopping of the clock at nine this morning. And this I can guarantee you: The clock will never be started again, except to save our lives. Not for oil would we do it. Not for territory. Not even to shorten a war, as you did.

"Guarantee us our lives as a nation, and our fingers will not go to the trigger. That we pledge. After all, we are a nation that's thirty years old and we've been living all of it with our fingers on one trigger or another, and with one weapon or another at our heads. We're sick of it."

The ambassador paused. "Threaten our survival again, and again we'll do everything we can, use any weapon to save ourselves. That's a promise, too. The price of permanent immunity from Israel is permanent life for Israel. No more, no less. It's not unfair, surely. Permanent existence of the nation is something every American takes for granted. I'm sitting here, content, because I feel Israel will now survive past 9 a.m. You, as an American, don't even think about a thing like that because . . ."

There was a sharp rap on the door and, without waiting for a "come in" from Shalzar, an aide stuck his head in and spoke quickly in Hebrew. Shalzar answered him briefly and then jumped to his feet, opened a door in a cabinet beneath a row of bookshelves to reveal a large TV set, which he switched on and turned to the UBC channel. A commercial was on. The ambassador took his seat again, and said, "I asked someone to warn me when the first coverage of the Middle

East was on, and apparently UBC just announced it would have a bulletin. It's got to be Kate Colby."

"My God, it will be," Maloney replied. "Glad you caught it because . . ." He swallowed the "I promised her I'd watch" and made it "I want to see what they say." Not even "what she says." Give her all the protection I can, the Secretary thought.

The anchorman was on. "Now here with that special bulletin on the Middle East crisis, UBC correspondent Kate Colby."

A cut to a medium close-up of Kate, wearing a light blue blouse.

"UBC News has learned, exclusively," she began, "that Israel and the Arab nations have agreed to a cease-fire in the Middle East, to go into effect one-half hour from now, at 9 a.m. New York time. We have also learned that the United States and the Soviet Union played important roles in working out the end of the fighting. Highly placed sources . . . ," and Shalzar and Maloney stared at each other for a moment, "told us the negotiations have been going on steadily since the Arabs attacked Israel at 9 a.m. Wednesday, New York time, and reached a successful conclusion only moments ago.

"Let me repeat that," she said, "a cease-fire will go into effect between the Arabs and Israelis a half hour from now. We have no details of the agreement at the moment, but we shall give those to you as soon as we get them."

The anchorman came back on; Shalzar stood, walked over and turned off the set, Maloney watching him, thinking of Kate. She hypoed the drama a bit, he thought, with that line about the agreement "only moments ago." And she seemed a bit chagrined at having to say "We have no details." But then who could blame her?

Shalzar sat down and said, half to Maloney, half to himself, "Well, I guess she's done it again."

What did he mean, Maloney wondered. Was there a special resonance in that? Maloney had to pretend there wasn't. "I don't suppose there's anything she can't handle," he replied, thinking: There, that's ambiguous enough.

They settled back into their old line of conversation, Shalzar pouring coffee for both, then saying, "I know you want more, but I don't see what I can give you and, honestly, I don't see what more in the way of assurances you have any right to expect. After all, preservation being the first law of nations, as well as nature, when our collective life is in danger, all assurances become meaningless, anyway."

Maloney saw there was nothing more to talk about, so, rising, he said, almost facetiously, "I've enjoyed our little talk, and the coffee, and I wish I could stay longer, but I've got a lot of work to do, including the pacification of our President." Maloney wanted the Israeli to know how much he had risked to push the Israeli demands through, and he wanted to soften Shalzar for a final thrust he'd saved for his exit. The Secretary waited until they were walking down the hall before thrusting.

"How about nuclear accidents, Dov? Can you be sure they won't happen? And can we offer any technical help?"

The ambassador looked at Maloney, smiling cryptically. A regular Mona Lisa, Maloney thought, reading into it strains of kindness, hostility, irony and derision, as well as amusement.

The smile broadened, but the answer was clipped, almost snappy. "Are you worried about our nuclear accidents? You with your reactors, power plants, stockpiles, silos, nuclear subs—worried about *our* accidents? Know how many *we've* had? None. Zero.

"How many have you had?" he asked, not waiting for a reply. "Never mind, I don't really want an answer. You've had some, let's just say that."

For a moment, Shalzar assumed a camaraderie Maloney had never seen in him before. The ambassador grabbed Maloney's left arm just above the elbow and spoke as if letting him in on a secret.

"I only wish you had as much reason to worry about *your* nuclear accidents as you have to worry about *ours*."

They said goodbye at the door, Maloney not yet having absorbed the ambassador's parting wish. But as he sat in his car, thinking about it, he asked himself: Why is he so sure the Masada Plan bombs couldn't go off by mistake—a technical error, a communications error? Then a suspicion that had been germinating in his mind since he first saw Kate's film suddenly sprang forth.

Suppose there were no nuclear devices in the nine cities? Suppose there were just a couple of sets of documents, which a few technicians could whip up in no time?

Suppose, in other words, the Masada Plan had been a gigantic bluff?

The Secretary of State slumped his exhausted bulk back on the seat and laughed. The biggest goddamned poker game in history, he said to himself, and we folded without ever seeing their hand.

And now we'll never see it. We'll never know.

He looked down at his right hand in its cast. It's been a hell of a thirty-six hours, he thought. I don't think I could ever get anyone to believe it. And what do you do for an encore? Will anything ever excite or frighten you again? How could it? Not even the fight with the President? Not even that, he thought. And he smiled again, this time in anticipation. It might be a hell of a fight, though.

If Maloney could find some stimulation in the prospect of a confrontation with the President, Kate Colby could find none in her impending meeting with Dov Shalzar. Only dread. And she'd begun feeling it as soon as the Masada crisis ended. It lurked in the background as she listened to Maloney explaining his negotiations; it faded, without ever quite disappearing, as she rode to the studio with Bill Brewster.

Not that Bill hadn't given her something to think about in the last few hours. Ten months ago she had parted from him wondering how she could ever have taken him seriously. Suddenly, in the last day, she had remembered: What in denigrating moments she had seen as indecisiveness, she now understood contained self-awareness; its stiffness contained elegance; the cold reticence, delicacy. She laughed to herself; she'd begun rewriting history. Well, she'd have time to sort all that out. First things first. Which took her back to the meeting with Dov and the vague tightness in the pit of her stomach.

Never mind Brewster and Shalzar, she told herself in the elevator. Concentrate on the story. You're miles ahead of anyone else on it. Get excited. Think about the special you should be doing on the Arab-Israeli fighting; you should be whipping it together to follow the 11 o'clock news tonight.

Oh no, she told herself, not tonight. Not me. There's a whole newsroom full of people, let them do it. First I need some sleep. First I need time to meet with Dov. Back to that again.

Then she was in the newsroom. She was at work.

A day in the company of Maloney and Shalzar had made Kate forget, temporarily, the pusillanimity and politics rampaging through the UBC news hierarchy. She had hardly stepped inside the entrance to the newsroom when she was reminded. Pussyfooting his way over to her, with all the speed his faint heart would allow, was the producer of the morning news, Ed Craven, whose name was a spectacular match for his courage.

"We've got to clear it with Ben, and I haven't been able to get hold of him yet," said Craven. Although he was slightly taller than she, he seemed to be looking up at her; he walked in a slump with his head down, so as few people as possible would notice him and perhaps ask, What does *he* do here? It was a habit he had developed in the army and honed to such a fine edge at UBC that though he had spent eighteen years in the newsroom, most of the brass didn't know who he was.

Craven's detractors, whose numbers were legion, claimed he didn't do *anything* before he cleared it with Ben Daniels, a vice president of UBC News, and periodically they put up a notice to that effect in the men's room. In eighteen years, Craven had never taken an initiative and never disobeyed an order, and having never looked ahead and always protected his flank, had outlasted many a better producer. The morning news was the ideal post for him because stories virtually never broke for his time slot, and he filled his two hours with repeats of last night's news, canned features, or live interviews, all of which could be approved in advance. To Craven, a breaking story, such as the one Kate now offered, was an unmitigated curse. The possibility of praise was meaningless to him because he had long ago given up on advancement; the prospect of blame was dark and threatening.

Kate had once said of him, "If I walked into the newsroom hand-in-hand with the Pope, to announce our elopement, *live,* on the morning news, Ed would want to clear it with Ben. This morning, she just said, "But Ed, it's almost eight and I wanted to lead the hour with it!"

Craven looked hurt. "No way, Kate! Even if Ben clears it, I couldn't juggle my lineup to make room for it this quickly. If we get his OK, we'll put you on right after the commercial break at the half hour." Then he tried an ingratiating smile. "The ratings are better at eight-thirty, anyway."

"I keep forgetting," she began, smiling back at him, "that the name of this game is ratings. I keep thinking it's getting on firstest with the mostest!" It's bad enough being a reporter instead of a doer, she thought, but it's worse when you're at the mercy of creeps like this one. And in television, you *were* at their mercy, she knew. Without air time you were a nonjournalist, and the air time was controlled by the Ed Cravens.

With Craven standing there, not daring to answer—he knew Kate was important, and he'd never risk offending her—she picked up a copy of the lineup and looked at some of the items in the 8 a.m. half hour: six minutes for the third part of a series on national parks; five on the pennant races; an eight-minute live interview with the author of a book on the romance of snuffboxes. Sure he couldn't juggle those, they were too hot to handle.

"OK, Ed, I know you've got a lot to do. I'll clear it."

He started to say something, but she stared at him until he walked away. Then she took a tiny address book from her purse, looked up Hannon's number and dialed it.

The wife of the news president answered. "Mrs. Hannon," Kate said, "I must talk to Dick; it's very urgent." Only then did she remember to say, "This is Kate Colby."

"Oh, hello, Kate. I'm afraid you can't, he's in the shower."

Kate had met Mrs. Hannon only twice and could not remember her first name. Another time she would have been embarrassed; now she had no time for it.

"I must ask you to get him out; that's how important it is. Right now, please."

"Well, all right." Her voice was cold. Being called by her first name by Kate Colby would have meant a lot to her.

Kate waited, then heard, "This better be good, Kate. I'm dripping all over my wife's new Moroccan rug."

"It's a big one, Dick. It's worth dripping all over your wife for, let alone her rug."

"Jesus, Kate," he replied, "don't your sources ever sleep?"

"Sorry about that," she said, "news is so undisciplined. I try to get stories to break at three-thirty, early enough for the seven o'clock news, late enough for you to get back from lunch. But the damned things just won't listen."

For you to get back from lunch *and* the three martinis which have made your hand steady enough to hold a piece of copy, is what she wanted to say, but didn't.

"Very funny for eight in the morning," he said. "Hope your story is as good as your wit."

"How about a cease-fire in the Middle East, to go into effect in one hour," she answered. "That good enough?" And then to save time she added, "Straight from the mouth of Peter Maloney, Secretary of State. *That* good enough?"

Hannon was a drinker and an office politician, but he had been a good newsman, and he could still keep a secret.

"Yeah, that's good enough, kid. In fact, that's great! Great! I mean that, Kate. Glad you're on our side."

She smiled at that. On whose side am I? she wondered. "OK, Dick, then will you talk to Craven now and tell him to give the kid what she wants?"

"Sure, Kate. And congratulations. Again."

"Thanks, Dick. Now hold on." To Craven she shouted, "Ed, pick up the phone, will you?" She watched the look of subservience come over his face as he heard Hannon's voice. They spoke for a minute and Craven hung up. The producer looked at her and let a flash of hatred slip through his façade.

"Right after the commercials at the half hour. How much time you need?" He had gotten his way about the 8:30, slimy devil, she said to herself. She looked at her watch. It was 8:05; she had to write the bulletin, change her clothes, go to makeup, then get to the studio. Hell, she needed the time, she was too tired to fight, and she had been through too much to bother with this thimbleful.

"Twenty seconds is all I need, and you can follow it with an update on the fighting." Then she buried her head in the typewriter. Her work from that point to the time she went on the air with the bulletin should have been a triumph; yet she hardly paid any attention to it. Her thoughts were whirling around Shalzar and the meeting she knew she had to have soon.

By the time she got off the set, washed off the makeup, returned to her office, it was 8:50. Had she called him then, she would have interrupted the end of his meeting with Maloney. But she found reasons to delay. She called her kids at camp; they were out on canoe trips. She got herself a container of coffee from the cafeteria, sipped it. At 9:05, she dialed his private number.

"I must see you as soon as possible," she told him, expecting him to be surprised. Instead, Shalzar surprised her by responding, calmly, "Yes, I must talk to you, too."

"When?"

"Why not in a half hour? Or as soon as you get here. Before all the machinery we're setting up starts clanking too loudly. Before we all collapse of exhaustion."

"All right," she answered. "I'll grab a cab and be up there in about fifteen minutes."

Not much of a conversation, she thought, for two lovers who hadn't spoken since the resolution of a crisis they'd been through together. No "thank God it's over." No congratulation, no "dear," no "sweetheart." Not by either of them. So, she told herself, something is as cockeyed from his point of view as it is from mine.

In the cab, Kate thought of her two years with Shalzar. That was over, she knew. Whatever happened now, however the spying resolved itself, the old relationship was no more. It had ended the moment she walked into that embassy with the camera and the tape recorder, and had *not* said: Look what I've got and look what they want me to do. *They*. The fact was, at the dinner, *they* had become *we;* she had cut herself off from Dov Shalzar and aligned herself with the Americans. She had spied on Shalzar for them, when she might as easily have spied on them for Shalzar. She had spent the crucial waiting hours in the suite of the American Secretary of State when she might as easily have spent them in the Israeli embassy. And she wasn't sure why.

She felt now it had been inevitable. But why? Because she was an American? Because her feelings for Dov were not what she had thought they were? Because she had really made the reasoned determination that her best chance to save the world was as an American spy, not as an Israeli spy? She didn't know.

And why hadn't she agonized more? How had it happened so easily? Oh come on, she told herself, it wasn't that easy. Was she now forgetting the agony? Was she now just imagining an inevitability? She didn't know.

The one thing she was sure of was, she'd walk in and tell Dov she had been a spy, and tell him why. And see what happened. Had she any real expectation he would throw his arms around her and tell her all was forgiven? Did she really believe he would ever trust her again? Suppose the situation were reversed? Would she forgive him? Would she trust him?

How would he react?

Well, I'll find out soon enough, she said to herself, as the cab stopped on the corner of Madison and Seventy-third. Kate walked along Seventy-third and was joined in a moment by an Israeli security man who led her through the rear entrance and into the library where Shalzar was waiting.

His embrace was as reserved as hers. I wonder why, she asked herself. I know why mine is—because I've double-crossed him. But what about him?

"Hello, Dov." She looked into his eyes as she said it, and suddenly all the emotions she had ever felt for him, all the closeness, all the expectations for the future, spoken, suggested, were in his eyes.

"Hello, Kate."

Oh my God, I mustn't, I mustn't, she said to herself. But tears came, and slid down her cheeks.

He made an elaborate gesture of wiping them with his handkerchief. He smiled at her, a smile of such sadness and resignation, she was puzzled by it. Again, she thought, I know why I'm sad—because I've double-crossed him. But why is he?

"So we've been pulled back from the brink, for a while," she said to him.

"Yes," he answered, "I just heard it from Kate Colby on UBC, and if she says it, it must be so. I don't know where she gets her stories, but she's never wrong.

"Yes," he said. "We've been pulled back from the brink . . . for a while. In Israel, we'll have a lot of repairs to make. And a lot that can never be repaired. But we're no longer at the edge of extinction and that feels good, anyway."

This was the time to jump in, with both feet, she decided. "You know, Dov, I played a certain part in that," she began.

"Yes, I know you did, and I want to thank you for it," he broke in quickly. Kate turned pale. He knew! No, it couldn't be. "Without your getting me through to Brewster and Maloney the way you did, the negotiations might not have worked out."

My God, she thought, I did that, didn't I! Years ago. Yesterday morning. I sat with Dov and Bill at the Unity. And I was on Dov's side of the table. Now I sit across from him, playing my cards while he plays his. No, I didn't come here to play cards. I came to confess. To try to get back on his side of the table. I think.

"You're welcome, Dov, but that's not what I'm talking about. The part I'm talking about is something entirely different, something I want to tell you about, that I want you to listen to without stopping me."

Kate leaned forward and grabbed his hand, that tough, bony hand which she had held, which had held her, so often. "This will be hard enough for me to tell. Please just listen till I'm finished. Then ask what you want and say what you want. OK?"

"OK."

Kate released his hand and clasped hers together in her lap. She remained sitting forward, and she began.

"You must understand, Dov, that there was a point, not too many hours ago, when Maloney, and the President, would not have given an inch to your demands, for the simple reason they didn't know what the Masada Plan was threatening.

"They also didn't know—they still don't—why you wouldn't tell them straight out. They did know you couldn't get what you wanted based on what you were saying. So Maloney felt they should try to find out more about the Masada Plan. The question was, how?

"You see, Dov, the world could have been blown up through a mixed signal, through Maloney's not knowing how serious you were. So they asked me to find out more. For the sake of America, and Israel, and the world. And you. I found their reasoning persuasive. I still do."

Kate paused and looked at Shalzar. Although she had said she wanted to tell the story straight through, she would have welcomed an interruption. He kept silent. So she went on.

"There were two ways I could get information. The first was simply to persuade you it was to your advantage to disclose more. I tried that when I came to dinner yesterday. It didn't work."

Now came the hard part. Her eyes dropped; she couldn't look at him.

"So I had to try the second way. I came in here as your guest, as your lover. I drank your wine, I enjoyed your trust . . . and I spied on you. I came in here with a tiny camera in my purse and a tape-recorder in my bra. Never used the recorder. But when you and Weismann rushed out after the explosion, I took the camera, walked over to Weismann's briefcase, which he hadn't locked, opened it, found the documents and snapped pictures. And took them to the Secretary of State.

"When Maloney saw what the Masada Plan was, I can tell you he was impressed. He started the negotiations that led to the cease-fire."

For the first time since she had mentioned the word "spied," Kate dared to look up. Shalzar's face was startling in its inscrutability. There was no disapproval on it, certainly no surprise.

"I spied on you, Dov. That's my confession."

She waited.

Shalzar looked straight back at her, his face graver, yet warmer than it had been a few minutes before, but giving no clue of what was to follow.

"Kate, I have something to tell you, too.

"We knew you spied. We let you. We wanted you to. We fed you the Masada Plan so you could photograph it. We left Itzhak's briefcase out and open deliberately. The explosion was planned as a device for getting us out of the room." He paused.

"The death of the young man was not. He shouldn't have been there. He didn't follow instructions." Shalzar shook his head.

310

"But the ruse worked. You were alone and near the documents. We set you up. That is my confession."

She turned pale. Her eyes widened. Much as she wanted to say something, nothing would come out. He waited. She could not speak. He went on.

"And like you, Kate, I have an explanation. You see, ever since there was a Masada Plan, there was the determination never to reveal it ourselves, from our mouths. We recognized the necessity for a Doomsday device; we don't apologize for that. At the same time, we knew the horror of it and regretted it. We knew, too, anti-Semites the world over would jump on it as the kind of pretext they're always looking for. So we decided, rather than disclose it, we would leak it, off the record—yet authoritatively enough to make it utterly convincing."

At first, she sat and listened, numb. Then the implications of what he said began to click, and her mind worked on them feverishly. But she didn't speak and he continued.

"We were as anxious as anyone—no, *more* anxious—that the Masada Plan do its work by *not* being used. But to do its work it had to be known, without our revealing it. The leak would have to be aimed at the right person; the source would have to be impeccable and the means of access plausible. What could be better than from Weismann's briefcase, to you, to Maloney. Our relationship made you the perfect person."

Our relationship, she thought. How convenient! What a lucky fringe benefit of a love affair! Only which was the by-product, the leak or the love affair?

Shalzar sat there waiting for her to speak but again she was both stunned and feverish, her mind full of myriad questions jammed together, fighting to get out. The first of them she directed to herself. Earlier she had asked herself: Could I ever trust someone who'd done to me what I'd done to Dov? Now she knew Dov *had* done it to her, perhaps worse. Could she ever trust him?

But that could wait; it might never be answered.

Shalzar, anxious at her silence, was relieved when at last she asked, "How did you know I would spy? Suppose I hadn't. What would you have done then?"

"We didn't know it," he replied. "But we felt they would come up with the idea, knowing as they did that you had access to me and the embassy. We felt there was a good chance you might be persuaded and we then proceeded to create the proper circumstances.

"If you hadn't? Why then we had alternatives. One of them could possibly have been to hand the plan to you and ask you to deliver it. Maybe, if desperate enough, we would have just given it to Maloney. We had others, too. But we didn't need them; our way worked."

He had told the truth, but not the whole truth. They had followed her espionage indoctrination through the eyes and ears of Linda Janowitz.

But even some of the truth appalled Kate. "Dov," she said, "all your talk has been in the first person plural. 'We' did this and 'we' felt that. This is Kate, Dov, remember me? Answer something about the first person singular, Dov Shalzar, the 'I.' Did you—the singular you—not have any thoughts, hopes, about whether the woman you loved would spy on you?"

More than at any other time during the conversation, the mask came away from Shalzar's face. He smiled sadly. "You mean did my ego surface at any time and make me hope you would show enough blind loyalty to reject the pleas to spy—maybe even come over to us? Did I have moments of fervent rooting for it to happen? Of course. I should hope you'd know that.

"But with my country being torn apart and time running out, the ego, those moments, were luxuries. I had no right to them; my only right was to root for you to spy, so the Masada Plan would be transmitted quickly and authoritatively, and acted on. So Israel's agony would end."

Sally was reminded of his words, only a little more than twenty-four hours ago—it just *seemed* like forever—about his country's coming first and there being no second. He had meant that; she, being romantic and an egotist, hadn't really wanted to believe it. But he had meant it. She wasn't even in second place.

"The camera," she went on weakly. "The film. Now there's tangible evidence of the plan, the kind of hard historical documentation you wanted to avoid. That screws up your plan."

He hesitated, then shook his head, and said merely, "There is no more evidence."

"What do you mean, there is no more evidence? I took pictures. Pete Maloney saw them. He has them!"

"You may have taken them," answered the ambassador, slowly. "Pete Maloney may have seen them. But he doesn't have them. There is no more evidence. Can I make that any clearer? Perhaps I can, but I'm not going to."

"You mean the pictures have been destroyed? And you know it?" Then the truth dawned on her. "No, you had it done!"

Shalzar just looked at her as she spoke and said nothing. He continued silent after she had finished. To her, his silence was a yes. Then she reached the most difficult question of all, and could barely bring herself to ask it. She began circling.

"How long ago was the Masada Plan conceived, Dov?"

"About five years ago, why?"

"And when it was formulated, was the method of delivering it—with the unofficial contact and leak—was that thought up at the same time?"

"I believe it was," Shalzar answered. "But tell me, as the judges say, what's the purpose of this line of questioning?"

"Well, it suddenly occurred to me," she said, "that when you and I first met, two years ago, I was a perfect fit for the plan. Is it unreasonable to wonder if, from the week you arrived in New York—that week I met you—you were looking around for such a perfect fit?"

Dov looked at her and began to get angry. She saw it, yet had no wish to stop; she hoped her occasional cowardice would not take over now; she raced forward to keep the momentum going. "The purpose of this line of questioning is to ask if, for the past two years, I have been part of a love affair or a Doomsday device. Do you now, or have you ever . . . ?"

The gathering anger flashed and then his eyes stopped revealing anything. "Let me say it straight out, straighter out than you were able to manage. Do I love you, have I ever loved you, or was I using you? For most of the two years we have known each other, we have been telling each other that we love each other, and presumably believing it. Now, after two years of such protestations, you ask me if mine were ever real.

"What does that say about me and my emotions, if after two years of hearing, seeing, feeling, tasting, smelling my 'I love yous,' the object of them cannot tell for herself whether I meant them or was faking? To me, it says that either my emotional sending apparatus, or your receiver, or our love affair is faulty."

He no longer seemed angry, just distant. "I can't see how a one-word answer now will satisfy what a two-year . . . relationship could not. Besides, if I'm Machiavellian enough to have faked and manipulated for two years, do you think I'd stop at lying to you now if I thought it would do any good?

"In short, there's no point to my answering you." He stared at her.

"To me, you sound more Jesuitical than Machiavellian," responded Kate. "Sometimes the need for reassurance goes beyond the boundaries of the syllogism. And the refusal to give it says more about one's heart than one's logic.

"However," she added, "I'm not going to press it. I'm going to get on a political and journalistic level again, so you can get comfortable."

Kate straightened up as if trying to shake off the subject of love as if it were an unwanted shawl. "As I see the situation, Dov . . ." She had almost said Mr. Ambassador. "It occurs to me that aside from the documents I saw and photographed, no one has any evidence of atomic bombs in nine cities. All we have seen is pieces of paper. What gives them validity, among other things, is the way they were discovered—secretly, cleverly, boldly—in the lion's den, by the Daniel of the Upper East Side, Kate Colby, girl spy. But we now know, she *didn't* discover them. She was *fed* them. She was not a Daniel, but a patsy.

"My question is: Was I merely a cog in a Doomsday device? Or, even more humiliating, a cog in a *phony* Doomsday device? Did I enter the lion's den only to mistake a paper lion for a real one?

"To put it another way: Would Israel have blown up the world? *Or were you just bluffing?*"

The Israeli ambassador hardly hesitated before replying.

"Kate, what kind of people do you think we are?"

It was the first of many times the question was to course through her mind and she was no more capable of an answer then than she was afterwards.

But before she could say anything, an Israeli official entered to say Shalzar was wanted on the telephone by Tel Aviv. Maybe it was a new hostility, maybe paranoia, but she felt Shalzar had called the man in or planned his entrance—Dov was good at that, she told herself—to end the talk.

"I'll be back very soon. Will you wait?"

"I guess so," she replied, knowing she would not.

Two minutes after he departed, she got up and strode quickly toward the Seventy-third Street entrance, determined to walk right through anyone who tried to stop her. No one did, and she found herself out on the street, on a warm, hazy summer morning, Shalzar's question resounding in her head.

What kind of people do you think we are?

But what was the answer?

The first possibility came quickly and easily. It was: We're fighters; we would not shrink from it. That's why we called it the Masada Plan.

The second came just as easily. We Jews are far too civilized a people to blow up the world.

What kind of people do you think we are? Bluffers?

What kind of people do you think we are? Nuclear killers?

Which one?

Walking down Madison Avenue, she smiled. A perfect ambiguity. Perfect.

Will I ever see him again?

Then her own questions poured out.

Will I ever be so close to the nerve center again?

Will we ever be so close to the brink again?

Will I ever take this walk again?

Walking slowly down the avenue, the heat of a placid July morning beading perspiration on her forehead, she came to see that all her questions about Dov Shalzar were one question:

What kind of man do I think he is?

Which was really the same as his question:

What kind of people do you think we are?

And she knew the answer to neither.

314